praise for tara johnson

"*All Through the Night* strikes all the right notes in a Civil War drama. Principled yet flawed characters grow with every chapter, a multifaceted setting brings the era's turmoil to life, and intrigue and danger keep the pages turning. Inspired by a real woman, this novel sings with spiritual truths sure to harmonize with any reader's life story. Another winner from Tara Johnson."

JOCELYN GREEN, CHRISTY AWARD–WINNING AUTHOR OF *VEILED IN SMOKE*

"A soul-satisfying story, peopled with characters who shine all the brighter against the dark backdrop of the Civil War. *All Through the Night* will leave you with a song in your heart and a deeper appreciation for the courageous men and women who endured and changed the course of history by their stand for truth."

LAURA FRANTZ, CHRISTY AWARD–WINNING AUTHOR OF *THE LACEMAKER*

"The tumult of the Civil War serves as a fitting backdrop for this story of two wounded people searching for purpose and approval. Cadence and Joshua are endearing characters, each seeking to do the right thing and bring healing to a broken world, no matter the cost. Tara Johnson has penned a romantic and touching tale that also highlights a little-known and sinister aspect of Civil War history. *All Through the Night* is a memorable novel not to be missed!"

SARAH SUNDIN, BESTSELLING AND AWARD-WINNING AUTHOR OF *WHEN TWILIGHT BREAKS* AND THE SUNRISE AT NORMANDY SERIES

"Tara Johnson is one of those rare writers who can weave history and fiction so seamlessly the reader is never sure where one ends and the other begins. A true talent and author to watch."

ELIZABETH LUDWIG, *USA TODAY* BESTSELLING AUTHOR, ON *ALL THROUGH THE NIGHT*

"*All Through the Night* is full of rich details that bring the Civil War to life and a delightful romance that is sure to warm readers' hearts. Those who enjoy engaging historical romance novels will fall in love with the strong but wounded hero, Dr. Joshua Ivy, and the talented yet hesitant heroine, Cadence Piper. The extra touch of suspense will keep readers up late and turning pages until they reach the very satisfying ending. Well-written and highly recommended!"

> CARRIE TURANSKY, AWARD-WINNING AUTHOR OF *NO OCEAN TOO WIDE*

"This is the kind of story that makes you want to cry, cheer, sometimes raise a fist, and other times sit back in your chair and go, 'Hmm.' The Civil War period is delightfully captured in all its definitive glory in *All Through the Night*, another memorable tale from author Tara Johnson that you won't want to miss."

> MICHELLE GRIEP, CHRISTY AWARD–WINNING AUTHOR

"Tara Johnson's *All Through the Night* will captivate you from page one. Beautifully written, the tale weaves you, the reader, into the story, until you walk with Cadence and Joshua. It's a must-read!"

> ANE MULLIGAN, AMAZON BESTSELLING AUTHOR OF THE CHAPEL SPRINGS SERIES

"Johnson returns to the Civil War for another exciting inspirational romance featuring a dedicated, devout heroine. . . . Johnson embeds the story with her customary attention to historical detail, but the deeply wounded characters remain the focus of this ruminative investigation into the personal toll of war. Johnson's Christian elements are subtle, allowing Cassie and Gabe's perseverance to provide inspiration and hope. Fans of Lynn Austin will enjoy this."

> PUBLISHERS WEEKLY ON *WHERE DANDELIONS BLOOM*

"*Where Dandelions Bloom* is a refreshing historical romance with surprising takes on gender roles. . . . Subtle messages about the power and necessity of forgiveness weave in."

> *FOREWORD* REVIEWS

"A beautifully written love story that takes place amid the horrors of the American Civil War . . . [with] the message of the peace we can have in the Lord in spite of turmoil, hope instead of despair, the importance of forgiveness, not only toward others but also toward one's self, and of not wasting the life God has blessed us with."

CHRISTIAN NOVEL REVIEW ON *WHERE DANDELIONS BLOOM*

"Bringing facets of Civil War history to life, *Where Dandelions Bloom* is an engaging journey of hidden identity and of discovering what's most important in life—and in love."

TAMERA ALEXANDER, *USA TODAY* BESTSELLING AUTHOR

"In her sparkling debut . . . Johnson crafts an inspirational tale of love, fortitude, and what it means to do the right thing when the very concept of 'right' is challenged."

PUBLISHERS WEEKLY*, STARRED REVIEW OF *ENGRAVED ON THE HEART

"A timeless and timely theme of helping persecuted people blooms into an unusual Civil War romance that explores Keziah's search for a purpose, the intersection of faith and practice, and how single acts have far-reaching effects."

FOREWORD* REVIEWS ON *ENGRAVED ON THE HEART

"Debut novelist Johnson does not shy away from the horrors of slavery and the important role of the Underground Railroad, but the tone of this historical romance is much lighter than expected. . . . Fans of the genre will be pleased."

LIBRARY JOURNAL* ON *ENGRAVED ON THE HEART

"Keziah and Micah brave danger and death to help slaves journey to freedom, reminding readers that choosing right often involves great sacrifice."

CBA *CHRISTIAN MARKET* ON *ENGRAVED ON THE HEART*

"A truly lovely debut novel. [Told] through the eyes of an unlikely heroine awakening to the injustices of slavery, *Engraved on the Heart* brings

Savannah, Georgia, during the Civil War to life. . . . A book to savor and an author to watch!"

SARAH SUNDIN, AWARD-WINNING AUTHOR OF *THE SEA BEFORE US* AND THE WAVES OF FREEDOM SERIES

"Set amid the beauty of Savannah, Georgia, at the onset of the Civil War, *Engraved on the Heart* is a story that is as spiritually profound as it is romantic. . . . A remarkable, memorable debut!"

LAURA FRANTZ, AUTHOR OF *THE LACEMAKER*

"Lovers of Civil War fiction will rejoice to add *Engraved on the Heart* to their collections. I'll be looking for more from Tara Johnson!"

JOCELYN GREEN, AWARD-WINNING AUTHOR OF THE HEROINES BEHIND THE LINES CIVIL WAR SERIES

"Blending realistic, relatable characters and the heartrending issue of slavery against a beautifully painted backdrop, Tara Johnson presents a debut novel that will leave you satisfied and yet still wanting more. . . . I highly recommend this engaging and intriguing historical novel."

KIM VOGEL SAWYER, BESTSELLING AUTHOR OF *BRINGING MAGGIE HOME*

"Tara Johnson delivers a stirring tale of danger and hope in *Engraved on the Heart*."

ROBIN LEE HATCHER, RITA AND CHRISTY AWARD–WINNING AUTHOR OF *YOU'LL THINK OF ME* AND *YOU'RE GONNA LOVE ME all through the night*

all through the night

A NOVEL

TARA JOHNSON

Tyndale House Publishers
Carol Stream, Illinois

Visit Tyndale online at tyndale.com.

Visit Tara Johnson's website at tarajohnsonstories.com.

TYNDALE and Tyndale's quill logo are registered trademarks of Tyndale House Ministries.

All Through the Night

Designed by Eva M. Winters

Edited by Danika King

Published in association with the literary agency of Books & Such Literary Management, 52 Mission Circle, Suite 122, PMB 170, Santa Rosa, CA 95409.

Unless otherwise indicated, all Scripture quotations are taken from the *Holy Bible*, King James Version.

Scripture quotations marked NIV are taken from the Holy Bible, *New International Version*,® NIV.® Copyright © 1973, 1978, 1984, 2011 by Biblica, Inc.® Used by permission. All rights reserved worldwide.

For information about special discounts for bulk purchases, please contact Tyndale House Publishers at csresponse@tyndale.com, or call 1-800-323-9400.

ISBN 978-1-4964-2839-4

Printed in the United States of America

26	25	24	23	22	21	20
7	6	5	4	3	2	1

Dedicated to two amazing women, born decades apart

*For Gladys Meier, a woman of many talents whose determination
and spirit has helped make me who I am today. Thank you for
being such an amazing cheerleader, Grandma. I love you.*

*For Leah Barley. Friend. Confidante. Fighter. Sweetness
personified. Your life on this earth seems short in length of years,
but you lived them wisely, shining like the purest star.
You, more than any other, capture the spirit of Cadence Piper.
My life is richer for having known you. Until I see you
again, dear friend . . .*

*"A friend is someone who knows all
about you and still loves you."*

—ELBERT HUBBARD

prologue

MARCH 1861
WASHINGTON, DC

"Yea, though I walk through the valley of the shadow of death, I will fear no evil: for thou art with me." I will fear no evil. I will fear no evil . . .

Cadence Piper walked down the darkened street, clutching her reticule to her middle. Her booted footsteps clicked loudly against the gritty walk. She winced at the echo that drifted back from the inky alley to the right. A chill crawled down her spine. Why hadn't she left the Ladies Aid meeting sooner?

Thunder grumbled overhead as the scent of coming rain filled the air. Would Father be worried? Since they'd moved here from Boston, he'd been so occupied setting up the business he'd not had much time to escort her around town. She'd not minded overly much. Until now.

Straightening her shoulders, she lifted her chin and prayed the action would settle her quaking stomach.

A portly man in a dark coat and tall hat approached, his steps rapid. She stiffened and tucked her head down, only to release the pent-up breath when he passed a moment later without sparing her a glance. She was overreacting. The circles of gaslights dotted the streets. A slow, soft drizzle started, creating a layer of silver dew on the sleeves of her dress. Just a few more blocks.

The faint sound of crying drifted through the night. She paused. Not the wail of a man or woman, but the heartbroken cry of a child. Her heart tugged, even as the odor of rotting garbage and the stench of urine assaulted her.

Pausing, she squinted, peering down another alley to the right. The crying was coming from its depths, she was certain. Dare she look further?

A shiver skimmed her skin. The thought of stepping foot into that black corridor made her tremble, but she could not leave a hurting waif alone. What if the child were sick or had been abandoned? A hundred scenarios peppered her imagination. She'd not sleep a wink tonight unless she checked. Wincing, she slowly entered as the drizzle turned into a steady rain. The darkness tore at her remaining courage.

She jumped when the toe of her boot bumped an empty glass bottle littering the ground. It rolled, and the strident sound bounced through the hollowed, eerie space. The faintest beam of light illuminated the alley wall. The rest was black as coal.

The crying grew louder.

Cadence braved a word. "Hello? Are you hurt?"

The crying muted into a soft whimper.

"It's all right. I won't hurt you. I only want to help." Her fingers scraped wet, gritty brick.

Silence.

"You're not in trouble. I promise."

Sniffle.

Poor lamb. Cadence felt through her reticule for the stick of hard candy that was always present. "Here. I don't have food, but I have a peppermint stick. Would you like it?"

Another sniffle. "Yes'm."

She smiled. "Then you must come to me. I can't see you."

Shuffling.

"Follow the sound of my voice."

Small, cold fingers grasped her arm. Cadence patted the frigid hands, trying to impart what warmth she could. "There you are, love." She pressed the peppermint stick into the child's hands and stooped down. The little body leaned close, seeking her warmth. Crunching sounds broke the quiet of the night.

"Do you live here?"

A smacking sound. "No."

"Then how did you come to be here?"

"I'm alone."

The way the girl said it, so matter-of-fact, pierced her to the quick. Cadence found the child's back and stroked it gently. "I understand. I lost my own mother. It hurts deeply, doesn't it?"

Another sniffle, followed by more crunching. She could not leave this little mite to fend for herself. She would not.

"Do you know what I do when I miss my mother?"

"What?"

"I pull out a memento she gave me and hold it close to my heart. One of her lockets or handkerchiefs. Do you have a special keepsake from your parents?"

The girl shook her head in the darkness, her body bumping Cadence's. "No, ma'am. I have nothing."

Swallowing a swell in her throat, Cadence dug through her reticule, fingers skimming the fabric until she found the desired object. "Here." She groped for the child's hand and set the cool object in her palm.

"What's this?"

"One of my mother's hairpins. I take it with me everywhere." She wrapped her hands around the child's cold, sticky fingers. "Take it."

The child gasped. "For me? Truly? But it was your mother's."

"I have others. Let it remind you that you're never alone."

She sniffed. "I feel alone."

"God is watching over you."

Silence, save for the drip-drip of water from the rooftops.

"What else do you do when you're lonely or afraid?"

Cadence stroked the child's wet, stringy tendrils of hair. "I sing."

"Sing what?"

Clearing her throat, she lifted her voice softly.

"Jesus, lover of my soul,
Let me to thy bosom fly,
While the nearer waters roll,
While the tempest still is high.
Hide me, O my Savior, hide,
Till the storm of life is past;
Safe into the haven guide;
O receive my soul—"

"Are you mad?"

Cadence's heart strangled at the masculine voice. Heavy footsteps stomped toward them. She pushed to her feet as the child clutched her damp skirts. Cadence's pulse clattered to a halt. The large form of a man hovered over them, his shadowed outline boding danger.

But then he turned to the girl. "I thought I'd lost you. You must stay with me. It's far too dangerous. No wandering off."

"Yes, sir."

"Come." The clipped command grated.

As the child moved to his side, Cadence lurched forward, took her hand, and hissed, "What do you think you're doing?"

He whirled around. "Pardon?"

"How dare you bully this poor child and steal her away. She's naught but a poor orphan and a hungry one at that!"

"Oh, really?" Amusement colored his deep baritone. "Is that what she told you?"

Cadence swallowed. "Of course."

The imposing man inclined his head to the girl. "Did you tell her you had no parents?"

The child mumbled, "No, sir. I told her I was alone."

Confusion ribboned through Cadence's middle. What was going on?

The stranger sighed. "You're alone because you ran off. This poor woman thinks she's aiding a hungry orphan living on the street. Not a girl who disobeyed her father."

The child's voice was meek. "I'm sorry."

The man turned to leave and Cadence grabbed his arm. Something was odd about the whole affair. "Sir, if you please, how do I know you're speaking the truth?"

He whirled back, his face mere inches from her own. He was so close, she could see the faint outline of his angular jaw and lips, despite the dark shadows cocooning them. The scent of bay rum and shaving soap filled her nostrils.

"Miss, if you'd be so kind, I'd like to take my daughter and return home before she catches her death of cold. That is, if your singing hasn't alerted every pickpocket and troublemaker to our presence already."

Blood drained from her head as he scooped up the girl and departed. Along with the sound of his fading footsteps, Cadence heard the child's faint call.

"Thank you, miss."

Cadence pressed a hand to the pulse thrumming in her throat. A waft of dank air slapped her face as more thunder rumbled.

What kind of father roamed the alleys at night with his young daughter in tow? A disreputable one, no doubt. Still, she couldn't suppress the irritation that flamed when she considered the confusion that had occurred. How was she to know *alone* didn't mean abandoned? And she'd given away one of Mother's hairpins because of her impulsiveness. Louisa was correct. She was far too rash in her decisions.

She could afford no more excursions into dark alleys.

chapter 1

"What do you think, Songbird?"

Cadence turned and smiled at her father's familiar nickname as they stepped into his toy shop and surveyed the space. The narrow display windows were filled with lace-trimmed dolls on one side and toy soldiers acting out battle scenes on the other. She had already witnessed young children pressing their eager faces to the glass, although Father had not yet opened the store for business.

The gleaming shelves were lined with dominoes and ninepins, whistles and cinch puzzles, harmonicas and marbles. Large baskets were strategically located throughout, filled with ball-and-cup toys, blocks, balls, and a variety of carved animals. More complex games like chess and checker sets rested along the higher shelves. Paper dolls and tea sets, trains and gyroscopes . . . even a spectacular telescope stood like a sentinel in the corner. Best of all were the glass containers filled with an assortment of

1

candy. Licorice, peppermint, lemon drops, butterscotch, sour drops, and cream candy provided a dazzling assortment of vivid, mouthwatering colors to old and young alike.

She propped her hands on her hips. "A bit more polish and I do believe it will be ready."

Her father's lips twisted in a soft smile as he studied his tiny kingdom, his blue eyes mellow with gentle sadness. "Do you think your mother would approve?"

She rose on tiptoe and brushed his cheek with a kiss, enjoying the slight scratch of his shaven jaw against her skin. "She would be delighted."

He sighed. His shoulders seemed a bit more stooped of late, though fifty-three was far from old. The silver threading his hair was more noticeable than the dark brown. Still, the laugh lines around his eyes and mouth were not deep. He was tall and slim. A handsome man. Perhaps she should encourage him to remarry.

The thought stung. Mother had been gone two years, but sometimes it felt like a lifetime. Cadence tried to fill the void as best she could, but a daughter was a poor substitute in companionship. In truth, Father seemed not to notice her attempts to try.

She longed to see the sad, haunted look swept from his eyes. To know in the dark of night he was not lonely, for most assuredly he was now. Why else would he sit in front of the parlor fire with naught but Dickens and Defoe to keep him company into the wee morning hours? She'd caught him reading late into the night more than once. Each time he claimed to be absorbed in the story, unable to put the volume down, yet he'd read the books numerous times. Knew the plots by heart.

As did she.

They had both hoped the move to Washington would be

a fresh start, a way to eradicate the dark memories and ghosts that haunted them in Boston. What could be done when ghosts occupied a heart?

The bell over the door jangled and three men swept into the room, each wearing a somber black coat and tall hat.

Father donned a welcoming expression and spread his arms wide. "Mr. Dodd, how wonderful to see you again! You are one of the very first to visit, and visit before the store is open to the public, I might add."

The youngest-looking man, shorter than the other two with barely a hint of silver at his temples, smiled widely and clasped Father's hand with a hearty chuckle. "Then I consider myself most fortunate indeed." He turned to his companions. "Gentlemen, may I introduce my good friend and one of our newest residents of Washington, Mr. Albert Piper."

The other men, a Mr. Brooks and Mr. Simmons, each shook his hand, their own welcome somewhat less jovial, though Cadence noticed they took in the store's inventory with a gleam of approval. Mr. Dodd turned in her direction. "And who is this beautiful young lady?"

Father placed his hand on the small of her back. "This is Cadence, my daughter."

Heat brushed her cheeks at their open stares, but Mr. Dodd nodded kindly. Lifting her fingers to his lips, he offered a chaste kiss to her hand and murmured, "Enchanted."

She cleared her throat. "Thank you, sir. Likewise."

He released her and winked at Father. "Where have you been hiding such a beauty, Albert? If Washington's social set knew she was here, your door would have been pounded down with suitors ready to stake their claim."

Father laughed weakly and tugged at his collar. "Why do you think I keep her at home?"

Her neck burned, but she forced a shy smile. "Our recent move has kept me busy setting up house."

Dodd nodded. "No doubt. Once that tedious task is finished, you must come dine with my wife and me."

"We would be delighted."

"It may be a while yet. At least for Cadence. Setting up a household takes quite some time, you know."

She frowned. Unpacking was nearly finished. Did he not wish her to visit Mr. Dodd?

Shouts erupted from beyond the door. A crush of people streamed past the window, the forms of men and women alike scurrying in a blur of color.

Mr. Dodd stepped toward the window. "What on earth?"

The door flew open, slamming against the wall with a bang. A newspaper boy stood in the open space, his satchel bulging. Behind him, shouts intensified.

"Did you hear the news, gentlemen? It's just come across the telegraph."

Father took a step toward the gangly youth. "What news? Why the melee?"

The boy straightened his thin shoulders. "Early this morning, Confederates under the command of General Beauregard opened fire upon Fort Sumter in Charleston, South Carolina."

Cadence heard Dodd suck in a harsh breath. Father bowed his head. She bit her lip. "What does this mean?"

Dodd's dark brows knit together. "I'm afraid, Miss Piper, this means we are now officially in the thick of war."

Joshua Ivy crammed his hands in his pockets and walked quickly down Fourth Street, his thoughts tumbling one over another.

Not a week after the firing on Fort Sumter and Washington

had already been transformed. The approach of summer usually meant a sleepy time of relative calm working at Washington Infirmary. His lips firmed into a tight press. This summer would be different.

People streamed into the city in droves. Hotels strained to bursting, even as new ones were hastily being constructed overnight. Train whistles blasted day and night and the streets were always crowded, with nary a moment's rest. And with President Lincoln calling for seventy-five thousand militiamen, things would only grow worse.

More upsetting still, the morning's newspaper had announced with bold letters: "VIRGINIA SECEDES." How many more would follow?

Madness.

Papa John would have been heartbroken. And how would this affect his own work at the hospital?

Keeping his head down, he turned onto E Street.

"Feel like trying your luck, sir?"

Joshua stopped and stared at the shyster eyeing him from the corner. The kid couldn't have been more than sixteen or seventeen at best. Three battered tin cups sat before him on a rickety table. The shell game?

Resisting the urge to laugh, Joshua sauntered closer. "I've naught but a nickel."

The fellow's eyes lit up. "A nickel will do. This game is simple." He began shuffling the cups around, his dirt-stained fingers moving in a blur. "Guess which cup is holding the ball. Not difficult for a man of distinction such as yourself, am I right?" The lad was laying it on thick.

"Indeed."

When he'd finished shuffling, Joshua tapped the cup farthest to the right. "There."

The boy lifted it and groaned. "By the saints, you've done it. I should have known better than to challenge a man with such astute powers of observation. Shall we have another go? Double or nothing?"

Joshua smiled. "Why not?"

The shuffle of cups, the scraping of tin on wood. The lad stopped with a flourish. "Tell me, where is the ball?"

Joshua lifted a brow. "In your hand."

The lad's composure faltered. "What's that you say?"

With a frown, Joshua lurched forward and grabbed his hands, wrenching them open to reveal the ball tucked inside the left palm.

The boy paled. "How—how did you know?"

Joshua pursed his lips. "Let's just call it a hunch. First rule of running games: Don't get caught. Ever. Word gets around." He released the lad, who blinked as if he'd been slapped.

Joshua's heart tugged. "You got family?"

"A mother. Little brother."

"Your father?"

"Dead."

Joshua scooped up the nickel and tossed it to him. "Here. Take it. Where do they live?"

The lad mumbled the address, and Joshua tried not to wince. The slummiest part of the city. He made a mental note to take them some food later.

"What's your name?"

"Thomas Moore."

"Well, Thomas Moore, you seem like a bright young man. Too bright to be wasting your life running games and tricking folks out of nickels and dimes. If you ever want honest work, come find me."

The boy nodded, his neck mottled red. "And where would that be?"

"Washington Infirmary. My name's Dr. Joshua Ivy. Oh, and, Thomas?"

He looked up, his pale-blue eyes wide. "Sir?"

Joshua leaned in, dropping his voice to a whisper. "Second rule of running games? Keep alert. There's a police officer right across the street and he's noticed your cups. If I were you, I'd act as if I was taking a drink from one of them and move along."

Thomas swallowed. "How did you know that?"

Joshua winked. "I keep alert."

"Cadence. Sing me a song."

Mother's weak voice trembled in the low light, wavering like the flickering flame of the spent candle near her bed. Cadence reached for her hand. Cold. So cold.

"Wh-wh-what do you want me to sing?"

"Anything. Everything."

Cadence closed her eyes, a hundred melodies flying through her mind before she landed on the perfect words.

"Meet me by moonlight alone,
and then I will tell you a tale.
Must be told by the moonlight alone,
in the grove at the end of the vale . . ."

The candlelight faded as darkness closed in. Cadence snatched Mother's hand closer, but her fingers were slipping away. Her eyes burned like coals through the encroaching shadows.

"Save me, Cadence. Save me . . ."

Tears streamed as she tried to hold Mother's cold fingers, but the tighter she gripped, the quicker Mother slipped from her grasp. The bed plunged her into a black abyss as all the light was snuffed out.

"Father! Tate! Help me!"

Cadence stumbled through the clawing darkness, but it panted against her heart like a beast waiting to snap her up. No light, no path. No one could see her. Hear her. She was alone.

Alone. Alone.

"No!"

Warm air invaded as her eyes snapped open. Something fluttered over her face. Her sheets? With a cry, she yanked the offending fabric away and breathed in long pulls of night air. Moonlight cut silver swaths of light across her room. Gasping, she collapsed against her pillow.

It was only a dream.

Sweat glued her nightgown to her skin. Her heartbeat slowed as she twisted to stare up at the ceiling.

Only a dream, and yet it wasn't.

Mother was gone, and she was to blame. Tate had fled and Father had little to do with her. Tears pricked her eyes as her throat swelled. In the ways that mattered, she was alone.

Even now, surrounded by darkness, long-held childhood fears reached out to choke her. Terrified of being noticed while yearning to be seen, truly seen and loved, despite her flaws.

Clutching the sheets between her fingers, she held them to her chest and willed the tears to flee.

God, did you see me then? Do you see me now?

chapter 2

CADENCE SIPPED HER WATER and studied the candlelit table as she reminded herself not to trip over her tongue.

Cut-crystal dishes twinkled in the soft light. Wine-colored jellies glowed atop the white lace tablecloth. Fluffy bread and pressed balls of cold butter, stuffed pork, and creamed peas made for a sumptuous feast, but she could barely eat a bite . . . not with the Dodds' son staring at her with such open admiration.

Mr. Dodd had been true to his word. Four days after he'd visited the shop, Cadence and her father had received a dinner invitation in the post. What she'd not expected was to find three other couples present, along with the Dodds' son, Stephen. From the moment she'd entered, he'd watched her with an attentiveness that caused her to squirm. She wouldn't be able to manage a sip of water if he continued . . . not with those stormy gray eyes fixed upon her continually.

Nevertheless, he was handsome, if a bit intense. The other

couples at the table were closer to Father's age. Perhaps Stephen was only relieved to find someone of his own age in attendance.

Mr. Dodd chuckled, drawing her attention back to the conversation at hand.

"Bully good story, James, although Mr. Piper may disagree, seeing as how he's from Boston."

Father laughed. "No longer. Cadence and I are Washingtonians now and happy to be so."

A wiry fellow sitting near the end of the table chewed slowly. "Odd time to be putting down roots, yes? What with the city in such upheaval."

Father offered a wry smile. "We have nothing to compare it to, so I supposed the activity in Washington the norm."

Another man, thinner and sallower than his companions, shook his head, his limp jowls swaying like a hound dog's. "I barely recognize the place."

His wife, a buxom woman swathed in silk, sighed melodramatically. "I agree. It's dreadful. So many people crowding in. I went shopping just yesterday and could barely get down the street. Pickpockets and beggars will be swarming soon enough. The War Department thinks the number of people flooding in will only grow worse."

Mr. Dodd nodded. "Undoubtedly so, especially since President Lincoln has called for volunteers."

Painfully thin Mrs. Simmons leaned forward, her hawkish gaze fixed on Stephen. "Will you enlist, Stephen?"

Straightening, he lifted his chin and darted a quick look to his parents. His father nodded. His mother lowered her face, her gaze fixed on her plate, lips trembling.

"Yes, ma'am. I have already done so. Just this morning, in fact."

Father's eyes softened. "God be with you."

Mr. Bagwell's voice boomed. "We are proud of you, young

Dodd. You go and whip those Rebels. Should only take a month or two at most."

"Hear, hear!"

Glasses lifted around the table. Stephen beamed, yet his mother's eyes shimmered like crystal.

Mr. Dodd's voice was far more subdued as they drank. "What of you, Simmons? Your boys planning to enlist?"

"Of course, of course. Mark and Peter will be joining the fight on the morrow. Our youngest is champing at the bit, but I've told him fourteen is too young."

His wife frowned. "Indeed."

Mr. Bagwell turned to Father. "I suppose you need not worry about such things, Albert, seeing as you have only your lovely daughter to attend to. Shame not to have a son who can fight for the family honor, though."

Cadence sucked in a light breath. The man couldn't know how deeply the remark stung.

Dodd took another sip. "Albert, I thought you mentioned having a son. Am I mistaken?"

Father cleared his throat, his expression grave. "You are not mistaken, Justus. I have a son."

Simmons's brows rose high. "And when does he plan to enlist?"

Father studied his plate. "I have no idea. I've not seen him for several years."

Silence settled like a heavy blanket. Tate's choices had already cost them dear friendships in Boston. Would he curse their life in Washington too? Cadence kept her gaze averted.

Mrs. Simmons murmured, "A pity."

Her husband's shrewd eyes narrowed. "Especially during a time when the honor of one's family—and country—is so vitally important."

The man's tone dripped with derision. Cadence slipped her

hand into Father's and squeezed. How dare they judge him and find him lacking, especially for failures that were Tate's alone to bear. Father pulled his hand away.

Dodd broke the strained silence with a gentle admonition. "Each of us is accountable to the Almighty for the decisions we make. We answer only for ourselves. May each of us strive to please him and do our part in this conflict, for truly we can do nothing less."

Cadence offered him a grateful look as the guests murmured their agreement and resumed their dinner.

Tate had dishonored Father, left a path of destruction in his wake, and left them to pick up the pieces. Her brother might not be able to represent their family as he ought, but perhaps there was something she could do. A way to serve for honor, love, and country and gain Father's admiration in the process.

But how?

"Miss Cadence? There is a visitor here to see you."

Cadence looked up from unpacking the last crate of china in the dining room to stare at the housekeeper in surprise.

"I was not expecting any callers."

Louisa's dark eyes twinkled, her teeth flashing in her mahogany face. "Yet one is here just the same. A young man. Handsome too."

Warmth seeped across her skin. She gently placed the rose-trimmed plate back in the straw-filled crate. "Look at you, Louisa. Grinning like a fox."

The older woman cackled. "About time you had someone calling, as pretty as you are. Go on. See to your young man. I'll finish unpacking and bring in something to drink in a few minutes. Make sure you're properly chaperoned."

Cadence shook her head. "I don't have a young man." Still, she offered Louisa's arm an affectionate squeeze on the way out. Dear woman. She paused before the parlor, attempting to smooth her hair and brush the dust particles from her blue skirt. She must look a sight. With a pinch of her cheeks, she walked into the room and stopped.

Stephen Dodd stood, his gray eyes alight with pleasure, dark hair gleaming from the sunlight seeping through the curtained window. "Miss Piper, forgive my unexpected call."

"No need to apologize, Mr. Dodd. I trust you are well?"

"Quite well now." He smiled and her hands felt oddly clammy. "How lovely you look this afternoon."

She dropped her gaze to the flower-patterned rug. "You're very kind. I fear you caught me unpacking the last of our belongings."

"Anything I can do to lend my assistance?"

"Thank you, no. Louisa is finishing my task." Ill at ease, she gestured to the chairs. "Please, take a seat."

He settled into a stiff-backed upholstered chair. She sat across from him and smoothed her skirts as an uncomfortable silence descended. What could he possibly want with her? The soft ticking of the mantel clock counted off the seconds.

Tick, tick, tick, tick . . .

Finally he cleared his throat and offered a tight laugh. "I don't recall ever being this nervous." He cast her a sideways glance. "I fear you tie my tongue in knots, Miss Piper."

"You have nothing to fear from me, Mr. Dodd."

"Please, call me Stephen."

She nodded. "All right. Stephen. Only if you call me C-C-Cadence." She winced. Not now, of all times . . .

He seemed not to notice her nervous tongue. "I confess I've rarely met someone who has so entranced me as you have.

From the moment you walked into our home last evening, I was smitten."

Her breath thinned at his blunt confession.

His gray eyes filled with earnestness. "I'm aware we know nothing of each other. Not yet, but—" he leaned forward and reached for her hand, lightly gripping her fingers between his—"but I would very much like to know you more."

"I . . . I'm flattered, sir."

Lines appeared between his brows. "I have no business requesting to court you, not with my recent enlistment, but I would desire your permission to write while I'm away." He cleared his throat. "Would you grant me permission to do so?"

Her thoughts spun. What harm could come from letting him write? "Of course."

A wide smile blossomed. "Thank you, Miss Piper. Cadence."

She gently retracted her hand and tucked it back into her lap. "I should be happy to hear from you. In so many ways, I wish I could go and fight as well."

His lips pursed. "Ladies should never be subjected to such things."

A sudden image of Mother's limp, pale form flashed before her mind. The days that bled into nights, cold compresses and pungent teas . . . none of it was pleasant. At least Cadence had been able to bring her a measure of relief. Afforded her a respite from her suffering.

She swallowed. "But to have a purpose. To know your task and give your life to it with all your heart. There is nothing more noble or honorable. Surely it must be highly satisfactory. A filling of the soul."

"Of course, but I'm a man." His brows lowered. "It's different for women. The gentler sex should be content at home."

Should they? Cadence had felt a gnawing at her spirit ever

since Mother had passed. The disquiet had grown steadily worse. It was not enough to keep house for Father and attend social gatherings. Of late, even the charitable organizations left her hollow. She longed to do something. To matter.

Or was she merely running from the darkness again?

The sudden memory of sitting in the phrenologist's office as a girl of twelve sliced through her mind like a shard of glass. She remembered the warm, stuffy air. How his breath had smelled of peppermint. The way his fingers had roved through her hair as he'd felt across her scalp, probing bumps and contours.

"I'm afraid she has a congenital malformation of the speech apparatus. Perhaps of the respiratory organs as well. You should not expect much from her . . ."

She'd replayed his stinging words a thousand times, yet her heart had not grown calloused to the pain.

Defiance rose up like a beast inside. She could do something to aid the cause, surely. She must do something.

"D-do all feel that women have no part to play in the conflict?"

Stephen paused, his face thoughtful. "I suppose not. Just this morning I heard a rumor that Secretary of War Cameron is considering appointing Dorothea Dix as superintendent of nursing."

"Miss Dix? I've heard of her hospital work for the insane."

He nodded. "Some say she's brilliant and others believe she's a harsh taskmaster, but from what I understand, everyone believes she is a woman who can achieve results."

"But everyone knows the army only employs male nurses."

"Yes, but apparently Cameron is considering letting Miss Dix organize her own nursing corps made up of female volunteers." Stephen frowned. "The notion will never fly, I say. Too scandalous."

An idea ignited a flame of hope inside Cadence's heart. Her blood warmed. The idea was ludicrous. What would Father think?

But the longer she pondered, the more certain she became. She must try.

———— ✲ ————

Cadence clutched the scrap of paper in her gloved fingers and peered up at the simple but peaceful-looking home tucked away along the end of the street. She eyed the covered porch and green shutters from beneath the brim of her wide bonnet. The fluttering in her stomach quickly spread to her limbs until she feared she would rattle apart like a string puppet.

Courage. If men like Stephen Dodd could enlist, she could muster up enough bravery to ask Miss Dix for a nursing job. Father deserved to have his name mentioned with honor, not with the disgrace Tate had thrust upon him. She could do the work. Hadn't she proven so when Mother lay dying?

With trembling legs, she climbed up the steps and rapped on the door. Muted footfalls sounded somewhere beyond. A woman opened the door, her skirts swishing as if she'd rushed to answer. Her face was calm, however, her features serene as her gaze swept over Cadence, her expression giving nothing away.

"How may I help you?"

"My name is—" she paused—"C-Cadence Piper. I would like to request an audience with Miss Dix if she is accepting callers."

The woman offered a wry smile. "When is she not? You may come in. Miss Dix is currently answering correspondence, but I'll see if she's willing to receive callers."

"Thank you."

Cadence followed the servant through the tidy foyer and into a small parlor. Perching on the edge of a gold brocade sofa, she slipped her gloves from her fingers, removed her bonnet, and smoothed her gray dress. With a gentle tug on her lace collar, she straightened her spine and waited. Nursing was a serious affair, and she intended to look the part.

Her gaze roved over the simple furnishings to the dining room beyond. Crates of every shape and size filled the room, stacked along the walls and floors . . . some even piled on the table itself. Odd. Perhaps Miss Dix had only just moved to Washington and had nary a moment to unpack. With the War Department's demands, such a thing was not unlikely.

The soft rustle of a skirt sounded in the hallway. Cadence's heart thumped so loudly she feared she might faint.

A slim, rather retiring woman stood in the parlor doorway. Cadence rose to greet her. The woman was wearing black, no jewelry or baubles to boast of. Her dark hair was parted down the middle and pulled into a severe knot, save for two wide dips she allowed over her ears. Shadows circled her eyes as if she'd spent many a night deep in study or some other intellectual task, but her bearing was regal . . . like a queen holding court.

"Miss Piper?"

Not knowing what else to do, Cadence offered a curtsy. "Forgive my unannounced call, Miss Dix. I've come on a matter of some importance."

A small smile appeared. "Everything seems to be of importance these days. Please sit. I'll call for tea."

She rang a porcelain bell sitting on a table beside her chair and sat, her back as straight as a metal rod. Placing her hands in her lap, she studied Cadence and waited, silent. Her gaze was piercing, dreadfully astute, missing nothing. Cadence fought the urge to squirm. Miss Dix would not make this task easy.

She cleared her throat. "I fear I've caught you at an inconvenient time."

Miss Dix waved her hand toward the dining room. "War changes things. No doubt you saw the supplies filling my dining area."

"Those are supplies? I assumed you'd recently moved to Washington."

Her lips twitched as the servant swept into the room with a tea service in hand. She placed the laden tray on the table and left as silently as she'd entered. Miss Dix poured them each a steaming cup and handed one to Cadence. She grasped it but feared her nerves would cause the tea and saucer to clatter.

"You are correct on both counts. No sooner did I move here than I was appointed superintendent of nurses. Now donations are pouring in faster than I can organize them. I daresay they will soon overtake my house."

Taking a sip, Cadence set her tea aside. "Actually, your new appointment is why I'm here."

Miss Dix remained silent. Cadence swallowed and blurted, "I want to be a nurse."

"I see."

Forgetting her nervousness, she leaned forward. "I can do the work. I know I can. I nursed my mother when she lay dying. I held vigil for months with little sleep. I found gr-gr-gratification and p-p-pur-pose." Cadence let her eyes slide shut. *Not here. Not now.* Heat engulfed every fiber of her body. Clenching her fists, she fought for calm. She opened her eyes, took a deep breath, and spoke slowly. "All I ask is a chance to prove my mettle."

Miss Dix studied her carefully. After a painfully long stretch of silence, she sighed. "Have you ever been inside a hospital, Miss Piper?"

"No, but—"

"It is not for the faint of heart. Disease and filth. Blood and dysentery. Men burning up with fever, others crying out in pain. The odor of urine, sweat, and less pleasant aromas that have caused grown men to pass out. Days are long and tempers are short. It's a far cry from keeping a lone vigil at a beloved's bedside."

Cadence felt the knot tightening her middle. "Of course. Surely the work is strenuous for even the most hardened nurse, but the need is great, is it not?"

Miss Dix continued as if she hadn't heard. "And then there are the men themselves to consider. We mustn't tempt them. My nurses will retain the highest standards of dress and decorum. No bows, hoops, or jewelry of any kind. Not even lace." Her sharp gaze dropped to Cadence's lace collar.

Cadence's cheeks warmed and she fought the urge to finger the collar. Surely Miss Dix wouldn't hold the requirements against her before she'd begun, would she?

"I understand."

Miss Dix sighed. "I like you, Miss Piper. I think you have gumption. Your eagerness is to be commended. You actually remind me a great deal of myself at your age. In a world where there is so much to be done, I felt strongly impressed that there must be something for each of us to do."

At least Miss Dix understood. "Yes, precisely. I long to serve, to be a part of something bigger than myself."

"This makes what I have to say all the more difficult."

Cadence's pulse halted.

"I'm afraid I must decline."

Humiliation washed over her in a cold wave. "I don't understand."

Miss Dix's brows lowered. "It's nothing you've done, my

dear, but I must consider the soldiers. How easily they form attachments to sweet nurses with lovely faces. Reputation and honor . . . these must be guarded with all diligence. The single most important requirement for my nurses is that they be older women, preferably married or widowed and plain of face."

Cadence blinked. "You're saying I'm . . ."

"Too young and far too pretty."

Never had a compliment held such a bitter sting. She grasped for any argument that might sway the woman's opinion.

"I'll be eighteen in but two months. Surely by then—"

Miss Dix frowned. "Eighteen may be the enlistment age for our soldiers, but our nurses must be far older. Even if you were forty, you are far too comely to be a nurse. I'm sorry."

Mouth dry, she stood on shaking legs and scrambled for a semblance of reasonable thought. "I—I'm sorry to have wasted your time."

Her throat burned. She hadn't realized how desperately she'd longed for the opportunity until it had been denied her. She had turned to leave, blinking back the tears threatening to spill, when Miss Dix's soft voice caused her to pause.

"Miss Piper?"

"Yes, ma'am?"

A sympathetic compassion flooded the woman's face. "Do not despair. There is still much to be done. Find out what task Providence has ordained you to do and then do it."

Cadence hated the traitorous tremble of her chin. "This is all I've wanted. I fear there may be no task for me."

Miss Dix's lips formed a thin smile. "There is always something. I think lying on my bed I can still do something. Whatever the work is, do it with all your heart."

The only thing Cadence longed to do had been denied her.

What else could there be for her, the slow-to-speak daughter of a toymaker?

She wasn't enough. Never had been.

With a nod, she spun on her heel and left.

———— ⚬⚬⚬⚬ ————

Joshua crept into the darkness of the littered alley, resisting the urge to shift his weight. One ill-timed sound could destroy everything.

Where was Zeke? He prayed his friend had not met with any trouble.

Releasing a tight breath, he blinked away the grit coating his eyes. Work at the hospital had been grueling. The never-ending stream of patients chipped away his time during the daylight hours, but it was here, during the darkness of night, that the work he felt most passionate about took place.

A door slammed in the distance. His nerves tightened. Boisterous laughter burst from a group outside a large building at the end of the alley. The masculine voices melted into less mirthful tones. Quieter, but carrying the hard edge of inflamed zeal.

"We must protect ourselves and our property, and those who will not help us will help our enemies. This is the way we are forced to reason the matter, and every true man who believes in individual rights will join the Knights without trouble. Those who will not join, we know are not true to our cause."

Hair prickled on the back of Joshua's neck. Forcing his step to be light, he braved a footfall in their direction. Then another and another. He hunkered low as they walked closer.

"We must work in unison."

"I quite agree." The third man's voice was deeper and rough, like the sound of wet pebbles tossed into a can. "We have made our oath. Nothing but blood shall satisfy against all men of the

North who are not friendly to our cause. Our emblems are the constant reminders . . . death to abolitionists and traitors."

His companions grunted their agreement, their heavy steps growing louder as they approached down the alley. Joshua held his breath as they passed. There were at least five of them, but the darkness made it impossible to gauge any details.

When he was certain he was alone, he rose, his thoughts troubled.

Just who were the Knights?

chapter 3

"I'M OFF TO OUR GRAND OPENING. Wish me luck."

Cadence looked up from clearing the breakfast table. Papa looked so handsome in his brushed black coat and starched white shirt. His eyes held a twinkle that had been absent far too long.

"You don't need luck. You've always been a success." Rounding the table, she straightened his tie and kissed his cheek. "Nevertheless, I shall wish you luck all the same."

He chuckled. "Thank you."

She bit her lip. "Are you sure I can't come assist you? I don't mind."

He waved his hand. "You'd be bored stiff. Watching people come and go, making small talk with customers. Hardly work for a lovely young lady. No, your place is at home with Louisa." He avoided her gaze, fiddling with his coat cuffs instead. Father was always kind, but he never let her assist him in the shop, nor had he let her help in Boston. The few times she'd attempted, he'd humored her . . . until customers arrived. Then he shooed her away with haste.

What was she to do at home all day? Needlepoint? Stare at the walls while Washington filled with soldiers waiting for troop assignments? Even elderly matrons were allowed to change bloody bandages and soothe fevered skin. They all had purpose. Destiny. And what did she have? Nothing. No great calling. And every time she attempted to latch on to one, her attempts were soundly thwarted.

"There is still much to be done. Find out what task Providence has ordained you to do and then do it."

Miss Dix's admonition rolled through her mind like a beating drum. What task of great worth could she possibly accomplish trapped at home?

Before she could utter anything more, Papa patted her shoulder and left her alone in the empty dining room. She gathered up the last of the breakfast dishes. Every clink felt loud and echoing, a yawning void of hollow space gnawing at her soul.

She could hear the housekeeper's gentle hum as she heated water for washing. Even the cheerful melody failed to soothe.

A sharp rap sounded at the door. Puzzled, she discarded the dishes in the kitchen and walked to the front door. She opened it to reveal a familiar face.

"Elida!"

The pastor's wife of Christ Church leaned forward and brushed her cheek before pulling back to offer a gentle smile. Blonde curls peeked out from the sides of her black bonnet.

"Forgive me calling so early, but I needed to speak with you, and I was already in the area, so . . ."

"Think nothing of it." Cadence grasped her arm and drew her into the parlor. "You know how much I enjoy your company.

Come. Sit down and let's enjoy a visit. Yours is one of the few friendships I've made since coming to Washington."

They eased down beside each other on the parlor's settee. Cadence smoothed her skirts to accommodate the wide hoops. Drat the fashion!

Elida took her hand. "Since the moment we met, I felt like we could be the greatest of chums." Her gaze dropped to her lap as she released Cadence's fingers, her brown eyes filling with sadness. "Which is what makes this visit so difficult."

Cadence puzzled over Elida's words. "What's wrong?"

"My husband and I are leaving Washington. He's given up his appointment at Christ Church."

Cadence sucked in a light breath. "I had not heard."

Elida's brow furrowed. "He's taken the pastorate at a smaller church in Fredericksburg. He believes our work here is coming to an end, and that, combined with the changes war will bring to Washington, makes it the ideal time to leave." Her shoulders sagged with an unseen weight.

"You and your husband will be missed. Your leadership and spiritual guidance have blessed many. Although we are new to the church, your influence has been easy enough to see." Cadence spoke past the cotton in her throat. "And I shall miss our visits most of all."

Elida's brown eyes became glassy. "We will write. Yes?"

"Of course."

Heaving a tremulous sigh, Elida shut her eyes for the briefest of moments. "Which brings me to my favor. Do you remember me telling you about my baby girl, Rose? It was one year ago I lost her to influenza."

Cadence's throat ached at the sorrow shadowing the woman's face. "Yes, of course I remember. A more painful loss I cannot imagine."

"The past year has been the most difficult of my life, but God has been faithful. I know I'll see my baby girl again." She looked up at Cadence. "The most difficult thing about leaving Washington has been the thought of not being near my Rose's grave." Her eyes filled with tears. "Not being here to check on her, to put flowers on her headstone, to keep vigil over her resting place—" her lips trembled—"it shreds my heart."

A vise squeezed Cadence's chest. "Would you like me to care for her grave?"

Elida expelled a tight breath. "Would it be a terrible inconvenience? It would bring me such comfort to know her resting place was being tended by loving hands."

Cadence's eyes stung. "I would be honored. I'll visit every week, and if you send me your address, I'll even write and let you know how things fare."

The young mother's face crumpled as she fell into Cadence's embrace. "Bless you. May the Almighty repay you for your kindness."

As she rubbed her friend's shuddering back, Cadence forced down her own tears. It wasn't nursing, but it was something she could do.

"Find out what task Providence has ordained you to do and then do it."

"Come. Show me Rose's resting place and I'll make sure she is loved and looked after. I promise."

⸻

OCTOBER 1861

Cadence placed the bouquet of red mums at Rose's headstone and adjusted the snowy-white bow before easing back on her heels. She smiled as she patted the still-green grass and allowed her skirt to billow around her as she settled to the ground.

"Good afternoon, sweet Rose. Your mother sends her love. She misses you terribly but knows Jesus is taking such good care of you."

She breathed in the fresh scent of the autumn air. Sunshine mingled with the cool nip of approaching change. In the distance, the steady thumps of drilling soldiers, with their synchronized footfalls and rat-a-tatting drums, charged the air as they marched down Pennsylvania Avenue in a grand parade. The continual, frenetic buzz of Washington contrasted with the serenity of the cemetery. Fresh mounds of churned earth filled every corner and row. She sighed. The war was only supposed to last a month, two at the most. It was now approaching six with no end in sight. How many more plots would be filled by year's end?

She returned her attention to the tiny headstone. "Perhaps it's silly to always sing you a lullaby, but I can't help but think that you would love a song. If I were a mother, I would want someone to sing to my baby girl. I've not yet sung you this one, but it's my favorite. One my mother sang to me. I always feel closer to her when I hear it."

She closed her eyes, remembering Mother's dark, silky hair, the way her eyes would light up when she was excited . . . how her laughter sounded like silver. Papa said she and Mother looked so much alike, save Cadence had Papa's bright-blue eyes. With a deep sigh, she cleared her throat and sang.

"Sleep, my child, and peace attend thee,
All through the night.
Guardian angels God will send thee,
All through the night.
Soft the drowsy hours are creeping,
Hill and dale in slumber sleeping,

I my loved ones' watch am keeping,
All through the night."

A gentle breeze rife with the loamy scent of leaves closed the lullaby like a whispered benediction.

"You are an angel if ever I've heard one."

With a startled gasp, she turned to see a middle-aged man staring at her. He boasted bushy whiskers and was well dressed in a finely tailored suit, a gold chain winking from his vest. His eyes were both intelligent and sorrowful. She rose on wooden legs.

"Forgive my frivolity, sir."

"Do not ask forgiveness for such a gift. Your voice is exquisite. I've never heard such beauty."

Her cheeks warmed. "Thank you."

He nodded toward the headstone. "Your child?"

Smoothing her skirts, she shook her head. "No, the daughter of a friend. I visit her grave as a promise since her mother cannot."

"Kind of you. I come to visit my son, killed at Bull Run."

"My condolences."

He quickly shuttered his stark pain behind a gentle smile. "He fought bravely. I could ask for nothing more."

"Yet you miss him."

"Desperately." He gave a slight shake of his head. "My apologies. I've not yet introduced myself." Bowing, he grasped her hand and lifted it to his lips before brushing it with a genteel kiss. "Congressman Daniel Ramsey, at your service."

She curtsied as he released her hand. "Cadence Piper. It's an honor to make your acquaintance, Congressman."

"The pleasure is mine. Join me for a stroll?"

With a nod, she slipped her hand into the crook of his elbow as he led her through the rows of headstones. He seemed so solemn a man, yet not cross.

"Have you fared well these past months, Miss Piper?"

"Better than most, given the state of affairs. My father is too old to fight and has opened a business that has seen a fair amount of success, considering the circumstances. My mother has already passed on to her reward. I have no sweetheart away fighting, no other siblings I need fear for."

She refrained from telling him about Tate. What good would it serve?

He sighed, his barrel chest heaving. "Indeed, you have been blessed. Untainted in some respects. We have two sons. One lost to us, the other not yet old enough to enlist."

"Your wife?"

He shook his head. "Luke's death has been difficult for her."

The soft hiss of grass beneath their shoes broke the silence. "You bear a heavy burden, sir. Both at home and politically."

"Indeed." A sad smile tugged his whiskers. "Though now perhaps you understand why your song moved me so. Beauty, grace, truth . . . these things become all the more sacred for want of them. Thank you for such a gift on a difficult day."

She didn't know what to say. Singing a lullaby didn't feel like a gift, but who was she to argue with a man who needed such simple encouragement?

He lifted his wiry brows. "Are you ready to leave?"

She looked back at the tiny grave. "Yes. I'll return soon."

"I'll walk you out."

They strolled in companionable silence down the gentle rise of the hill, past the iron boundary, and back into the bustling streets. The noise and clamor seemed twice as thick as only an hour before.

"Where do you wish to go?" He had to raise his voice to be heard over the hawkers, rattling wagons, and shouts.

"I live on Judiciary Square. It's not far."

He frowned. "I'll escort you. I hate to see any lady walking among such disquiet."

As he maneuvered them through the clogged streets, the throng suddenly parted. Congressman Ramsey halted, his entire form stiffening at the sight crossing the road before them. Cadence looked down the street and gasped.

Hundreds of men shuffled past, all of them filthy and emaciated in battered blue Union uniforms. Their complexions were sallow and chalky beneath their scraggly beards and long hair. They sagged along in the shadow of the US Capitol dome, but they looked beaten down . . . haggard and near death.

"Oh, Mr. Ramsey, who are they?"

"Our poor soldiers returning from the battlefields." He released a long exhale and bowed his head. "God, have mercy." A muscle twitched near his eye.

"Such brutality." She blinked. "I don't understand it." Something inside her spirit churned. If she could only do something . . .

Congressman Ramsey turned to her, a fire blazing in his expression. "Sing for them."

"Pardon?"

"Will you sing for them, Miss Piper? Fan the flames of their patriotism. Give them hope."

She stared at the pitiful souls shuffling by. "I am nobody, Mr. Ramsey. I haven't the ability to do such a thing."

"The Almighty moves hearts, but he has given you a voice so his message can be heard. Just sing from your heart and let him do the rest."

One of the soldiers turned and looked at her then. The emptiness, the hollow ache shook her down to the core. She nodded and allowed the congressman to lead her to the line of soldiers slowly scooting by.

He held up his hands, his voice booming through the air. "Gentlemen, we stand here before you today a grateful people."

Some of the soldiers paused and glanced at him. Others kept looking straight ahead as if they didn't hear. Regular people in the street stalled, observing the odd spectacle. He continued.

"Though our hearts and minds cannot imagine the horrors you've endured, we humbly thank you for your service. Thank you for your courage. Thank you for protecting our children and daughters. Thank you for protecting our freedom and for your fight to preserve this great Union. Do not give up. Stand strong. Salvation is of the Lord!"

He turned to Cadence and gestured for her to begin. Every limb quivered like preserves, but she inhaled a fortifying breath.

"O say can you see, by the dawn's early light,
What so proudly we hailed at the twilight's last gleaming . . ."

From the corner of her eye, she watched the soldiers stop. Men and women, children and the aged, all of them circled around her.

"Whose broad stripes and bright stars through the perilous
*   fight*
O'er the ramparts we watched were so gallantly streaming?"

Men removed their hats. The thin soldiers stiffened to attention. Several of them lifted their shaking hands into a salute. Her heart pounded against her ribs.

"And the rocket's red glare, the bombs bursting in air,
Gave proof through the night that our flag was still there."

Voices lifted in unison around her. Some robust, others hoarse, but it didn't matter. A swelling of sound filled the street so strong, she felt as if she could fly. She lifted her face to the sky and smiled.

"O say does that star-spangled banner yet wave
O'er the land of the free and the home of the brave?"

A moment of silence held suspended as she finished the last note, followed by thundering cheers and applause. She looked down to realize the soldiers had dropped their knapsacks at her feet. Tears were streaming down their grimy faces.

"Thank you, miss. Thank you."

Congressman Ramsey wiped his eyes. "Well done, Miss Piper. Would it trouble you if I asked your father's permission to have you sing for other patriotic events in the city?"

"I—uh, I'd be honored."

Her mind spun as she was crushed by well-wishers and admirers. Who would have thought singing a lullaby in a grave-yard would have led to this?

-------- ✦ --------

Dr. Joshua Ivy looked over the group of soldiers walking into the hospital. These men deserved better. Those who were saved would likely be sent straight back to the battlefield, and those who were wounded badly enough would probably never leave the hospital alive. The disturbing reality ate at him like a cancer.

The line of soldiers entering suddenly ended. He frowned. The captain had said there should be at least one hundred more.

Walking out the hospital doors, he glanced down the street lining Judiciary Square. A crowd had gathered, and he could hear . . . singing?

He walked toward the crush of people: starving soldiers, residents of Washington, men, women, and children. All of them were focused on one person. He pushed his way through the crowd and stopped.

In the midst of the throng stood a young woman, the most beautiful woman he'd ever seen. Her dark, glossy hair was pinned up, but the pins did little to hide her thick mane of curls. Sky-blue eyes. Her lips were full and pink, framed on either side by dimples. Her cream-colored bodice highlighted every womanly curve she possessed, accentuating her tiny waist before flaring into a wide skirt. But it was the lush melody spilling from her lips that held him spellbound.

She sang, her voice lilting like a spring breeze, yet it was not breathy. No, it wrapped around him like an embrace, tugging, binding him without touch. His pulse skittered when the melody lifted on tiptoe. Gooseflesh broke out on his arms when her voice tapered back down to earth, spinning him around and around.

Cheers and applause broke the sacred spell. He startled back to reality with a snap. She stood among the soldiers, accepting their handshakes, their tears as if, as if . . . she were the object of their worship. They'd even dared to throw their knapsacks at her feet. He bristled.

Who did this vain slip of a girl think she was, parading her beauty about like a peacock? He'd seen her type before. Young girls with romantic ideals about war. Miss Dix had done an admirable job keeping them out of his hospital, yet nothing stopped them from seeking the attention they so desperately needed elsewhere.

Clamping his jaw, he strode forward. "I'm the head physician at Washington Infirmary. If you're a wounded soldier, we will be administering your health examinations posthaste."

Several of the soldiers turned to stare at him before picking up their knapsacks, their former excitement replaced with looks of resignation. He marched back to the hospital, sneaking one more glance at the woman as he departed.

Just what he needed. A mockingbird perching right outside his roost.

chapter 4

THE BELL IN FATHER'S TOY SHOP jangled overhead as Cadence pushed the door open, a laden basket in her arms. A mother and child were at the counter paying for their purchases. Father looked up as he bade them good-bye. When he spied Cadence, a smile stretched his mouth wide.

"Well, if this isn't a pleasant surprise!"

She nodded upon passing the mother and child, but when the door closed behind them, she moved to kiss his cheek. "How are things in the shop today?"

"Better now that you're here. Something smells heavenly." He sniffed in a melodramatic fashion. "Louisa's fresh-baked biscuits?"

"Of course, along with blackberry preserves and cheese, and I made cinnamon cake this morning."

He placed his hand over his stomach. "Is it my birthday?"

She shook her head. "Am I not allowed to spoil my father

from time to time? Besides, I have an errand to run and thought I might as well visit you while I'm out."

He took the basket with a chuckle and unpacked its contents. "I'm glad you did. As to business, things have been quiet this morning. I pray it's only a temporary lull."

Cadence unwrapped the fluffy biscuits and studied his careworn face. "Is there news I've not heard?"

He sighed. "Nothing overly alarming. This morning's paper held tidings of battles heating up in Virginia. The gentlemen I've spoken to believe Congress is worried. Things are not looking favorable for the Union."

She pulled the preserves from the basket and glanced out the front window, watching the people scurry by as if they too were abuzz with some kind of frantic worry. "Do you ever wonder if Tate is—?"

He looked away, his shoulders slumping. "All the time. But it serves no purpose to dwell on it or wonder."

Her throat constricted. Indeed. Her brother had chosen, albeit poorly, and now he must live with the consequences. If only Mother hadn't died.

If Cadence had been a better nurse, Mother might have lived and Tate would still be with them.

Dorothea Dix might have been right to turn her away.

Forcing a brightness she didn't feel, she spread the food before Father.

He studied her face, his brows pinched. "You've set two places here."

"I thought we might enjoy a midday meal together."

The slight wince in his expression stung, despite his quick attempt to mask it. "As much as I would enjoy it, my dear, I'm afraid I simply haven't the time to visit. Customers, you know."

"I thought you said it had been quiet."

He looked away, refusing to meet her eyes. "Afternoons are always busier than the mornings. You understand, don't you?"

A cold feeling washed through her chest. Pasting on a smile, she attempted a chirpy response. "Of course. Customers always come first. I have an important errand to run anyway."

He smiled and gave a sigh of relief. "Good, good. Thank you for the lunch, Songbird. You're a good girl."

Ignoring the sharp twist in her stomach, she took her leave, her sights set on Washington Infirmary. She would think about Father another time. She must find out what had happened to those poor wounded soldiers. They'd haunted her sleep last night and every waking moment since. They'd been so beaten down. So . . . lifeless. Until the simple strains of an anthem ignited a spark not yet extinguished.

Her heels clicked against the street as she wove between hordes of moving people, creeping wagons, and peddlers. A cool gust of wind cut through the air and slithered up her skirt. She studied the darkening October sky and winced. Thick rain clouds hung low. The breeze had already picked up, carrying with it the odor of rotting garbage mingled with baking bread. She reached the hospital just as the first raindrop hit her cheek.

Pushing open the heavy door, she stood inside the foyer and took note of the gleaming wood floors and sterile white-painted walls. She shook away the crimson leaves clinging to her skirt and sniffed. The sharp sting of ammonia hung in the air. She wrinkled her nose against the smell and braved a glance up and down the hallway. No one coming or going. Somewhere beyond the corridors she could hear chatter, people conversing. A low moan. More indistinguishable sounds before silence settled.

Should she search for someone to speak with? Make her presence known? Feeling as if she were shattering some sacred, invisible barrier, she walked to the left and followed the long corridor until it turned sharply to the right. A swell of noise and activity beckoned just beyond a closed door. With a fortifying breath, she pushed open the door. It gave with a gentle swish. She stopped and stared.

The room was large, almost cavernous. Tidy rows of beds lined each side. Men wearing Union uniforms scurried back and forth, all of them intent on some errand. Two or three matronly women clad in black walked among ill patients tucked within the confines of the cots. A man in the back corner cried out, thrashing against his blanket.

The veil to the inner sanctum had been lifted. This was what had been withheld from her. Why should age or appearance be a qualification for compassion?

Her presence must have been noticed, for one of the nurses approached. Her gray hair was pulled back into a severe bun. Why, the nurse's pins must be jabbing her so sharply, she no doubt suffered from a headache.

"Pardon my intrusion. I found no one in the foyer. I met some of the newly arrived wounded yesterday and wanted to check on them. How are they?"

The elderly nurse sighed, her expression revealing shadows of fatigue. "On the whole, not well. Most have pneumonia. All of them are severely malnourished and dehydrated. Others suffer from a host of other ailments which I should not discuss if you have delicate sensibilities."

Cadence winced. "How dreadful. Is there anything I can do to be of service?"

The nurse tipped her head, her brow furrowed. "Did Miss Dix send you? I'd not heard of—"

"There's the singer!"

A gravelly, masculine voice interrupted their conversation.

Cadence turned to see one of the patients smiling at her. The man's cheekbones protruded sharply in his face, but his eyes were alight with pleasure. "Aren't you the miss who rallied our spirits yesterday?"

Cadence approached his bedside. "I am. I came today to see how you all fared."

"Not so well." He coughed and cringed, his entire frame convulsing. "But better now that you're here. Private John Carter, at your service."

She forced her tongue to obey. "Cadence Piper."

His glassy eyes studied her face, a small smile hovering over his cracked lips. "Cadence. What do ya know? Perfect name for a songbird, don't ya think?"

She laughed and noticed that the nurse was smiling as well.

"Will you favor us with a song?"

"I don't know . . ."

Private Carter lifted his ragged voice to the other soldiers nearby. "Listen up, boys. The singer is here. You want her to share another song?"

Weak cries peppered the air. Cadence turned to the nurse. "May I? I'll not do it if it causes you any trouble."

The matron shrugged. "I don't see it causing any harm. If anything, it will brighten their spirits."

Nodding, Cadence directed her focus to Private Carter. "What shall I sing?"

He settled back against his pillow, his face pale. "Anything. Everything."

A hundred songs flitted through her mind, but one settled and refused to budge.

> "Rock of ages, cleft for me,
> Let me hide myself in thee;

Let the water and the blood,
From thy wounded side which flowed,
Be of sin the double cure,
Save from wrath and make me pure."

Private Carter sniffed. "Reminds me of my ma. Sing another verse, please."

"Could my tears forever flow,
Could my zeal no languor know,
These for sin could not atone;
Thou must save, and thou alone.
In my hand no price I bring;
Simply to thy cross I cling."

When she'd finished that hymn, a different soldier requested another. After singing a total of four songs, the nurses asked if she would help dictate a letter for a soldier who wanted to write home. Before she realized it, her short visit turned into two hours.

Two beautiful hours, and she'd never been more fulfilled.

Joshua dragged his hand down his face, attempting to wipe his mind free of the look in the soldier's eyes when he'd delivered the news. No man wanted to hear his leg must be amputated, but this soldier had resembled a wounded, panicked animal trapped in a cage.

How many more would share the same fate in the coming months? Defeat clawed at Joshua's mind like a vulture.

He should try to get some rest before the surgery. Check on his other patients. Private Campbell's chest sounded far too congested, and Private Donovan looked as if he might be suffering from scurvy.

Slipping through the hallway, he walked into the patients' quarters and froze.

It was her. That singer. He could never forget her dark, glossy hair nor those blue eyes. She was leaning over a bedside, pressing a cloth to a patient's head. The man said something and she smiled, a dimple emerging in her smooth cheek.

Joshua studied her slim form. She wasn't wearing black. Miss Dix hadn't sent her. Why on earth was she here?

An itch formed between his shoulder blades. He marched up to Nurse Meyers and blurted, "What is she doing here?"

The elderly woman whirled to him with a start, her eyes wide. "Who?"

He clenched his jaw. "The young miss attending Private Scoffield."

"Ah yes. Miss Piper. She arrived just past noon and inquired about the health of the newly arrived soldiers. Claimed she'd met them yesterday and was concerned about them. Nothing more." Nurse Meyers's face creased into a hundred wrinkles as she smiled. "You should have seen them when they recognized her. It was like the sun had risen. They asked her to sing." Her eyes actually misted, for heaven's sake. "Such an angelic sound I've never heard. After a time, I put her to work with other tasks. The men are loath to see her depart."

Private Scoffield laughed, snagging Joshua's attention. Miss Piper squeezed his hand and stepped away.

Was it any wonder they didn't want her to leave? He quelled an angry retort.

"Should I dismiss her, sir?"

He pursed his lips. The men clearly wanted her there, but her presence breached Miss Dix's protocol for nurses. There was enough to do without having to worry about a vain popinjay flitting through his hospital. An idea formed.

"No need, Nurse Meyers. I shall take care of it." Strolling to the young woman's side, he cleared his throat. "Miss Piper?"

She turned to him, eyes blinking. Words fled as he looked down into her upturned face. Her eyes were even bluer than he'd imagined. The color of the Potomac on a sunny day.

"Yes? May I be of some assistance?"

He straightened. He would not fall under her spell as the others had. He leveled a hard stare into her eyes. "You do not meet Dorothea Dix's requirements for nurses, so enlighten me . . . how did you manage to sneak into my hospital?"

chapter 5

CADENCE TOOK A STEP BACK, her breath thinning as she stared at the stranger before her.

He would have been handsome, strikingly so, with his strong build, chestnut hair, chocolate eyes, and chiseled jaw, save for the fierce scowl marring his expression.

His gaze raked over her, and she fought the urge to rub her arms. Surely January's wind held more warmth.

"I'm waiting, Miss Piper."

She licked her lips, her voice suddenly uncooperative. "I—I merely stopped by to check on the soldiers I met yesterday. They asked me to sing, and—"

"And you decided to indulge some romantic notion of being a nurse in their hour of need."

Heat scurried up her neck and bloomed in her cheeks. "No! I merely want to help."

"That's good to know, because I have need of a nurse."

She clasped her hands and nodded. "I know little, but I'm happy to assist however I can."

"Good. Follow me." He walked briskly through the room, motioning to two stewards on his way. "Please bring Private Sanders to surgery."

She struggled to keep pace with his long strides, even while her mind scrambled. Surgery? She had no experience in such things. Alarm iced her veins.

Behind her, she could hear men grunting as they lifted the patient's bed through the hallway. The doctor led her into a smaller room, but one much brighter with an entire wall comprised of rain-splattered windows. Watery light filtered through the glass, revealing the cloudy skies beyond. Long rows of cabinets lined the opposite wall. Tables were filled with every kind of instrument imaginable. An odd assortment of aromas hung in the air. A large stack of towels sat on a table in the corner. A long, flat table stood squarely in the middle of the room.

"Dr. Ivy, would you like us to transfer the patient now?"

The handsome doctor nodded at the two stewards as he pulled various bottles and instruments from the table. A cloth folded and sitting erect like a cone, long tweezers, and a . . . saw? Cadence gripped the edge of the closest table. Surely he wasn't going to . . .

The stewards lifted the sheets underneath Private Sanders, transferring him, bedding and all, onto the surgery table with a groan.

The soldier's complexion went gray. "You sure, Doc? Please. How am I gonna farm without a leg?"

"I'm sorry, Joe. I wish there were another way, but once gangrene has set in, it's only a matter of time before it not only takes your leg but your whole life." He squeezed Private Sanders's shoulder. "You'll be amazed what you'll be able to do once you get used to being without it."

The young man squeezed his eyes shut. Sweat beaded on his upper lip. "I don't know if I can do this."

Dr. Ivy looked up at Cadence. "Hand me the anesthesia cloth, please."

Mouth dry, she studied the assortment of instruments he'd arranged closest to the table. With trembling fingers, she handed him the tented cloth. He took it without a word.

"Chloroform."

Scanning the labels, she felt a surge of triumph when it only took her two seconds to locate the correct bottle.

"Unbutton the patient's collar."

She stared at him. His brown eyes flared with something akin to amusement.

"We're not at a garden party, Miss Piper. I assure you, he'll not think you forward." A wicked grin tipped his lips. "Not overly much, anyway."

The cad. She'd never so much as exchanged words of endearment with a man, save for familial affections with her brother or father. Unbuttoning a man's collar seemed far too intimate.

Dr. Ivy's sigh sliced sharply. "Sometime today, Miss Piper."

Whether it was anger at him for being so infuriating or at herself for allowing him to fluster her so, she couldn't tell, but before she knew what was happening, she watched her fingers fly over the buttons of the patient's shirt, revealing his hair-covered chest.

Dr. Ivy's chuckle snapped her back. "No need to completely undress him."

She clamped her teeth together. Was the man always so churlish? Her gaze flickered to the patient's, who looked away. Crimson mottled his neck.

Dr. Ivy leaned over Joe, his expression gentle. "We're ready. I'm going to pray, if that's all right."

Joe nodded, and the surgeon closed his eyes. "God Almighty, I humbly beseech you to guide my hands. I ask that you watch over Joe. Bring him healing, quick recovery, and long life. I ask these things in the name of your dear Son, Jesus. Amen."

Cadence stared. Who was this man? Infuriating one minute, petitioning Providence the next. Grabbing the tented cloth, he held it over Joe's nose and mouth before allowing drops of chloroform to saturate the tip of the cloth.

"Breathe normally. You may feel odd, but I assure you all is well."

Joe's eyes widened. "I can't breathe!"

Cadence reached for his hand, but he pushed her away, his fingers flailing, grasping at the air. Dr. Ivy seemed unconcerned.

"You're not suffocating. Chloroform feels strange, but your body is getting all the air it needs. Relax. There you go."

Joe's eyelids began to droop. His body twitched sporadically. His eyes rolled back in his head before his weight sank into the operating table.

After another few seconds, Dr. Ivy removed the cloth cone. "There. That should last awhile."

He pulled down the blankets covering Joe's lower body and unwrapped his right leg. A putrid stench filled the air, so foul Cadence gagged. She barely got a glimpse of the blackened flesh before her vision swam. Nausea clawed up her throat. The world tilted. Dr. Ivy's commanding voice swarmed through the tumult.

"Have you seen gangrene before, Miss Piper?"

She attempted to straighten and keep the bile in her throat down. "No, I have not."

He smiled tightly. "It's not nearly as romantic as dabbing fevered brows and singing to lovesick soldiers, is it?"

She offered no reply. She couldn't. The smell . . . heaven help her, the smell was more than she could bear.

He wrapped a tourniquet above the patient's knee before grabbing a small handsaw and positioning it just below Joe's kneecap.

At the first sight of crimson, the room spun. Her vision narrowed to tiny pinpoints. She could no longer contain her nausea. Her knees wobbled. Dr. Ivy's voice sounded far away.

"Miss Piper . . ."

A shout for the stewards, the floor rushing up to meet her, then merciful nothingness.

"Miss Piper?"

A baritone voice beckoned her, prodding her senses. Warm fingertips pressed against her neck. Forcing her eyes open, she gasped to find the handsome face of Dr. Ivy hovering over hers, his chocolate eyes intense. Was that compassion flickering in his gaze? He snatched his fingers from her collar as if he'd touched a burning coal. His eyes shuttered, the concern replaced with something altogether different.

"Go home, Miss Piper. This work is not for you."

She pushed herself up. She was in an empty examination room. Had she missed the entire surgery?

Lifting trembling fingers to her brow, she fought to push away the haze clouding her mind. Private Sanders. Chloroform. And then Dr. Ivy unwrapping his infected leg . . .

She'd fainted. Made a spectacle of herself in front of not just Dr. Ivy, but the stewards as well. Humiliation, anger, frustration . . . all of it rolled through her in waves as hot tears pricked her eyes. Images blurred.

Cupping her hand over her mouth, she stumbled from the room, searching through the maze of corridors until she found the door. She had only one destination in mind.

Home.

Joshua gouged the sockets of his eyes with the palms of his hands. He ought to be horsewhipped. He'd thought if he but mentioned the word *surgery*, Miss Piper would run home, but she'd held her ground. Not just held her ground but done her best to assist. Even when he'd shown her gangrene, she'd not succumbed as he'd wagered. Instead, she'd forged ahead with far more pluck and starch than he'd given her credit for.

Unease gnawed his middle. He'd only meant to scare her away. She had no business working in the hospital. She was far too attractive. Far too impressionable and innocent. His jaw cramped as he ground his teeth.

No. He couldn't risk it. The work was too great.

Growling, he pinched the bridge of his nose. He'd never expected her to faint. Run out of the room? Yes. On all counts, Miss Piper had surprised him.

After the stewards had taken Joe to recovery, he'd attended to her. Watched the gentle thrum of life in her slender neck, admired the curve of her cheek, the long sweep of her lashes. She was so feminine and fragile . . . too much so to be mingling among blood and disease. No, in every way it was a bad idea.

She thought him a monster, and rightly so. Better she believe him to be a beast than allow her to destroy herself or her reputation.

Cadence smeared away the tears that refused to stop falling as she lay on her bed. The rose-patterned wallpaper had blurred before her eyes for two hours, and still her sobs had not ceased. She stared at the embossed blossoms but saw only blood, could still smell the putrid stench of decay. Had Dr. Ivy mocked her

48

when she'd succumbed? Surely he must have. A nurse who couldn't endure the odor of infection . . . his derision must have been slicing. Humiliation covered her like a wet cloak.

A soft knock sounded. Louisa's voice drifted through the door. "Missy, you been in there a long time. You feeling okay?"

If she said no, Louisa would insist on seeing her. If she said yes, she would wonder why she'd not yet emerged since it was past time for supper. Father was likely already home.

Sighing, she brushed at the escaping tears. "I'm not feeling well."

"May I come in?"

"Yes."

The door creaked open. Louisa's face appeared, concern lined in her gentle features. "What's got my lamb crying so?"

A sob scraped Cadence's chest. Louisa's knotted fingers rubbed her back in circular motions as she and spilled out the horrid story.

"Land sakes, ain't had no idea you even wanted to become a nurse, much less tried to go into that hospital." Louisa clucked her tongue. "Hard work, child. Mighty hard."

Cadence sniffled. "I was so sure I could do it. Things were going so well too, until Dr. Ivy . . ."

Louisa harrumphed and Cadence sat up, wiping away her tears. "What?"

The housekeeper frowned. "Sounds to me like that doctor was trying to scare you away."

She sucked in the remnants of a sob and let her mind wander over the events of that last miserable half hour. "I don't know." His terseness. The way she'd been taken from transcribing letters and moved to assist a surgical amputation. The steward's look of sympathy. Her throat clamped.

Dr. Ivy had indeed chased her away. Her nostrils flared. "Why, that no-account, low-down—"

Louisa grabbed her agitated hands. "Calm down, missy. Cool that temper. What that doctor did wasn't right, but neither were you."

The accusation stung. "I didn't do anything."

The servant arched a brow. "Come now. You may have wanted to check on those soldiers, true enough, but that was done in five minutes. What you really wanted was to try your hand at nursing, which those women let you do readily enough, even though Miss Dix already told you no."

Heat crept up her collar. She dropped her gaze to the bed. "I suppose there's a measure of truth there. My motives weren't quite as pure as I painted them to be. Not that it matters." She blew out a breath and rubbed her temples. "Clearly I'm not cut out to be a nurse."

Louisa shook her head. "I didn't say that. Seems to me, no one is born a master at their craft. All of us got to learn. Even that surgeon. We learn and we grow. We's all born naked, knowing nothing. We learn one skill at a time. You ain't been taught nothing about nursing yet, but two things you got that I know would make you an excellent nurse."

"What's that?"

Louisa cupped her cheek, her brown eyes filled with tenderness. "You love people, child. You love 'em so deeply, you hurt when they hurt. You'll do anything and everything to take that pain away, even if it means sacrificing yourself."

Cadence's lip trembled.

"And two, you've got the Almighty. If it's his will, he'll provide a way. Why, look what he's already done in your life. Remember what that phrenologist said all those years ago? And look at you now."

Cadence offered no rebuttal. She dared not share how much she still hid in order to fit in. How many times she still clamped her lips shut so the dreadful malady would not be noticed. How many words she substituted to avoid the ridicule, the embarrassment.

"You pray. Wait and see."

Wrapping her arms around the housekeeper, Cadence inhaled Louisa's unique scent of cinnamon and soap. "Thank you. I don't know what I would do without you." She released Louisa and straightened her shoulders. "Tomorrow I'm going back down to the hospital to apologize for my weakness. I'll march in there with my head held high. Miss Dix and Dr. Ivy may not allow me to nurse, but at least they'll not say I ran crying from the building in disgrace."

Louisa chuckled. "Make that three things you've got in your favor."

"What's that?"

"Gumption. You never, ever quit."

The next morning, Cadence squared her shoulders and opened the doors of Washington Infirmary. This time, instead of an empty foyer, Nurse Meyers greeted her, her arms filled with clean linens. Upon spying Cadence, she paused, sympathy lining her aged face.

"It's good to see you again, Miss Piper. How are you faring?"

She lifted her chin. "Qu-qu—well now. Thank you, ma'am."

Nurse Meyers leaned forward and dropped her voice to a whisper, her mouth puckering into a pinch. "That was a nasty trick Dr. Ivy pulled on you. He's usually so kind. I've never seen him behave so."

She had no gracious reply. The better road would be one that rose above backbiting. "I may not be adept, nor permitted to be a nurse, but if there is ever anything I can do to help, anything at all . . ."

Nurse Meyers smiled. "I will be sure to let you know. The soldiers are quite fond of you." She winked. "As are we."

"Thank you."

She watched the older woman carry the linens down the hallway and disappear from sight. She closed her eyes and blew out a thick breath. It had been difficult to swallow her pride and walk in, but if she could somehow lend a hand to help the Union or ease the burden of those nursing the suffering soldiers, she'd do it. Even if it meant scrubbing filthy linens.

"I didn't expect to see you again."

Her eyes popped open. Dr. Ivy stood before her, his head tilted, regarding her with that brooding, dark stare of his. Her heart hammered, but she refused to look away. She would not be intimidated by this man again. She would *not*.

"You'll find me to be full of surprises, sir."

A flicker of amusement twitched his mouth. "No doubt."

Cadence twisted her hands together, then forced them apart, not allowing herself the luxury of fretting in front of the surgeon who so flustered her. "I came to apologize."

"Whatever for?"

She lifted her chin. "For collapsing in the operating room yesterday. I'm not proud of it, and I pray I did nothing to impede the soldier's surgery."

Dr. Ivy studied her so long, she felt the urge to squirm. "No apology necessary, Miss Piper. You're not the first to faint in such circumstances. You'll not be the last."

His understanding unraveled the anger that had wound itself around her heart.

"I must ask, sir, did you intend to scare me away or merely test my mettle?"

The hint of a smile appeared. "Tell me, did you interview with Dorothea Dix?"

Why would he not answer her question? "I did."

"And did you meet with her approval?"

She squared her shoulders. "I did not."

"I see."

She tried not to notice the way the light caught strands of his chestnut hair, turning them golden brown.

"What reason did she give?"

"Miss Dix said I was too young."

"What that all?"

She remained silent.

His mouth tipped into a lopsided smile. "Knowing Miss Dix as I do, I would say she also judged you to be far too comely to be among sick and wounded men. Am I correct?"

She nodded, hating the admission. Her cheeks scorched under his perusal.

He sighed and pinched the bridge of his nose. "There's nothing for you here, Miss Piper. Please, I beg you, go home."

"But I—"

His gaze grew fierce. "You cannot serve here."

She took a step back, her trembling fingers groping for the door.

His expression was stormy, though his voice was soft. "If you return, I'll throw you over my shoulder and march you home myself."

She blinked hard. "You'll not see me again."

Then she turned and left, letting the door shut behind her with a resounding click.

chapter 6

FEBRUARY 1862

"When other helpers fail and comforts flee,
Help of the helpless, O abide with me."

Cadence finished the last note of the hymn and bowed her head. Christ Church was full for the night of revival and prayer services. Hearty *amen*s punctuated the air. With a cleansing exhale, she lifted the hem of her skirt and returned to her seat beside Congressman Ramsey and his wife.

Thelnita grasped her hand. "Beautiful solo, my dear."

"Thank you."

Cadence let her eyes slide shut for a brief respite. How she longed for a cool breath of air instead of the stuffy atmosphere of the overly warm room. Her traitorous gaze trailed to the window once again, where the outline of the hospital sat merely a block away.

Stop it! You're not wanted. The admonition stung, but it was a familiar sensation, like the stab of a needle in a calloused finger.

Since being forced from Washington Infirmary, her days had been dull. A listlessness ate away at her spirit. Father refused to let her assist him at the shop, and Louisa tried to include her in household tasks, though they both knew Cadence wasn't truly needed. The only things that brought her purpose were her trips to baby Rose's graveside and the memories of helping the wounded soldiers months before. Even donating her sewing projects to Union charities failed to ease the ache inside.

She forced her attention to the front lectern, where Reverend Quattlebaum took his place, clutching his thick black Bible.

"Thank you, Miss Piper, for leading our hearts to the throne of God with such beauty. Congressman Ramsey has done nothing but shout your praises."

She felt her cheeks heat as several people turned to stare. She bobbed her head and lowered her lashes.

"Among our honored guests this evening is famed orator and poet Fanny Crosby."

Cadence startled and clutched Thelnita's arm, leaning in to whisper, "Miss Crosby is here?"

The older woman's dark eyes shone. "Indeed she is. She spoke at the Capitol building this morning. My husband invited her to come tonight."

Cadence pressed a hand to her suddenly nervous stomach. She was glad she had not known the acclaimed poet was among them before she sang, otherwise she would have been too shaky to have uttered a note.

The reverend continued. "Miss Crosby is also quite a talented singer. I asked her if she would mind sharing a hymn with us tonight, but our dear sister is recovering from the quinsy, and with her earlier speaking engagement to Congress, her voice is tired. Please pray for her recovery and for her safe travels as she returns to New York to join her husband, Mr. Van Alstyne, in their ministry work." His smile stretched wide. "Miss Crosby, upon your next visit, I look forward to hearing one of those hymns you told me you were starting to write. No doubt you shall be as successful in composing sacred lyrics as you have been with poetry."

"Thank you, sir."

Cadence couldn't see her, but the voice from the corner of the room was soft and light.

The pastor turned toward the congregation. "And now, please open God's Word to Genesis chapter 45, verse 27. 'And they told him all the words of Joseph . . .'"

The crush of people exited Christ Church and spilled into the darkened street. Congressman Ramsey and his wife were saying their good-byes to Reverend Quattlebaum when a gentle voice inside the church beckoned Cadence.

"Are you Miss Piper?"

She turned to see a tiny woman gripping the corner of a pew. Her dark hair was pulled back in a severe bun. Her features could be described as nothing but plain, yet her smile was sweet. The eyes behind her round, darkened spectacles were unfocused. They traced no movement. Sightless.

"Yes, ma'am. Miss Crosby?"

"Yes, my dear. Forgive me if you must hasten away. I only wanted to say how much your singing and your song selection spoke to my spirit tonight. Thank you."

Cadence moved to stand before the diminutive woman. "A greater honor you could not bestow upon me. My father and I have long admired your work, ma'am. When I discovered you were in attendance, I admit a whole swarm of butterflies took flight in my stomach."

Miss Crosby laughed. "Anxious to impress a blind woman? Sit with me if you have a moment so we may become better acquainted."

"I would be honored."

The poet felt her way along the pew and eased down, making room for Cadence.

Studying the woman she'd heard so much about, she was suddenly tongue-tied. Many questions rolled around her brain, yet none surfaced into coherent thought.

"I'm astounded at my good fortune in speaking with you. My father will be amazed. We've read your poems and anthems for years. He's especially fond of the ones printed in the *Saturday Evening Post*."

"Ah, yes. The *Post* has been most kind to me."

"I doubt it had as much to do with their kindness as with your talent. And to hear you are to begin writing hymns. How delightful!"

Miss Crosby leaned in and dropped her voice low as if sharing a secret. "To be honest, my dear, I've been writing music and lyrics for quite a number of years with my dear friend George Root, but most liturgical circles have not been aware of it. They would disapprove, you see."

"I cannot fathom why."

Miss Crosby smiled slyly. "My earlier works are used in secular song-and-dance shows."

Cadence suppressed a grin. "Ah, I see. Not so well received among high society."

"Nor among some Christian circles, I fear, though there is nothing scandalous about them. Still, I've busied myself of late writing patriotic songs but find the Almighty is drawing me more and more toward hymns . . . songs that bring me close to his heart."

Cadence breathed. "Knowing how splendid your poetry is, I cannot wait to hear your sacred work. Perhaps I'll sing them one day and be able to say I met the composer herself."

Miss Crosby blinked as if shaking away a deep musing. "Enough about me. Tell me about yourself. I already know God has gifted you with a golden voice. Are you using it for him?"

Miss Crosby did not believe in dancing around a topic, that much was plain to see. "I'm trying. Mr. Ramsey has been very gracious to me, inviting me to sing at patriotic rallies for the Union and revival meetings. It's something I can do to help, I suppose."

"You suppose? What else occupies your time?"

"Looking after my widowed father, though he stays busy since opening his shop. And there's the promise I made to Reverend Goodwin's wife before she moved. Their baby passed away while they ministered here, and I promised her I'd watch over their little girl's resting place. I visit each week and keep the grave decorated."

Miss Crosby's expression shifted as if a veil had been draped over her countenance. "That's extremely kind of you. I—" She stopped short and swallowed, the muscles moving in her neck. Cadence waited, but Miss Crosby's mouth lifted back into a shaky smile. "Very kind."

"To be honest, I still find myself longing for something I do not have. I've begged and pleaded with God to open a door, but thus far, he has kept them all barred and shut to me." Unexpected tears welled as her throat constricted. "I should be content with singing, encouraging others and caring for my father, yet I'm not. My heart yearns for more. I know he can but say the word. Why would he deny me something that would only bring good?"

"Would it? Are you God? Can you see tomorrow's sunrise or next month's or next year's? No, my child. What seems good to us may bring untold pain in the future, could we only but catch a glimpse beyond the bend."

"What shall we do then? Never hope? Never pray or dream?"

"No. Pray—not for your own glory, but rather for his to be displayed. Pray for his great name to be made powerful in your weakness. He may grant your petition with favor. Sometimes he still says no, as he did with me when my child was swept into his arms."

Cadence took a sharp breath. Miss Crosby's lips trembled even as a tender smile lifted. Her vacant eyes behind her spectacles held peace. A serenity infused with strength. Cadence reached for her slender hands and squeezed.

"I'm so sorry."

"My child is with Jesus, and a more wonderful place to be, I cannot fathom. Whether her passing was providential care to prevent some unforeseen disaster, or rather a flaming arrow flung by the enemy, I do not know. So I stand with Shadrach, Meshach, and Abednego of old and say I know God is able to deliver, but even when he does not, he is still good, and I choose to follow and obey."

Miss Crosby squeezed Cadence's hands, and she felt a rush of peace settle over her like a gentle breeze. "You are an inspiration, Miss Crosby. Thank you for your encouragement. So I trust God and keep serving."

"Indeed. I visited a prison here in Washington only just yesterday, and do you know what captured my attention? One man. One lone man crying out from the depths of his cell as we passed. He was whimpering, 'Don't pass me by. Don't forget about me!' There are so many who need help, my dear. We need not wait for a divine revelation. We just do the next thing until God opens a new door."

"Just do the next thing." Yes, she could do that. "What a lovely thought. Love the broken. Give water to the thirsty. Feed the hungry. Just do the next thing."

Miss Crosby patted her hand. "It's been a joy visiting with you, Miss Piper."

"Likewise."

As they stood to depart, Cadence turned back. "You know, that would make a wonderful hymn."

Miss Crosby's brows rose. "What would?"

"About the prisoner crying out. 'Pass me not.' You should use that in a song, Miss Crosby."

A light warmed the woman's vacant eyes. "Perhaps I shall."

Father grunted and took another pull of his coffee as he perused the morning newspaper.

Across the table, Cadence looked up from her plate of eggs. "Bad news?"

"Nothing but." He peered over the top of his reading spectacles. "The Union's western campaigns are not as successful as the generals had hoped they'd be."

"That's a diplomatic way of saying they failed."

Father harrumphed. "Quite. And this—" he slapped the newsprint—"leaves me questioning the morality of mankind."

"What is it?"

"It seems a group of men had a bit of a skirmish, unrelated to the war. One of the men was shot and the rest made haste to his home to divide up ownership of his slaves. They plundered the best of his slaves and killed an infant slave boy when his mother protested being taken away."

Cadence shuddered. "How terrible."

"Authorities are reported as saying it's a closed case." Father frowned. "Odd, that. Shouldn't they be doing more?"

She took another bite of her eggs and dabbed her napkin to her lips. "It's been strangely silent here all winter. Why? And not only with the local authorities. You'd think the Confederacy would be champing at the bit to attack the capital, unless they feel they have no shot of capturing it."

Father rubbed his chin. "Perhaps. Then again, General McClellan has done nothing but sit all winter long. No campaigns, no advances, and no apparent plans to do so. Odd state of affairs. And this—" he jabbed the paper—"beats all I've ever heard."

"What is it?"

He pushed the spectacles higher up his nose. "With the Fugitive Slave Act and so many disreputable bounty hunters roaming the countryside, abolitionists are trying a new tactic to free slaves. Buying slaves themselves."

Cadence put down her fork. "That makes no sense."

Father offered a wry smile. "It does if they buy them only to set them free."

Her mouth dropped. "But how do they keep from being recaptured?"

"The article doesn't say, but I imagine if they have the means to buy the slaves, they also have the means to transport them north and give them the proper paperwork to ensure their freedom. Of course, Confederates are fit to be tied at the abolitionists, but what can they do? It's perfectly legal for a man to do what he wants with his own property."

"Beating them at their own game." She shivered. "I'll never forget the photographs I saw in that gallery you took me to in Boston. Remember? The ones showing the slaves' backs who'd been whipped?" Nausea bubbled up at the horrific images stirred by the memories. "Such brutality should never be embraced by any people."

Father shook his head. "Yet the Rebels call us the barbarians."

She leaned back in her chair, her stomach sour. "Still, we endeavor to preserve the Union through guns and bayonets, slicing apart those who disagree with us. Are we any different?"

Father stilled and gave her a sad look. "War is nasty business, darling. There can be no peace without war. No victory without struggle and no beauty without pain. The Almighty knows the end from the beginning. We seek him and leave all else in his hands."

She nodded. There was wisdom and a measure of comfort in what he said.

"Have you heard from Stephen Dodd lately?"

Her eyes darted up and regarded Father sharply. If she didn't know better, she'd suspect him of hoping for a match. She spoke slowly. "Yes, he wrote just last week."

"And what does he say of events?"

What could she possibly share? Stephen's letters held little of the conditions of war. Instead, he wrote of how he admired her beauty and wondered if she thought of him as much as he thought of her . . . things far too intimate considering how little they knew of each other or what little relationship they actually enjoyed. She'd not encouraged Stephen in the slightest, however, keeping her own letters breezy and cheerful, albeit formal. She could tell Father none of this.

"Not much. I fear he does not want to bore nor alarm me with the worst of the horrors of war. All he mentions is that the drilling is monotonous and the men are weary of staying put."

"No doubt. Yet I do not wish them to be in harm's way either."

She sighed. "I don't know what to pray anymore."

A sharp rapping sounded on the front door. Startled, she looked up. "Are you expecting company?"

He shook his head. "I'll answer it. Louisa just left for the market."

Nodding, she stood to clear the dishes. "I'll clean up." She gathered an armful of dishes and carried them into the kitchen. She had just begun shaving lye into the steaming wash water when Father reappeared.

"You have a caller, Cadence."

She wiped her hands on a cloth and straightened. "Who?"

"A young man. He says he knows you. Dr. Joshua Ivy."

If she'd been holding a dish, she would have dropped it. She heaved a breath. "Did he say what he wanted?"

Father studied her carefully. "He did not. Judging by your reaction, I take it his arrival is unwelcome?"

How to answer? "Yes. Possibly. That is, I shouldn't judge him too harshly, should I?"

"No. Not until you've heard him out."

The question in Father's blue eyes spoke volumes. Guilt gnawed her middle. She'd not told him of her visit to Miss Dix nor to the Washington Infirmary. He'd only worry unnecessarily. Or would he even care?

She pushed away the uncharitable thought. Of course he cared. He was her father, after all. Since Mother's death and then Tate's departure, he'd simply been lost in a world of his own. Perhaps keeping her dreams and whereabouts quiet had been unwise. Surely he'd want to know of her longings to become a nurse. But would he support them?

"I'll see him in the parlor."

"I'll accompany you."

The very idea of Father being present for whatever humiliation Dr. Ivy might impose caused a cold wash to skitter down her spine.

"I'll be fine. Thank you, though. I'll leave the parlor door open and call should I need you."

He frowned. "Five minutes. I'll not have you go unchaperoned a minute longer." He departed, giving her a knowing look.

Mustering her courage, she dropped the cloth on the counter and walked slowly toward the parlor. What possible reason could Dr. Ivy have to seek her out? And why now, months after he'd barred her from the hospital?

She paused at the parlor door and gripped the jamb, staring. He paced before the crackling fire, oblivious to her presence. Even with his head bent, he was taller than she remembered, broader across the shoulders but trim. His chestnut hair shimmered almost golden between the firelight and the morning sunshine streaming through the window. But it was the shadows beneath his eyes that tugged her heart. He looked weary, far more exhausted than she'd last seen him.

"Dr. Ivy?"

His head snapped up. He froze upon seeing her in the entryway. Something flared in his eyes, though she could not read his expression.

"Miss Piper." He bowed his head. "Thank you for receiving me." He lifted a brow. "I wasn't sure if you would."

She clasped her hands together. "In truth, I wasn't sure if I should."

He smiled then, and she marveled at how it transformed his face. The man was handsome but such a genuine smile . . . the effect was altogether unsettling.

Swallowing, she gestured toward the chairs. "Please feel free to sit. I can offer you some tea if you'd like."

"Thank you, no." He took a seat but perched on the edge,

leaning his elbows on his knees as if in a hurry to state his business. She sat in the stuffed chair across from him and waited, her stomach in knots.

He wove his fingers together and frowned before lifting his gaze. "I'll come straight to the point, Miss Piper." He cleared his throat. "I need you."

Fire scorched her cheeks. Rational thought fled. "Wha—?"

Crimson streaked up his neck as his eyes widened. "I didn't mean that the way it sounded. I—" He jumped up and kneaded the back of his neck before whirling back to her once more. "I need you as my nurse."

Never would she have dreamed he'd come to request such a thing. A wicked part of her longed to watch him squirm, but needling him over his boorish behavior wouldn't be kind. Still, she couldn't form a coherent answer.

She must have taken overly long pondering what to do, for his deep voice cut the silence.

"Are you waiting for me to beg, Miss Piper?"

"No. I'm simply too shocked for words. Your request is far different from your threat months ago when I believe you told me . . . What was it? Ah, yes, that you would toss me over your shoulder and c-c-car—" she cleared her throat—"hoist me home if I dared enter your hospital again."

He blanched and tugged at his collar. "Forgive me, Miss Piper. It was wrong of me to have treated you so. Surely you understand that I must strive to obey protocol. Miss Dix is quite firm in her requirements for nurses, and I would have received no end of trouble had I defied her wishes." He offered a lopsided smile. "Surgeons and nurses alike don't call her Dragon Dix for nothing."

Cadence could well imagine. There was steel beneath the woman's satin gentility.

"Have the requirements changed, then?"

His brown eyes flickered with hesitancy. "No, they have not."

"Then why ask me for help?"

He sighed. "To be honest, I'm losing nurses left and right. Influenza has exacted a heavy toll on my most reliable ones. Three of my best have passed away. Four more are convalescing in their homes and may not be able to return for a month, perhaps longer due to their age. Several others have left to nurse their own sons who were wounded in battle." His jaw tightened. "And I tell you this under the strictest confidence, Miss Piper. A Union general told me only just yesterday that a flurry of fighting is predicted to occur in Virginia in the coming months. If that comes to pass as he thinks it might, casualties will be transported—"

"To Washington." She finished his sentence in a whisper. Could the already-overcrowded capital city hold hordes of wounded? It was bulging at the seams. Each week the streets grew more clogged, the beggars more abundant, the structures of newly constructed tenement buildings more pronounced.

"I know you're aware of the fire that destroyed Washington Infirmary in November."

"Yes. Most unfortunate."

It had only been a week after he'd chased her away that the hospital building had caught fire. She watched from her vantage point in the cemetery as firefighters attempted to douse the licking red flames.

"I'm resettled in a new hospital now, and we've been commandeered by the military. I've already sent a request for more nurses, but with resources needing to be stretched across so many, I fear the reinforcements will come too late. I need nurses now so I can train them before the bulk of new casualties arrive." His eyes trailed to hers and held fast, causing her heart to squeeze. "You have fortitude and compassion. Several women I've tried to train of late didn't have the stomach to even set foot in the room with gangrene, much less try to battle through to be of any help. You did."

She looked away, hating the flush creeping over her skin. "But I fainted."

His chuckle caused her to snap her eyes to his.

"Do you think you're alone in that reaction? My first encounter with gangrene left me heaving into a chamber pot for the better part of an hour." He shrugged. "You get used to it. It's part of the training." He smiled, and her shame melted away. "I wager you'll not faint again. You have grit and plenty of it. Why do you think I came here, ready to humble myself and beg?"

Dr. Ivy could be quite charming when he wanted to be. Hope beat against her ribs like a bird longing to take flight. "But what of Miss Dix? Nothing changes the fact that I am young and unmarried. She denied me before. She'll do so again."

His mirth faded, replaced by somber gravity. "Necessity demands much. In times of war, things like age and appearance don't seem to matter so much. I'll arrange it."

"What if she doesn't agree?"

He looked away. "There are ways of making it work."

His answer seemed elusive, but he knew that world far better than she. Dare she hope? Could God really be giving her the desire of her heart?

Glancing into her eyes once again, he frowned. "I'm far from perfect, Miss Piper, as you're already well aware. In surgery I can be demanding and tend to speak first without thought of softening my tone. But if you can be patient with me and forgive my faults, I would be happy to train you."

He'd already torn her heart to pieces in two brief encounters. How would she manage to work alongside such a man day after day? Still, the thought of her dream so close to her fingertips was far too heady to be ignored.

"What say you, Miss Piper?"

Her pulse drummed slowly in her ears as she stared at his hopeful expression. How could she say no?

"On one condition."

"What's that?"

"My father must agree." She could win him over. And how good it would be for him to be able to tell his friends, *"No, I have no son fighting, but my daughter is a nurse for the Union."* He would have no cause to bear the disgrace of Tate's shortcomings any longer.

He nodded. "A reasonable request."

She held out her hand, and he clasped it with his own. "Provided my father agrees, then yes, Dr. Ivy, I shall be your nurse."

chapter 7

Cadence dipped a cloth in the basin of water and squeezed out the excess, mopping it across the fevered soldier's neck. With half of his head and face bandaged, she could make out little of his features, but at least he was calm, despite the severity of his injuries. That could not be said for many in the hospital.

She kept her voice light and cheerful as she worked. "What battle did you last engage in?"

"Kernstown, ma'am." His lips quirked. "We whupped them Rebs good, though I imagine I look like I came out on the losing end."

She chuckled and dropped the cloth back in the basin. "You're alive, and that is what matters, soldier. You make us all proud."

He smiled fully then but winced. "Don't imagine my eye will look the same when all is said and done."

"Perhaps not, but you'll have a badge of honor that tells the story of your heroism. Here now." She opened an envelope of laudanum powder and sprinkled it into a tin cup of water next to his bed, stirring it with a spoon. "Dr. Ivy wants that high fever to break. You need rest and liquid. Drink this and sleep."

The soldier gulped down the medicine in four long pulls and grimaced before falling back into his bed. "Bless you."

She placed her hand on the thatch of wheat-colored hair sticking up above his bandage and prayed. *Heavenly Father, heal him if it be thy will. Bless him with long life and purpose to love and serve you.*

As he drifted into sleep, she placed the cup, washbasin, and empty medicine envelope on the serving tray and stood, moving to the next patient. Her back ached and her eyes blurred from hours spent hovering over small beds, but she regretted not one moment. Caring for the wounded had given her greater satisfaction than she'd dreamed possible.

Moving to Private Taylor's bedside, she frowned. He was another of the casualties of the battle at Kernstown, and his leg had been crushed in the skirmish. Dr. Ivy had amputated as soon as he'd arrived, but the poor soldier continued to weaken. The arduous journey to Washington might have been more than he could endure. She studied his pasty complexion dotted with beads of sweat. His eyes were pinched closed, yet he trembled violently as he fisted the covers close to his body.

Kneeling at his side, she placed a calming hand over his clenched fists. "Private Taylor, how are you feeling?"

He trembled through gritted teeth. "M-m-mighty p-poorly, Mrs. P-Piper."

She didn't correct his use of *Mrs.* Dr. Ivy had given her a cheap wedding band to wear at the hospital to protect her reputation and perhaps her job. She pushed the guilt of the deception aside. The good she was doing justified the means, didn't it?

She smoothed his sweat-matted hair from his forehead. "I'll fetch the doctor. Stay strong."

She rose and looked for Dr. Ivy. Seeing no sign of him in the large room, she walked quickly down the corridor to his small office and peeked in. He sat hunched over his cluttered desk, hastily writing amid haphazard stacks of papers and medical journals. The man was a constant enigma. Patient and kind one minute, gruff the next. In the past two months he'd been training her, they'd worked remarkably well together, likely because he knew nurses were scarce and he must be on his best behavior. Still, she'd never seen anyone so tender with the patients. His office always looked as if a cyclone had struck, but his mind was razor-sharp, quick, and discerning.

She cleared her throat and he looked up with a start.

"Nurse Piper? Did you need anything?"

"I'm sorry to disturb you, but it's Private Taylor. His color has worsened, and he has cold sweats and tremors. It would relieve my mind if you'd be so kind as to examine him."

Frowning, he stood and grabbed a stethoscope on his way out. She led him to the bedside and waited, watching as he placed the cone over the ill soldier's chest and listened through the earpieces. He moved his fingers to the patient's wrist, checking the young man's pulse. After examining the young man's neck, eyes, and stomach, Dr. Ivy straightened. His face was granite as he watched the soldier moan and thrash in his delirium.

"What's wrong?"

"Blood poisoning." He scrubbed his hands across the back of his neck. "He's the eighth one in the past fortnight to succumb. If I could just figure out why they're all contracting it . . ." He let his words trail away, his brows low as he puzzled it out. "I clean the wounds as best I can, yet still they fall ill to the poisoning."

Her heart ached at the stricken look on his face. "You're doing all you can."

A muscle in his jaw twitched. "Unfortunately, that brings little comfort to the dead or their loved ones." He looked at her then, his face unreadable. "Keep him as comfortable as you can."

She nodded as he brushed past her, rubbing his temple on the way out. He was correct. There was little solace in doing your best when men still died. She cooled Private Taylor's neck and face with a damp rag and managed to slip a couple spoonfuls of diluted laudanum water between his cracked lips before she found herself drawn to Dr. Ivy's operating room.

Walking slowly through the small space, she carefully studied the assortment of vials and medicines, the washbowls and clean towels ready to be used. The surgical instruments were lined in rows.

She mentally rehearsed the order Dr. Ivy used in his amputations. *Fold and shape cloth into a cone. Hold above the patient's nose and mouth. Apply three to five drops of chloroform on the cloth until patient is asleep and breathing peacefully. Tourniquet above the part of the limb about to be removed.*

That's where things changed. Different amputations required different saws. Different instruments and techniques. She could see nothing in the earlier part of the operation that would cause blood poisoning. It must have something to do with the instruments . . . but what?

And many of the patients they received had already endured surgery in a battlefield hospital. In truth, Dr. Ivy had only performed a few surgeries in the past month. What was causing the men to suffer so?

She glanced across the corridor to see Dr. Ivy hunched over his cluttered desk, his head in his hands, hair fisted in his fingers.

Was the burden of his patients what weighed on him so heavily, or was it something more?

———— ⚘ ————

Joshua stared at the low flame licking the wick of the sagging tallow candle on his desk. Twilight had descended, snuffing out the sunlight and plunging the hospital into darkness. The soft glow of lanterns lined the corridors and wards. His eyes burned with fatigue. Any more correspondence would have to wait for another day. One particular letter seemed to bore through him from the mess stretched across the desk. He capped the inkwell and set the pen aside. He'd have to give the general his answer soon. A muscle in his neck spasmed.

If he were to agree to travel with the Union troops for a time, what would become of his carefully laid plans? The operation he'd so painstakingly put in place? Then again, discovery was much more likely if he grew lukewarm and stagnant. Several times in the past few months, he'd sensed someone watching him. Perhaps with a change of pace, a change of scenery, new contacts, he'd lessen the risk of discovery. But what of the children?

Enough for one day. He must sleep. He blew out the candle and pushed back from the desk with a scrape. The acrid stench of smoke filled his nostrils as he stood and stretched his stiff limbs. He reached for his coat on the rack. No, not the green one. The brown. He slipped into its warmth and walked down the hallway. In the distance, he could hear the sharp click of booted heels. A patient coughing. Murmured words of comfort. And . . . singing.

The soft melody grew louder as he wound his way into the largest ward. He stopped to see Miss Piper sitting next to Private Taylor's bedside, her hand holding his as his chest faintly rose and fell. A single kerosene lantern sat on the bedside table, illuminating her perfect profile.

> *"When we've been there ten thousand years,*
> *Bright shining as the sun,*
> *We've no less days to sing God's praise*
> *Than when we'd first begun."*

For a moment, he closed his eyes, letting her sweet voice and the comforting words wash over him like rain on parched ground. A sniffle caused his eyes to fly open.

Tears fell down her smooth cheeks, leaving golden tracks in the lantern light as she watched the soldier's face. Joshua's gaze shifted to the soldier. Private Taylor's chest was no longer moving.

He walked to Miss Piper's side, placed his hand on her shoulder, and offered a gentle squeeze. "I'm sorry."

She wiped her face with shaky fingers and smiled despite her tears. "I know it's silly to be weeping. I knew he was going to pass. Men die here every day, yet I hurt for them. Hurt for their families." She looked up at him then, her blue eyes large in the soft light. "Does it ever get easier?"

He sighed and knelt before her. "If you grow calloused to pain and suffering, then yes, it gets easier. If you don't, it still hurts." He swung his gaze to Private Taylor. The shadow of death had already stolen the look of life from his face. "Did he ask you to sing to him?"

"No. In truth, I don't even think he knew I was here, but—" she looked into Joshua's eyes and his chest tightened—"no man deserves to die alone."

He nodded and tore his gaze from hers. "Kind of you." He stared at his hands and fumbled for the words he wanted to say.

"I never told you before—I mean, I should have, but, well, your voice. It's beautiful."

"Thank you."

"Where did you learn to sing like that?"

A sad look drifted across her face. "I don't know. I've been singing for as long as I can remember. It's always been my escape." She looked into some place he could not see. "Music speaks when words don't suffice."

"Rather cryptic."

"Perhaps."

"The patients love it, so however you came by this gift, I'm grateful."

The ghost of a smile played around her mouth. "Why, Dr. Ivy, I do believe you're warming up to me."

He dropped his jaw and placed his hand to his chest in mock outrage. "The cranky Dr. Ivy?" He smiled. "Yes, Nurse Piper, you've taken to nursing with remarkable ease. I'm most pleased with your work."

She bit her lip and glanced down at her lap but not before he witnessed the telltale blush springing pink to her cheeks. Was his praise so rare that it actually elicited the bloom of heat? He struggled to think of any praise he might have doled out in the past week to Nurse Piper, Nurse McDougal, Nurse Pearson, or any of the other nurses. His mind came up blank.

He must remedy such pitiful oversight.

"Forgive me for not saying so earlier. You are one of the brightest nurses I've ever worked with."

"Nurse Piper?"

Both of them looked up with a start at Nurse Meyers's soft call. The elderly woman stood in the doorway.

"Pardon the intrusion, but I could use your help distributing the next round of medicines."

Miss Piper stood and offered a small smile. "Thank you, Doctor. Your praise means much."

He rose and stuffed his hands in his pockets. "I don't offer praise often or lightly. Something I intend to remedy."

Nodding, she took another long look at Private Taylor. "Should I stay until—?"

"I'll call for the night steward to take Private Taylor away. He'll be prepared for burial on the morrow."

She pressed a solemn kiss to the dead soldier's hand and slipped away into the darkened corridor. Joshua watched her go, his chest tight.

Ever since the day he'd witnessed her standing on the street singing Francis Scott Key's anthem surrounded by war-weary soldiers, their knapsacks at her feet, the woman had been a constant surprise. Had he really thought her shallow and vain? The idea seemed ludicrous now. Not after witnessing her determination and compassion.

He rested his hand gently on Private Taylor's shock of blond hair and bowed his head, murmuring a silent prayer for the Almighty's blessing over the young man's memory. Singing a dying man into Jesus' arms. Joshua's throat cramped. Miss Piper was far more than a nurse. She was an angel on earth.

Sighing, he turned away. An angel he'd spent far too much time thinking about of late. He couldn't, wouldn't let himself grow attached to her or any other female. His work called. Voiceless faces silently cried out for help, both in the hospital and beyond. He'd not compromise freedom's cry for the hopelessness of chasing daydreams.

A patient thrashed two beds away, his hoarse pleas slurred in his delirium. "The snake! The order! They's comin' for me!"

Joshua rushed to his side and grabbed his flailing arms before he hurt himself. The bearded soldier bucked, his eyes wild as he locked on to Joshua's face. His pupils were large, his eyes darting about as if he were frantically trapped in some hellish nightmare.

"Calm now, McHenry. You're safe. No one's going to hurt you here."

McHenry tried to shove him away with a shriek. Joshua fought to control the thrashing man. Every muscle strained to keep him down.

"The Knights! You don't understand! My brother turned to the order. I saw the emblem of the snake. They'll kill my wife! Please!"

The Knights? Struggling to make sense of the frantic cries, Joshua yelled, "Steward Swindle! I need my bag! Now!"

Within moments, the lanky man was running toward them, bag in tow. As the steward held down the thrashing soldier, Joshua filled the syringe with the hastily mixed morphine solution before injecting it into McHenry's leg. Within moments, the delirious soldier had slipped into the blessed ignorance of slumber.

Swindle wiped his sweaty brow with the back of his wrist. "Land sakes. What was that about?"

Joshua clenched his jaw and shook his head, his own chest heaving as he watched the spent patient. "I don't know. He kept hollering something about snakes and the Knights."

Swindle shrugged. "He's just out of his head with fever."

Joshua frowned. "Perhaps." Or was he? Suspicion took root and lodged deep.

Steward Swindle straightened McHenry's covers. "I wouldn't put too much stock in anything this here fellow has to say. I mean, I know it's my duty to care for him and all, but what I've seen, he ain't exactly the most respectable sort. Heard one of the other men in his regiment call him white trash."

A sudden memory surfaced. Sour breath and chipped, broken teeth. A sneer. A giant looming over Joshua as he curled in on himself, holding his aching ribs from the swift kick to his middle. His six-year-old body trembling as he peered through his swollen eye.

"Yer nothin' but trash. Garbage!"

Joshua slammed his eyes shut, as if the action could sever the lash of the taunt from so many years ago. It never had, though he tried time and again.

He studied the sleeping soldier, his chest twisting. What was it that tormented him so?

Turning away, he sighed upon seeing the still form of Private Taylor. Arrangements had yet to be made for the lad. If Joshua blinked, he could still see Miss Piper keeping watch over the dead man's body. He swallowed and looked away.

Miss Piper was far too good for the likes of him and he'd do well to remember it.

Angels and sinners didn't mix. They never had and they never would.

chapter 8

Dear Miss Piper,

Can it be mere months since I last beheld your winsome smile or kissed your hand? Time seems to have stretched into an endless cycle of drills, marches, and terror. I thought the bleakness of winter would never cease, but the spring campaign has been far worse. The skirmishes have been difficult. I shall not tell you more, for I fear your delicate nature could not bear it. Only know I covet your prayers.

You inquired how we fare on our rations. Were it not for coffee, I believe we would all languish. Hardtack is common, but the wafers are baked so hard, we have taken to calling them sheet-iron crackers. Private Newton asked the captain if our last batch had been passed down from the Mexican War. Captain Driggers was not amused. We were given a ration of pork last week, but it had gone rancid and we spent a miserable few days in agony.

Cornmeal and coffee make the days bearable. How I long for my mother's table!

I enjoyed reading of your singing endeavors. An admirable contribution for a young lady to bolster the war effort. With Providence's blessing, we should crush the Rebels in only a few more weeks and I shall return home to bounty, family, and best of all, you. It is the thought of your smile, and a future with you, that keeps me pressing forward. Dare I hope you feel the same?

Until then,
Stephen Dodd

Cadence lowered the letter, her heart twisting. She enjoyed hearing from Stephen as a friend, but she'd never encouraged him beyond that. Yet with every passing missive he presumed more. She must be firmer in her intentions. How could she do so without stealing hope from his already-discouraged soul?

"Letter from Stephen?"

She looked up from her seat in the parlor to see Father enter, a cup of coffee in his hands. Steam rose in ribbons above its rim.

"Yes." She finished folding the note. "He is well, although he reports the soldiers are weary. Food is far from plentiful and poor in quality."

He grunted. "I'm afraid that's to be expected. Too difficult to bring in proper nutrition for the troops while winding through marshland, fording creeks, and dodging cannon fire."

She tapped the letter against her lips. "Scurvy will set in if something isn't done soon. And dysentery . . . it's killing more of our men than Rebel bullets are."

Father frowned and squirmed in his chair. "You know far more than you should about such topics."

"I'm a nurse, am I not? Such things are a matter of my work."

His brows lowered, his lips pursing in a manner that boded no good. "Perhaps you should not be nursing then."

Her pulse galloped. Surely he would not deny her this. The letter slipped from between her fingers and fluttered to the floor. "But, Father, you granted me permission. The hospital needs me. The soldiers are in so much pain, and there aren't enough nurses to bring them relief. If—"

"Calm down." He held up his hand. "I'm not refusing you."

She fought to still her racing heart.

He studied her with sad eyes. "But disease, death . . . these are things you should not be forced to wallow in. Not at your age, not for your gender."

She sighed. "Times are changing."

"Is it wrong to want to shield you from the harsh cruelty of life?"

Slipping from her chair, she knelt at his feet and clasped his hands. "I'm not a fragile china doll. I want to serve. To be useful. For me, a life of ease is a life wasted."

"They are not having you diagnose ailments, are they? Mix medications for the soldiers? I feel such tasks are beyond your understanding."

She bristled at the insinuation. "No, Father. The physicians are assigned to those tasks. Not I. The nurses change dressings, dispense the medications, and write letters home for the soldiers who are too ill to do so." She pressed her lips closed. He did not need to know more. Such knowledge might cause him to relinquish his permission.

A thick sigh escaped his lips. "How you managed to convince Miss Dix to allow you to be a nurse, I'll never know."

Guilt stabbed her afresh. When she'd begged him to allow her to work with Dr. Ivy, he'd assumed she'd first received permission from Miss Dix. She'd not corrected him, only remained silent. Her sin rose up before her now, taunting her with its venomous shadow.

Liar.

The long-ago phrenologist's face drifted through her mind, his sour breath sharp as it had been then.

"You should not expect much from her. She hasn't the capacity, you see. A language problem like hers is a sign of impaired brain function . . ."

Fraud.

Liar.

She swallowed. Was it that Father was worried about her sensibilities or that he thought her incapable of doing the work? Something hot and strong rose up inside.

Tell him the truth.

She tamped down the urge burning for release. The phrenologist had been wrong. She could do the work. A slow tongue did not make a slow mind.

She would prove him wrong, and then his dreadful pronouncement and its haunting refrain would finally be silenced.

"Nurse Piper, could you see to filling the linen closet with fresh sheets before going home for the day?"

Cadence turned to smile at Nurse Meyers. The widowed woman's eyes were ringed with dark circles, her shoulders slumped.

"Of course. You look done in."

Nurse Meyers arched her back, placed her hands in the small of it, and winced. "I know I'm not as old as some around here, but I feel my age around you, being a spring chicken like you are." She laughed lightly. "Being up on my feet all day makes for a stiff back."

Cadence giggled. "If it makes you feel any better, I return home at night with my entire body aching."

"I believe it. This work is not for the faint of heart or body. By the way, I asked the stewards to sprinkle more lime over the pit where we empty the chamber pots in back."

"Thank you." Cadence shuddered at the memory of the ghastly smell that had emanated from the waste pit behind the hospital that morning. Washington as a whole was beginning to reek from the overflow of people and garbage littering the roads. With the added stench from the hospital waste pits, the odor was unbearable.

Nurse Meyers gave her a concerned look. "You've been working more hours than any of us. You must rest, dearie."

"I know. I promise to return home within the half hour. I did want to have Dr. Ivy check on a new patient, though. His fever is not breaking as it should."

"I'm afraid Dr. Ivy has already left for the day."

Cadence couldn't stifle her surprise. "So early in the evening? It's not like him."

The nurse leaned forward and dropped her voice to a whisper. "He's a mystery, that one is. Disappears sometimes, always wearing that ratty green coat he keeps in his office."

"How long?"

She shrugged. "Sometimes just for the evening. Sometimes longer. Once he was gone for nearly four days without a word of explanation. When he returned, he acted as if he'd never been away." She pinched her lips in a smirk and narrowed her eyes. "Nurse Pearson thinks he slinks away to drink, but I think he keeps a lady, if you catch my meaning."

Nausea crawled up her throat. A cold feeling curled through her middle, swiftly melting into a sting of betrayal. She pushed the odd sensation aside. Dr. Ivy owed her no explanations. He was nothing to her . . . so why the sharp pang of disappointment?

She fumbled for some sort of gracious reply. "Did anyone ever ask him where he went on his excursions?"

"One of the stewards did once. The doctor told him it had nothing to do with hospital business and refused to speak further on the matter."

"Perhaps it's nothing of import."

"Then why hide it?"

Why, indeed. Cadence had sensed something troubling Dr. Ivy for the past few days. Several times she'd walked past his office only to see him hunched over on his chair, his elbows on his knees, absently rolling a coin between his knuckles. From the quiet of the corridor she'd watched, marveling at the way he slipped the quarter from knuckle to knuckle, gliding it along with careless ease. Side to side, over and over.

Something haunted him, that much was certain.

Pounding steps echoed down the hallway. She turned, eyes rounding to see Father running toward her, his chest heaving. "Father! What's wrong?"

"It's your brother. Tate . . . he's hurt . . . just outside of Richmond. He's asking for us. We must go to him."

Cadence gripped the bars of the rumbling train through gloved fingers. It belched black smoke, quivering as if it too wanted to flee the Confederate capital with all haste. Behind her, Father murmured in her ear, "Courage."

She descended from the train car and stepped foot on the train depot's boardwalk, clutching her reticule with a tight grip. All around her, gray-clad Confederate soldiers swarmed the station. She barely noticed Father's hand at the small of her back, prodding her forward . . . straight into enemy territory.

Richmond was a hornet's nest of activity. Men and women, soldiers and officers, peddlers and the hungry all crowded the streets around the depot. Wagons and buggies rattled past, stirring up clouds of dust. A galloping horse cut through a crowd down the far side of the street opposite the train station, causing a string of gasps to rise from the crush of people clogging the walkway. Its rider paid no attention, intent as he was on his mission. Buildings, offices, and homes closed in on every side. In the distance, Tredegar Iron Works rose up like a giant in the sky.

She was suffocating.

Father leaned in close, his whisper taut. "Remember, speak as little as possible. We need only find the boardinghouse where Tate is recovering."

Nodding tersely, she followed him through the maze of people. He hailed a hack and gruffly gave the address Tate had mailed to him, saying little so as not to betray his Northern accent. The driver flicked the reins, setting the carriage into motion, maneuvering through the congested streets with silent aplomb. When he pulled the horses to a stop before a modest two-story boardinghouse, Cadence breathed a sigh of relief.

After paying the driver, Father rapped on the front door. A robust woman with a round face and narrowed eyes opened it. "May I help you?"

Father took off his hat and worried the brim between his fingers. "We're looking for Tate Piper. Is he here?"

Her dark brows rose. "He is. You're his father, I take it?"

"Yes, ma'am."

She stepped aside to allow them entrance. "It's good you've come. He needs more help than I have time to provide. Got my hands full feeding the other boarders. Follow me."

Cadence bit back a retort. This woman was sorely lacking in grace. Poor Tate. She glanced back over her shoulder as the woman led them through the boardinghouse.

"My name's Mrs. Dupree. Can't say I'm going to be sorry to see young Mr. Piper go. The other boarders never did take a fancy to him, you see. Though he seems a bit more subdued now." She sniffed.

Mrs. Dupree's manner set Cadence's teeth on edge. Still, what had Tate done to cause such a reaction among the others? Father said nothing.

Finally they came to the end of a hallway and Mrs. Dupree opened the door. "I'll give you all some time alone."

Cadence slipped her hand into Father's and they entered the dimly lit room. The curtains were drawn, casting a dark pall over the scant furnishings, yet the light from the hallway illuminated the lone figure on the bed.

Even with his left leg wrapped and splinted, and his torso stripped and covered by poultices and large swaths of bandages, she'd know that shock of dark hair, those cheekbones, that mouth anywhere. She breathed his name. "Tate."

Father fell on the bed, sobbing as he clutched Tate's hand. "My son, my son! Praise God! He returned you to me."

chapter 9

CADENCE LEANED FORWARD and slipped another spoonful of willow-bark tea between Tate's dry lips. He blinked in the near darkness, the lone candle casting dancing shadows across the right side of his whiskered jaw. The sun had long since set and Father had retired to catch some needed rest. It had taken all of Cadence's pleading, but he had finally acquiesced. It would do no good if he fell ill too.

Mrs. Dupree had tolerated their presence with a long-suffering air, offering them a room and a meal of stew and biscuits. Food, Cadence had learned, was harder to come by in Richmond than it was in Washington. No doubt the boardinghouse mistress would be relieved to see all three of them gone.

She felt Tate's steady gaze on her but concentrated on slipping another spoonful of tea between his lips.

He swallowed and whispered, "I can't believe you came."

She lowered the spoon. "Of course I came. You're my brother. How could I not?"

"After what I did, how I treated you and Father . . ."

"It doesn't matter. It's in the past."

He pinched his eyes closed, his face drawn and tired. "If only I could forgive myself as easily. When Mother died . . ." He released a long exhale. "I lost myself."

She reached for his hand and squeezed. "I know."

Opening his eyes, he returned his focus to her face. "I pushed you and Father away. The drinking and gambling, cursing and carousing. You must have been happy to see me go."

"Never believe such a thing. We were worried sick. Father turned Boston upside down searching for you." Her curiosity could no longer be quenched. Her breath snagged in her chest. "Where did you go?"

He blanched. "All over. I stayed drunk most of the time and only sought work when I needed more money to put me back in the gaming halls for cards and cups."

"What kind of work did you do?"

He looked away as a streak of crimson crept up his neck. "I worked as a bouncer for, uh, places of ill repute."

She'd not push him further.

"I tried to return home once, you know."

"I didn't know that."

He nodded, his eyelids heavy. He let them slide shut as if remembering something painful, then lifted his gaze to hers. "By then, you and Father had moved away. Mrs. Harvey from the neighborhood told me you had packed up and gone to Washington."

"So that's how you knew where to write to us."

He swallowed. "When too many people began coming after me, I decided to head south. I was tired of living hand to mouth, barely scraping by. I discovered a way to make good money. Fast money, so I threw myself into it with gusto." A thick breath escaped between his lips. "God forgive me."

"Tell me. You'll not receive any condemnation."

He looked at her with sad eyes. "Don't promise something you can't deliver."

"Tate, please."

He hesitated only a moment. "I'm a . . . a slave trader."

Horror iced her veins. Tate—her big brother, the one she'd looked up to since she was a child—was responsible for ripping babes from their mother's arms? Shackling men and women like beasts? Buying and trading them like animals? Subjecting them to cruelty beyond comprehension? No, such a thing could not be.

She fought to school her reaction.

"So you're a Confederate then?"

"No." His face was bleak. "I'm nothing, Cadence. Nothing but a fool. I've benefited from the slave trade but have no particular love for the Confederacy. All I've done has been to line my own pockets. Nothing more." He stared at her hard. "I repulse you, don't I?" He looked away, his jaw hard. "I repulse myself."

As she searched for words, he stared out the window. "I never thought much about it. I didn't start slavery. The institution doesn't rise or fall with my word, so I reasoned, what difference would it make if I gained money from it?" Stark pain flooded his eyes, turning them glassy.

"One day I bought a slave woman from the auction block. She was weeping and wailing. Her child had been sold, torn from her, and sent to another plantation down Georgia way."

A knot lodged in Cadence's throat.

"That woman clung to my arm, pleading with me to help, tears running down her face. She kept saying, 'Help me. I can't live with this pain. Oh, please, help me!'" Thick tears ran down Tate's face, swallowed in the stubble of his jaw. His lips trembled as he turned to stare at Cadence. "Those were the very last words Mother said to me before she passed." A sob escaped and he covered his face. "Same words. Same plea, and I did nothing to help either of them."

Father, help me love him the way you do. A wave of mercy and love so deep rose up inside, it nearly caused her to weep. Scooting forward, she cupped his face in her hands. "I love you, Tate. Nothing changes that. Nothing."

He clung to her and shuddered in her embrace.

When the worst passed, she released him and smoothed his hair. "You still haven't told me how you came to be injured. A gunshot wound to the knee, multiple stab wounds to the torso . . . those aren't accidental."

"No, they're not. A fortnight ago I was returning from delivering two slaves to Lumpkin's Jail in Shockoe Bottom. It was dark and I was accosted by a group of men."

"Do you know who they were?"

"I'm not sure. I didn't recognize any of their voices, and I couldn't make out any faces. Not after they'd pulled me into the alley. They asked me if I was the no-account slave trader. I denied it, but they knew better. They started beating me with their fists, kicking me, all the while muttering things like 'The Almighty will punish you scum.'" He rubbed his hand over his face, as if reliving the memories was too much to handle. "I suppose they were some sort of abolitionist radicals."

Nausea rose within her. "Fighting for abolition is one thing. What they did is hate, pure and simple."

Fatigue shadowed his eyes. "I deserve worse, in truth. What I did . . ." His throat bobbed, cutting off his words.

"What happened next?"

He inhaled a steadying breath. "I managed to fight my way free from the worst of them in the darkness. As I took off running, one of them pulled out his gun and fired. Hit my knee. As I lay there bleeding, two of them came up behind me and stabbed me multiple times before running away. When I came to, a physician was pulling lead from my knee."

Her heart burned for what he'd endured, some of it through his own poor choices. But the stabbing, the gunshot . . . such hate was beyond the pale.

"I didn't know abolitionists roamed Richmond."

"They don't. Not openly, anyway. They work in secret, just as Confederate sympathizers do in Washington."

"What is to be done about your attackers?"

He looked away. "Friends have vowed to see justice meted out." His fingers fisted the quilt, worrying the fabric into tight bunches.

She frowned. "What friends?"

"Don't ask questions!"

She startled at his snapped retort. He forced the agitation from his face with a sigh. "I shouldn't have asked you and Father to come. It's too dangerous."

"Nonsense." She smoothed the quilt under his fingers. "But staying here in Richmond—you know we cannot."

"I know. Nor should you."

"As soon as you're able to travel, and if you're willing, we'll take you home. We have a friend who's a congressman. He's already provided all the necessary paperwork to ensure our safety."

His chin quivered. "You would so readily embrace me after all I've done?"

She pressed a kiss to his bruised, cut knuckles. "Love can do no less."

The next day, Cadence handed a coin into the driver's hand and descended from the hack near Richmond's most populated markets. Father had been only too eager to sit with Tate and tend to him, freeing her to search out an apothecary for medicines to aid his recovery. Her brother would benefit greatly from slippery elm and chamomile, and an envelope or two of morphine would be helpful in his return trip to Washington, though it was doubtful she could procure it. Such medicine came dear now.

Clutching her reticule, she hastened toward the cluster of buildings, eyeing the food available for purchase. Loaves of bread for a quarter apiece and eggs being sold for a dime each. Who could afford such prices? She wrinkled her nose as she passed a cart loaded with salted fish. A swarm of flies buzzed around the fare, rising from the catch in a dark cloud as her shadow passed it. She swatted the pests away and shielded her eyes from the sun's rays. Where was the apothecary shop?

A figure crossed the street in front of her, shoulders hunched. The man wore a tall hat—a tar bucket, as Father called them—and kept his hands shoved in his pockets. She would have paid him little mind save for his stride. Something about his manner and build seemed so familiar. He wore a green coat despite the warm spring day. A green coat frayed around the cuffs.

She gasped. Dr. Ivy? She nearly called out to him, but with the distance and his swift stride, she knew he'd not hear her. What was he doing in Richmond?

She scurried toward him but found her way blocked by shoppers. She bit back an oath of frustration as she watched his long-legged stride eat up the distance away from the markets. Lifting the edge of her skirt so as not to tangle her hem, she walked as fast as she dared and followed. At the corner of an intersection, he looked to the right and darted sharply to the left.

Cadence fought to keep him in sight. He acted as if he was trying to hide something. She caught up just in time to see him turn down another street. She paused, heaving against her stays, and scanned the crowded street for his green coat. Had he eluded her?

There! She caught sight of his broad shoulders heading toward a building marked *Lumpkin's Jail and Auction*.

She froze. Wasn't this the same place her brother was leaving when he was attacked? The very place they took slaves to hold before selling them? A stone sank to the pit of her stomach.

She scanned the signs mounted around the building. *Jail*, *Slave Pen*, and *Auction Block* marked off the sections of the building. A man and woman walked past, casting a condemning look at the structure.

"The devil's half acre." The man's murmur caused a shiver to course down Cadence's back.

Mouth dry, she followed Dr. Ivy inside, sure her soul was tainted just by stepping foot across the threshold.

A crowd of men had gathered in a large room, their booming voices ricocheting against the hard walls. Amid their grating conversation, the sound of scraping iron could be heard, drawing ever closer. A man appeared moments later, a long chain in his hand. Five shackled slaves bound by iron ankle cuffs shuffled in behind him, their heavy chains clanging across the floor. The first two were brawny men, their clothes tattered. Their faces were solemn, but their onyx eyes glittered defiance. The third was a much lankier man, stripped to the waist. His expression was void, his eyes empty. The fourth was a small child, a boy of no more than six or seven. The fifth was a woman. She was completely naked and her hair had been shorn.

Bile rose in Cadence's throat. She averted her eyes as her face burned. She should not have come. No one should.

"Five specimens up for bid today, gentlemen. The first is hale and hearty. An excellent field hand. Stronger than three horses! The bidding starts at eight hundred."

A heavyset man with side-whiskers called out, "Not a penny will be bid until I see his teeth."

The man holding the chain barked, "Show them your teeth!"

All five slaves opened their mouths wide to let the crush of people examine their teeth. Cadence had never felt such revulsion. Barbaric. And Dr. Ivy was among them.

"Bidding starts at eight hundred for specimen one."

"Eight hundred!"

As the men haggled, Cadence held back against the far wall, squeezing her eyes shut. She couldn't believe Dr. Ivy was party to such a dreadful thing. Yet hadn't Nurse Meyers intimated he had secrets? Never would she have dreamed it was something as vile as this.

What if he bid on the naked woman trembling at the end of the line? Unable to stomach any more, Cadence fled the building on shaking limbs.

How could he? The refrain beat round and round in her head like a drum.

Once she was sure she wouldn't cast up her accounts, she pushed away from Lumpkin's outer wall, prepared to flee from the dreadful place and never look back, when the sight of a green-coated figure caught her attention. He was holding the hand of the small child who had been on the auction block inside.

Something white-hot licked her insides. So Dr. Ivy had bought the poor child like he was nothing more than a pet, had he?

Before she could consider her actions, she followed them, her fury mounting with every passing step. The doctor took the child down one alley, then another and another. What was he doing?

Her heart hammered as she finally caught up. Dr. Ivy was kneeling in front of the boy, who was nodding solemnly. Another man appeared, and Dr. Ivy handed him some papers. What was going on?

Scoundrels!

From the end of the alley, she shouted, "Stop!"

All three of their heads snapped up. She rushed for the slave child as Dr. Ivy turned toward the strange man.

"Go! Now!"

The man scooped up the child, spiriting him away before Cadence could draw him into the comfort of her arms.

"No!"

Her fingertips managed only to grasp the edge of the man's tattered coat before he disappeared. Strong arms lifted her from the ground. She squirmed and kicked, fighting with all her might, but she was no match for the muscled strength subduing her.

"I mean you no harm!" The harsh whisper cut through her screaming thoughts. Hands pushed her up against the brick wall of the alley. She stilled, fighting to catch her breath. When Dr. Ivy realized whom he held in his arms, his face went slack.

"Miss Piper?"

chapter 10

JOSHUA GRASPED MISS PIPER'S SLENDER ARMS, watching her chest rise and fall, her blue eyes flash fire, and was rendered speechless. He didn't know whether to shake her or kiss her. Never had anyone caught him before.

Her nostrils flared as she stared at him, and one thing was abundantly clear: she was furious.

"What are you doing here?"

"Me?" She tried to pull free, but he held her fast. "I'm not the one on trial here. Buying children as if they were chickens or sows at market?"

"Please, Miss Piper, I need to know. What are you doing here?"

She seethed. "If you don't release me at once, I shall be forced to scream."

"If you scream, I shall be forced to kiss you to keep your silence."

"You wouldn't dare."

"Try me."

She must have sensed he would carry out the threat, for her muscles relaxed a fraction under his hold. "If you must know, Father and I received word my brother was badly injured and requested us to retrieve him home. He's here in Richmond."

So that explained it.

"If I let you go, do you promise to keep quiet?"

Her jaw jutted forward, but she gave a terse nod.

With slow movements, he uncurled his fingers and released her. She stepped away, her blue eyes narrowed to slits of ice.

"How could you?"

"How could I what?"

"Go to an auction house and buy people made in God's image, as if they were chattel? That poor child." She choked then, her eyes filling with tears, and his chest twisted.

How he wished he could tell her. Comfort her. Unburden himself of the truth. He steeled his softening heart. It would jeopardize everything.

"You bought him and then sold him again without so much as a blink."

"You stumbled upon something you know nothing about."

"I know you're a monster." Her words found their mark. *Monster, trash, rubbish.* He'd been called all of it before. His heart had grown scarred and jaded with the old barbs. Yet hearing it from her lips, his soul gave a cry of anguish.

Stiffening, he stretched to his full height. "Go home. Forget what you saw."

"Forget? How can I forget?"

He ground his jaw, yearning to tell her the truth.

"Things are not always what they seem, Miss Piper."

———— ✦ ————

Cadence yanked at the sheets twisting around her legs. The stale, warm air of the narrow room stifled her breath. Far more troubling was the thought of the slave child helplessly shoved from hand to hand. The poor waif had made no protest.

And Dr. Ivy . . . why had she ever thought him to be a man of honor?

Heat rolled through her middle once again. Sleep would never come at this rate.

A large moon cast silver rectangles through the boarding-house windows. The pewter glow lent enough guidance for her to find her robe and don its modest protection. She could do nothing about Dr. Ivy's betrayal or the poor child's fate except pray, but at least she could be a help to her father. He might appreciate a break from his nighttime vigil.

She slipped down the hallway, her bare feet padding against the wooden floor with light slaps. As she approached Tate's room, the low murmur of masculine voices drifted through the cracked door. Father and Tate were up at this hour? She leaned close, her ear to the gap.

"It hasn't been the same without you, Son."

"I'm sorry for all I've put you through. I thank God you've had Cadence. She's been both son and daughter to you."

Father's sigh was deep enough to extinguish a candle. "She's a good girl and has taken excellent care of me since your mother passed." Father's gentle sobs rent the air then. "But it's been you my heart has longed for. My son . . ."

Cadence stumbled backward, her heart throbbing.

But it's been you my heart has longed for. . . ."

She pressed her fist to her trembling lips as salty tears filled her mouth. She hadn't been enough. She was never enough. Not for Mother. Not for Father. Not for Dorothea Dix. Not for anyone. The truth shredded her heart, clawing its way up her throat.

"You should not expect much from her."

The phrenologist's sharp admonition rose up in her memory. Father had pleaded with the physician.

"Can nothing be done?"

"A French doctor, Hervez de Chegoin, has proposed that stammering occurs because the affected person's tongue is too short or incorrectly attached to his or her mouth. Surgeries are one means to provide relief, although a number of patients have bled to death from the procedure." The phrenologist had sniffed. *"I myself believe it to be a deficit of mental acuity. There is no cure."*

Cadence's chest squeezed as the realization stabbed afresh: Father's attitude had changed toward her from that day forward.

A sob rent her chest as she fumbled down the hallway and flung herself on the lumpy bed, crying until the piercing pain dulled into a quivering ache and dawn's light turned the inky darkness to crimson once again.

Joshua leaned against the building beside Lumpkin's Jail, rolling a nickel between his knuckles, keeping his head ducked low underneath his hat. This costume was altogether different from his clothes of yesterday. He couldn't risk being recognized. Not after buying little Thomas . . . even if he had used a false identity to do so.

He eyed the group of men hastening into the building. Evil vipers. The auction would begin soon, judging by the stream of visitors. Minutes later, the raucous calls of bidders bellowed through the building's frame. Time for the performance to begin.

Pulling out a deck of cards, he slid the nickel into his pocket and flicked the deck from one hand to the other like the wide pump of an accordion. He flashed a bright grin and let his voice boom over the people passing through the crowded street.

"Ladies and gentlemen, step right up and try your luck. As the demon Yankees oppress our rights, our children grow hungry. Try your hand at making a nickel or two. Bread in their stomachs or a drop of candy to sweeten their tongues."

Children slowed to stare, tugging their mothers' hands. Men and women alike paused to watch him. A young maiden turned his way and he winked, causing her to blush.

"You, miss. Mightn't you care for a pretty new ribbon?"

Her cheeks dusted pink, but the vixenish gleam in her eyes told him she was not as innocent as she seemed.

"I have no money with which to play." Her Southern accent dripped honey.

Slipping his hand into his pocket, he pulled it back out with ease and moved his fingers to her ear, wiggling his hand with a flourish. The nickel appeared at the end of his fingertips, and the gathering crowd gasped. Her green eyes rounded as the crowd clapped.

Joshua bowed and offered a rakish grin. "Now you have money to play, do you not?" He fanned out the deck of cards facedown. "Pick a card, but do not show it to me. Memorize it well."

She removed one from the stack of pasteboards. As she studied it, he stacked the remaining cards with a quick scoop and split the deck in half.

"Place your card facedown here."

She followed the instructions. He smiled to himself, remembering the card in the stack before hers was the queen of spades. Wiggling his eyebrows, he began dropping cards on the whiskey barrel, turning over an occasional card to keep the crowd wondering. When he found the queen of spades, he knew hers was next.

With a grin, he held up the two of hearts. "Is this your card?"

Her jaw dropped open. "Incredible!"

The crowd murmured in awe as he bowed. "Anyone here care to best me for a nickel? I assure you it can be done."

Man after man came forward. On occasion, Joshua purposefully fumbled to keep people gambling. His pockets were soon jingling with coinage. From the corner of his eye, he spied a potbellied man striding from the auction house, his buttoned vest straining. George Proctor. Joshua had heard the odious man bragging yesterday that he intended to buy another slave girl to warm his bed, but this . . . Disgust coated Joshua's tongue. The mite walking meekly behind him, bound by wrist cuffs, wasn't more than ten at best.

He must act quickly. "You, sir! You!"

Proctor turned his way and glared, the sun glinting off his bald head. "You calling me, boy?"

Joshua smirked. "That I am. Care for a gentlemanly wager?"

Proctor sneered. "I have better things to do with my time."

"I understand if you don't have the courage for it. It's a man's game, after all."

The crowd around them snickered. Some whistled low. Proctor's round face flushed red. He ambled forward, the girl meekly trailing behind. His gaze raked the whiskey barrel and pasteboards. "I suppose I have enough time to teach a guttersnipe a thing or two. What's the wager?"

Joshua flashed his teeth in an effort to both charm and rile. "Whatever pleases you, sir."

Lifting his nose in the air, Proctor pulled a bill from his pocket and laid it atop the barrel. People gasped. Joshua fought the urge to smirk. A twenty-dollar Confederate note. The man was feeling proud of himself today. Like a peacock . . . either that, or terribly insecure. The two extremes were odd bedfellows.

Joshua whistled. "That's a heavy bet, sir."

"If you're not man enough for it—"

Joshua raised his hand. "No, no. I asked you for a wager, and I'm a man of my word." He grabbed the deck and shuffled, keeping his eyes trained on Proctor's beady stare, though his concentration stayed on the tiny girl chained behind him. What possible future would she have in Proctor's house? Misery, anguish, death.

Joshua's gaze snagged on Proctor's black lapel. A gold pin gleamed in the light. The carved image of a snake coiled into a circle.

Snakes . . .

What was it about the image that triggered something sinister in his memory? He shook away the wayward thought.

"Pick a card, but don't let me see it. Memorize it."

Men whispered around them while he shuffled. He lifted the stack and noted the card facing up. Ten of diamonds. "Place your card here."

Proctor returned it, and Joshua repeated the same trick he'd used on the others. He pulled a card up for all to see. "Jack of clubs. Is this your card?"

Proctor's face mottled a ghastly hue of scarlet when the crowd whooped. He banged his fist on the table. "Impossible!"

An onlooker chuckled. "He's good, Proctor. Been beating us off and on for the better part of an hour."

The bulbous slave owner fumed, spittle flying from his mouth. "I demand a chance to win my money back!"

"Of course." Joshua waved his hand. "What else have you to bet? I'm happy to oblige if you've more Confederate notes you'd like to be rid of."

Men laughed uproariously. Proctor patted his pockets and searched the linings, finding naught save a few paltry coins. He growled. "I've nothing else."

Joshua tsked. "Spent it all on the girl, did you?" He snapped his fingers. "Say, there's a thought. Wager the girl. If I win, I keep her. If you win, you keep her, the twenty you've already lost, and bragging rights that you beat the best pasteboard player east of the Mississippi." Laughter peppered the air.

"But I paid eighty for the girl!"

Joshua shrugged. "Makes no never mind to me. I can walk away now a much richer man either way. Your choice."

Indecision warred on Proctor's face before his pride took over. "Fine!"

People swarmed around them, chattering excitedly. The bait had been cast and the fish was on the hook. All Joshua had to do was reel him in. While he shuffled the pasteboards, a man walked up to Proctor's side and whispered in his ear. Had he slipped something into the slave owner's hand? Joshua narrowed his eyes.

His palms were damp as he spread the deck out in its facedown position. "Pick a card, but do not let me see it. Memorize it."

Proctor took his card, but a smug gleam shone in his narrow eyes. Something was wrong. Unease gnawed Joshua's gut. He folded the deck and divided it. "Place your card here."

Proctor's gloat had already begun, and the game had not yet concluded. Had the man given Proctor an extra card to throw Joshua off the trick?

Sweat trickled down his back as the crowd watched with bated breath. Slowly he counted out the cards, flipping some over, dropping others facedown. What should he do? He'd all but lost his chance to save the slave girl from Proctor's cruel grip. His eyes roved over the onlookers and froze.

Miss Piper's blue-eyed gaze stared back. Confusion, disgust, concern . . . all of it warred in her lovely face.

His stomach soured. Not once, but twice she'd seen him playacting. He didn't know whether to laugh or weep at the absurdity of it. He'd wanted to keep her at arm's length and surely he'd accomplished it. No doubt she thought him the vilest human being alive.

Proctor hissed, "Quit stalling!"

There was only one option before him, and it was not defeat. Joshua slowly held up a single card, but instead of offering his standard question—"Is this your card?"—he flung the entire deck in Proctor's face. Pasteboards flew in every direction. Joshua lunged forward, scooped up the slave girl, and ran with all his might. Shouts and cries of confusion rang all around him.

"Get him!"

The waif quaked in his arms as he ducked into an alley. Feet pounded behind him. Proctor's furious bellows of outrage receded as Joshua sprinted between buildings. His pulse thudded in his ears. *Turn left, right.* His legs burned as he fought for breath, weaving his way through alleys. This was not the shortest way to meet Zeke, but it was better than being caught. The girl clutched the lapel of his jacket and whimpered.

"I'll keep you safe. You have my word."

They were close now. He turned and ran down a long alley, nearly tripping over a broken bottle. Zeke was waiting at the end, the wagon ready.

He breathed against the girl's neck. "Do you know the man I took you from was a bad man?"

She nodded, her eyes large.

"The man up ahead is a good man. He will carry you someplace safe. You must crawl in the back of his wagon to the secret box and remain quiet. Don't make a peep. Can you do that?"

She nodded again.

"Good girl."

He slowed just long enough to open the secret compartment of the wagon and urge the girl inside. She gave him a questioning look for only a moment before wordlessly crawling inside.

He offered a tight smile and whispered, "God be with you, little one."

"What do you think you're doing?"

He spun to see Miss Piper sprinting toward him, panting like a caged animal, her dark hair slipping from its pins, eyes blazing.

With a growl, he closed the compartment and Zeke snapped the reins of the horses, jerking the wagon from the alley and emerging into the bustling street. Hopefully, toward freedom.

Miss Piper stomped up to him. Shouts of angry men drew closer. He yanked the hat from his head and removed the shabby coat, praying it was enough to cause the irate men to pass him by. He stuffed the costume in a discarded crate and turned to face her wrath.

"Absconding with a child! Wha—?"

He grabbed her arms. "I can explain, but now isn't the time. You're in danger. Come with me."

He attempted to pull her along, but she jerked her hand free, standing her ground.

"Who do you think you are? I'll not allow you to kidnap me as you did that poor girl. If my—"

The shouts grew ever closer. He growled. "Hush! Or I'll be forced to silence you myself."

"I'd like to see you try, you brute!"

Pounding feet would burst down the darkened alley any moment. With no other alternative, Joshua grabbed Miss Piper and pulled her toward him, crashing his mouth against hers.

She squirmed only a moment, then stilled, as did he. She was sweet and soft, tender and tantalizing. His heartbeat raced in his chest and he let his hold shift, moving his hands to feel the length of her back, the gentle curves, the silky threads of her hair.

Sweet saints above, she was heaven. The feel of her beneath his fingertips set his blood on fire.

A flurry of bodies rushed by, ignoring both of them, no doubt thinking he was a drunk enjoying the lewd pleasures of a soiled dove. Miss Piper didn't even seem to notice, for she was not only allowing his kisses but was kissing him back, her fingers roving through his hair, and—

She jerked away with a gasp. Cool air rushed between them. His breath was ragged as he stared at her swollen lips. Her chin trembled and he knew she understood. The kiss had been a diversion.

Self-loathing flooded every pore of his wretched body. "I—I'm sorry. I had to quiet you."

Even in the shadows, he could see the flush staining her cheeks.

"You most assuredly accomplished that."

He rubbed his eyes and paced. How had this happened? He'd never meant to drag her into this. Never meant for anyone to know. He braved a glance. She was staring at him, her expression fearful.

"Who are you?"

He sighed. "I'll tell you everything, I promise, but it's not safe here." He held out his hand. "Come with me and I'll explain."

She blinked at his outstretched hand and hesitated. Would she judge him and find him lacking? It had been so all his life. He'd not blame Miss Piper if she did the same.

Still, a spark of delight flamed to life inside his chest when she nodded before slipping her slender fingers inside his.

"Let us make haste."

chapter 11

PERSPIRATION GLUED CADENCE'S BODICE to her skin. The spring day was not overly warm, but chasing a surgeon through the streets of Richmond had heated her body in an unexpected way. As had his kiss.

Her face flushed hot at the memory of his embrace.

Stop!

She studied the man walking beside her through the Richmond cemetery, his hands stuffed deep in his pockets. He still looked warily at their surroundings as if waiting for some unforeseen foe to jump him. It had been over an hour since he'd managed to weave them safely away from the heart of Richmond to the relative quiet of a secluded cemetery. What had Dr. Ivy gotten himself into?

Father was likely worried sick. Twice now she'd gone to retrieve medicine from the apothecary and twice Dr. Ivy's horrifying behavior had disrupted her. He and Tate would be wringing their hands.

Or would they? Father's remark from last night rose up to taunt her once again. A cold fist squeezed her throat. Perhaps he was not concerned at all.

Blinking back the sting of unshed tears, she lifted her chin. "Now, if you would be so kind as to explain why you felt it necessary to kidnap a child and then abscond with me, I'd be ever so grateful." She heard the sarcastic bite in her tone but didn't care. She had ceased understanding the doctor and made no more pretense of trying.

He sighed and rubbed his hands across the back of his neck. "Please know I had no idea you'd be in Richmond, Miss Piper."

"Yes, it would have been more convenient for your nefarious dealings if I'd remained away, wouldn't it?"

"That's not what I meant." He frowned and turned to face her. "I just . . . I'm sorry for confusing you so. No doubt you think me the most despicable man alive."

She said nothing. Indeed, she'd mentally accused him of that very thing within the past day.

His brows furrowed as he studied her face. "Do you believe slavery is a righteous institution, Miss Piper?"

"Absolutely not."

"Neither do I."

"But I saw you buying a slave yesterday."

"Yes, you did."

She expelled a thick breath. "You speak in riddles, sir."

He chuckled low. "I know. It seems an odd thing to do for a man morally opposed to the institution, but it would only be odd if I were to keep the slave. I do not. I free them."

Understanding dawned. It was the very thing she and Father had discussed over the morning paper not long ago. "That man I saw you talking with yesterday . . . the same one driving the wagon today—"

"Yes. He's a freed man who helps me smuggle slave children into free states."

Her mind raced. "How many others do you work with?"

His lips pressed into a firm line. "I cannot say. I should not have even told you this much, but I feared what you would do or think if your suspicions were left unchecked and ungrounded. I know how it appears." He winced. "Please be assured I was only playing a role."

Relief so thick filled her chest, she could do nothing but stare. "I understand. I must say, you were quite impressive as the street performer. Where did you learn such tricks?"

But instead of smiling, his mood darkened. "It doesn't matter. It serves an end."

She swallowed. This man was a mystery. A storm. Beautiful and intense. Ever changing, sweeping in and out with ferocity, but touching everything in his wake.

He walked several more steps, his hands shoved in his pockets, head bent. "Tell me, Miss Piper, when I speak the phrase 'A dog is barking,' what do you envision?"

She pondered the thought for a moment. "I think of Domino, my dog from childhood. He was a little ball of black-and-white fluff, always barking at strange sights beyond the window. A falling leaf, running squirrels."

He stopped and turned to her, his expression somber. "Do you know what I think of? Mean, starving dogs covered with cuts and nosing through garbage in back alleys. I envision snarling teeth and slobbering tongues snapping at children as they sob, desperate to protect the small morsel of food they have tucked to their chest." His lips firmed. "You and I have lived very different lives, Miss Piper. There is a whole world beyond those streets you know nothing about."

A yearning gripped her. "Let me help you."

His dark eyes widened. "No. Absolutely not."

"Why not?"

"It's too dangerous."

She propped her hands on her hips. "You take the risk. Why should I not? I'm unattached, with no husband or children dependent on me. I can be of service."

He snorted and turned away. "Do you always need to prove your worth, Miss Piper?"

She jerked back as if slapped. Was that what he thought she was doing?

"How dare you!" she whispered. "Lest you forget, it was you who begged me to work in your hospital. It was I who found you after remembering what alley you and your friend met in yesterday. You're the one who botched things today. Not me."

His jaw twitched as he stepped close, his nose mere inches from hers. "Proctor cheated!"

She softened her voice, knowing vinegar with this man would accomplish nothing. "Please. I only want to be of help. Let me."

He hesitated and opened his mouth before closing it once more.

"What is it?"

He grimaced. "I must ask you, why did you say you're in Richmond again?"

She frowned at the odd change in topic. "To retrieve my brother. He was injured. Father and I plan to bring him home with us to Washington."

Dr. Ivy nodded slowly but kept his gaze averted, his face serious. "And what is his name?"

"Tate Piper."

"And what is his profession?"

"He's a——" She stopped, choking on the answer. His eyes lifted to hers, sorrow flooding their depths. Dr. Ivy knew.

"He's a slave trader. That is, a former slave trader." Her voice shook, dropping to a hoarse whisper. "You knew?"

"Suspected. I knew of a Tate Piper by reputation only."

She grabbed his arm. "But he's different now. He wants to change. Father and I didn't even know about what he was doing until two days ago. Surely—"

Dr. Ivy shook his head. "You would not be trusted, Miss Piper. Not with such a person in your family. I'm sorry, truly."

Heat licked her middle. "So I'm to be condemned for the actions of another?"

"Not by me."

She looked into his eyes and knew he spoke the truth. It made no difference to him, but those helping him would view her through jaded eyes.

"I'm sorry."

She gave a terse nod. "Perhaps there's a way I can contribute financially. Surely such an endeavor is costly. Buying slaves from the auction block takes funds. If I were to—"

"You would be caught." His shoulders sagged. "The expenses are routed through a long chain of donations, none of which know about the rest. Having a benefactor working side by side with me is too risky." Sighing, he looked over the gentle slope of the cemetery. "You must return to your father soon. Say nothing of this to anyone. When we both return to Washington, act as if this conversation never happened. This day, these memories . . . erase all of them from your mind."

Was such a thing possible?

"And, Miss Piper—" he winced—"forgive me for my earlier, uh . . . passion." Crimson crept up his collar. "I had few options."

She bit her lip. "I understand. I shall do my best to forget if you can."

He leveled his gaze to hers. Something in her stomach flipped.

"I doubt such a thing is possible, Miss Piper."

It was suddenly hard to breathe.

She turned to go, but his gentle call turned her back.

"Miss Piper?"

"Yes?"

He offered a lopsided smile. "Considering all we've been through, might I ask you one question?"

"Of course."

"What's your Christian name?"

A tiny ray of sunlight pierced the muddled emotions shrouding her heart. She fought to control her wayward tongue and answered slowly. "Cadence."

"Cadence." He repeated the name with a smile hovering around his mouth. "It suits you. And a beautiful name for a songbird at that."

She smiled slowly. "But now you must tell me yours, Dr. Ivy."

"Joshua."

Strong name. The name of a warrior.

"Joshua Ivy. That has a nice ring to it."

"Let me walk you back to your boardinghouse." He grinned, his white teeth flashing. "In Washington, I'll be Dr. Ivy. I can't handle impertinent nurses . . . Cadence."

She tossed a saucy glance over her shoulder. "You'd better be on your best behavior then, *Joshua*."

❦

WASHINGTON, DC

Cadence studied the soldier's exposed neck and pursed her lips.

The young lad chuckled. "Do I look as bad as all that?"

116

Forcing herself to lighten her expression, she shook her head. "Of course not, but this rash is troublesome. Tell me again why your captain insisted on delivering you to Judiciary Square?"

He coughed weakly, his eyelids drooping in his too-thin face. "Ain't got no stamina, seems like. Can't hardly walk a straight line no more. Between the vermin, the vittles, and those blasted Johnny Rebs, is it any wonder?" He reddened and rubbed a hand over his shock of white-blond hair. "Pardon my language, ma'am."

She chuckled. "Pardon granted."

"Came down with the malaria, but our field doc gave me some quinine and it seemed to do the trick." He squinted up at her. "Think I've had a relapse? I've been getting the shakes again."

Pressing a cool cloth to his forehead, she murmured, "Perhaps, but that rash is not a sign of malaria."

"I'll be the judge of that."

Cadence tensed at the masculine voice behind her. The military had wanted to ensure Joshua had enough surgeons on hand for the expected influx of patients and had sent half a dozen new physicians to the hospital. Several had been contract surgeons, meant only to handle the less severe cases. The rest were skilled surgeons, but none of them had an ego as big as Dr. Perritt's.

Whether it was the man's small, spindly stature or the prickliness from his oversize, bushy mustache, Cadence didn't know, but he was forever belittling the nurses, continually reminding them a woman's place was in the home. He took special delight in tormenting Cadence. He was not liked by the stewards, and the nurses loathed his overbearing presence.

Cadence turned to see Dr. Perritt scowling. "Doctor, may I help you?"

"You may tell me why you presume to give a medical diagnosis when you have no medical training."

She clenched her teeth until she feared they'd break. "But I have, sir. Dr. Ivy trained me himself."

He snorted and laughed as if she were a simpleton. "The training of a nurse to change linens and empty bedpans is hardly the same training one receives to become an astute physician. Stand aside."

She moved to make room as one of the stewards came up behind her. He leaned in, crossing his arms. "What's got his knickers in a knot today?"

She suppressed a smile. "He caught me using my brain."

Steward Swindle's eyes rounded in mock horror. "Traitorous!"

Dr. Perritt swiveled and glared at both of them. Steward Swindle's face turned purely angelic. Cadence had to bite the inside of her lip to keep from laughing.

He straightened. "This soldier has nothing more than a case of the scabies. Clean him up and send him back to his regiment."

"But, sir—"

The doctor glared. "Nurse Piper, might I remind you who diagnoses patients in this hospital? It is not the nurses, however earnestly they might strive."

Steward Swindle scratched his head. "With all due respect, that there ain't no scabies, sir."

"And who are you to contradict me?"

He bowed low and smiled, revealing crooked teeth. "Just a lowly steward and recovering soldier. Honest Swindle's the name." He rocked back on his heels and hooked his thumbs under his suspenders. "With a name like Swindle, people wonder if I'm a thief. Well, I won't pick your pocket, but I might pick your brain."

"How droll." Dr. Perritt spoke through gritted teeth.

"When I was in the army, I saw a lot of illness in camp,"

Swindle continued. "That isn't scabies. And scabies don't cause muscle weakness and fatigue like Private Richey here has. I've had the Virginia quickstep from eating those desecrated vegetables and embalmed beef, and watched several in my regiment fight off the malaria too." He shook his head. "This ain't like a vermin or skin disease. Not the diarrhea nor malaria either."

Dr. Perritt's eyes narrowed to slits. "You're merely a steward. You know nothing. What does Nurse Piper think ails him?"

She gathered herself and spoke slowly. "Based on the type of rash, its placement and his symptoms, I would think he might be suffering from—" she winced—"the red measles."

Steward Swindle snapped his fingers. "That's it! That's what our field surgeon called it."

"Preposterous!" Dr. Perritt huffed. "Another reason why females have no business in hospitals unless they are dying."

Footsteps approached. Cadence turned to see Dr. Ivy standing behind them. She groaned inwardly.

Since those baffling days in Richmond two weeks ago, Dr. Ivy had said little more than a short string of words to her. They'd each returned to the hospital in Washington, but when he'd walked in and her face lit up, he'd not even glanced her way. In the days since, he'd done little more than grunt and attend to patients. When he'd operated, he'd called for the other nurses' assistance, not hers.

She'd been thoroughly and completely ignored.

It was as if Richmond had never happened at all.

"What seems to be the trouble?"

She lifted her chin but said nothing as Dr. Perritt scoffingly told Dr. Ivy how his nurse had dared to suggest a diagnosis for the ill soldier. "A diagnosis completely erroneous, in my opinion."

Steward Swindle's eyes twinkled. "Here's a lark for you. Let's hear Dr. Ivy's opinion on the matter."

Her gaze flickered to his. The ghost of a smile played around his lips as if he were enjoying the predicament. "Sounds like a fair way of handling the matter."

He took a moment to examine Private Richey and ask him the same questions Cadence had. He nodded and padded the lanky lad's shoulder.

Dr. Perritt arched a single brow. "Well, what say you? Scabies, isn't it?"

Dr. Ivy's face lit in surprise. "Not at all. From my observation of the rash, as well as his other physical maladies and symptoms, I'm positive Private Richey is suffering from red measles."

Cadence released a breath she wasn't aware she'd been holding. Honest Swindle whooped as Dr. Perritt's face flamed and the older man stomped away.

"Just like Nurse Piper said! Don't that beat all?"

Dr. Ivy turned to her, his chestnut eyes dancing. "Was that your diagnosis as well?"

She nodded, suddenly shy at the attention.

He winked. "I best be on my guard or the hospital will be replacing me with my best nurse." He chuckled. "Well done. If left untreated, those measles could have turned into pneumonia."

Steward Swindle puffed out his chest. "That's why our Songbird is the pride and joy of Judiciary Square Hospital. Of the whole Union!"

Her face flamed when Dr. Ivy leaned in and whispered, "Amen."

If only her father felt the same . . .

Turning to Steward Swindle, he placed an order for medicine

to be brought immediately. "Make sure Private Richey takes it all."

"Yes, sir."

His focus centered on Cadence. "Follow me."

Was she in trouble? She followed his quick stride down the corridor, cringing at the sound of their shoes clicking against the polished floors. With the vacant empty halls, every noise echoed. Hollow and empty.

He led her to his office and picked up the morning paper, handing it to her with a roguish grin. "Did you hear?"

"No. What?"

She hadn't seen a newspaper since their return to Washington, as she had been avoiding breakfast with Father and Tate completely. Father now acted as if she didn't exist, doting on Tate's every whim. The few times she'd attempted to check on her brother's progress or clean his wounds, Father had shooed her away. At least she could be of use here.

She grabbed the oily paper and scanned the headlines. There in bold letters, the type announced: "Slavery Abolished in the District of Columbia."

She gasped and lifted her eyes to his. Joy danced in their depths. "Can it be?"

"I know it's only one small step, but to know Washington, DC, is free of slavery's disease is immensely gratifying."

"I should say so." She returned the paper to his hands. "Now to only see it rid everywhere."

Sadness drifted across his face. "I pray to God it would be so." He blinked and the shadows snapped away like a window shade that had been raised. "This is not wholly why I asked you to come. It seems Congressman Ramsey and his wife have planned a huge benefit to raise funds for our soldiers. There's to be a dance and auction. They'd like to showcase the work that goes on here at Judiciary Square Hospital as well. Perhaps raise some funds for our needs. They've asked me to speak and have requested you speak also. Sing some patriotic songs." His face shone when he gave her a tender smile. "The Ramseys do nothing but shout your praises."

Her heart slammed against her ribs. Singing was well and good, but speaking? She couldn't. She could still feel the phrenologist's fingers roving over her scalp. Could still hear the taunts of her schoolmates as she stood in the classroom, stammering over the recitations that refused to be coaxed from her lips. She'd barely held back the burning tears amid her shame as she stared at her buttoned top boots, stammering over the words stalled in her throat. Lizzie Johnston's taunts yet burned her ears and branded her soul.

"C-c-cat g-got your tongue, C-C-Cadence P-P-Piper?"

She watched Dr. Ivy's mouth move.

"The benefit is set for next Friday evening. I'd be honored if you'd let me escort you for the evening." His brows rose. "What say you, Miss Piper?"

She licked her lips. The thought of standing before hundreds of people, listening to murmurs, their snickers and taunts and ridicules, caused a swell of panic to burst in her chest.

"Forgive me, but I cannot."

She turned and fled.

Joshua gripped the doorframe and silently cursed himself. Why did he think she would want to attend the benefit on his arm? He who had forced himself upon her, tasting what he had no right to taste. Even now, the memory of her honeyed lips burned his.

He was a fool.

Cadence was right to keep her distance.

Cadence shut the front door behind her and dropped her reticule onto the foyer table with a weary groan. A steady *thud, thud, thud* told her Tate was approaching the entryway. He appeared seconds later, cane in hand.

"Good evening." His warm greeting cheered her. She offered a tired smile in return.

"Had a profitable day?"

He shrugged. "If you consider reading half the morning, taking an hour to dress, eating, and napping profitable, then yes."

She stretched up on tiptoe to buss his cheek. "Be patient with yourself. You've been through much. Is supper ready?"

Louisa bustled by, carrying a soup tureen. "Just 'bout ready to call everyone to the table. Good to see you here before eating time, missy. You've been burning the candle at both ends lately. Getting too skinny." She frowned. "Just felt like coming home earlier than usual?"

Cadence took a sudden interest in her nails. "Guess I'm missing your delicious meals."

"Glad I am of it. Sit. Eat."

Cadence would never tell her the reason she'd left the hospital early. Since denying Joshua's request to attend the benefit, she'd felt him watching her all day. She could not tell him why she refused to participate in such a noble event. The confession would be too humiliating.

Father opened the front door, sniffing. "Is that chicken and dumplings I smell?"

Louisa beamed. "Yes, sir. Everybody enjoy them. Flour prices are rising. Might be the last ones we have for a while."

Father stopped when he saw Cadence. "You're home early, my dear."

She smiled weakly. "A little more tired than usual, I suppose."

"I think your charity work at the hospital is too much for you. Perhaps it's time to set it aside."

A frisson of alarm skittered down her spine. "What do you mean? I love helping the soldiers."

"I know, darling, I know, but your brother is home now. His healing is coming along nicely. I understand that you wanted to do your part in the great conflict and step up for our family's honor. You've done so. But now—" he offered a smile filled with hope—"don't you think it's time to put an end to it?"

She stepped back, shaken. All this time she'd thought Father understood, at least in part, her desire to find purpose. To serve. To be something more than a listless spinster floating through the house. He'd said he was proud of her, boasted of her to his friends. And now he would ask her to give it up?

A fist squeezed her heart.

She forced herself to speak slowly. "The hospital depends on me, Father. I can't just leave. The physicians, the other nurses, the patients . . . I can't abandon them."

"No one is irreplaceable."

"Of course not, but—"

Father looked toward Tate and beamed. "Congressman Ramsey is working on getting your brother a job at the Capitol when he's ready. Oh, I know it will be a lower-level secretarial employment of some kind, but still, that's something, eh?"

Cadence looked to her brother. He was staring at her, apology in his solemn eyes. He was as uncomfortable as she with the turn of events. Bitterness coated her tongue.

"Yes, that's something all right."

Father patted her shoulder. "All I'm saying is that it's not proper for a genteel woman to work among disease all day long. I strongly urge you to resign your post."

Before she could respond, he turned to Louisa with a smile. "Now, let's eat. I'm famished."

As chairs scraped and dishes were filled, she stood still in the foyer, dismissed.

One thing was abundantly clear: she should not have pushed Dr. Ivy's invitation away so swiftly. Clearly he was one of the few who understood her.

Perhaps the only one.

chapter 12

Joshua swallowed against the tight collar constricting his throat, but it was the loveliness of the woman on his arm that rendered him breathless. Cadence's gloved fingers dug into his arm as if she were terrified. He glanced down to her petite frame wrapped in lavender silk. Her bare shoulders were like cream, and with her glossy curls swept up, it was all he could do not to stare at the slender curve of her exposed neck. The gown's bodice revealed her slim waist and feminine form to perfection before flaring out into a billowing skirt. Yet she trembled like a leaf in a spring gale.

He had no idea why she'd recanted on her initial refusal to attend, but he was thankful.

As they stood in the darkness before the steps of Society Hall, with the bright lamplight pouring from its windows and the sound of revelry vibrating through its foundation, he placed his free hand on the gloved fingers she tucked in the crook of his arm.

"You look stunning, and I have no doubt you'll do Judiciary Square Hospital proud."

She looked up at him then, the traces of window light dancing across the gentle curves of her face. "I pray so. Are you nervous?"

He tipped his head. "A little. Giving grand speeches is not my strong suit." He winked. "I prefer surgery."

She smiled. "Or barking at nurses."

He feigned horror. "Never!"

"Joshua, I—I don't think I'll be able to speak."

So that was her concern? His shoulders sagged with relief. He'd thought she didn't want to be accompanied by him. A ribbon of hope unfurled through his chest.

"You needn't if it upsets you. Many people are terrified of speaking in public. I'll speak for the both of us. I'll tell Congressman Ramsey you're not up to talking or singing, and—"

She placed her free hand on his chest. "No. That's not what I meant. I'll happily sing. Just not give a speech."

Curiosity flared. "Of course, if that's what you desire." He would think singing would be twice the torment of giving a speech. Why the angst?

Her entire body relaxed and she looked at him, her eyes large and bright. "Thank you."

"Think nothing of it. After all, I must pamper my best nurse."

He led her inside to the dazzling bright gaslights and swirling colors of silks as couples spun their way through a Virginia reel, lining up and clapping in time to the sounds of jaunty violins. Shoes stomped in rhythm to the music, vibrating the floor beneath. An array of booths lined the great hall, decorated with brightly colored bunting, some serving food and drink, others collecting donations for various charities. A number of black-clad widows and clergymen manned the tables, doing what they could to seek help for those in need. The crush of people was overwhelming.

"Oh, my," Cadence breathed at his side. "I had no idea there would be so many people."

He chuckled. "When Congressman Ramsey does a thing, he does it up big."

As if summoned, the large man appeared, his wife at his side. "Dr. Ivy! Miss Piper!" He shook Joshua's hand and gave Cadence a gentle kiss on the cheek. "So glad you could both attend."

Mrs. Ramsey took Cadence's hand and squeezed. "Oh, do tell me you'll sing tonight, my dear."

"Yes, that is, if you and your husband still desire me to do so."

"Of course!" The congressman chuckled, eyes twinkling. "How could we have a benefit without hearing from the Songbird of the North?"

Two bright spots of crimson stained her cheeks. "Oh, dear, you've heard the nickname then?"

He grinned. "Yes, from several of the soldiers who have been discharged from Judiciary Square Hospital. It seems many have an especial fondness for Nurse Songbird and her gentle way of bringing comfort to the ill."

Joshua smiled at Cadence's discomfiture. And to think he'd once thought her vain. How wrong he'd been.

Congressman Ramsey turned to him. "Please tell us whatever you'd like about the hospital, Dr. Ivy. How many patients you're attending each week, what your needs are, about the soldiers, anything. Paint a picture that will help people understand the depth of need."

"Yes, sir. Tell me when you'd like Miss Piper and me to do our part, and we'll be ready."

"Very good. In the meantime—" the congressman turned to wink at his wife—"I believe my lovely bride owes me a dance. Dr. Ivy, Miss Piper." He whisked his wife away.

"He's a good man. I like him."

Cadence watched him spin his wife into the reel with a laugh. "One of the k-k-kin—" she abandoned the vexing word—"uh, nicest souls I know." She looked away.

"He's given me a wonderful idea."

"And what's that?"

"I do believe it's time for a dance."

His chest pounded when she answered with a saucy smile and slipped her gloved fingers into his waiting hand.

"Lead the way."

"May God save the Union! The red, white, and blue,
Our states keep united the dreary day through;
Let the stars tell the tale of the glorious past,
And bind us in Union forever to last."

Applause erupted as the last note died away. Cadence let her body relax and curtsied to the cheering crowd. She'd done it. Her gaze landed on Congressman Ramsey and his wife, beaming from the side of the hall. They were pleased with her. A buzz of giddiness swept through her chest.

After receiving congratulations and more enthusiastic introductions, Cadence walked out of the hall, blessedly free of the stuffy air, and fanned her overheated face. The relative cool of the evening was a welcome reprieve after dancing, singing, and greeting people congratulating her on a job well done. Her shoes pinched and her back ached, but the evening had been grand. The dance still continued inside.

She looked up into the night sky, drinking in the sight of scattered diamonds stretched across a canvas of ink. And Dr. Ivy . . . *Joshua* had been the perfect escort. Who could have imagined that the gruff, demanding surgeon who'd tried so desperately to chase her away mere months ago could be such a gentleman? And a charming one at that.

She'd noticed the way the other women stared at him tonight, as if he were a prize they longed to dig their fingernails into. And when he'd arrived to escort her to the benefit and she'd seen him in his suit, looking so tall and handsome and strong, his eyes studying her in that intense way he had, her knees had felt strange. Weak and watery.

Odd.

The urge to cool her too-warm skin caused her to extend the lacy fan. The puffs of air toyed with a curl against her neck.

"You align yourself with danger."

A cold sensation slithered down her spine. Gooseflesh rose on her arms. She froze and spun, looking for the source of the pebbly voice. A man stood watching her in the shadows of the building. She shivered.

"Who are you?"

"Tell the doctor the Knights see all. Have a care, Miss Piper. The Knights of the Golden Circle come for you next." His shadowy presence fled.

She lurched backward but couldn't suppress the question begging for release. "Wait! What do you mean?"

But he was gone, evaporating like a spirit.

Joshua sipped the punch, letting the flavors of lemon, black tea, and rum coat his tongue. A bit strong for his taste. He never had developed a fondness for spirits. Papa John had seen to that.

He set aside the cup and strolled through the crowded room, eyeing the brightly decorated booths and clusters of boisterous people. Where was Cadence? He had lost sight of her after her performance, so pressed was she with admirers, and rightfully so.

Large potted palms in the corners of the room provided auspicious alcoves to catch one's breath . . . or hide from ardent pursuers. Perhaps she had sought refuge in one of these corners.

Weaving his way through the crowd, he explored the quiet spaces behind the palms. Nothing but a shadowed corridor. Did the passageway lead outside? Shoving his hands in his pockets, he followed the papered hallway lined with gaslit wall sconces. Raised masculine voices came from behind a door on the left. The barest crack in the door left its secrets unguarded, its occupants' voices clear as angry tones vibrated through the slit.

"Poppycock! I don't care if Barrister was dead! Parading right up to his house to claim his slaves and divvy up his property was a foolish thing to do. Have you no sense?"

Joshua frowned. Congressman Ramsey? He'd never heard the statesman sound so riled.

"How were we to know the papers would get wind of it? Bunch of no-good, mealymouthed . . ."

The unnamed man let out a string of profanities so vile, Joshua cringed.

Glass shattered, effectively silencing the cursing form.

"I have Miss Piper singing the Union's praises for us so we can move freely. Do you not understand what we are doing here?" Congressman Ramsey's voice was low. Controlled. Then it burst in a yell of fury. "There's too much at stake!"

His voice grew louder, his footfalls heavier. He must be approaching the door. Joshua pressed himself against the wall, frantically searching for a quick escape. Then the footfalls faded again and he breathed once more. The congressman must be pacing.

"I'm doing all I can from the inside. Don't you think it kills me to extol the Union day and night, much less that insipid Lincoln? Show some self-control. That's all I'm saying . . ."

Joshua swallowed hard. What could this mean?

". . . not tolerate any further outbursts. Oaths require blood. Do I make myself clear?"

A heavy silence descended.

"Perfectly."

"Good."

Their footfalls grew heavy again. Rapid. They would leave the room in a matter of seconds. Joshua hastened back down the hallway, his mind reeling.

He burst onto the crowded dance floor and inhaled long pulls of sticky air.

Never would he have thought freedom could be found in such confusion.

Cadence's heart hammered. Her throat pinched. *Tell the doctor the Knights see all.* The doctor. Did the stranger mean Joshua?

"The Knights of the Golden Circle come for you next."

Her eyes slid shut as she placed a hand to her quivering stomach. She should go back inside. It wasn't safe here.

"There you are."

The masculine voice caused her to jump. Gasping, she whirled, only to see Joshua staring at her.

"Forgive me. I didn't mean to startle you so."

"I—uh, no. It wasn't you." She shook her head. "It's nothing."

His eyes narrowed. "No, it's not. Something has frightened you. What is it?"

Cadence's breath thinned as she stared into his face. Could she trust this man so full of secrets with moods as unpredictable as a spring storm? The stranger had issued a warning to both of them. What danger might befall him if she were remiss in telling him the truth?

Please, God, help me know what to do.

He stepped close and tenderly cupped her shoulders. "Did someone hurt you?"

She shook her head. "No, but a stranger was here. Lurking in the shadows."

He frowned and glanced around. "Where?"

"Over there." She pointed. "He fled moments ago after uttering a warning."

"A warning? For whom?"

"Both of us." Her voice felt strained.

A frightening intensity flooded his face. "Tell me."

"He said . . ." She shut her eyes to remember all he'd relayed. It had happened so quickly. "He said I had aligned myself with danger. Wanted me to tell the doctor that 'the Knights see all.'"

Joshua was silent for a long moment, his face granite. "Did he say anything else?"

"Yes. He told me I should have a care. The Knights were coming for me next." Her brows pinched. "Who are they, Joshua?"

A muscle twitched in his jaw as he grabbed her wrist and tugged. "Come."

"Where?"

Fire blazed in his dark eyes. "I'm taking you home. Immediately."

She yanked away from his hold, fearing his harsh reaction would draw the attention of people outside the hall. "Why? What are you not telling me?"

"The less you know, the safer you are."

"Joshua, please—"

"Don't you see?" He drew her so close, his warm breath fanned her cheek. She could smell the clean scent of his shaving soap. "I never should have brought you here. I didn't know . . ."

Despite the shadows of the evening, the stormy conflict in his eyes was plain to see. That, and the tense coil of his muscles. She fought to keep her voice soothing. "I wanted to come."

"What I'm engaged in, what I do . . . I never should have involved you. Just being around me is a danger."

"What if it's a risk I'm willing to take?"

His jaw firmed, lips pressed tight. "But it's not one I am willing to take." He signaled for a hack passing by and helped her inside.

After Joshua settled across from her, the carriage lurched into motion. The clip-clop of the horses' shoes was loud against the road in the silence of the enclosure.

He dropped his head in his hands. "I'm sorry, Cadence." His voice was hoarse. "You cannot be anywhere near me. Not at hospital benefits nor anywhere else."

Sharpness pierced her chest. "What are you saying?"

His eyes slid closed. "Your work at Judiciary Square Hospital is henceforth no longer needed."

Blood leached from her face. She grasped his hand and curled her fingers around his. They were limp. "Joshua, no! You can't do this."

He lifted his head as he slumped across the back of the seat. "You're the finest nurse I've ever worked with, but for your sake, for your protection, you must stay away."

"I will not." Would she forever be doomed to being ordered about by demanding males, denied her passion and purpose?

"You know what good I can do there. What help I can be. Please—"

"Your position has been terminated. I'll—" He cringed. "I'll write Dorothea Dix if I must."

He wouldn't. He couldn't be so cruel. Not after he'd begged her to return, taught her so much, become her friend . . . he'd then cast her aside like a worn rag?

With a start, she realized he *was* her friend. Probably the dearest one she had. When had he slipped from greatest foe to most treasured confidant?

"You needn't worry about that man and his threats. I'll be careful. I'll have an escort at all times. I can hire Steward Swindle to walk with me everywhere. Why, I'll even—"

"Cadence." Her name on his lips silenced her. He reached over and stroked her chin with the pad of his thumb. "I'll not be deterred. You're too precious to be sacrificed because of me."

Her pulse raced at his gentle touch. What was happening? He suddenly dropped his hand as the hack lurched to a stop. They had arrived at her home.

Joshua opened the door and helped her down. Her heart felt like lead as she trudged up the steps to the door. He released her hand.

His soft whisper tugged. "God bless you, Cadence."

And then he was gone.

chapter 13

CADENCE WIPED A BEAD OF PERSPIRATION from her brow as she knelt in front of the tiny grave and yanked a handful of weeds away from the headstone. The air was sultry and thick, far too warm despite the cloudy skies swirling overhead. Storms were approaching, without a doubt.

"There, little one. Your spot looks tidy now."

She laid a bouquet of wildflowers just below Rose's name and adjusted the scarlet ribbon, praying the coming storm would not abscond with the bright treasures. Searching the ground, she grabbed a handful of pebbles to anchor the flowers and pressed them into the soft earth, using the stones to keep the stems in place.

Low thunder grumbled overhead and she sighed, rising and snatching up the cumbersome carpetbag at her feet. She must hurry if she was to deliver the books to Judiciary Square Hospital before the rain began.

Her heart ached with every step that brought her closer. This was madness. The past two weeks had been utter misery. The walls of her home had shrunk with each day that passed. Father's continual pampering and praise of Tate nearly drove her mad. He'd refused to let her help in his shop, so she'd done little but assist with the meager chores and baking Louisa had conceded to her care. She was going crazy with the need to do something. Every thought brought her back to the hospital, to the soldiers, to treatments and fevers and Dr. Ivy.

"Just do the next thing."

Miss Crosby's gentle admonition from months before had needled Cadence until an idea had formed. Recuperating soldiers often grew weary from months spent in bed. Why not organize a book drive for them? She'd spread the word through Mrs. Ramsey, and already the donations were pouring in. The first load of books had been delivered to each of the area hospitals. Only one remained: Judiciary Square.

She lugged the heavy bag up the steps and knocked lightly on the door before pushing her way inside. Everything was the same. Polished floors, white walls, the scent of ammonia, the sound of heels clicking up and down corridors, the faint coughing of patients far away, muted conversations. Her chest twisted. She should be here. This was her home.

Steward Swindle rounded the corner. His eyes grew wide. "Nurse Piper! Glad I am to see you. Please tell me you've got word about Dr. Ivy."

Confusion flooded her. She dropped the bag of books to the floor. "What do you mean? I haven't seen Dr. Ivy for a fortnight. I only came to deliver book donations for the soldiers who are convalescing."

Steward Swindle frowned as he wrung his hands. "It's like the man just disappeared."

"Please." She placed her hand on his arm. "Tell me what happened."

"Three days ago, Dr. Ivy said he had some business to take care of on the morrow. Not to expect him the next day. All right, we said. His day away passed, but two more days have come and gone and he's nowhere to be found. The nurses don't seem worried a mite. Some say he's a scoundrel, off with a woman, but I don't believe it." Honest Swindle's green eyes were lined with worry. His red hair stuck out from under his cap as if he'd been running his fingers through it over and over. "Something's wrong. I can feel it in my bones."

A stone sank in the pit of her stomach. The man in the shadows. The threats. What if something had happened to Joshua? What if one of his escapades had gone awry? A hundred scenarios flitted through her mind, none of them good.

An idea formed. She looked into the steward's face. "I know I no longer work here, but might I be allowed to enter his office?"

He looked up and down the hallway. "If anyone asks, I haven't seen you today. Be quick."

She nodded and raced down the corridor to Joshua's office. The normal stacks of journals and papers lay scattered in disarray over every surface. She looked to the coatrack. His frayed green coat was missing. Nausea curdled.

She must discover where he lived. That would be the first place to start. He'd never given her one clue about his private life. Everything about him was wrapped in secrecy. She shuffled through his papers, wincing. Such an invasion of privacy, but if he was in trouble, she must know.

If she could find anything—an envelope or letter, anything at all would help.

There! A letter lay among a stack of correspondence, but

this one did not bear the address of the hospital. Instead it was addressed to Dr. Ivy on a street on the other side of Washington. Dare she? She grabbed a pencil and a scrap of paper and scribbled down the address. Stuffing the scrap into her dress pocket, she braved a glance down the hallway. Empty. Voices drifted. Time was running out.

With a prayer that she wouldn't be discovered, she hastened down the corridor and slipped out of Judiciary Square Hospital. A crack of thunder shook the sky. A fat raindrop hit her cheek as she hailed a carriage.

Storm or no, she would not rest until she'd found Joshua.

Cadence glanced up at the two-story house squatting in a modest part of the city. The street was lined with other clean, well-cared-for houses, but the worst of Washington's slums lay only blocks away. Was this Joshua's home? And if so, why was it so far from the hospital?

She clutched the scrap of paper in her fingers and climbed the three short steps to the door. The yard needed tending, and several plants looked wilted from lack of water. This was a fool's errand. What made her think he was even here?

Still, Steward Swindle's worry propelled her feet forward. If the easygoing soldier sensed danger for Dr. Ivy, she must do something.

She lifted her hand and rapped on the door, counting the seconds under her breath. The rain came in earnest now, dampening her hair and tickling her eyelashes. A raindrop found its way down the back of her neck and slipped under her collar.

He wasn't here. Having no other leads, she turned away only to hear the door open with a soft squeak.

A young girl of no more than ten stood in the doorway.

Her bright-red hair was plaited into two braids, and a spray of freckles kissed her nose. Startling green eyes stared at Cadence solemnly.

This wasn't his house. Words fled from Cadence's mouth as the wide-eyed girl stared at her. "I—I'm so sorry to disturb you. I must have the wrong address. I was hoping to find a Dr. Joshua Ivy."

The girl tilted her head, curiosity darkening her eyes to emerald. "What's your name, miss?"

"Cadence Piper. I work at Judiciary Square Hospital. Well, I used to."

The young girl looked over her shoulder as if uncertain what to do. After a long moment, she lurched forward and took Cadence's hand. "Can you treat a gunshot wound?"

Cadence's pulse tripped. "I know how to clean the wound to stave off infection, though I've never performed surgery to remove a bullet."

The girl looked into Cadence's eyes, searching for something, then nodded silently. "Come with me."

She tugged her into the dry warmth of the house. All was silent save for the soft ticking of a mantel clock. The sprite released her hand. "I can take you to Dr. Ivy, miss." Her green eyes glassed with unshed tears. "Please help him."

Alarm wrapped cold tentacles around Cadence's heart. She knelt before the child and squeezed her shoulders. "I'll do all I can, sweetheart."

The girl nodded and wiped her eyes.

"What's your name?"

"Penelope."

"Well, then, Penelope, let's find Dr. Ivy."

She led Cadence past the parlor, down the first-floor hallway, and pushed open a door on the left. Cadence peeked inside.

Joshua lay on a bed, his color ashen. His bare chest peeked out from the blanket covering his still form. A bloody bandage was wrapped around his middle. His eyes were closed, pinched as if in pain.

Her throat constricted. She fought against the tears threatening to fall. He needed her help, not her tears.

Forcing a smile she didn't feel, she cupped Penelope's cheek. "Sweetheart, would you mind helping me gather a few things? I need some warm water, fresh cloths, soap, and any whiskey you might have on hand."

She bit her lip. "We don't ever keep whiskey here, but I'll see what I can find."

"Thank you."

As the girl turned to gather the supplies, Cadence neared the bed and grasped Joshua's hand. His fingers were warm.

"Dr. Ivy, you're not supposed to be the patient."

His head moved against the pillow, his eyes cracking open to slits. A tiny line marred the skin between his dark brows.

"Not safe . . . for you . . . to be here."

"Hush." She silenced him with a soft whisper and pushed his chestnut hair away from his forehead. His skin was feverish to the touch. "You need help."

He shook his head. "Must leave."

Stubborn man. She straightened and propped her hands on her hips. "You'll have to forcibly remove me, and we both know you can't even rise from that bed."

A lopsided smile lifted the corner of his mouth. His eyes shut. "Bossy."

"You sass an awful lot for someone too weak to move."

He chuckled, then groaned, his face contorting.

She sobered. "What happened?"

He cracked his eyelids open again and studied her. "Slave-buying operation went bad." He swallowed. "Fight broke out. Pulled a gun on me. Shot in the abdomen."

She winced. "And the child?"

"Escaped with Zeke . . . but barely."

She let her eyes slide shut. So dangerous. "You play at life and death like it's a game of faro."

"Worth it . . . to see those children taste freedom."

"But who will fight for them if you perish?"

"We're all going to perish at some point. We must live with abandon for as long as the Lord sees fit."

"Live with abandon." Something about the phrase resonated deeply, but she couldn't figure out why. Wasn't that what she had been doing? Fighting to live a life absent of regret? To live without fear or constraints? Yet there was something intrinsic and foundational about Joshua's passionate heartbeat. What? And why did she have such a hard time grasping it?

"Need you . . . to remove the bullet."

"It's still in there?"

He nodded curtly, his jaw tight.

Her heart slammed against her ribs. "I've never done this before."

"But you've assisted me dozens of times. Don't fret. I'll talk you through it." He pinned her with a stare. "You can do this."

"How do you know?"

"I was lying here, asking God what to do, and he brought you to my door." The ghost of a smile teased his mouth. "And I trained you. I'm a good teacher."

He trusted her. It was written all over his face. Her chest swelled. "I'll do my best."

"My bag is on the bureau."

She crossed the room and reached for his bag, opening the treasured possession with a snap. The door opened, and

Penelope entered with a pitcher of warm water, lye soap, and towels.

"Thank you."

Cadence laid out the surgical tools on a clean cloth and studied them under the lamplight. She plunged her hands into the washbowl and scrubbed them with the warm water and lye soap. Her mother's admonition from years before drifted through her mind. *Cleanliness is next to godliness.*

She glanced over at his instruments, used countless times to treat the maimed and wounded. An idea niggled.

"Purge me with hyssop, and I shall be clean: wash me, and I shall be whiter than snow."

Before she could talk herself out of it, she dunked the instruments into the warm, soapy water and scrubbed.

"What are you doing?" Penelope's soft voice intruded.

"Cleaning Dr. Ivy's instruments."

The little girl said nothing, only watched in wide-eyed wonder. Who was this redheaded flower? Joshua's little sister perhaps? There would be time enough to ask later.

She carried the now-clean instruments over to the table beside the bed and urged Penelope to go heat more water for cleaning the tools again later. The child should not be subjected to watching surgery. Cadence's own nerves were tight, fraying like a spent rope.

"I—I'm ready."

Joshua drew a breath. "Pull down the cloth covering the bullet wound."

She lifted it carefully away, wincing when Joshua hissed through his teeth as cool air made contact with the raw wound. Angry red tissue puckered around an oozing hole in his side.

"Now." His voice was low and tight. "You must use the

pliers to extract the bullet. Be careful, though. It might be best to probe with your fingers first so as to minimize any bleeding the pliers might instigate when entering the tissue."

Lifting a prayer for help, Cadence gently massaged her forefinger into the hole. Blood oozed around her finger, making it difficult to see anything. Joshua writhed, a guttural groan causing his entire body to stiffen.

"I know it's difficult, but you must relax," she said, recalling the guidance Joshua had given patients when she witnessed the surgeries he performed. "The bullet will be difficult to extract if surrounded by tight muscles."

Joshua nodded tersely and blew out small, short breaths. Blood ran in rivulets down his side. She grabbed several towels and tucked them around the wound and under him to sop up as much mess as possible. Her finger scraped something hard. Bone? No, too small. The bullet.

Sweat beaded her upper lip as she kept her left index finger near the round ball of lead and reached for the pliers. She pushed aside the flesh, and a scream tore from Joshua's throat. Her hands shook. She looked up. His face was the color of paste. His body slumped, going limp. Her heart climbed in her throat until she realized his breath was steady. He'd only fainted. Her mouth turned to cotton. How would he talk her through the rest? Her pulse thrummed dully in her ears.

She removed the piece of lead with the pliers, dropping both into the basin of water now turning pink. Blood spilled from the hole in his side. She dunked her hands in the water once more to remove the sticky blood from her fingers. Pressing a clean cloth to the wound, she waited for a long moment until the worst of the bleeding had stopped; then, reaching for a needle and thread, she began to stitch up the wound.

When she'd finished, she used her wrist to wipe away the

sweat dotting her brow. Done. Her hands trembled, but she'd done all she could. *Please, Lord, let him live.*

Penelope returned with clean, steaming water. Cadence poured a small cupful over the stitched incision site and gathered up the cloths from his bed. After washing her hands, she dunked the instruments in soapy water and heaved a thick sigh. Joshua was stirring.

Penelope stared from the foot of the bed, her chin quivering. "Will he live?"

Cadence rubbed the girl's small shoulders. "I pray so. God is the Great Physician. We've done all we can, so we petition him and trust."

Footsteps padded down the hallway. The door opened, and Cadence whirled. Two dark little bodies entered: a small boy who looked to be perhaps seven years of age and a tiny girl of no more than three. Their eyes looked to Penelope, but it was the boy who spoke.

"Penelope, you're gonna be in trouble! You know you ain't supposed to let strangers in!"

Penelope frowned. "This lady works at Judiciary Square Hospital. She just removed the bullet. He's got a fighting chance now."

Cadence knelt and smiled at the adorable children. "My name is Miss Piper. And who are you?"

The little boy studied her with suspicious eyes but answered respectfully. "The name is James. And this here's Etta."

The toddler ducked behind the young boy and stuck her thumb in her mouth, shyly glancing around his pant leg. Cadence fought a grin.

"It's a pleasure to meet you, James and Etta. Are you friends of Penelope's?"

"We're more than that."

Cadence felt as if she were in the middle of a puzzle she couldn't piece together. "Oh? How do you all know Dr. Ivy?"

Sheets rustled. She turned to see Joshua shifting, pain clouding the hue of his eyes, but his gaze was fixed steadfastly on hers.

"I think I can explain, Cadence." His chest gave the slightest heave. "I'm their father."

chapter 14

CADENCE'S BREATH THINNED as she gripped the nightstand by his bed. "Your . . . children?"

A dozen emotions ripped through her with the speed of a cyclone, but only one horrifying thought rose to the surface. "Forgive me. I shouldn't be in here, alone with you like this. Your wife. She'll . . ."

Shame burned her from the inside out. Images blurred as a hand encircled her wrist. She glanced down. Joshua.

She lifted her eyes to his. His expression was unreadable.

"I have no wife."

Three children and no wife? Her head ached.

"It's not what you think. I'll explain. Soon. Don't leave."

Her thoughts were in a tangle, and she longed to do nothing more than flee to the comfort of solitude, but at his pleading expression and the solemn gaze of the children, she hesitated. She ought to at least listen. Slowly she nodded, and he released her.

His focus drifted toward the little ones. "It's all right. You can come closer."

James and Penelope moved near the bed, though Etta stayed firmly tucked behind her brother, her thumb ensconced in her rosebud lips.

James frowned. "You gonna be okay, Papa Gish? Penelope said this lady took the bullet out."

Joshua smiled weakly. "That she did. She's a good nurse. I trained her myself."

Penelope grasped his fingers. "Is there anything I can get you?"

He moved his hand to cup her freckled cheek. "Not a thing, dumplin'. Just help Miss Piper out with whatever she needs."

Cadence cleared her throat. "Penelope has been an excellent help already. She assisted with your surgery, preparing the hot water, towels, soap . . . she did all of it so I could focus."

Penelope's cheeks tinged pink, but her eyes shone with pleasure at the praise. Joshua beamed through tired eyes. "That's my good girl."

"Me, me!"

Little Etta must have come to life, for she pushed past her brother and jumped up and down.

"Yes." Joshua smiled. "You're my good girl too." He looked at James. "Where's Miriam?"

"In the kitchen, preparing supper for later. Etta and me just returned from the market with her."

He nodded and let his eyes slide shut. "Good. Tell her Miss Piper is here and that she removed the bullet. You three go play for a little bit. You can come eat supper with me."

They murmured their agreement, but before leaving, Penelope leaned over and placed a kiss on his cheek. "I'm praying for you, Papa Gish."

"Thank you, dumplin'."

They departed, leaving only silence in their wake. Cadence felt strange. Her hands suddenly seemed too big. He owed her no explanations, no answers, yet she craved them all the same.

Spinning from his perusal, she rifled through his bag.

"What are you doing?"

"Looking for an envelope of pain powders for you. You need them."

"I need to talk with you first."

Her breath hitched. Did she want to know? "You don't need to tell me."

"Perhaps not, but I want to."

She stilled and waited.

He sighed. "In Richmond you wanted to know how I learned to play street tricks like I did. How I could command the crowd and sweet-talk them into giving away their coinage." He swallowed. "It's easy enough to do when it's all you've grown up knowing."

Her lips parted.

"I was a child of the Philadelphia streets, Cadence. My father abandoned my mother and me when I was just a small boy. When my mother died, I lived in alleys, foraging for food, begging." His jaw tightened and he looked away. "As more than one person reminded me, I was gutter trash."

Shards of pain sliced her heart afresh. What he must have suffered. A knot lodged in her throat.

"Hunger causes you to do strange things." He offered a sad, lopsided smile. "I began to watch the shysters and pickpockets. Studied the card sharps and gamblers. As I grew, I learned the art of deception. I had no conscience to sear as I lined my pockets because filling my belly was all I cared about. That, and sharing food with the other kids just like me who lived in the alleys."

The light in his eyes shifted to something soft. "That all changed one day when I picked the pocket of the wrong man." A brief chuckle shook him and he winced. "John Hopper caught me. Instead of dragging me to the authorities or thrashing me as he should have done, he brought me to his house, where his wife, Ann, fed me. His children welcomed me with smiles. John and Ann were Quakers, and they told me about God and his love. Told me it didn't matter what I had been told about who I was or where I belonged." His eyes glassed. "John said throwing a work of art in the trash doesn't devalue the work of art. It only shows the lack of wisdom and judgment in the person who so carelessly tossed it aside. For the first time I realized just because people had told me all my life I was worthless didn't mean it was true. Jesus had died for me, and that made me priceless."

Tears ran in rivulets down her cheeks. She tasted salt and wiped them away with shaking hands. "What a beautiful gift."

"The Hoppers adopted me as their own. Father Hopper was a healer of sorts, a wonder with herbs, and had a rudimentary knowledge of medicine, especially with animals. He taught me much and encouraged me to pursue an education in medicine when he saw my interest. They sacrificed and saved to send me to medical school. When I came here to work at the hospital, I was shocked to find so many homeless children running the streets of our capital." He paused. "I couldn't ignore them. That had been me. In some ways, it's me still."

Her lips trembled. "You began taking them in, caring for them, didn't you?"

"Yes. I gave them medical care. Providing food whenever I could. Finding them homes. And when I discovered abandoned children hiding in broken crates and barrels, their bellies bloated for want of food, I knew I had to do something. The organization I work with provides the funds and the network to get them into free states. Still—" he glanced down at his bandaged middle—"we draw the slaveholders' ire. Abolitionists always do. Father Hopper always did too."

She leaned forward. "And Penelope, James, and Etta?"

His eyes slid shut. "Children I found abandoned in the slums of Washington upon my arrival here. They had nowhere else to go. So I brought them here and hired an older woman I trust named Miriam to care for them while I work or am away."

"I see." She sat back, stunned by all he'd revealed about his past. "They called you Papa Gish."

A small smile tugged. "Gish was my nickname growing up. Don't know why. I guess some of the smaller children couldn't say 'Joshua.' Came out as Gish and just stuck that way. Seems safer to let my children call me that. The more identities, the less likely rabid slaveholders will come gunning for me and them, don't you think?"

She'd not thought of that. "I suppose so."

He sobered, his expression grave. "You are one of the only people I've entrusted with this information. Please, tell no one. Not your father or brother. No one."

She braved a touch, reaching out to grasp his fingers. His hand curled around hers.

"I promise."

He relaxed into his pillow. "Thank you." A shadow crossed his features. "And now I must beg you to leave."

Leave? "I will do no such thing! You need proper care. You're running a fever, and the children—"

"Have Miriam." His eyes flashed. Even ill, she knew the stubborn jut of his jaw meant no good would come of the conversation. Still, what could he do this time? Nothing. He was as weak as a newborn lamb.

"I'm staying." She crossed her arms and glared. Daring him. She expected to see anger, rage, but something altogether different clouded his expression.

"Please." His voice was hoarse. "If something happened to you because of me . . ."

"Hush." The admonition came out harsher than she intended. "What harm could befall me here? Besides, the best way for you to throw me out is to heal quickly, which you need my skills to do. Then you can boss me and be back to your grumpy old self and toss me out on my ear."

He blanched. "I really was insufferable, wasn't I?"

"You still are," she teased. Spying a glass of water on the table, she offered him a drink and replaced it before straightening. "Sleep. I'll go home, pack a bag, and return shortly."

His eyelids drooped with fatigue. "Stubborn woman."

She paused with her hand on the doorknob. "I should be. I learned from the best."

chapter 15

"'AND SO, THE PRINCESS TRIED HER BEST to convince the old queen she was a real princess, but the old queen did not believe her, soaked as she was from the terrible storm. Water ran down from her hair and clothes. It ran down into the toes of her shoes and out again at the heels. No matter how regally she acted, nor how she displayed her royal lineage, the old queen was not persuaded.

"'"But I am a real princess," the drenched princess protested.

"'*Well, we'll soon find out,* thought the old queen.'"

Penelope looked up from the thick tome containing "The Princess and the Pea," opened wide on Cadence's lap, and asked, "How could the old queen ever manage such a thing?"

Cadence tugged the girl's red braids. "You'll have to listen and see."

James frowned. "Seems to me the queen shouldn't've been so worried 'bout whether the girl was a real princess or not. Who cares if her son wanted to marry a real princess? The girl was cold and wet. She needed shelter. Just give her a bed and food."

Cadence grinned at him. "You're a very wise boy, James."

Little Etta snuggled against her chest, her pudgy body warm and soft. "'Tory."

Penelope giggled.

Cadence laughed. "Forgive me. I forgot I was supposed to be reading a 'tory." She cleared her throat melodramatically and continued.

"'The old queen said nothing but went into the bedroom, took all the bedding off the bedstead, and laid a pea on the bottom. Then she took twenty mattresses and laid them on the pea, and then twenty eiderdowns on top of the mattresses. On this the princess had to lie all night. In the morning she was asked how she had slept. "Oh, very badly!" said she. "I scarcely closed my eyes all night. Heaven only knows what was in the bed, but I was lying on something hard so that I am black-and-blue all over my body." Now they knew she was a real princess because she had felt the pea right through the twenty mattresses and the twenty eiderdowns. Nobody but a real princess could be as sensitive as that.'"

James grunted. "That's silly. Why would feeling a pea through a bunch of mattresses make you a princess?"

"Because it meant she had a sensitive heart."

The masculine voice in the parlor caused all four of them to turn. Joshua stood there, his complexion still pale, but blessedly alert. He had managed to don pants and a shirt over his bandaged torso but gripped the doorway. The past three days had been precarious as he fought off fever and recovered from the bullet extraction.

"Papa Gish! You're up!" Penelope bolted from the floor and

ran to his side, gripping his free hand. He looked down at her and winked.

"Of course I'm up. The Almighty knows you three need someone to keep you out of trouble." They laughed as Penelope led him to a chair. He captured Cadence's gaze.

She asked, "No dizziness?"

"Only at first. Not now. Just a little weak."

"Miss Piper is reading us a story." James grinned.

Etta pulled her thumb from her mouth as she burrowed deeper in Cadence's lap. "'Tory."

He gingerly settled into a chair. "Don't let me keep you from finishing."

Cadence glanced back down, suddenly uneasy as she felt Joshua's gaze upon her. "'So the prince took her for his wife, for now he knew he had a real princess, and the pea was put in a royal museum, where it still may be seen. They lived happily ever after.'"

Penelope sighed. "So romantic."

James huffed. "Seems like a waste of a pea to me."

Cadence laughed. "In the few days I've been here, I've noticed you're awfully fond of food, young man."

"Of course." His white teeth flashed. "Girls only cause trouble. Food is lots better."

"You don't have a romantic bone in your body, James Ivy!" Penelope glared. "The point of the story isn't the pea. It was about discovering the identity of the princess."

Joshua interjected, his voice low. "In some ways, you could say it was about the princess laying aside the need to prove herself and rest in the knowledge of her royal identity, whether anyone else knew it or not."

Cadence looked up to find him watching her. Her skin

warmed. Was he speaking to her? *"Laying aside the need to prove herself and rest in the knowledge of her royal identity . . ."*

She swallowed.

Miriam bustled into the room. "All right now, children. You done wore out Miss Piper. I've got some shortbread and milk on the table for you. Go on and eat some and then it's time to get back to working on your sums."

With a groan, they plodded from the room, all except for little Etta, who turned to study Cadence. Her fingers cradled Cadence's face before she planted a sticky kiss on her lips.

"Tisses."

Delighted, Cadence wrapped her arms around the plump body. "I love your kisses, sweetheart."

Squealing, Etta toddled from the room, chasing after her brother and sister as fast as her dimpled knees could carry her.

"You're good with them."

She smiled, toying with the edge of the book of fairy tales. "They're delightful."

"How old are you, Miss Piper?"

He'd dropped the use of her first name the past several days, a change that had not gone unnoticed.

"Nineteen. And you?"

"Five and twenty." He closed his eyes. "Some days I feel older."

She laughed lightly. "A man of five and twenty with a daughter of ten."

"I suppose they are more like adopted sisters and a brother, but I believe they like thinking of me as their father. Makes them feel safe somehow."

"I can understand that. There's a measure of protection only a father or husband can provide."

Her thoughts drifted to her conversation with Father only two days before when she'd returned home to pack her bag. He'd accepted her explanation that she was needed to nurse a dear friend and take care of her friend's children. Guilt pricked. She'd led him to believe the friend was a fellow nurse at the hospital and he'd not questioned her further. Still, he'd been too busy gushing about Tate's new position working for Congressman Ramsey to pay Cadence much mind. If she thought to move his heart by showing him her compassion for the ill, she'd been sadly mistaken.

Anymore she resembled a wandering soul, a child without a home, desperate for the approval that never came.

Pushing aside the gloomy thought, she rose and moved to Joshua's side. "Let me check your wound."

"It's fine."

She gave him a pointed look, and he clenched his jaw. With short, jerky movements, he unbuttoned the lower portion of his shirt, exposing the bandage that swathed his middle. As gently as possible, she curled the cloth back. The flesh was healing nicely. No infection or oozing fluids.

She didn't realize how close their heads were until she heard his hoarse whisper.

"Cadence."

Her gaze slowly lifted. His dark eyes were mere inches from her own. Something indefinable pulled between them. Her breath caught, suspended. Her pulse pattered an uneven staccato as his fingers reached up and tenderly brushed wayward tendrils of hair from her face. His fingertips trailed down her cheeks to the hollow of her throat. His gaze dipped to her lips and lingered. Warmth twisted her insides.

"What does one do when he has a real princess in his grasp but he himself is not a prince?"

Her heart felt bruised at the pain lacing his voice. "I see a prince before me."

His eyes flickered. "I'm no prince, but I see your worth. There's no need to prove it to me."

His thumb roved over her lips. A heady rush filled her senses as his lips nuzzled her hair, her forehead . . . trailing down to her ear. Her skin prickled with the sensations flooding her.

"Cadence . . ." He breathed her name like a caress. "Promise me something."

She leaned in to his touch, their lips not yet meeting, yet chasing, drawing . . . so close.

"Anything."

"Stay away from Congressman Ramsey."

Her eyes flew open.

Joshua reached to trace the curve of her cheek, his dark eyes intense. "Promise me."

"But why?"

"There are things about him you don't know. I care about you too much to see you tangled up in something you don't understand. Please. For me?"

"Something you don't understand." Did Joshua believe her to be a simpleton too?

Pulling away from his touch, she stiffened. "Congressman Ramsey has been nothing but kind to me. And you want me to discard him on a whim?"

Joshua glowered. "Not a whim. Because I'm asking. I overheard him threatening someone at the benefit. Please believe me. To blindly tie yourself to him would be foolish!"

Stung by the harsh edge of his tone, she fumbled to her feet and forced down the ache in her throat. Joshua was just like Father. Just like the phrenologist. Viewing her as too dull-witted to make decisions. To think. To be of use.

"So I'm foolish?"

"No, I didn't say—"

Her stomach tightened. "Congressman Ramsey has been the only one who has treated me as an equal. The only one who has lifted me up instead of belittling me and telling me I'm too inept to rise to whatever the occasion might demand. I will not cast him aside merely because you said I'm too simple to understand."

"Would you let me speak?" Joshua's nostrils flared. "You didn't hear what I heard. Ramsey is not the man he pretends to be in public. He's using you. Having you sing for patriotic events to disguise his true agenda."

Cadence propped her hands on her hips. "Which is?"

Joshua cast about for words. "I—I don't know yet."

"You want me to discard him based on conjecture?"

"I want you to leave him be, based on my wishes."

Cadence crossed her arms. "Lest you forget, *Dr. Ivy*, I no longer work for you. You cannot order me about and expect me to fall into line."

A muscle twitched near his eye. "You're right. I don't need you as my nurse, nor does Congressman Ramsey need you to sing. You're nothing more than his puppet, Cadence!"

She stepped back, stung. Unshed tears burned her throat. "Since I'm not needed, I should go."

"No, Cadence, I didn't mean it like that. I—"

His words were lost, and she ran to the room she'd occupied, crammed her scant belongings into her bag, and fled the house.

The tears didn't fall until she stepped onto the uneven street. She'd not even been able to tell the children good-bye.

And it was good-bye. Her heart could bear no more encounters with Joshua Ivy.

----- ❧⊱❧⊰❧ -----

The front door slammed behind the swishing of skirts. Silence descended. His heart swelled until he feared it might split.

He collapsed into the stuffed parlor chair and cradled his head in his hands, sucking in a sharp breath against the searing pain in his side . . . pain that somehow seemed far less than the aching throb in his soul.

He was a fool. She'd misunderstood him completely. He didn't need her as a nurse. He needed *her*. Her compassion, wit, and beauty brightened every room she entered.

Every fiber of his being yearned to chase after Cadence. To pull her toward him and apologize for his poor choice of words. More than that. To confess what was trapped inside, but he could not. Perhaps it was better this way. Being tethered to him would mean heartache. The bullet hole in his side was burning reminder enough of what could happen.

Etta wandered into the parlor, cookie crumbs sticking to her round cheeks. "Mith Pi-puh?"

His chest constricted as he reached for her chubby fingers. "Gone."

"'Tory?"

Bitterness wrapped cold tendrils around his heart.

"No, Etta. No more stories. No happily ever afters. Not today."

Her lower lip protruded, and as she buried her face in his knee, he brooded.

There were no happily ever afters when a man fell in love with a woman he could not have.

chapter 16

JUNE 1862
OAK GROVE, VIRGINIA

A piercing whistle raised the hair on the back of Cadence's neck just before the ground beneath her feet quaked. Her teeth rattled in her head. That one was close. Far too close. The soldier at her feet groaned, recapturing her attention.

She poured a cupful of water from the bag strapped to her back and held the dented tin cup to his dry lips.

He gulped down the sustenance, nearly choking in his eagerness. "Bless you."

She forced a smile, trying to ignore the sight of his bloodied legs, crushed to a pulp below his belt. How he'd lived this long was a wonder. The woods beyond the battlefield were full of the wounded and dead. Some had crawled to the shelter on their own . . . large boulders, hollowed logs, and thick brush provided ample hiding places. Others had been dragged by fellow soldiers. Moans and cries of the wounded rose up all around. Surgical tents were being hastily constructed not more than thirty yards away. The white canvas quivered every time another cannon found its mark just beyond the line of trees. Smoke colored the woods a hazy blue.

"Mercy! Someone have mercy on me."

A soldier to her left was reaching out. His arm lay at an unnatural angle, twisted backward like a snapped tree limb.

"I have water."

As she knelt, she hummed the melody to "Fairest Lord Jesus," though she doubted the tune could be heard above the dull thump of cannons, the explosions of gunfire in the valley below, the rat-a-tat of drums, or the moans of the dying.

A hand squeezed her shoulder. She turned to see Nurse Nelson looking down at her with anxious eyes.

"A far stretch from Judiciary Square Hospital, no?" She practically had to shout the words to be heard.

"Indeed." When the call had gone out for more nurses at the battlefront, Cadence had gladly volunteered. Father had shown little resistance, consumed as he was with Tate and his shop. As taxing as nursing was, at least she was needed . . . and wanted.

Nurse Nelson jerked her head toward the nearest surgical tent. "Dr. Price needs a nurse who can administer a chloroform cone. I told him I have no experience but you might."

"Yes, I am able."

She nodded. "Good. I'll give them water. Make haste, for he has a slew of amputations to perform."

Her stomach clenched as she hurried to the surgical tent. With her wrist she wiped away the perspiration running in thick beads down her temple. She ducked under the white canvas, letting her eyes adjust to the interior. Instead of blessed relief from the late-June heat, the tent's air was even more sweltering and oppressive.

Dr. Price scurried around a makeshift table, laying out equipment. The elderly physician's gray hair stuck out like tufts of combed cotton. His apron was soaked with crimson.

"Nurse Piper?"

"Yes, sir?"

He speared her with a sharp eye. "Can you handle a chloroform cone?"

"Yes, sir."

"Excellent." He nodded at a stack of cloths and a handful of brown bottles. "Make haste. We will begin any moment."

"I need only wash my hands first."

He stared at her as if she were daft. "Why? You're not performing the surgery, only applying the anesthesia. We don't have time to waste on such frivolities." He snapped his fingers toward the blue-clad ambulance runners at the tent flap. "Bring in the first one."

Cadence folded the cloth into a tent and placed it over the soldier's nose before applying three drops of chloroform at the peak, slowly counting as the delirious soldier began to twitch. The moment brought to mind another surgery so many months before.

If he could only see how far I've come.

How was Joshua faring? Had he returned to work at Judiciary Square? Likely he had pushed too hard, resuming his duties long before he was ready.

And the children . . . what had they made of her hasty departure?

No. She would not think of him. Of them. She pinched her eyes closed to the memories. If only her mind could blot out images as easily as her eyes.

Cadence sat at the edge of a small creek and splashed her face and neck with water, wishing she could wash away the memories of the past few days as easily as she could the dirt and sweat from her skin. How many amputations had she assisted in now? Fifty? Seventy? More?

Death saturated everything. Her ears rang with screams and explosions, the shriek of horses and shouts of panicked surgeons. Her nose was filled with the metallic odor of blood and the stench of decay. Yet the mounds of the dead, the dying, the wounded continued to grow, covering the hills.

The battles had raged for three days. Or was it four now? She kneaded the muscles of her shoulders and stretched the kinks from her back as she sat on her heels. Every muscle in her body ached and her eyes burned with the need for sleep. She'd only snatched scant hours here and there, trading off with the other nurses. There was too much work to be done. It was impossible to rest when moans of agony flooded her tortured dreams.

Footsteps crunched through the brush. Nurse McDonald appeared, her face drawn and haggard.

"Cadence, I thought you were sleeping."

"I did for an hour or two."

"That's not enough."

"It's hard to sleep when so many are suffering."

The older woman's face softened. "I know, but they count on you for help, which you cannot give if you fall ill yourself."

She nodded and let her fingers cut swirls through the cool water.

Nurse McDonald sighed. "If I can't convince you to rest longer, there are men beyond surgical tent number five who could use water."

"I'll go to them." Cadence rose and shook loose twigs and dirt from the hem of her skirt. She'd not sit idly by while men languished from lack of water.

As she tromped through the woods toward the wounded, a thought skimmed over her mind.

"You could say it was about the princess laying aside the need to prove herself and rest in the knowledge of her royal identity, whether anyone else knew it or not."

She gritted her teeth and pressed forward. Why wouldn't the story or Joshua's remark leave her be? That wasn't what she'd been doing, was it? Becoming a nurse to prove something to herself or to her father, to find her significance or fill some kind of emptiness inside? Ridiculous. She longed to help people. Nothing more.

Then why the yawning emptiness in the dark of night when the world was silent? Why the sting when Father failed to praise her accomplishments?

She shoved the musing aside. This was not the time. Men needed her. One of the stewards passed her a water bag and she took to her task, kneeling, murmuring words of comfort, dribbling sustenance between parched lips and praying over those whose time was near. In the distance, the battle raged as fiercely as it had days before.

A sharp wail split the air. "Mama! Mama, please! Help me!"

A lad of no more than sixteen or seventeen lay on the ground. Crimson bubbled from his mouth. Cadence's heart shredded at the tears glazing his eyes. His outstretched hands begged for comfort.

"Mama!"

She rushed to his side and cradled his head with one arm while clutching his flailing hands with her free one. "Shush. You're not alone."

"Mama." His cries turned to whimpers. Poor lad. In his

delirium, he thought hers to be the comforting arms of his mother. She'd not tell him differently.

He looked up into her face as a single tear rolled down his filthy cheek. "Help me." The words gurgled in his throat.

Tears warmed her skin. Her throat cramped. She loathed this war, the hate, the blood, the violence. She despised everything about it.

The memory of a tiny grave in Washington coaxed a melody to her lips, even as her eyes burned. Rose's grave.

"Sleep, my child, and peace attend thee,
All through the night.
Guardian angels God will send thee,
All through the night.
Soft the drowsy hours are creeping,
Hill and dale in slumber sleeping,
I my loved ones' watch am keeping,
All through the night."

He quieted, as did the cries of the hurting around him. She looked up at the hazy sky, willing herself to see past the smoke, the disease and blood. To see beyond the grip of death tainting everything around her. Salt filled her mouth as she lifted her voice louder.

"Sleep, my child, and peace attend thee,
All through the night.
Guardian angels God will send thee,
All through the night.
Death will not have the victory,
To paradise Jesus will lead thee,
All through the night."

She glanced down to see a faint smile hovering on the soldier's face. Air left his lungs in a gentle whoosh as his body went limp in her arms. A sob shook her chest. She kissed his bloody face, rested her forehead against his, and wept.

———⋐◉◈◎⋑———

"Death will not have the victory,
To paradise Jesus will lead thee,
All through the night."

Joshua knew that voice. He stepped from the surgical tent and froze, his breath coming in labored pants. It couldn't be. Not here. Yet it was.

Cadence sat in a field of the wounded, cradling a dead soldier and weeping over him.

When the Union had contracted him to work as a field surgeon for several months, he thought it would be a wise decision. It would get his attackers off his tail, thereby providing an extra measure of safety for the children. He left them in Miriam's capable hands, although he already missed them terribly, and had hired Zeke to protect them as a bodyguard in his absence.

And he'd prayed the turmoil of war would keep his mind off a certain blue-eyed beauty.

He'd never dreamed she would be here. Hot anger lashed his insides. Why had her father permitted such a thing?

Stepping back inside the confines of the tent, he took a deep draft of stale air. He'd just keep his distance. He had to.

For her sake.

chapter 17

THUMP, THUMP, THUMP.

Would the pounding of cannons never cease? Cadence's head throbbed with the monotony of it. Then finally, after seven excruciating days, the battle fell into ominous silence. Finished, leaving carnage in its wake.

She picked her way carefully through the pockmarked battlefield, wincing at the sight of bloated bodies now festering in the summer heat. Flies buzzed in thick swarms around corpses. Bullet-riddled horses and splintered trees made the scene even more ghastly. Yet it was the eerie, ghostly moans of the survivors that made the entire atmosphere feel like the bony hands of a specter shadowed the land.

She lifted her skirt hem, watching for signs of life among the dead as she directed ambulance runners to carry the living to surgical tents. The slightest twitch of fingers, the shallowest intake of breath could make all the difference.

A blue-clad soldier lay facedown in the dirt. His limbs were motionless, yet she watched as the cords of muscle in his neck flexed. He attempted to lift his head and fell limply back into the dust.

"There!" She pointed the wounded man out to the runners, who hurried to lift him into a stretcher. They carefully flipped him, exposing a dirt-crusted bullet wound to his left thigh. The man moaned, but his eyes fluttered open. Despite the growth of beard covering his jaw, something was familiar about him.

He croaked, "Miss Piper? Am I dreaming?"

"Mr. Dodd?" It seemed a lifetime since the dinner so long ago in the Dodds' home, yet despite Stephen's agony, his stare was piercing.

"I can die a happy man now." His voice was gravelly. Weak.

"Hush. I'll not hear that kind of talk. You must endeavor to fight."

"For you I shall."

"You must fight for your own sake, Mr. Dodd. You have much life to live."

The ambulance runners whisked him away, and she murmured a prayer for his healing.

As afternoon slipped into the lengthening shadows of evening, the fatigue of the past week soaked into her bones. Nurse McDade tugged her toward the nurses' tents with a stern frown, the light from nearby campfires dancing across her high cheekbones.

"You're about ready to fall over, dearie. You must sleep. Nurse McDonald and I will take the watches tonight."

Cadence was too exhausted to argue. Half-asleep on her feet, she was plodding toward the row of tents when the snap of a twig behind her caused her senses to roar to life.

"Mighty dark night to be walking alone."

She spun around. A lone soldier stood mere feet away. The silver moonlight was bright, yet his kepi shadowed his bearded features. The glitter of his eyes was plain enough to see. A shiver coursed down her spine.

"Not alone, sir. Only joining those in my company."

He came closer, and she took an instinctive step back. "You look alone to me. Alone and lonely." He tilted his head. "I'm lonely too, if you catch my meaning."

Cold fear snaked around her stomach. "I do not. Alone and lonely are two different things. I'm neither."

He lurched forward and grabbed her by the arms, pulling her roughly to him. "Don't you long to forget?" His sour breath fanned her cheek. "Help me forget. Just for tonight."

He smashed his mouth to hers, and shudders racked her body. She tried to jerk away, but his wiry frame was far too strong. She whimpered against his punishing touch, but he only pressed harder. She bit down on his lip.

"Ouch!" he roared but didn't release his grip.

Her pulse pounded dully in her ears as a maniacal gleam shimmered in his eyes. He shoved her to the ground. Pain exploded in her back. A scream was trapped in her throat when his hand clamped down on her mouth. He straddled her, muttering oaths as he fought the fingernails she clawed into his face, his arms.

"Fight all you want. The outcome will be the same." The teeth flashed.

Nausea climbed up her throat. *Jesus . . .*

His weight was jerked from her in a sudden whoosh. She gasped and rolled onto her side, her heart slamming into her ribs like a runaway wagon. A shadowy figure circled the soldier and attacked, landing punch after punch to his face. The soldier cursed and connected his fist to the stranger's jaw with a sharp thud. He stumbled back and rounded on the soldier. With a sickening crack, the stranger landed a blow to the soldier that dropped him to the ground in an unconscious heap.

Cadence's chest heaved as the intimidating man approached. His steps seemed slow. Calculated. Would this man do the same as the soldier had? Terror rendered her unable to move, to breathe, to think.

He crouched and his features grew clear in the silver light. Her breath fled.

"Joshua."

―――――― ✦ ――――――

Joshua's heart tripped as he stared at Cadence. Her hair was mussed, the sleeve of her dress torn. A sick sensation crawled through him. If he hadn't come down the pathway at that particular moment . . .

He reached out to smooth her hair but stopped short and dropped his hand. "Did he hurt you?"

She blinked up at him, her large eyes luminous in the moonlight. She shook her head.

He cupped a hand under her elbow to gently lift her to her feet. Her body quivered.

"You're trembling."

She wrapped her arms around her middle. "I didn't know you were here."

He turned to yank the unconscious soldier to his feet.

"What will become of him?"

Her soft voice scraped his heart. He turned and studied her. "He'll be hauled to the captain and likely be court-martialed. Punished."

She nodded but said nothing more. When he returned from hauling the unconscious soldier to his superiors, he stretched out on the ground in front of Cadence's tent to keep watch as she slept.

No one would attack her again. He'd make sure of it.

———— ⌍⌐⌍ ————

Cadence looked for Joshua the following day but could not find him anywhere; however, she did notice the two soldiers now stationed as guards over the nurses' tents. Joshua's doing? Likely.

She'd suffered no more than a few bruises, broken fingernails, and a bad fright, yet the memories of the foul man's groping hands left her feeling vulnerable and exposed.

Suppressing another shiver, she pushed back a wayward lock of sweaty hair with her wrist and carried the basin of clean water into the surgical tent where Dr. Price awaited. Only the smallest amount splashed on her dirty apron.

Nurse McDonald passed and wrinkled her nose. "Trade with me."

Cadence smiled. "Why? What doctor have you been assigned to assist today?"

The matronly nurse's mouth pinched into a frown. "You'll never guess. The most handsome one this side of the Mississippi. Dr. Ivy is here. Can you believe it?"

Cadence looked down at the basin of water. Her watery reflection stared back at her.

Nurse McDonald grabbed her arm. "Oh, please, trade duty with me. You always had such a way with him. You were the only one who could manage him when he was in one of his moods, and merciful saints, he's in a foul one today."

Cadence hesitated. She longed to have the opportunity to thank Joshua for saving her last night, but she'd promised herself to stay far away. She mustn't give in. Not even a little.

"I'm sorry. I already promised Dr. Price my assistance for the day."

Nurse McDonald's mouth puckered like she'd bitten into a pickle. "Can't say I blame you, but I'll not be held to account if there is one more casualty added to the list."

Cadence chuckled as the disgruntled nurse stalked away. Nurse McDonald would have to learn to deal with Joshua's tempestuous perfectionism just as she had. Her heart could bear no more.

Indeed, she feared she'd already given it away.

chapter 18

"HERE. TAKE THIS." Cadence scooped a spoonful of mashed blackberries into the soldier's mouth.

He kept his eyes closed and chewed slowly. "After months of beans, coffee, and teeth grinders, plain old berries taste like heaven." He smacked the purple juice appreciatively. She could barely see the gray eyes opening beneath the bandage wrapped around his head.

"Teeth grinders?" She used the spoon to keep juice from dribbling down into his beard.

"That's what me and the boys call hardtack."

"Ah. Well, one of the nurses found a huge blackberry patch by the creek." She leaned in and whispered conspiratorially, "Dr. Price thinks it will aid with, uh, dysentery."

He stared at her blankly.

She cleared her throat. "The Virginia quickstep."

Comprehension dawned. "I understand. I'm beholden to

you if it helps. Ain't nothing caused me more misery these past months than that."

She straightened and smiled. Most of the men were sweet and grateful. The talkative ones, anyway. The others, well, the rest hovered between life and death.

A mosquito buzzed near her ear, and she swatted it against her neck with a slap. A sweltering heat lay over the valley, causing the stench of decaying bodies to rise thick. Soldiers could not get the dead buried quickly enough. The nauseating stench coated her nose and tongue. Little respite from the heat could be found within the shade of the tents, for no breeze stirred within.

The elderly Dr. Price walked by, the bags under his eyes puffier and more pronounced than usual. "Nurse Piper, we are out of chloroform and I have a number of amputations to perform this afternoon. Could I trouble you to find some?"

"Where would I need to go?"

He waved his hands. "We have several supply tents set up that way. For the most part, we surgeons take what we need. I require chloroform and whatever you can find of the quinine." He frowned, his small jowls sagging. "Malaria is rampant."

"Yes, sir."

She picked her way across the uneven ground and closed her eyes in bliss when the faintest breeze stirred. Pewter clouds were gathering in the distance. Rain. If only rain would come and wash death and disease away.

She ducked into the first tent in the direction Dr. Price had indicated. Crates were stacked and filled with medicines and bottles of every shape and size. She blew a tendril of hair off her forehead and began sorting through the brown bottles. Calomel, slippery elm, vinegar, and whiskey. No chloroform. Other crates revealed large stores of bandages and lint, as well as quinine. She grabbed one bottle and slipped two more into her apron pocket.

Leaving that tent, she glanced around. Hadn't the doctor mentioned several supply tents? Perhaps the next one over would provide the chloroform.

She ducked and stepped carefully inside the shadowed darkness of the next tent. This one was smaller than the other. A cot stood against one wall of the canvas-draped frame. She frowned. Surely this wasn't a supply tent. A valise and bag had been tossed in the corner. Several small crates were stacked along the opposite side. An assortment of medicines were strewn across their tops.

Odd place to store medicine.

She moved to the glass bottles and squinted to read the labels in the dim light. As she held up the largest, her eyes adjusted enough to see the bold block letters: *CHLOROFORM.*

She had whirled to leave when the canvas flaps flew open, admitting a swath of light. Joshua stepped inside, drawing the flaps shut behind him, plunging them both back into shadows. Upon seeing her, he froze. Her hand flew to her heart.

"You frightened me."

A muscle ticked in his jaw. "I frightened you? Tell me, Miss Piper, do you always make it a habit of marching into places uninvited?"

Heat scorched her cheeks. "I was not uninvited. Dr. Price sent me here to acquire medicine."

His brows rose. "Here? To my personal tent?"

Blood leached from her face. "I d-didn't know. I only s-saw the medicines and thought—"

Fury thundered on his face as he stepped closer. "That's the problem, Miss Piper. You don't think. You do whatever comes into that pretty little head of yours."

Her voice strangled. "Why are you acting this way?"

"If you must know, I just lost a patient, so I'm not in the mood for lies." His eyes narrowed to slits. "What did Price send you in here to steal?"

She gasped and tucked the bottle against her chest. "Steal? He did no such thing! How dare you!"

"Then show me!"

Tears stung her eyes. "You're nothing b-but a b-bully, Joshua Ivy!"

"What is it? What did you take?"

She shook her head. "It's nothing. Just c-c-c—"

The word stuck, stalled on her tongue as if wading through frozen honey. Hot tears made tracks down her cheeks.

"C-c-c—"

"Say it!"

"C-c-chl—"

A sob escaped. Something flickered in his eyes. The shutter masking the hard edge snapped, revealing a tumultuous yearning. A rushing sound filled her ears. He pulled her to his chest and cupped her face in his hands.

"Oh, Cadence."

His voice was strained, a tortured whisper before his lips claimed hers, hungrily devouring, exploring. Her heart quavered as his hands slid through her hair, down the curve of her back, and up again, as he murmured against her lips, "Forgive me."

Her sobs found release and calmed as she melted into his touch. She was falling. As his lips explored her face, her jaw and neck, the world faded away. There was only him.

"Cadence," he whispered against her skin, his lips chasing hers. "What have you done to me?" He gentled his hold and kissed the tears from her cheeks, her lashes, before claiming her lips once more. Her pulse roared in her ears. "I was content in my work, my life until the day you walked into the hospital. Now I can think of nothing else, no one else. Nothing but you."

Her spirit found flight. She could feel the rapid thrum of his heartbeat beneath her fingertips as her hands pressed against his chest. Her breath was ragged as she gazed into his eyes . . . eyes flooded with desire and longing.

"Joshua, I thought you believed me simple."

He nuzzled her cheek. "Never."

"My father, he treats me as if I'll never measure up to some intellectual standard. I'm sorry I believed you to be the same. I've tried to push you from my heart, but—" another kiss—"I can't."

He stepped back and tenderly stroked her face with the pad of his thumb. "I'm a fool. After the benefit, I thought the best thing would be to keep you at arm's length. The thought of losing you merely because you were associated with me was, and is, unthinkable." He shook his head. "But I can't. God forgive me, you're in everything. Everywhere I turn, in the songs I hear . . ." His gaze darkened. "Even in my dreams."

Her breath snagged as he lowered his head once more.

In the distance, Dr. Price's gruff bellow drifted. "Nurse Piper, have you found that chloroform?"

She sucked in a breath. Slowly she pulled the glass bottle away from her chest and held it out to him.

"Chloroform?" His brows lowered. "Why didn't you just tell me so?"

Her chin trembled. "Because I wasn't able."

She couldn't stay. Couldn't bear his pity or her own shame. "I must go."

"Cadence, wait—"

Air stirred and light invaded as she pushed free of the canvas flaps. Her lips burned from Joshua's kisses. Could everyone see? Keeping her head down, she hastened to the surgical tent.

If only chloroform could heal a wounded heart.

Wearing her somber black dress and pinched expression and holding open a small journal, the superintendent of nurses for the Oak Grove campaign stood before the line of women just after sunrise the following morning. The fatigue lining her face brooked no argument about the day's coming assignments. Soldiers were still hard at work burying the dead. Many of the wounded were being loaded onto wagons so they could be transported via boat up the Potomac to hospitals in Washington. The nurses were to occupy the last of the boats back to the capital. Until then, they would continue to treat the wounded as best they could.

"Nurse McDade, you'll be the main assistant to Dr. Abernathy today, and Nurse McDonald, you'll be assisting Dr. Price."

Nurse McDonald heaved a sigh of relief. "Thank you, ma'am."

The superintendent nodded curtly and ran her finger down the column of names. "Nurse Sewell, you'll be overseeing the less experienced nurses as the ambulance runners carry wounded to the dock. Private Greene has a wagon ready to transport you. And, Nurse Piper, you'll be assisting Dr. Ivy today. Any questions?"

Cadence's eyes slid shut. The rest of what the superintendent said was drowned out by the buzzing in her ears. Work side by side with Joshua after what had transpired yesterday? His outburst of temper, then passionate kisses? Worse yet, she'd stuttered like a fool, then received his ardor like a loose woman. What did he think of her? Heat crawled up her neck.

Yet as she'd lain in the dark of her tent last night, she'd replayed the moment over and over, savoring every touch, every murmured word of affection. And she knew then, as the tears poured down and found their mark on the scratchy woolen blanket beneath her skin, she was in love with Joshua Ivy.

She trudged toward the surgical tents and rolled up her sleeves. She poured a bucket of clean water into an empty basin and lathered her hands with sharp-scented lye. She eyed Joshua's surgical tools. Dr. Price had not let her wash his, but Joshua might think differently. He'd long sought a way to lower the cases of blood poisoning among the wounded. Surely cleaning the instruments wouldn't hurt, would it?

She paused in indecision before scooping up a handful of the tools and dunking them into the tub of soapy water. She'd just begun to scrub when a masculine voice near her ear caused her to jump.

"What are you doing?"

She whirled. Joshua stood staring at her, looking far too handsome. A tender light shone in his eyes.

"I—I, that is, I just thought, for bl-blood p-poisoning . . ." She forced a calming breath. "I thought to clean your instruments."

His brows rose. "Interesting theory. You think this may help reduce infections from surgery?"

Warmth flooded her cheeks. "I thought it might help. If washing hands aids in reducing illness, washing instruments should do the same."

He said nothing, only stood rubbing his chin in thought.

"Dr. Price would not let me touch his instruments, so I have no way of knowing if it is beneficial."

His mouth tipped. "Let's try it."

"Really?" Her heart fluttered.

"I think we'll know soon enough whether it works, based on the number of patients who recover with this new method. The idea has merit."

She was spared saying anything further when runners brought in the first soldier for surgery. She swallowed at the sight of Stephen Dodd on the stretcher. Despite the early morning's relative cool, sweat dotted his ashen face. Upon seeing her, his pain-stricken expression brightened.

"Miss Piper." He croaked the words, each one costing him considerable effort. "How I prayed to see you again."

"Save your strength, Mr. Dodd." She reached for a tin of water and let some dribble into his mouth. "You must rest."

Joshua leaned over him and smiled gently. "Private Dodd? I'm Dr. Ivy. I see you've sustained extensive damage to your leg from a minié ball. It has shattered bone and severed tendons and muscle. Infection has set in. Do you understand what must be done to preserve your life?"

Stephen nodded curtly, his lips pressed into a firm line. "Do what you must, Doctor. It would not be what I would choose, but if I would dare claim to be willing to give my life for the glorious cause, I should not be ashamed to give my leg."

Joshua squeezed his shoulder. "You have great courage, soldier."

Stephen's gaze flickered to Cadence as Joshua turned to ready the tools he needed to operate. "I only fear I should not be able to dance with you as I told you I wanted to do when I wrote."

Joshua paused and Cadence stiffened, sensing his sudden unease.

"You and Nurse Piper know each other?"

Stephen gazed at her with tenderness. "Quite well." His gaze returned to Joshua. "Her father gave me permission to court her with plans to one day make her my wife."

Her heart thudded to a painful stop. The silence was dreadful.

Finally Joshua spoke. "I see."

Stephen reached for her hand and she fought the urge to yank it away. He didn't understand. He'd never understood, no matter how many times she tried to gently redirect his interest. And now Joshua thought . . .

"It was the hope of knowing she was waiting for me that got me through." His eyes were bright in his too-thin face. "Despite the grueling marches, the nightmares I've endured, it was the promise of a future with Miss Piper that gave me the strength to keep pressing forward."

How to dispute the tender hope of a gravely injured man? She couldn't crush him. She wouldn't.

She extracted her hand gently and forced a smile. "Rest." She braved a glance at Joshua. He was looking away, his brows lowered.

Nor did he look at her the rest of the day.

chapter 19

Cadence directed the stewards carrying in yet another wounded soldier. She pointed to one of the few spots left in Judiciary Square Hospital's overcrowded rooms.

"There. That corner will hold three more men before we'll be forced to start lining them up in the hallway."

"Yes, ma'am." They obeyed, and she paused only long enough to wipe a trickle of sweat from her flushed skin. She'd prayed Washington would be cooler than Oak Grove had been, but when she'd stepped foot on the dock two hours ago, her hopes had been dashed. The heat was enough to nearly make her dive into the Potomac.

Tonight. Tonight she would bathe at her own home and sleep in her bed. A real bed. Not a lumpy bedroll or the unforgiving ground. The past fortnight at Oak Grove had been grueling. Far more taxing than she'd dreamed possible.

She'd just stepped outside the hospital doors to gauge how many more soldiers needed admittance amid the flurry of bustling nurses and stewards when she was suddenly surrounded by a flock of men in suits, all of them brandishing small journals and sharpened pencil stubs.

"Miss Piper? Are you Miss Piper?"

"I am." She drew back at their inquisitive stares and loud voices.

Yet they pressed in all the more eagerly, circling, their smiles wide, eyes bulging as they scribbled.

"Miss Piper, when did you return to Washington?"

"How long have you been a nurse?"

"What songs do you most often sing to the soldiers?"

She couldn't breathe. They surrounded her like a pack of wolves. She stepped back and bumped into a warm body.

"Easy now. You're scaring the young miss."

She looked up to see Steward Swindle glaring at the lot of them. He tugged his cap low. "What's all the fuss about?"

A young man with pomaded blond hair and a thick mustache pushed his way forward. "I'm a reporter with *Harper's Weekly*. Miss Piper, one of our sketch artists was at Oak Grove and caught you singing to one of the wounded soldiers. He captured your likeness and printed up the story. Here." He tugged a copy of the periodical from his jacket pocket and thrust it into her hands. "The entire town went wild over it. Rumors have abounded over the woman dubbed the Songbird of the North."

Mouth dry, Cadence scanned the oily newsprint. Sure enough, there in the middle of the page was her likeness, sketched in pencil as she wept over a dead soldier. Her throat constricted. It was him. The young man who had cried out for his mother, who had rent her heart open with his pleas.

"Don't you know?" The reporter's breathless voice startled her back to the present. His eyes were bright. "You're famous, hailed as a beacon of hope amid the ashes."

She lowered the paper. "I—I don't know what to say."

"Will you answer a few questions?"

The reporters collectively held their breath, pencils poised and ready.

"What would you like to know?"

───────── ⁕ ─────────

Joshua rubbed his bleary eyes and dropped the meticulous notes on his desk. Every single patient's name, diagnosis, treatment, and scant history had been detailed and recorded. With the hospital bulging at the seams, keeping the information straight was a difficult task, but thankfully, he'd not had to perform any surgeries this day.

He'd had his fill of amputated limbs.

Rolling his head from side to side to loosen the tight muscles, he pursed his lips and ran his fingers down the list of amputees. Of those he'd operated on at Oak Grove, only eight had succumbed to death. The rest, thus far, had survived. The majority of those who were healing quickly were those he'd operated on since Cadence began cleaning his instruments after each surgery. He rubbed his chin. Most interesting.

Cadence. Just the thought of her caused an ache to form in his chest. Since they'd returned to Washington, he'd avoided her. He'd let his feelings burst free and scared her senseless. If he'd but known she'd pledged herself to another . . .

He could still taste the sweetness of her lips, feel the soft curve of her back against his fingertips.

And yet . . .

She'd kissed him back.

He scrubbed his hands down his face and slapped them against the desk.

Please, Father, sever this longing I have for her. You've given me the children. A calling to heal and to help others find freedom. It is enough. Help me be content.

It would be better for her not to be entangled with him. So why couldn't he make his heart obey?

Last week's edition of *Harper's Weekly* taunted him from the stack of papers on his desk. His chest pounded, just as it did every time his gaze traitorously returned to it. He ought to throw it out, but he couldn't seem to obey that directive either.

He ran his finger over the penciled sketch of Cadence cradling a dead soldier in her arms. Her dark tresses were artistically drawn in sweeping waves over one shoulder. The faintest pencil lines of tear tracks shadowed the curve of her cheek as she wept over the soldier, his head back, mouth slack and opened wide to the sky. The artist had captured the moment flawlessly, yet he'd not been able to re-create the song spilling from her lips. That melody was forever tattooed on Joshua's heart.

"I my loved ones' watch am keeping, all through the night."

Since returning to Washington, Cadence had become such a celebrity, she'd not had as much time at the hospital as before. Ramsey bade her sing at his every whim and pleasure. It seemed to Joshua she was always fighting to prove herself for some unknown reason. He sighed and pushed the journal away.

Rising, he walked toward the great room where the majority of the patients lay on lumpy, unforgiving cots. He'd make final rounds for the evening, then go home, where three smiling faces would greet him.

He stopped at various bedsides to administer a word of encouragement or issue a medication order to a nurse or steward.

As he passed the foot of one bed, its occupant softly called out, "I never did thank you, Doc."

He paused and turned. Stephen Dodd lay watching him from the bed. Joshua nodded slowly. "No thanks are needed. I only wish I could have saved your leg."

Dodd offered a faint smile, his eyes ringed in shadows. "Me too, but it was preferable to losing my life."

Joshua moved to stand near the head of his bed. "Are you comfortable?"

"Enough." His eyelids were heavy as he blinked. "One of the nurses changed my bandages a bit ago and gave me some pain powders. It's odd, though. Some days I have sharp pain, almost like my leg is still there."

"You are one of many to complain of the same malady. Some say it's as if their limb cramps with the most excruciating pain, but they feel as if they are losing their mind since the limb is gone."

Dodd's eyes rounded. "Yes, that's it exactly."

He grunted. "I've seen recent journal articles about this very thing. Some physicians believe it's related to damage done to nerves running through the amputated limb. No one is sure yet, however."

"Will it get better?"

"I pray so. Nerves are slow to heal, but time and rest work wonders."

Dodd studied him. "I'm thankful to you. Many others have battled infection, yet I have remained unscathed."

He swallowed, hesitant to say her name. "I cannot take credit. The glory goes to the Almighty and Miss Piper. She suggested washing all the surgical instruments before each operation. It seems to be quite successful in reducing infection and blood poisoning."

Dodd relaxed against the pillow. "She is a wonder. The day I met her, I knew I wanted her as my wife."

The confession pierced sharply. Joshua looked down. "How did you two meet?"

"At a dinner held by my parents. Miss Piper was quite shy, of course. She spoke very little, but her father said I could visit again. I saw her just before I was sent into duty, and she granted me permission to write her. My feelings have only grown in the meantime."

One visit? Dodd had only called on her once and had declared her to be his future wife? Unease niggled.

Forcing a tight smile, he squeezed Dodd's shoulder. "Rest well tonight. I'll be around in the morning to check on you. Call one of the night stewards if you have need of anything."

"Thank you."

As Joshua trudged home for the evening, Dodd's words replayed over and over in his mind.

Was Cadence actually betrothed to Dodd? And if not, what game was she playing with the man?

Father adjusted the spectacles perched on the end of his nose as he perused the morning paper over the breakfast table. Cadence picked at the eggs cooling on her plate. The potato cakes held little appeal. Fatigue weighted her body like a blanket. She only half listened to him read the headlines, though Tate leaned forward, eagerly lapping up the latest tidbits of war.

He tapped the newsprint. "Look there. Belle Boyd has been captured." He shook his head. "It's about time."

Tate bit into his toast and jam and washed it down with a sip of weak coffee. "Past time. The woman has been a menace."

Cadence blinked. "Belle Boyd? I've not heard of her."

Tate glowered. "Monstrous woman. Some call her the Siren of the Shenandoah. Just last summer, it was reported she shot and killed a Union soldier who, she claimed, insulted her and her mother."

Cadence gasped. "Why was she not already in prison then?"

Father peered over the top of his spectacles. "According to the papers, the commanding officer inquired into the circumstances and judged her to be innocent, though witnesses believe Miss Boyd beguiled him with her charm into seeing things her way." He snorted. "The papers state she is quite bold and outspoken, daring and desperate to be seen."

Tate pursed his lips. "There is talk that Miss Boyd may very well be a spy for the Confederacy and reports directly to General Stonewall Jackson."

Cadence dropped her fork with a clatter. "A female spy? Is such a thing possible?"

Tate grinned. "Why not? You're a female nurse, are you not? You were bound and determined, and despite your age and the rules you plowed ahead. Why is Belle Boyd any different?"

She fell silent. The comparison to the bawdy Belle rankled. Surely Cadence wasn't desperate for attention like the infamous Confederate, was she? Impossible.

Father continued, scanning the tiny type with a sharp eye. "At any rate, she'll be held at Old Capitol Prison. Perhaps they'll have the good sense to keep her locked up longer than they did Rose Greenhow."

Tate's brows rose. "Did you hear? Mrs. Greenhow plans to travel to Europe to rally aid for the Confederate cause." He smirked. "Perhaps she will seek an audience with Napoleon III."

Father's eyes twinkled. "Well, Cadence's appearance at the Union Aid Society is likely to meet with more success."

She smiled faintly. She'd sung at a benefit or gathering nearly every night for the past two weeks. Her body begged for rest. There had been no time to recover after Oak Grove.

Tate put down his fork. "Another performance? The press and charities refuse to give Cadence a moment's peace."

Father sipped his coffee, his focus on the paper. "Your sister has expectations to meet for the good of our glorious cause. They are depending on her."

Tate leaned forward. "But what does Cadence want?" His gaze swung to hers and held fast. In truth, the demanding schedule of events was exhausting. She felt crushed on every side. She longed to flee to the confines of Judiciary Square, back to the routines of soothing fevers and comforting scared soldiers.

Father looked up from his paper and speared her with a sharp look. Her wishes shriveled, wilting like a parched flower. What would they think of her if she told them no? What would Father think? People all over Washington were hailing her as the Songbird of the North. Father beamed every time she walked into a room. Doted on her in front of crowds, carrying on as if she were his pride and joy.

She could not lose his affection.

"I—I don't mind."

Father nodded with satisfaction. "See there? Such a good, giving daughter. What will you be singing tonight?"

She pushed aside the uneasiness his words drummed up in her middle. "A new song by a very talented abolitionist, Julia Ward Howe, titled 'The Battle Hymn of the Republic.' The words are quite stirring. It was printed in the *Atlantic Monthly*, and I was told President Lincoln is quite fond of the lyrics." She pushed back her plate. "I sang it a fortnight ago and it was well received."

"Splendid." His eyes shone. "Your mother would be so proud."

He'd said the same thing several times within the past few days, yet the thrill it initially gave her was growing faint. Since returning from Oak Grove to her newfound celebrity, Father had seemed more attentive. Perhaps too attentive. Or maybe he was truly seeing her for the first time in too long.

Sighing, she picked at her eggs. Perhaps she'd only been overly sensitive when Tate was recovering. Father had simply been elated to see the wayward son he thought he'd lost. He hadn't been ignoring her, merely preoccupied. That was all, wasn't it?

It didn't matter any longer. Tate had healed well and was content with his new job working for Congressman Ramsey. And she . . . she was as busy as ever. The pull of so many responsibilities suddenly weighed on her like a wet cloak.

She hadn't even been to baby Rose's grave since returning to Washington. Guilt pinched.

Busyness was best. It kept her from thinking. Thinking about handsome doctors and three sweet children across town. Thinking about hurting soldiers lying helpless on scratchy cots. Thinking about bloody fields and the screams of the dying calling for their mothers.

Applause could drown out the sound of much.

Joshua shoved his hands into his pockets and hastened toward home. Evening had already blanketed the city in darkness, though many other men yet roamed the streets, some clad in suits and ties, others in the humble attire of common laborers.

All Joshua wanted was to see the children and fall into his own bed. The demands of the ill begging for relief in the hospital never ceased. He frowned, puzzling over Private Watson's troubling ailments.

"You're being watched, Doc."

The low voice called from the shadows of an alley. Joshua stopped, peering into the darkness, but made no move to step closer.

"Watched?" He glanced around, making sure no one approached. "By you?"

"No, not me. The Knights of the Golden Circle. They watch you."

Joshua's blood simmered. He stepped closer. "Who are you? Show yourself!"

Cigarette smoke wafted toward him in the darkness. "Calm yourself. Outwitting the Knights takes cunning and patience."

"Why would I need to outwit them?"

A long moment of silence. "If you don't, they will destroy everything you hold dear."

Joshua's heart squeezed in a vise. "Who are you?"

"Meet me here in one week's time. Midnight."

"What's your name?"

But the retreating footsteps told him the stranger was gone.

chapter 20

CADENCE BLINKED against the too-bright lights. The hall holding the evening's benefit for the Union Aid Society was far too cramped for the crowd pressing in. Heat and the odor of thick perfume suffused the air. How she longed for a fresh, cool breath.

Few were brave enough to dance in the sweltering heat, though at least a dozen still managed to swirl through the waltz playing gaily from the corner of the room. The violin seemed out of tune, its sound strident, instead of the soothing ebb and flow she was accustomed to. She feared it was not the musicians but her. She was in a dour mood this night. She cringed, thinking how her nerves would strangle her later in the evening when the brass bellowed out rousing patriotic songs. Thankfully, they'd agreed to remain silent during her own rendering of "The Battle Hymn of the Republic."

"Miss Piper?" A man with red hair, wearing a blue uniform and a hopeful expression, appeared on her left. He held a cup in his hands. "My name is Theodore Cummings." He bowed and looked up. "Forgive my forwardness at not having myself properly introduced to you, but I could not seem to restrain myself. I so longed to meet you."

Cadence forced a smile. "It's a pleasure to meet you, Mr. Cummings."

"I don't know if you remember, but I heard you sing outside of Judiciary Square Hospital last year when the wounded were marching in from battle. It was so inspiring, I decided right then and there that as soon as I turned of age, I would enlist."

"And it seems you did."

His chest lifted. "I turned eighteen just last week and joined right up. I'm ready to do my part. Ready to fight!"

Her smile wobbled in the face of his blind enthusiasm. Was he ready? So many others thought they were as well, but they hadn't been prepared for the horrors they witnessed. For the hand of death that sliced down their friends like a scythe.

"Mama, please! Help me!"

". . . just wanted to say thank you." His mouth creased as he held out the cup. "And here, I brought you some lemonade." A blush crept into his face. "I'm sorry they have little else, but with the rising prices of food and goods, I suppose it was the best they could do."

"It's fine. Thank you." She took a sip of the sweet-and-sour liquid and studied the young man, so full of life.

With a small nod, he began to excuse himself. "Well, I'll not bother you further. I just wanted to thank you for the inspiration."

"Mr. Cummings?"

"Yes, miss?"

Words stalled. What could she possibly say to prepare him for all he was about to endure?

Giving him a small smile, she reached out and grasped his hand. "Stay close to the Almighty. May he go with you."

The boy's eyes sparkled. "And with you."

As he walked away, her stomach clenched, but she had no more time to consider Theodore Cummings before she was surrounded yet again by admirers.

When the evening afforded a brief lull, she excused herself and pushed through the crowd to the powder room, seeking a moment of peace. She let the door fall shut behind her and sighed. The dull roar of the laughter and music, tinkling glassware and heavy footfalls faded behind the thick wooden door. She leaned against the papered wall, fingering the pendant dangling from the delicate chain around her neck.

She glanced down at the sparkling teardrop sapphire and blinked moisture away. Mother's pendant. She hadn't even known Mother had possessed such a treasure until that very afternoon, when Father had rapped on her door and presented her with the beautiful gift.

"For you, Cadence." His eyes had been tender as he opened the black velvet box to show her the sparkling necklace inside.

She had breathed, "Oh, Father. I couldn't accept such a token."

"Don't fret. It was your mother's. I should have given it to you long ago. In all honesty, it had slipped my mind until yesterday. But when Louisa mentioned needing to press your blue gown, it jogged my memory." He swallowed hard. "Such a beautiful dress and beautiful girl deserve a lovely bauble to go with them."

"Thank you."

She'd thrown her arms around his neck and inhaled the scent of him. Peppermint and cherry pipe tobacco.

"Here. Let me put it on you."

She settled on the vanity stool and watched her reflection in the mirror as he fumbled with the clasp before slipping the sparkling necklace around her neck. The pendant felt cool against her skin.

"Your mother would be so proud if she could see you now."

Cadence swallowed. Something cold twisted within. "Now?"

He beamed. "Of course. Seeing how famous you've become. You're a beacon of inspiration in Washington, my dear. Your golden voice, you know."

She watched a tiny line appear between her brows in the looking-glass reflection. "But you and Mother would be proud of me even if I couldn't sing, wouldn't you? Even if no one noticed my voice or cared how I sounded?"

Father's smile dimmed. "Of course, but that's not the case."

She rose and twisted her fingers together, looking out the sun-dappled window and back to Father's puzzled expression.

"What troubles you, Cadence?"

"The singing. I used to love it. It made my heart soar. I felt closer to God when I lifted my voice, but—" she struggled to find words—"not anymore."

"What are you saying?"

"It's tiresome. It feels like a chore. I no longer connect to the lyrics, the melody." She bit her lip. "I'm weary of it. Weary of performing every evening and greeting people and acting like I'm cheerful all the time." Her chest heaved as she spilled the burning admission. "I just want to nurse."

Father's expression was grave. "Cadence, people look up to you. They count on you to bolster their spirits. Think of how many you'll disappoint."

"Think of how many suffering men I disappoint every time I fail to show up at the hospital."

He sighed. "We've already discussed this." He ran his hands

down his face. "Emptying chamber pots and breathing in diseases . . . it's not fitting for a young lady."

"You've allowed me to do so until now."

He frowned. "It seemed to give you a goal to work toward. I honestly didn't think . . ." He fell silent.

"You didn't think I could do it, did you?"

He blanched and looked away. Something inside her wilted, crushed like vellum in a fist.

"You accomplished it nonetheless. But Providence has laid this new opportunity before you. You should make the most of it. Not to mention preparing yourself to be a wife someday." He smiled weakly. "Stephen Dodd is so fond of you."

She gripped the edge of her vanity, fighting the turmoil churning her middle. "I don't love him."

"Love grows. All I'm saying is you should enjoy this time. So many are looking to you as a bright light in the darkness. Don't be too hasty to throw it away." He had patted her shoulder and left.

The room seemed to close in around her at his words. She couldn't breathe. She was drowning. And the despair had only grown since.

Now the floor rumbled underneath her feet as she clutched the pendant in her white-knuckled fingers. She was boxed in. She could not disappoint Father, nor would she hurt Congressman Ramsey, not after all he'd done for the family. Yet she could not forget the faces of moaning, miserable men writhing in agony inside the hospital. The other nurses, the stewards . . . all teetered on the brink of exhaustion. One less person to help was more work for the lot of them to do. Meanwhile, scared young men were on a battlefield somewhere being sliced to ribbons by bayonets and muskets. Who would attend them? Who would comfort them as they lay dying? And baby Rose's grave? Was it overgrown with weeds by now? No matter where she turned, she was letting someone down. She couldn't do it.

It was too much. The demands. The expectations. Life was drained of color, washed only in shades of gray.

She couldn't sing. Not another note.

Yet somehow she must.

Joshua's smile felt starched as he answered the same questions over and over. The Union Aid Society had pledged to donate funds to Judiciary Square Hospital, and his attendance was required to meet patrons and explain the hospital's needs, but the press of people, the repetitive questions, and his fatigue mingled to cause him a pounding headache.

He forced his attention to remain fixed on the matron before him, who was chattering like a fussy hen.

". . . and when I saw the newspaper, how dreadful our soldiers looked and what a hard time they had of it, I just knew I must do something." She shook her head, her jowls swaying. "It's our Christian duty, is it not?"

"Of course. And the men appreciate any help you can give."

Her plump, gloved hands fanned her face so rapidly, the movement resembled a hummingbird's wings. "I just never imagined they would endure so much." Her lips pursed into a frown. "Why do they suffer from so many ailments of the stomach, Doctor?" Her eyes narrowed to slits. "They aren't imbibing, are they?"

He suppressed a laugh. "Not to my knowledge, ma'am. From what I've witnessed, their stomach distress and weakened conditions come from malnourishment. The food that provides optimum nutrition is either too expensive for the government to supply or cannot endure the rigors of travel. The men would greatly benefit from fresh fruit to prevent scurvy and similar ailments, but there is none to be had, save for any wild-growing berries or fruit they discover as they march. Meat turns rancid very quickly as well, even heavily salted. The men are often reduced to a diet of coffee, hardtack, jerky, cornmeal, and beans. Sometimes less."

"Pitiful." She clucked her tongue. "Why don't they hunt for fresh game?"

He paused and tried not to laugh at her earnest puzzlement. "Because they are too busy hunting Rebels, ma'am."

"Oh yes. I suppose that's true. Well, I'm sure my husband and I can spare some coinage for the cause." She sighed melodramatically. "Although it won't be as much as I'd hoped, not with food prices rising as they are. I've lost a great deal of weight since this horrid war started."

He tried to school his reaction. The woman looked as if she'd not missed a meal in the past decade. Instead, he nodded. "I hate to think of you suffering so."

She sniffed. "Yes. But we must all make sacrifices. I shall do my part. 'Give me liberty or give me death' and all that, you know. Thomas Paine said that."

"Or was it Patrick Henry, ma'am?"

She frowned and shook her finger in his face. "It was Paine. You should have paid better attention in school, young man."

He coughed back a laugh as the musicians ended their time of rest and took their places on stage. The crowd of chattering people must have sensed a shift, for a hush fell over the hall. A pencil-thin man with wiry gray hair and a gray mustache that reminded Joshua of a broom walked across the stage. Red, white, and blue bunting was draped overhead, hanging low from the ceiling.

The elderly man smiled widely and let his voice boom. "Good evening, ladies and gentlemen. Thank you for attending the Union Aid Society benefit this evening. Your generosity has been overwhelming. Thanks to you, we will be able to supply our soldiers with new shoes and blankets and supply our doctors with morphine, quinine, and other medicines. With your help, we will fight the good fight and bring our boys home safe and sound, claiming the victory and reuniting this land as it was created . . . one nation under God!"

A roar of applause and thundering cheers rose. When the wild frenzy died down, he lifted his hands. "As a gift for your incredible generosity, we have a treat for you this evening. A musical guest who will thrill your soul and stir your heart. A woman of pure patriotism and renown. Please welcome Miss Cadence Piper!"

Joshua's breath caught as the deafening applause drowned out the sound of his hammering pulse. He hadn't said more than a few mumbled words to Cadence since Oak Grove. His heart twisted when she walked gracefully across the stage in a stunning sapphire gown that accentuated her feminine form to perfection. The gloss of her dark hair in the lights, the dimples in her cheeks when she beamed at the crowd . . . He didn't know if his bruised heart could stay. It was too much. His feelings were just as strong as they'd ever been.

She turned to nod toward the musicians, and the hall was swept into a flood of melody.

⸙

Cadence smiled through stiff lips as she turned to face the crowd. The lights were too bright, the air stuffy, and her throat far too dry. All she wanted to do was escape. Run away from inquisitive stares and expectations.

The strings trilled her cue, and she inhaled as deep a breath as she could manage against her tight corset.

"Mine eyes have seen the glory of the coming of the Lord . . ."

She closed her eyes, desperate to connect to the emotion of the stirring song, but she felt nothing. As she reopened them, she could see the delight on the faces of men and women pressed around the stage. Perhaps the song itself was enough, even if she wasn't communicating it well.

As the verse swelled into the chorus, the musicians increased their volume to a forte.

"Glory, glory, hallelujah . . ."

Several women were dabbing their eyes with delicate lace handkerchiefs. Men cleared their throats. Cadence glided through the other verses with ease. As they launched into the final chorus, the music dramatically rose into a heavy fortissimo. She could feel it now. The emotion, the grandeur of the moment. Gooseflesh rose on her arms as she shut her eyes again and reached for the highest note of the melody.

"Glory, glory, hallelu—"

The note strangled. Her eyes snapped open. A strange sound burst from her throat. A screech, like the brittle strike of an unrosined violin bow across the strings. Men and women were whispering behind fans and gloved hands. A dizzying heat flushed her face. She must finish.

"Our God is marching on."

Something was wrong. Every note of the last phrase was strained and scraped. Panic clawed. Amid the sea of faces, one stood out above all others: Father's crestfallen expression.

She remembered little of what happened afterward. A hasty curtsy amid polite applause. Blurring faces. She slipped from the stage and scurried into the darkened corridor, seeking the solace of shadows. What must everyone think? If Father was mortified, she would find no sympathy from anyone else. Nausea crawled up her throat.

Air. She needed air.

Lifting the hem of her wide skirt, she hurried down the corridor to the door used by servants to carry food in and out of the hall. She pushed open the escape and nearly wept when a puff of clean night air brushed her face. Soft gaslights illuminated the road in front of the hall, but here along the side, she was blessedly safe from prying eyes.

She pressed a hand to her forehead and gave in to her trembling lips. Tears fell as she spied a bench and eased onto it with a sob. The sound of crickets was her only friend. Footsteps approached long moments later. Forcing back her cries, she straightened and swiped the moisture from her cheeks. She looked up. Joshua stood before her.

She flushed hot, then cold. Why him? Why now? She'd barely spoken with him since their clandestine exchange of affection at Oak Grove. Her heart and mind had tried to keep thoughts of him at bay. Working was easier than feeling. Must she confront her feelings as well as her humiliation?

"Cadence?" He moved closer. "I thought I heard someone weeping. Why are you crying?"

She watched the pewter moonlight shift across the strong lines of his jaw and cheekbones. "Joshua. I didn't think to see you tonight."

"In truth, I wasn't sure I'd come."

She toyed with the gloves in her lap. "You would have saved your ears much pain if you had not."

A puzzled expression drifted over his face. "You sang beautifully. I'd not heard that song until tonight. It's very moving."

Was he serious? She glared. "Have you been sniffing chloroform? My voice left me!"

To her surprise, he threw back his head and laughed. He fell onto the bench. "Sniffing chloroform?" He grinned. "You wound me, Miss Piper."

Her humiliation buoyed into something lighter. Shame fled for one blessed moment. "Forgive me. That was unkind. I have had a trying evening."

He chuckled and studied her. "So you made a mistake. Is that so terrible? In no way does it mean you need throw out the beauty of the rest of the evening."

She twisted her fingers. "There are some who don't feel as you do."

"Hm." He grunted and rested his arm along the length of the bench's back. "Their opinions shouldn't matter unless it's their approval you seek."

She fell silent, wading through his words. "How are the children?"

"They are well, although they ask about you often. It seems you made quite an impression on them. They want to know when my pretty nurse will return and read them more stories."

She felt the heat of a blush creep into her cheeks. She was thankful for the cover of evening's shadows, despite the bright moonlight.

"I . . . I would like that. Very much." A sigh escaped her lips. "Ever since returning from Oak Grove, it feels like I'm smothering. Forced to do so many things people expect of me. I've no time left to do what I love."

"And what is it you'd like to do?"

She bit her lip. "I want to nurse. Perhaps even in a field hospital again. I don't simply want to sing for charity benefits and soirees." She looked up, searching his eyes. "Does it make me a selfish person, that I don't want to sing for Washington society anymore?"

"No, not at all."

"But they say my songs give voice to the patriotism of the Union." Fatigue tugged her shoulders. "What if not singing for Congress or relief benefits means I'm refusing to use the gift God gave me?"

Joshua pursed his lips and looked across the night sky for so long, she feared he'd not answer. Finally he spoke.

"I was there, you know. I saw you holding that dying soldier in Oak Grove."

She inhaled a soft gasp. "You saw?"

"I did. I heard you sing as you wept over him. 'All through the night . . .'" His voice, a slightly off-key baritone, drifted over her like a gentle caress as he offered a smile. "What you sang tonight was lovely, but that? That moment on the battlefield, that song was true music. You weren't worried about an audience or what people thought. You were just . . . present. Ministering as best you could to a battered man with the gift God gave you."

Her throat swelled to a painful ache. "That's what is missing. Why don't I feel that same kind of peace singing here? I'm surrounded by comfort and food. No blood or mud or death, yet I'm suffocating in the excess. Drying up. Why?"

He sighed. "The gifts God gives only continue to flourish when we pour them out through love. They dry up when we use them motivated by any other purpose."

She frowned. "But I'm singing and going to all these charity events for them—for other people. Not for myself. I'm exhausting myself for them!"

He leveled his gaze. "Are you? Or are you doing it to fulfill some need in yourself?"

All rebuttals fled. Was she? Trying to sift through the exhausting emotions was overwhelming. She couldn't think, couldn't sort out the truth through the muddled mess in her bruised heart.

She sneaked a glance to see Joshua watching her. He quickly averted his gaze to study the ground.

"Sometimes I think you know me better than I know myself, Dr. Ivy."

He stared straight ahead for a long moment before turning to her. His eyes were gentle as he whispered, "Perhaps I do."

He stood suddenly and crammed his hands in his pockets before strolling away.

"Joshua?"

He turned, his face partially shrouded by the shadows.

"What will you do next?"

"I've told the Union I'm at their service. Whenever they beckon, I go to the battlefield."

He offered no other words of solace. Ever since Oak Grove, things had been stilted and strange between them. Did he regret his passionate outburst? Or perhaps after kissing her, he found her lacking.

She pushed past the quiver in her voice. "You will be in my prayers."

"And you in mine."

chapter 21

CADENCE WINCED at the bright sunshine streaming through her window, far later than her usual time to rise in the morning. The soft blush of sunrise had long since vanished. She was stretching her stiff muscles and blinking the lead from her eyes when the memory of the previous evening crashed over her in a rush.

Moaning, she pulled the covers over her head. She, Father, and Tate had left the benefit in silence. Upon arriving home, Father had mumbled something about praying folks forgot about the incident and then excused himself for bed. Tate had looked at her with pity, which had bothered her far more.

The aroma of warm oatmeal wafted toward her. Peeking out from under the covers, she spied a breakfast tray waiting along with the morning paper. Louisa was as constant as the sunrise.

Perhaps if she occupied her mind, thoughts of last night would flee. She reached for the newsprint and scanned the headlines. Battles, troop movements, editorials, casualty lists . . . She sighed. All the news was the same as the day before and the day before that.

Her gaze flickered over the society columns, though she cared little for the shallow fluff pieces they usually contained, until she spied her own name.

Acclaimed Singer Struggles to Impress at Union Benefit

Her breath thinned as the words swam before her eyes.

Spectators at the Union Aid Society benefit were thrilled to learn the capital's own darling, Miss Cadence Piper, was scheduled to sing Friday evening as part of the benefit's entertainment. The anticipation soon turned to concern as the acclaimed singer struggled through the first selection, her voice audibly straining through the melody's higher notes and causing the audience to wonder if the reputation of Washington's "Songbird" has been somewhat exaggerated.

Miss Piper is the daughter of Mr. Albert Piper and is said . . .

Cadence pinched her eyes closed and shoved the paper away, too sickened to read anymore. Not only had she humiliated herself, but she had inadvertently shamed her father as well. A lump rose in her throat as fresh tears pricked her eyes.

A soft knock invaded. She remained silent. Louisa's cheerful chirrup piped through the door. "You awake, Miss Cadence?"

She couldn't fool Louisa if she tried. With a groan, she mumbled, "No. I'm sleeping."

Louisa chuckled. "I know you're awake, missy. You gonna let me in or not?"

Pushing back the plump covers, Cadence sighed. "Come in."

Louisa entered, her face beaming. In her hands she carried a long, rectangular box trimmed with scarlet ribbon.

"What's that?"

Her dark eyes danced. "Don't know. It was just delivered for you, though if I were to judge by the fragrance, I would say someone has sent you some flowers."

Cadence sat up straighter and took the box from Louisa. "I can't imagine who they would be from. I had the worst performance of my life last night."

The house servant grunted. "Couldn't have been too dismal. Not if this is any indication."

Cadence tugged the card free from the ribbon and slid the message from its creamy envelope. Her heart gave a wild leap.

Cadence,
You have already been called worthy, daughter, and
loved by Christ. Embrace this beautiful truth. 1 John 3:1,
Galatians 1:10.

> *Your friend,*
> *J. Ivy*

Laying the card near her Bible, she slipped the ribbon from the box and lifted the lid to reveal a fragrant bouquet of pink roses and white daises.

Louisa's eyes rounded. "Land o' Goshen, who they from?"

"Just a friend."

"You want me to find a pitcher and put them in some water for you?"

"If you don't mind, that would be lovely."

Louisa nodded curtly and whisked the beautiful flowers away. "Won't be gone but for two shakes of a lamb's tail." She scurried from the room, mumbling about secret beaus, but Cadence paid her little mind.

Flowers. And a note. Her battered heart squeezed tight. She picked up Joshua's letter and reached for her Bible, flipping through the onionskin pages until she found the verse from 1 John.

Behold, what manner of love the Father hath bestowed upon us, that we should be called the sons of God.

She closed her eyes and meditated on the verse. Son of God. Daughter. Child. Adopted through the blood of Jesus. Her eyes flew open. If she was adopted by God, that meant he'd chosen her, wanted her, picked her. The sweet faces of Penelope, James, and Etta swam to her mind. Joshua had chosen them to be his family. He'd loved them too much to leave them as they were. Was that how God saw her?

Peering to see the second verse, she rustled the pages until Galatians 1:10 stared boldly into her soul.

For do I now persuade men, or God? or do I seek to please men? for if I yet pleased men, I should not be the servant of Christ.

Her hands shook, causing the words on the page to wobble under her touch.

"If I yet pleased men, I should not be the servant of Christ."

Had the apostle Paul struggled with the same thing? Had he stood before crowds wondering if he would be accepted? Had he lived in fear of being rejected? Had he scraped to prove himself amid a society that constantly told him he couldn't do something? He must have, for the word *yet* jumped out at her.

A new awareness washed over her like icy water. Had Paul been so desperate for his father's approval that he'd done nearly anything to get it?

Trembling fingers slowly lifted to cover her mouth. She tasted salt. Why hadn't she seen it before? All the working and striving and accomplishments . . . they weren't just because she wanted to help hurting soldiers. She was trying to capture Father's attention. She wanted his approval. She was sick with the need for it.

He had never seen her, truly seen her. Not the way her heart longed to be seen and known. Washington society had seen her but for all the wrong reasons.

That's why none of it had ever been enough.

Her nightdress billowed around her as she slid to the floor and dug her fingernails into the patterned rug.

Oh, God, forgive me. What a miserable wretch she was! Claiming to love the suffering, yet all the while trying to fulfill her own selfish needs. A sob shuddered from deep inside. Her nose ran as tears dripped from her wet lashes.

You are loved.

She sniffed and looked up. She'd heard no audible voice, yet the words felt as tangible as if someone had spoken aloud.

Cadence, I see you. I know you. Let me be your Father.

The sound of her own sobs flooded her ears. Father always wanted more from her. Congressman Ramsey never ceased praising her abilities. How had she let them become her gods? She had behaved as if they had died for her.

My love for you will never change. You are my delight.

Tears streamed down her skin.

"Father, forgive me. Forgive me for seeking love outside of you. Forgive me for building an idol from others' opinions and approval. I ask you now to be my Father. Heal me, Lord, for I am broken. Wash me clean through the sacrifice of Christ and teach me your way. Show me how to live for you alone."

Like a feather drifting down from a still sky, peace fluttered through Cadence's spirit. She sensed a warm presence surrounding her. A smile wobbled through her tears.

She felt Love.

Moving to the window, she pressed her face to the glass and looked into the heavens. "You are the God who sees me."

Joshua ground his jaw and shifted his weight as he stood in the shadows of the alley three blocks past Judiciary Square Hospital. He had lost his mind. He must have, to return to meet a complete stranger in the darkness.

Still, the Knights needled him. They were a mystery. And if the man was correct, he had much to lose by dismissing them and their threats.

"Doc?"

The low voice to his right startled him. The stranger had made no other sound. He must have been waiting in the shadows. Watching. Another streetwise fellow like himself perhaps? Respect for the stranger rose.

"Yes."

"Come."

Joshua reached out and snagged the man's coat sleeve in the darkness, stopping him with a harsh tug. "I'll not take another step until you tell me your name."

A sharp exhale. Even in the shadows, Joshua could tell the man was shorter than he was, stocky and muscular.

"My name is Edmund Warwick."

"Mr. Warwick, why should I go with you?"

The man grew so still, Joshua feared he wouldn't answer.

Finally he spoke, his voice thick. "I used to be a Knight. That is, until I became uncomfortable with them and their way of handling business. When I defied them, they murdered my wife and son."

"I cannot imagine a more terrible punishment. My deepest sympathies."

Edmund stepped close, so close Joshua could smell the traces of tobacco on his breath. "If you mean that, sir, I request your help. We must throw them down."

Joshua blinked. This Edmund was no guttersnipe. His speech was articulate, befitting the manners of a gentleman. Just what kind of men made up the Knights?

Joshua gripped his arm. "Show me."

Edmund led him silently down a maze of alleys, pausing only on occasion to ensure they were not being followed. He scurried down a final alley and halted behind a massive building. Most of the windows were dark, save for two on the upper floors.

"Where are we?"

"At the temple."

"What temple?"

"The Knights of the Golden Circle have secret temples in nearly every prominent town." Edmund reached down to fiddle with a basement window, but Joshua stopped him with a hand to his shoulder.

"Which towns? You mean the capitals? Washington and Richmond?"

The faint trace of moonlight overhead illuminated the arch of Edmund's dark brow. "No. I mean every prominent town in the North and South."

Joshua pulled away, astounded at the information. The secret society was that extensive? He swallowed, watching as

Edmund wiggled the window lock free, silently motioning him to slip inside.

Lifting a hasty prayer for safety, Joshua squeezed through the small space, quietly landing in the musty basement below. Dust tickled his nose, mingling with the odor of mold.

Edmund dropped down behind him, shook dirt from his coat, and whispered, "What I'm about to show you is something no other man save a Knight has seen. I'm showing you this because your name has been mentioned here. You're being watched. Targeted. I have no desire to see you destroyed the way the Knights have destroyed my family." He paused. "They may yet kill me, but you still have a chance to escape their wrath. But to do that, you need to know what you're up against."

Joshua's breath thinned.

"There is to be an induction of new Knights this evening. I know of a secret place where we can observe. Say nothing. Make no sound or we will be discovered and slashed to ribbons. The only way out is the way we've entered. Understand?"

Joshua nodded tersely and followed the intense fellow as he pushed open a secret panel next to a shelf of tools and old lanterns. A narrow hallway not much bigger than the span of his own shoulders loomed into inky blackness.

Edmund wordlessly moved into the chasm. Joshua inhaled a fortifying breath and followed, the shadows pressing around him. Muffled voices pounded dully through the walls, vibrating through the passageway like the faraway thud of distant drums. Joshua fought to keep his breath even in the cramped space, fighting the sickening knowledge of being trapped inside the temple's interior walls. Like a coffin.

Edmund turned a corner and stopped him with a gentle touch. Joshua nodded, hearing the clear sound of voices just ahead. They were headed toward the heart of the Knights' meeting rooms.

Light slowly invaded the inky tunnel, thin slits piercing the darkness. A portion of Edmund's face was illuminated, as was his hand as he gestured for Joshua to step closer. Carefully, quietly, he slid forward.

Half-inch decorative gaps in the temple's inner sanctum allowed them to watch unnoticed from the hidden tunnel.

The room was dark, made infinitely more so by the flickering torches placed ceremoniously along the walls. The slight stirring of air cast dancing shadows along the walls like frenzied demons. At least thirty or more men stood in a circle, murmuring quietly, most of them attired in robes of crimson velvet lined with silver lace. Ruby stars and emeralds bedecked the cuffs and hems. Each man wore a turban made of similar material. Joshua squinted to make out their identities but startled. Each Knight wore a flesh-colored mask over his face.

Large columns stood along the back wall, framed by draped fabrics. Between the columns hung the golden image of a snake curled into a circle. Skulls were mounted every ten feet throughout the sinister hall.

The thrum of voices died down as a door opened to admit five trembling men clad in average clothing. They took in the sights before them with wide eyes. A man carrying a sword stepped from the corner of the room, his mask and bearing remarkably deadlier than the others circling the cowering visitors.

"You seek admission to the secrets of a cause which will make your name, in ages yet to come, glorious in the bright page whereon the faithful historian records renowned men and famous deeds. As it is written, 'We are like the herb which flourisheth most when it is most trampled on!'"

Joshua whispered, "I don't recognize the quote."

"*Ivanhoe.*" Edmund frowned, his gaze fixed upon the scene

unfolding behind the slatted wall. "All the Knights favor it. They fancy themselves great warriors for justice and truth, like the knights of old." The lines around his mouth deepened. "How often the oppressors delude themselves into believing they are the oppressed."

Joshua grunted. A profound thought.

The intimidating orator continued. "Should you betray its truth, a fate more terrible than death itself awaits you! We visit revenge upon the weak and innocent. All whom you love— your wife, sister, child, aged mother, and everything on earth you call your own—all is forever lost to you if you breathe to mortal ear one word or sign of the secrets we confide in you. From this time onward, we own and hold your very life!"

Heat licked Joshua's insides as one of the men whimpered. The throng advanced around the shivering men, chanting in demonic rhythm.

"Whoever dares our cause reveal, shall test the strength of knightly steel. And when the torture proves too dull, we'll scrape the brains from out his skull, and place a lamp within the shell, to light his soul from here to hell. Cut him down, my men, with your good broadswords, and let the milk from his veins—we want no cowards."

The mob rushed forward, binding all five of the men by the hands and blindfolding them before knives were drawn. As the circle passed by each man, the tips of the blades occasionally drew blood, eliciting cries from the terrified inductees. The Knights chanted, "I know thee. Break not thine oath!"

One of the poor souls attempted to bolt. With a cry, he lurched forward, only to be swiftly caught up by the band of masked demons. Blindfolded as he was, he stood not a chance of escape. Joshua longed to burst through the panel, to do something, anything to save the poor creature. Edmund must have sensed his agony, for he placed a restraining hand on his arm and silently shook his head.

The leader's voice boomed. "Oh, so we have a coward already, have we?" He snapped his fingers, and a rope was brought from somewhere beyond the room. "Remove the blindfolds, and all shall see what is to be done with cowards and those who shirk the vow of Knighthood!"

A cry arose as the frantic man was carried into the middle of the room. His screams and writhing only seemed to feed the frenzied mob. The rope was strung from some scaffolding high above, the noose settled over the man's twisting shoulders.

"Let this be a lesson to all . . . no one defies the Knights of the Golden Circle!"

With a shout, five men yanked the rope, pulling the screaming stranger from the floor by his neck. Joshua lurched forward only to find his body jerked backward.

Edmund hissed into his ear. "You cannot act. You must not."

Fury filled his lungs. "But that man! Will no one stop them?"

"Such is the way of the Knights. Now you know the evil to which they stoop."

Joshua watched helplessly through the slit in the wall as the flailing man stilled, his body growing limp as he dangled from above. The raucous shouts mellowed into eerie chants.

"Death to traitors. Blood be required. Death to traitors. Blood be required . . ."

Joshua clenched his jaw, his hands curling into fists. What hellish evil could have birthed such a society? After long minutes, they lowered the body and murmured about who would receive the man's property and personal effects. Edmund's fingers flexed and relaxed, flexed and relaxed. Joshua could feel the man's ire rising as they stood side by side in the tight space, watching the dreadful scene unfold. The leader turned to the other inductees with a harsh eye.

"Have we any more who yearn to dissent?"

"No! Not I!"

The four remaining men shook their heads, visibly cowering under the glare of the Knights.

"Kneel, then, and take thine oaths."

As the trembling souls knelt to repeat the cursed words, Joshua tasted the bile rising in his throat.

"I will give my heartiest energies and my property to the cause of this order. It shall be my duty to sustain and cherish the institutions of the South against all adversaries. I do furthermore swear to bear hatred, that nothing but blood shall satisfy, against all men of the North who are not friendly to our cause. I swear to uphold the superiority of Southern gentlemen and hold inferior the Negro, the simple, the poor, the . . ."

Joshua could bear no more. "Someone must stop this madness!"

Edmund whispered, "You've seen enough."

With a small push, Edmund urged him back through the dark, tomb-like tunnels inside the temple. Cool air rushed in and brushed his face when they reached the opening to the basement. The silence of the room was a welcome reprieve from the demonic revelry they'd just witnessed.

Joshua gouged his eyes with the palms of his hands. "I can't believe what I just saw."

Edmund's brows lowered. "I'm ashamed to say I've lost count of such gruesome displays. The Knights, or Copperheads as they sometimes call themselves, are everywhere. They are the driving financial force behind the Confederacy." Edmund stepped closer, dropping his voice to a nearly imperceptible whisper.

"Political figures, congressmen, and military commanders have taken the very oath you just heard."

Nauseated at the thought, Joshua whirled away, pacing in the confined space. "What is to be done? Trying to topple such a network . . ."

"Not easily accomplished." Edmund shook his head. "Granted. But we can work to root out the corrupt in our own city."

"How?"

"It won't be easy. Their facades are many and varied. And the codes they employ are so nuanced, it's hard to pinpoint the origin and meaning of messages, much less the messengers. Knights excel at saying one thing and meaning another."

Joshua rubbed his chin. "Still, there must be some way."

Edmund squinted. "I have a plan, but it will take resources. I'll contact you within the week."

The stocky man moved to pull himself up through the window, but Joshua stopped him with a hand to his shoulder.

"Where shall I expect to find you?"

Edmund grunted. "Don't look for me, Doc. I'll find you."

chapter 22

"YOU SURE ABOUT THIS, ZEKE?"

His trusted friend crossed his bulging arms and nodded, his face a scowl. "I tell you, I've caught the man three times in as many days watching your house."

A cold fist sank into Joshua's gut as he stared at his friend from across his small library.

"Any possibility he's only after me and not the children?"

Zeke leveled his gaze. "He waits until you leave for work and disappears once you come home. He's watching the children, Doc. Looking for the opportunity to strike. What better way to crush an enemy than hit him where it hurts the most?"

Zeke was a man of few words, but what he said landed a punch. Fear, fury, nausea . . . all of it curdled through Joshua's middle and fanned out like poisonous fingers. "I always knew someone would come after me, didn't I?"

Zeke grunted. "We both got targets on our backs. Me, a freeman working to set my people free, and you a white man, going against those who want to keep us in chains." He shook his head. "Ain't the kind of thing that makes folks happy. We were bound to feel the lash of their anger at some point."

Joshua stared out the darkened windows and absently rubbed his fingers over his mouth. He had plenty of enemies. Zeke was correct. Such a thing was expected as an abolitionist. But what if the stranger watching the house was more than an ill-tempered Confederate?

His heart squeezed as he remembered the nightmare one of the stewards had unearthed yesterday at Judiciary Square. Joshua had been making his rounds to check on patients when one of the men rushed in and urgently whispered in his ear.

"I was sprinkling lime in the waste pit when I saw a man lying facedown near the back of the building."

Joshua had met the steward's gaze and saw the truth already settled in his countenance. Dead.

"Someone we know?"

The steward shook his head. "Leastwise not by me. Not hospital staff. Can you come?"

"Of course."

Joshua had followed the solemn man outside but felt all the blood drain from his face when he rolled the body over to discover the dead man was Edmund Warwick. Multiple stab wounds covered his bloody torso. One side of his head bore the telltale marks of a crushing blow.

Ambushed. And Joshua had known then . . . the Knights had discovered, or at least suspected, Edmund's plan to take them down.

Had Edmund been on his way to warn Joshua? And if the Knights knew of Edmund's traitorous turn, would Joshua and his loved ones be next?

His stomach soured as he recalled the mysterious man who

had approached Cadence the night of the benefit. He had warned her she aligned herself with danger. It had been more than a warning. It was a threat.

Joshua pinched the bridge of his nose. "Things cannot remain as they are. The Union is asking me to travel yet again to skirmish points and act as a field surgeon." A headache loomed in the back of his skull. "I cannot leave the children and Miriam for so long unprotected. Nor would I ask you to guard them and impose such a burden on you."

"I would do it for you."

"I know you would, but even the best of bodyguards need sleep. You can't be on alert all the time for weeks on end." He rubbed his eyes. "That's the problem. I never know how long I'll be gone when the generals call. It might be for a few weeks. It might be for several months or more."

Zeke ran his fingers through his black curls. "What other options do you have?"

He ground his jaw. "Only one that I can see."

"Which is?"

"I have to take the children with me."

Cadence inhaled a fortifying breath and lifted her hand to knock on Joshua's door, squinting against the bright sunshine and sultry July air.

When she'd told Father her decision to stop singing at benefits and rallies, he'd nearly been bowled over. He'd pleaded, begged, and even threatened to forbid her to step foot in a hospital again.

She'd almost broken under his barrage but kept her voice soft, her tone gentle. "You must do what you think is best, Father, but I cannot sing for these Washington events anymore.

I'm doing them for the wrong reasons. And the exhaustion is more than I can bear."

He'd just stared before turning on his heel to leave the room. The look of disappointment stung like a shard of glass embedded in her flesh, but alone in the parlor, she'd expelled a cleansing sigh. She'd done it. Her mind already felt more rested, despite the turmoil Father's displeasure had stirred in her heart.

For three days she'd done little more than read her Bible, tend to Rose's grave, and sleep, but the cluster of pink roses and creamy daisies on her dresser was a constant reminder of the person she had yet to thank.

She had attempted to find Joshua at Judiciary Square Hospital that morning. No one had seen him all day, so she'd visited the men, lent a hand to the nurses, and helped feed patients their noon meal. When it was clear he wasn't going to appear, she'd excused herself, hired a hack, and ventured the long trek to the far side of the capital city. Though the neighborhood he and the children lived in was comfortable, squalid streets lay just beyond the next block. The odor of rotting garbage drifted through the air.

She waited, wishing she could lift the thick snood away from her neck and cool her skin. Sweat trickled down her back under her corset as she rapped the door again and listened. She knew he was home, for she could hear the low rumble of his voice and then a higher-pitched one respond. She knocked harder.

Conversation ceased. Footfalls crossed to the door and it creaked open. Joshua stood before her, yet it was not him. Shadows rimmed his eyes. Golden-brown stubble covered his jaw. His hair was mussed as if he'd spent all morning digging his fingers through it.

"Cadence."

"Forgive me for calling uninvited. I stopped by the hospital, but you weren't there. I feared something may have happened again, so . . ."

The corners of his mouth tilted. "Nurse Piper to the rescue?"

Heat crept under her skin. "Something of that nature. I also wanted to thank you for the beautiful flowers." She swallowed. "And the c-c-c-card." She closed her eyes. She didn't want to stutter like a simpleton before this man.

It doesn't matter what anyone thinks. You are loved.

She blew out a small breath. "It—it changed my life."

His brows rose. "I would like to hear. Please, come in."

"Am I welcome? I mean, do you think it no longer dangerous?"

As he shut the door behind her, she could hear Miriam fussing. ". . . craziest thing I've heard in all my days. Taking them babies? Ain't got the brains God gave a goose."

When she saw Cadence enter, her dark eyes rounded. "Miss Piper! Law, but it's good to see you again."

"It's good to see you too." Cadence embraced the matronly woman, but she couldn't miss the tension filling the room. It was as tight as taffy.

"I'm sorry to have interrupted. If I need to leave, I'll be—"

Joshua held up his hand. "No. Please stay."

Miriam shot him a withering glare. "Mm-hmm. I'm sure you do want her to stay, so I'll hush up, but if I said it once, I'll say it again. You're crazy if you think we're going with you!"

Cadence looked between the two of them. Joshua was rubbing his temple, and Miriam glowered, looking like a bulldog who refused to give up a bone.

"What's wrong?"

"I'll tell you what's wrong." The older woman scowled. "This man thinks to drag them precious, innocent babies with him into war and wants me to go along, too, to wash all them Union boys' drawers. As if I ain't got enough to do in my old age!"

Shock rendered Cadence mute. Her gaze flew to Joshua. His eyes were closed and he spoke slowly as if trying to be patient. "Miriam, we've been through this. I would not be giving the children bayonets. They would be safely away from the fighting."

Propping her hands on her ample hips, she glared. "Oh, really? And where would we be?"

He smiled sheepishly, though it resembled more of a wince. "At a safe house near Bristoe Station."

She threw her hands up. "Land o' Goshen! Who living there? Yankees or Confederates? You even know? Could be anybody!" Stomping into the kitchen, she muttered, her temper rising with every step. "Done lost his mind . . ."

Silence descended.

Finally Joshua spoke. "My apologies. Miriam can be dramatic."

"Really? I thought she was rather calm."

He chuckled.

"So you're truly considering bringing the children with you when you work in the field hospital?"

"You think it a bad idea?"

She paused. She had no right to tell him what to do with his own children, but . . .

"Miss Piper!"

Penelope squealed and ran down the hall, launching herself against Cadence and wrapping her arms around her waist.

Cadence laughed and squeezed the precious girl, smiling down into her dancing eyes and freckled face.

"Penelope." Joshua frowned. "How many times have I told you? Ladies do not yell, run, or throw themselves at people they are happy to see."

"Sorry."

Cadence tapped her nose. "How is my favorite princess?"

"I'm fine. Etta is taking a nap, so James and I are painting. Would you like to come see?"

"I would love to."

Joshua tugged her braids. "Hold on, missy. I need to speak with Miss Piper for a moment in private."

Penelope's lower lip stuck out. "Okay. I'll go tell James she's here. He'll be so excited." She bounced on her tiptoes. "Can you read us a story?"

She smoothed the girl's hair and glanced toward Joshua. "If it's all right with your papa."

He nodded.

Penelope squealed and ran to tell her brother. Joshua called after her retreating form. "Young ladies don't run, Penelope!"

Cadence smiled. "She's excited, is all."

He offered a tired smile and motioned toward his library. "If you don't mind, what I have to say needs no listening ears."

He led her into the small room and closed the door behind him. The musty aroma of books and leather filled her nostrils. Papers and journals lay scattered across his desk here as well. Order was not his strong suit.

She turned to face him and once again noted the weariness lining his face. "What's wrong?"

"Someone is after my family."

A cold, sick sensation slithered down her stomach. "Who?"

"I have enemies, as you well know. It was the man I hired to guard the children who first noticed someone watching the house while I was gone. In fact, you've seen him before in Richmond." A wry smile tugged his mouth. "He often helps me in freeing slave children. His name is Zeke."

Cadence blinked, trying to absorb the information.

"There is a group of men called the Knights of the Golden Circle. Evil, power-hungry men who hate the Union and hate those who support abolition even more. I think they are behind the threat you received the night of the benefit."

She reached to steady herself. The night of the benefit. The warning.

"The Knights see all."

Her fingers dug into the upholstery of the wingback chair at her side.

"They are coming for me, Cadence. And now, with the Union summoning me away once again, I cannot leave my family here alone without protection."

"Your friend cannot protect them while you're gone?"

"He's only one man. He cannot guard them all day and all night. And there is no one else I trust."

Cadence watched the emotions dance across his face. Fear had burrowed deep inside him, gnawing away his normal control. "And you feel the only option is to take them with you."

He paced the length of the room. "I know it sounds crazy. Perhaps it is, but I heard regiments are allowed to bring up to four laundresses with them, something the War Department devised to help improve sanitation. The laundresses are usually wives of the soldiers and bring their children along as well. If I offered to bring a laundress for the surgeons to use, the War Department would likely approve such a measure and even allow the children to come. Miriam has flatly refused." He scrubbed his face. "I can't say I blame her. No woman in her right mind wants to launder bloody bandages and linen while cannons shriek nearby."

Cadence remained silent. She found nursing to be rewarding, but the laundering of soiled linens . . . remarkably less so. She could not cast fault with Miriam. Especially when the task involved watching three young children in the heart of the conflict.

"There are other options." Joshua paced rapidly, rubbing the back of his neck. "Less desirable in some ways but safer in others."

"What options?"

He sighed. "The safe house I mentioned near Bristoe Station. I have friends there. Friends who would shelter and protect them. At least there they would be away from the fighting."

"Have you told Miriam about the man watching the house?"

He winced. "Absolutely not. She and the children can't know. Miriam is as skittish as a flea. If she knew, she'd go into vapors. And I don't want the children thinking there is some horrid man waiting to kidnap them. That's a fear no child should live with. I'll tell them if I think I must, but for now, I'd rather they live in innocence."

He fell into a chair and dropped his head into his hands. "Please pray. I don't know how to protect them."

Awareness washed through her. *Just do the next thing.* This was something she could do. There would be no acclaim, no glory, but it would be sacrificial. The opposite of how she'd been living. Service based on pure motives. Giving to those who had nothing to give in return.

"I'll do it."

His head snapped up. "What?"

"I'll be your laundress. I'll care for the children . . . whatever you need me to do so they are safe and you are at ease."

He rose slowly, his jaw slack. "You would do that for them?"

"Of course." She smiled gently. "After how you've helped me, it's the least I can do."

He frowned. "I don't understand."

She twisted her fingers together. "The flowers you sent were beautiful, but the note changed my life." She lifted her face to his. "The verses, more importantly."

His gaze roved over her. "Tell me."

Breathing slowly, she fought to find the words she longed to say. "Ever since I was a little girl, speaking has been difficult for me. I stammer and stutter. When I was a child, it was especially dreadful."

His face registered surprise. "I've never noticed such a thing." Understanding lit his eyes as his expression went slack. "The day I caught you searching for chloroform in my tent . . ."

"Yes. I work hard to erase it as much as possible. Mother and Father insisted I visit a phrenologist when I was twelve. He declared I would never outgrow the problem because I bore the mark of an intellectual deformity of some kind." Her throat clogged as the horrid words were given voice once again. "He said my parents should not expect much from me."

Joshua rubbed his thumb against his clenched fist. "He was a fool."

She sighed. "Looking back, I believe he was in error, but from a child's point of view, I believed him to speak the truth. And I sensed a shift in how my father treated me after that day. He was still kind. Indulgent even, but—" she blinked away the burning sensation in her eyes—"something was different."

"And your mother?"

Cadence smiled. "Mother didn't change. Nothing ever persuaded her once her mind was fixed."

"She sounds like her daughter."

Cadence bit her lip. "I'd like to think so. She told me to pay the phrenologist no mind, but the words needled. So instead of forgetting about him, I set out to prove him wrong. I did everything I could to erase my stutter. I excelled at my studies . . .

all of it to prove my worth." Her throat swelled. "For so long I thought it was to prove it to myself, but I think it was even more to prove it to my father."

"Cadence." His voice was low and strained. "Is that why you didn't want to speak on the night of the benefit?"

"Yes. When I'm nervous, the problem roars back to life with a vengeance. And the day in your tent when you thought I was stealing . . ."

He blanched and looked away. Her heart sank. He regretted kissing her. Must she always fall short?

"I was an unforgivable brute that day."

"I couldn't spit out the words because I was so flummoxed." She pushed away the memories of his fervent touch and murmured words of affection. He hadn't meant it. She swallowed down the lump in her throat.

"The verses you wrote on the card helped me see I've been living for all the wrong things. I think, perhaps, even wanting to become a nurse was in part a way to gain Father's approval." His brows dipped low, but she continued. "You helped me see that approval and love are not the same thing. God has shown me I am loved already by him. I need not earn it." She smiled into his eyes. "Thank you, Joshua."

He said nothing for a long moment. A muscle worked in his throat as he stared at the floor. Finally he lifted his eyes and locked his gaze on hers. "I was wrong, you know. There is not one vain, shallow, or superficial bone in your body."

His fingers grazed hers. She sucked in a breath as he lifted her hand to his lips and pressed a kiss to her fingers. Ripples of pleasure skimmed up her arm.

"Let me help you. I've been to a battlefield, if you remember." She couldn't suppress her teasing tone. "I can do it. Let me help you keep your children safe."

He studied her for a long moment. "And what would moti-
vate you to do such a thing?"

"Love. Love for those children. Love for God. No other reasons, I assure you."

He released her hand, his eyes shadowed. Had she mis-
spoken somehow?

Finally he nodded. "Thank you. Only if you're sure."

"I'm sure."

He expelled a thick breath and laughed lightly. "Now how
do I tell the children they are going with me to war?"

"Might I suggest making it sound like a grand adventure?
Frame it as if they are the heroes in their very own storybook."

Her heart caught when he grinned. "Something tells me
they will care very little about where they are going, once they
hear you will be going as well." He turned toward the door. "I'll
call them and we can tell them together."

"You know what this means, don't you, Dr. Ivy?"

He turned back and lifted his brows in question.

She offered an impish smile. "This means we'll be working
together yet again."

He winked and she felt her knees weaken.

"I shall look forward to the challenge."

chapter 23

The barrage of cannon fire shook the ground beneath Joshua as the frame of the canvas-covered surgical tent rattled like a coin in a tin cup. He blinked away the sweat stinging his eyes to focus on extracting the bullet from the wounded soldier's arm.

"Got it." His sticky, blood-soaked fingers worked the clamps to drop the round piece of lead into the waiting bowl. He turned, handed the instruments to the steward, and barked, "Wash those instruments immediately!"

The steward shrugged and scurried away to finish the task. Shells whistled overhead. The explosion barely registered as Joshua hastened to sew the soldier back together. Ambulance runners were waiting at the tent flaps. Men screamed and wailed in pain. One man was carried to another surgeon in the large tent. Half of the soldier's face was missing. How was he even still alive?

This was far worse than Oak Ridge. His thoughts traveled to Bristoe Station. With the camp bulging at the seams, he'd had little choice but to turn to his friends for help. Elderly siblings Moxley Morris and Maisey Honeycutt had eagerly offered to house Cadence and the children until his duties were finished. Had he placed them far enough away from the fighting? Were they safe?

His crimson-covered hands shook as he wove the needle through torn flesh.

Father, protect them. Hell is being unleashed.

Cadence cuddled with the children inside the guest bedrooms of the elderly siblings' farmhouse as the dull thump of cannon shook the ground.

Despite their distance from the fighting, the acrid odor of smoke wafted through the air. Surely the fight wouldn't reach them, would it? Mr. Moxley had assured them Bristoe Station was miles from the conflict.

Or perhaps the fight was just that severe.

Cadence pressed a kiss to Etta's curly head. The toddler lay snuggled heavy against her chest. As soon as the cannon fire had sounded through the air, Etta had climbed into her lap, jammed her thumb in her mouth, and buried her face in Cadence's neck. Poor lamb.

Penelope was curled into her other side, saying little, clutching some hidden object in her fist. Cadence alternated between running her hand over the girl's frayed braids and massaging her back with small circular motions, but the skin beneath her freckles remained pale.

James tried harder to be brave, despite his mere eight years. He peered out the window, checking the yard for movement, his face somber. So young to wear the mantle of a man's burden.

She observed him tenderly, even as another rumble shook the ground. "Thank you for watching over us, James."

He swiped under his nose with his fist. "Ain't nothin', Miss Piper. Just doing what a man is supposed to do. Taking care of his women. That's what Papa Gish always says."

She smiled. "He's a good man."

"The best. Me and Etta was starving to death, living in an alley and hiding from paddy rollers, when Papa Gish found us. Gave us a home." He grinned, white teeth flashing. "Another sister too."

Penelope shifted at her side. "You're not always happy to have me."

He frowned. "Only when you take my best aggie."

Cadence laughed at the sound of Penelope's soft giggle. "How did you and Etta come to be alone?"

He looked down and picked at a thread on his trousers. "Pa and Ma escaped our master down South Carolina way. We traveled north following something Pa called the Railroad. Master caught up with us, though. Pa sent us on ahead and decided to sacrifice himself so we could have a chance of escaping." His lips curled downward. "Something went wrong. As we was running, we heard a gunshot. I looked back and saw Pa collapse."

Cadence's eyes slid shut. So much horror for a little boy to witness. "I'm so sorry."

His face was set. "Ma said real love means pain and Pa had real love for us because he gave up his life. And I know I had real love for him because it hurt so much when he died."

Her heart twisted. "I lost my mother. I had real love for her too. It hurt. It hurts still."

James nodded. "Ma was tough. Managed to get us all the

way to Washington, but she was scared. Didn't know where to go or who to turn to. She got bad sick and died just weeks after we arrived. It was just me and Etta left." His face brightened. "But then Jesus sent us Papa Gish."

Penelope giggled again. "Providence knew I needed some new aggies."

James rolled his eyes. The pounding of cannons intensified, rumbling the floorboards and rattling the glass globe of the kerosene lamp on the desk. Etta was limp against her neck, her breathing deep. Asleep.

Penelope huffed an impatient sigh. "How long will this go on?"

Cadence smoothed her hair. "At Oak Grove it went on for seven days."

"Seven days?"

"Yes, but in truth, it wasn't this bad. What's going on across the way at Bull Run—" she winced—"well, we need to pray for those men, sweetheart."

Penelope wrinkled her nose. "It sounds like Old Scratch is loose."

"Penelope! Where did you ever hear such a term?"

The little girl shrugged. "From Miriam. She calls the devil Old Scratch all the time."

James burst out laughing. Cadence shook her head. "Just because Miriam says it doesn't make it proper."

A bone-rattling boom shook the house. Penelope squealed and curled herself into Cadence's side. Cadence murmured a prayer for safety. She could only imagine what chaos Joshua faced in the surgical tent.

Penelope's thumb stroked the hidden object tucked in her fist.

"What do you have, pretty Penny?"

The girl shook her head and clutched her fist to her chest. "Just something someone gave me. A lady."

"Oh?" Her curiosity flared. "Who?"

"I don't even know her name, but I used to wish Papa Gish would marry her."

That comment stung far more than it should. "I see."

Penelope looked up into her face. "Now I wish he would marry you, Miss Piper."

Words fled. What could she say? With a startling clarity, she suddenly realized how very much she wished the same thing. She loved him. She loved him deeply.

"Would you marry him?"

James gasped. "Penelope Alice Ivy!"

She glared. "It's only a question!"

"It ain't a proper question."

Cadence swallowed, keeping her voice gentle. "Don't quarrel. It's not really a thing to argue about, is it? He has not asked."

"But would you accept if he did?" Penelope probed, her green eyes hopeful.

Should she answer? She could see no way around the pointed question without being deceitful. "Yes. I believe I would."

Penelope sat back with a satisfied smile.

"But he has not asked, so you should put the idea from your head, missy."

She burrowed deeper into Cadence's side. "I must think of something. Anything, or I shall go mad."

Cadence exhaled softly. "How about a story?"

The little girl nodded. "Yes, please."

"All right. Once upon a time, there was a lonely couple who desperately wanted a child. They lived next to a walled garden belonging to an evil witch named Dame Gothel . . ."

As the pounding of cannons plunged into the abyss of night, Cadence ventured from the room. All three children were blessedly asleep, tucked close to each other, breathing deeply in their innocence.

She crept down the stairs, toward a soft glow of candlelight beckoning from the kitchen.

Moxley and Maisey sat across from each other at the simple wooden table, a Bible open before them. Their silver heads were bowed as Moxley's deep voice murmured, "We thank thee, almighty God, for Miss Cadence and these precious children thou hast brought to our home. Bless them. Protect them. Be with dear Joshua. Guide his hands. Be our peace amid this troubled time . . ."

Cadence stilled, dropping her own head in reverence as the older man finished the prayer. At his *amen*, the siblings looked up with sweet smiles. Maisey's pale-blue eyes twinkled above her round cheeks. "I was preparing to come check on you, dearie. Are you and the children settled in?"

"Yes, ma'am. The cannons bothered them for a while, but they're sound asleep now."

"Glad I am to hear it. Come." She patted the chair next to hers and rose, shuffling to the stove to fetch the teakettle. "Nothing comforts the heart quite like the Good Book and a cup of tea."

Moxley grunted. "Coffee is better."

Maisey wrinkled her button nose. "Not if it's chicory."

The older man frowned before swinging his gaze to Cadence. "My sister refuses to brew chicory coffee. Near breaks my heart." He grimaced and pointed at his half-empty cup. "Serves me this female nonsense instead."

"Tea is just fine, and you know it. You just like to have something to grouse about."

"At my age, I've got nothing better to do." He winked and Cadence laughed. Such charming people.

Pushing back his chair with a soft scrape, he rose. "Think I'll check around the house. Sounds like the fighting has quieted some. Might as well make sure the barn critters aren't too riled either."

"Thank you, Brother." Maisey placed a steaming cup of tea before Cadence and eased back down into her chair before pushing the cream and sugar her way. "Don't be shy now. The Almighty's been good to us."

The heady aroma of peppermint rose up from the curls of heat ribboning over the cup's rim. Cadence added a splash of cream and a generous spoonful of sugar before sipping the warm brew with a murmur of satisfaction.

"Mm. Delicious."

"Thank you. I've always been a bit partial to tea. My father never did let us have it much. Declared it unpatriotic, something his pa told him after the War for Independence, but my ma would sneak a tin in the house from time to time. We both had a taste for it."

Cadence smiled at the impish gleam that filled Maisey's twinkling eyes. "Something tells me you might have been a handful when you were little."

The older woman chuckled. "Quite so. Not much like Moxley. He was always the obedient one. Oh, he had a way with people but was always a bit on the shy side, especially with females. Never did court a girl. He says one never caught his fancy, but I think it's because he was always too afeared to ask."

"And what about you? Did you have a beau?"

Maisey's eyes drifted to a faraway place, shifting into a

dreamy land of melancholy. "Oh yes. I had a beau. Sweetest boy I ever met."

"Did you marry?"

"Yes, child. We had eight beautiful months together. Until he caught consumption and passed."

Cadence looked down into her cup. "I'm sorry."

Maisey patted her hand. "Don't be. Most glorious eight months of my life. Wouldn't wish it any different. To love and be loved that fully is a blessing. My Walter was shy. Had trouble speaking, getting out what he wanted to say. But, my, he had the heart of a lion."

Cadence nearly dropped her cup as she leaned forward. "I struggle from the same malady." She bit her lip, hesitant to share such intimate thoughts with a stranger. "When I was a child, a physician told me my mental capacity was impaired because of my speech."

Maisey chuckled, her laughter like silver. "Sounds like your doctor didn't know his Scriptures."

"What do you mean?"

"Why, Moses, of course. Do you not remember, dearie?"

Warmth flushed through Cadence's cheeks. "I suppose not."

Smiling, the older woman sipped. "When the Almighty told Moses to return to Egypt to set his people free, old Moses balked and said he could never stand before Pharaoh because he was slow of speech. He had trouble speaking too. Yet God refused to take no for an answer. And I think Moses did a right fine job, don't you?"

Cadence felt her heart taking flight. "Yes, ma'am."

"If there's anything my Walter taught me, it's this: just because someone talks slow, or not at all, doesn't mean they're deficient."

Cadence sighed and took a sip of the peppermint tea, relishing its minty warmth. "I wish everyone shared your view."

Maisey leaned back in her chair, her work-worn fingers curled around her cup. "Remember, sweetie, a lie is only harmful if you believe it. Don't believe what others say about you. Trust what the good Lord says and all will be well. It didn't matter a whit to me that my Walter had trouble speaking." Her eyes danced. "And judging by the way our Joshua spoke of you, I doubt it matters a jig to him either."

Cadence could feel the telltale blush creeping across her skin. "I pray he's all right."

Leaning across the table, Maisey patted her hand. "If the cannons have stopped completely on the morrow, I'll have Moxley take you to him."

chapter 24

CADENCE CLUTCHED Moxley's calloused hand as she descended from the rickety wagon, releasing him once her boot sank into the earth.

Her eyes scanned the horizon and her breath fled as she drank in the sight of the valley below. She remained standing though her knees weakened at the images emblazoned against the reddening sky.

Thousands. Thousands upon thousands slain. Mangled corpses. Dead horses and snapped trees. Bodies were three feet deep in places. Ruddy pools of blood amid churned earth. A haze of blue smoke lay heavy, like the hand of death itself was ashamed to reveal the carnage.

"Dear God . . ."

The stench of smoke and decay rose up in a thickening fog. Moxley looked around at the devastation, eyes filled with sorrow, and shook his head. "You sure about this, missy?"

"I'm positive. The surgeons and nurses will need all the help they can get."

"Truer words were never spoken."

She turned to him, her brows pinched. "Are you sure it's not an imposition to leave the children with you for the day?"

"Nah. 'Course not. Maisey will be in heaven. And if their jawing gets to bothering me, I'll just hie myself to the barn." He winked. "I'm partial to children. Don't see near enough of them. If you see our Joshua, tell him I'm praying for him." He reached behind himself and pulled out a wrapped parcel, thrusting it into her hands. "This is from Maisey to him. She says he must eat it all."

The aroma of Maisey's biscuits wafted through the bundle, along with, perhaps, the spicy scent of ham. She slipped it into her pocket. "Thank you, Moxley. I'll make sure he obeys."

Nodding, he clicked his tongue and urged the horses forward. The wagon lurched into motion, leaving her alone in a field of thousands.

She turned in a slow circle. Corpses. Blood. Hands reaching out for mercy. Ambulance runners walking between bodies with stretchers, combing the scorched landscape for life.

There are so many, Lord. So many.

Acrid smoke stung her nose, smothering what once was clean air. Twigs and rocks crunched beneath her feet as her weight shifted.

Their moans rose up like a cacophony of diseased specters. Wailing. Crying for relief. For water. For death. The longer she stood, the louder they seemed. She shivered and covered her ears, trying to push out the sounds, but they crowded in, intensifying with every breath she took. How many were wounded?

Her knees weakened. It was too much. Too much to be done. Too many who needed help. Heavens, she couldn't even take a deep breath for the stench.

She slammed her eyes shut, gasping.

"Just do the next thing."

The next thing. That was all she could do. One thing at a time.

Blinking, she turned again. Focusing. The white canvas of the surgical tents shone just ahead. Her breath caught when the morning light revealed hundreds of wounded piled around the structures. Tears pricked her eyes. So many. As she approached, a moan sent shivers down her spine.

"Help me! Please! Don't pass me by . . ."

"Don't pass me by."

She froze. The drifting memory of Fanny Crosby and her recollection of the prisoner begging to be noticed assaulted Cadence like a slap. It didn't matter what she had been asked to do. She could not turn away from these men. The need was too great. Their suffering incomprehensible.

She knelt at the man's side before grasping his dirt-crusted fingers. Blood and mud coated his neck and torso.

"I'm here, sir. I'll not pass you by."

He wheezed, his face contorting in pain. "Water."

"I'll find some and return. I promise."

As the morning crept along, the mournful howls of the dying continued. Cadence walked from soldier to soldier offering a cup of water and praying, asking each man his name.

One soldier grabbed her wrist, his blackened fingers curling around her hand, causing her to spill the cup of water across his chest. His eyes were wide and panicked. "I ain't ready. I'm dying and I ain't ready."

She kept her voice calm. "Do you believe Jesus is God's Son? That he died for you and rose again?"

The soldier's eyes searched the sky, his throat convulsing. "I believe. I cast my soul on his mercy."

"Then go in peace."

A single tear trickled from his eye and slid into his beard. He coughed violently and curled into a ball. She held his hands, murmuring, "Jesus, be with him. Have mercy."

His body suddenly relaxed. A shadow passed over his face as his breath left him. Bowing her head, she sat back on her heels and rubbed her palms against her gritty eyes.

She turned slowly. Farther up the hill, a man sat outside the surgical tent, his head in his hands. Weariness weighted his broad shoulders.

Joshua.

She trudged toward him. Either he did not hear her approach or was too weary to care. She rested her hand on his shoulder. He didn't look up.

"There are too many, Cadence."

"I know."

He lifted his head. Heavy lines ringed his eyes. "Is it worth it?"

"What?"

"The price of freedom." He waved his hand over the valley. "Is it worth all this?"

She knelt at his feet and looked into his shadowed features. "Picture James or Etta and ask the question again. Is it worth it?"

His jaw firmed. "Yes." He drew his hand over his face. "I just feel helpless. I don't know how to help them all. I can't."

She sighed. "No, you can't."

He looked at her.

"You help one at a time and leave them all in the hands of the Almighty."

His hand lifted and grazed her cheek. He pulled her close and pressed his lips to her forehead. His breath hovered warm near her skin as he pulled away, his eyes dark. "Thank you."

Her throat was dry.

"Are the children managing?"

She swallowed. "Yes."

"That's good."

He had yet to remove his hand from her cheek. His thumb stroked her jaw and she feared she might collapse under his touch. What was it about this man that he could so completely undo her with the slightest brush?

Warning bells rang in her mind. She could not be swayed by her wayward emotions anymore.

"Maisey sent something for you. Here." She pulled the parcel from her skirt pocket. "I'm sorry if it's a bit crushed. She said you must eat it all."

A tired smile ghosted his lips. "Dear woman." He blinked up at her. "They are part of the operation, you know."

Those two elderly siblings helped set slave children free? Maisey was right. Appearances could indeed be deceiving. "I'm quite fond of them."

"They're good people. Tell Maisey I will eat every bite." He looked at her for a long moment. "Cadence, I—"

"I'm needed to distribute water. I should go."

She slid away from him and hastened toward the buckets waiting to be dispersed. Canvas and wooden poles were not enough barrier to protect her heart.

───── ❧ ─────

Hours ceased to have meaning as time was suspended in Manassas. Joshua felt his hands would never be clean again. Blood forever stained them. No sooner had he operated on one than a hundred more waited.

He turned to one ambulance runner. "How bad are the casualties?"

The runner wiped a forearm across his sweaty head and replaced his kepi. "Heard the captain say nigh unto ten thousand of our boys, but it looks like more than that to me. Word is the Rebs lost almost as many on their side too."

Joshua bowed his head, resisting the urge to spit out an oath. Such waste. "How could this have happened? And at the very spot where the Rebels surprised us only last year?"

The ambulance runner shook his head. "It's a pity. General Pope misjudged Lee somehow."

Joshua studied the hillside, covered with runners, nurses, doctors, and volunteers. Even more were scheduled to arrive throughout the coming days, but a thousand would not be enough to help twenty thousand wounded. Far too many would be dead before help could arrive. Even the land itself looked as if a massive twister had cut through, leaving nothing but destruction in its wake.

"Brawner's Farm will never be the same."

The runner studied him with a critical eye. "You need sleep, Doc."

Joshua frowned. "I can't sleep when so many are suffering."

"You'll not do them a lick of good if you succumb to exhaustion."

"I'm not to that point. Not yet. But I will gather some fresh air for a few moments."

The soldier nodded and grabbed the poles of an empty bloodstained stretcher, ready to resume his trek back down into the valley of the dying.

The children. Joshua had not checked on them since the battle started. How he missed them.

He had seen Cadence walking toward the laundering tents. Grabbing more linens or washing? Either way, he would welcome a minute with her.

He trudged forward, his feet feeling as if they were weighted with lead. He squinted against the midmorning sun winking through the trees. The only trees not severed like toothpicks from cannon and shell. He shuddered to think what would have happened if the battle had shifted farther south, toward the safe house.

The smell of lye stung his nose as he drew close. For a moment, he just slowed and watched.

Cadence presided over a washpot, stirring a bubbling cauldron of soapy water with a paddle. A roaring fire crackled underneath. Her cheeks were flushed and rosy from the heat, her dark hair coming loose from its pins. Despite her own exhaustion, here she stood, dutifully washing linens and bandages so the doctors could keep working.

She'd strung a long line of rope between thick pines, where other nurses were hanging dripping strips of clean bandages and cloths. An ambulance runner dropped sticks into a pile before adding another load of dirty linens to the stack near the cauldron.

"Thank you, sir." Cadence rewarded him with a wide smile. "Good help is hard to find."

The young lad's chest puffed out. "Ain't much, but I can haul wood. You gonna need more?"

"I'm sure I will. The casualties are massive. The doctors will have their hands full for days to come. The help you are providing will do much."

The runner nodded proudly. At Joshua's approach, they turned. Everyone in the tent smiled, save Cadence. Her blue eyes flared with something he couldn't quite place before she dropped her focus to the cauldron of soaking cloth.

"How do you fare, Dr. Ivy?" one of the nurses asked as she wiped away a bead of sweat.

"To be honest, the work is horrible. I have no idea when it will end." His gaze rolled to Cadence, but she studiously avoided looking his way.

The young ambulance runner approached and saluted. "Private Wilson, New York Fifth. I've heard the nurses saying what a skilled surgeon you are, sir, and, well, I just wanted to say I hope to be just like you someday."

Joshua offered a tired smile, heartened by the lad's enthusiasm amid such heartache. "If your fortitude and optimism today is any indication, I believe you will be, son."

Private Wilson beamed.

"Here." Cadence moved to Joshua's side, a cup of hot coffee in one hand and a tin containing a golden piece of fry bread in the other.

His stomach growled as if on cue. "Thank you."

A pretty blush stained Cadence's cheeks. She looked away.

Another woman approached—a short, plump woman with her thin brown hair pulled back into a strict knot. "Nurse Piper! Got more wash for you."

Cadence nodded. "Put it in the washpot. I just started more."

The woman panted as she struggled to dump the bulging basket into the cauldron. "There." The severe woman stared Joshua down, and he fought the urge to squirm as he swallowed his coffee. She reminded him a bulldog as she scowled and placed her hands on her hips. "Do you I know you, mister?"

His brows rose into his hairline. "I don't believe so, ma'am. My name is Dr. Ivy." He looked to Cadence.

"Pardon me. I failed to introduce both of you." Cadence gripped the wash paddle and held her slim hand toward the older woman. "Dr. Ivy, Mrs. Meade. Mrs. Meade, may I introduce Dr. Ivy, surgeon to the Union."

"Ma'am." He dipped his head and her scowl lightened.

"'Tis a pleasure, sir."

He turned to Cadence. "How were the children last night?"

Her shoulders lifted. "Truthfully? A bit frightened. The girls didn't like the sound of the cannons. Neither did James, though he tried hard not to show it. All of them were worried about you. It took quite a while to get them to sleep."

"But you settled in?"

"Yes, quite nicely. Maisey and Moxley are dears. And the children slept with me, so I think they felt safe."

"You two are married?"

The sharp voice caused both Joshua and Cadence to turn with a start.

Mrs. Meade stood staring at them and continued, "It's a mighty good thing. I was worried. Ain't safe for an unmarried woman out here. 'Specially a comely one like your wife."

Crimson streaked Cadence's neck as she dipped her head. Joshua tugged his collar. "No, Mrs. Meade, you misunderstand. Nurse Piper and I are not married. She is a laundress and nurse for the Union and has agreed to care for my children while I work."

The woman's gray eyes flashed. "In your tent?"

"No!" He winced at the panic lacing his tone. "No, nothing like that. Nurse Piper and the children are staying with some friends of mine. My quarters are near the surgical tent."

Mrs. Meade eyed him as if he were the very devil. "I see." Her gaze shifted to Cadence and a knowing glance passed between them. Cadence looked away.

Mrs. Meade forced a tight smile that seemed altogether opposite of friendly. "I'll bring you more wash soon."

She scurried down the hill, glancing backward at Joshua as she departed. He bit into the fry bread and chewed, his eyes narrowing. "I don't like that woman."

"Hush." Cadence frowned and sliced more chunks of lye into the boiling pot. Grabbing the paddle, she stirred. The steam dampened the tendrils of hair around her temples. "If she is intent on making trouble, you need not give her a reason."

"There is too much to do for her to make trouble."

"Precisely. Put her meddlesome ways from your mind and rest."

Despite the truth of her statement, Joshua couldn't shake the feeling Mrs. Meade could cause more trouble for them than he ever would have expected.

Hours bled into days. The moans of agony fell into silence as death stole the life from those they could not reach. Between surgeries, Joshua grabbed fitful snatches of sleep. On the fourth day, or perhaps the fifth, he stumbled from the surgical tent. His neck and shoulders ached. His vision blurred to the point where he saw double. He no longer felt hunger. His body craved only sleep.

He blinked against the afternoon light, though it was mellowed by the thick rain clouds rolling in overhead. In some spots they were as dark as charcoal. The farmland was yet covered with the dead. A sickening stench putrefied the air. Gravediggers worked furiously, but their speed was no match for the number of slain.

Joshua winced as he looked up at the darkening sky. The downpour would do no good for those exposed to the elements. Thousands lay prostrate on the open ground with naught but hay beneath for comfort.

The slim form of a young woman hovering above a dead soldier snagged his attention. Her shoulders sagged, then shuddered. She was weeping. Cadence.

He walked swiftly toward her and lifted her gently to her feet, wiping the tears from her eyes with the pads of his thumbs.

She sniffled. "Forgive me. Is it silly to weep over one when there are so many?"

Her lovely face was streaked with grime, but she had never looked more beautiful.

"No, it's not silly. Your heart is tender. Don't let the cruelty of this place harden it."

She nodded and swiped away her remaining tears.

"Where are the children?"

"With Maisey. I felt guilty for not coming the past two days, so Moxley brought me this morning." She fell silent. Her fatigue was palpable.

"Have the children been sleeping?"

"Some."

"How long has it been since you've slept well?"

She shook her head. "I don't know."

His eyes widened. "What do you mean?"

She looked down. "It's hard to rest knowing the men are suffering. And Etta . . . well, she misses you."

He blew out a heavy breath. This was taking a heavy toll on everyone.

"So you care for my children through the night and wash laundry and tend to dying men during the day." Stubborn, wonderful woman. "You must not continue. You'll collapse."

She lifted her chin. "And how much rest have you received, Dr. Ivy?"

He snapped his mouth shut. Her rosebud lips twisted into a saucy smile. "It appears we suffer from the same malady."

He chuckled lightly. "Yes, it seems so."

Heavy footfalls approached. Joshua turned to see Captain Archer striding toward him, his countenance stern.

"Pardon the interruption, Dr. Ivy. Miss." His eyes flashed toward Cadence before settling like ice on Joshua. "I must speak to you immediately about a matter of utmost importance."

Unease rippled through his middle. He nodded toward Cadence. "Rest while you can." He followed the captain's quick stride, his senses screaming. From the corner of his eye, he felt someone watching him. He turned his head to see the snide smirk of Mrs. Meade from beside a tent. An itch nagged between his shoulder blades as he entered the captain's tent and stood stiffly.

Captain Archer faced him with a stern eye. "Dr. Ivy, it was my understanding when you requested permission to bring your family, the female in question was your wife."

Joshua said nothing.

Captain Archer paced, his hands behind his back. "As you are well aware, regulations and rules in the military are not merely in place as guidelines. They are foundational to ensuring peace. They are for the good of both the soldiers and civilians."

He stopped and glared. "This is why I find it so troubling to hear accusations that the woman caring for your children is not your wife."

Joshua lifted his chin but made no rebuttal.

The captain's face mottled red. "Blast it, man, what have you to say?"

Joshua clenched his teeth. "As of yet, I've not been asked anything."

Captain Archer's nostrils flared. "Is the woman caring for your children, the woman hired as a laundress by the Union, your wife?"

"No, she is not."

He straightened his shoulders. "I see."

Joshua kept his gaze direct. He had no intention of looking away.

"Dr. Ivy, did you intend to deceive me?"

"I don't see how I could deceive you when you never asked."

The captain slammed his fist into his makeshift table, causing the inkwell to tip and the papers to scatter. "There is such a thing as propriety, Dr. Ivy! Christian behavior and decorum. I could scarcely believe it when Mrs. Meade told me. Especially when I witnessed your behavior with the young woman."

"My behavior has been nothing but honorable, sir."

The captain speared him with a hard look. "You may have kept your distance from her, but I witnessed your interaction with her several mornings ago." His lined face softened. "I may be gray-headed, but I am neither blind nor deaf, Dr. Ivy. I can recognize a man in love."

Joshua's breath snagged. "I was merely trying to comfort her. She had witnessed the devastation, and—"

"Enough!" He stroked his salt-and-pepper beard, his eyes shrewd. "I am not foolish enough to accept the word of one silly busybody. I have checked with several nurses working here, all of whom vouched for Nurse Piper's character after acknowledging they worked with her in Washington."

Joshua relaxed a fraction. "All is well then."

"No, it is not. You see, they were also under the impression Nurse Piper was married and insisted she wore a wedding band while working in the hospital. Miss Dix is quite adamant, as you well know, about the requirement for nurses. They must be either married or widowed to be considered, and Miss Piper is neither. We cannot have unmarried women mingling and treating men. It's unseemly, and we certainly cannot have them tending children for unwed physicians. So I'll be more direct. Is Miss Piper married to anyone?"

He paused for a moment, fearing his response would end the nursing career Cadence loved. *Forgive me, Cadence.* "No, she is not."

"Then there is only one solution that can resolve this matter satisfactorily to salvage both of your reputations."

"Speak plainly, Captain."

His whiskered jaw firmed. "You will either marry Nurse Piper immediately or you will be relieved from your post as physician. The choice is yours."

chapter 25

CADENCE KNEW SOMETHING WAS WRONG the moment Joshua stormed to her side and pulled her away from her washpot, yanking the paddle from her hand and tossing it into the grass.

"What are you doing?"

He cupped her elbow. "We need to speak. Now."

Her heart pinched as he led her into the privacy of the woods behind the laundering tents. Within the canopy of the forest, she turned to him and clutched his sleeve.

"What's wrong? Is it that man who was watching the children? Is he here?"

He blinked and shook his head. "No. No, nothing like that."

"Oh." Her heart resumed its normal rhythm. "Then what is it?"

He swallowed. "Captain Archer, with the help of Mrs. Meade, has discovered you are not married."

She studied him, trying to understand. "Am I supposed to be?"

"If you remember, according to Miss Dix, yes."

"But you came to me during the influenza outbreak and asked me to come to the hospital to work."

A muscle ticked in his jaw. "Why do you think I suggested you wear that wedding band while at Judiciary Square?"

"To eliminate questions. To protect my reputation. But you promised my unattached status would not be an issue. You said there were measures you could take to ensure I could continue working."

He rubbed the back of his neck. "Which is why I'm here now. And it's not just the fact that you're unmarried. Captain Archer also believes having you care for my children with both of us unwed is . . . indecent."

"He thinks we are—?"

"Yes." Sorrow clouded his expression as his gaze held hers. "Forgive me. In my haste to protect my children, I didn't consider every aspect of this situation. In the tumult of war, who could imagine superiors noticing or caring about the platonic arrangements between a laundress and a surgeon?" He blew out a thick breath. "I hold sway at Judiciary Square. I have none out here. The fault is mine."

"What shall be done then?"

His lips pressed tight. "We have two options. We either marry immediately or we return home, for neither of us will be allowed to treat the wounded any longer."

She stepped backward. Marry? Marry Joshua? She lifted her gaze, and a warm flush washed through her at the intense look in his eyes. Heat spread through her belly. "I—I don't know what to say."

"I know. It's a horrible shock. I don't want you to feel you have to choose, but Captain Archer has given us an ultimatum."

So she had been correct—Joshua didn't want her. Not really.

He needed to protect the children. He wanted to care for the wounded men. She was only the means to an end.

She fought the urge to cry as she felt a tickle rise in her nose. "And Captain Archer assures us both we can continue to doctor and nurse upon our marriage?"

"Yes."

"And you believe the children are still safer here than back home with Miriam?"

"For the time being? Yes."

She looked into his eyes and her world tilted. She loved him. How she yearned to have him love her in return, but she would not throw herself at his feet.

"What do you want, Joshua?"

She sucked in a breath when his warm fingers encircled hers. He stepped so close, she could feel his breath upon her cheek. Could see the golden flecks mingled with the chestnut-brown stubble lining his jaw.

His voice was low when he spoke. "Don't make the mistake of thinking Captain Archer is forcing me to do something against my will, Cadence. The situation is unusual, granted. But I promise you, you would give me no greater honor than becoming my wife. I promise to care for you and protect you with every ounce of strength I possess until I cease to draw breath."

Her heart quivered at his words. He was a man of passion. A tempestuous storm. Had she not tasted his intensity once? Surely he would grow to love her, wouldn't he?

God, help me be the wife he needs.

He lifted her chapped hands to his lips and pressed a kiss to the back. "Will you marry me, Cadence Piper?"

Lord, help me.

"Yes, I'll marry you."

Every fiber of Cadence's body trembled as she stood before the dour military officers under the grove of pines.

Once plans were made, Joshua had been granted leave to gather the children. Moxley, Maisey, Penelope, James, and Etta had all returned with Joshua and Cadence to the battlefield to make hasty preparations under the watchful eyes of Captain Archer.

The chaplain clutched his worn prayer book, swaying on his feet in exhaustion. Cadence's groom was nowhere to be found.

She rubbed her clammy hands down her skirt and winced. Her navy work dress. A poor wedding gown. Nothing about this moment was how she'd once pictured it.

The chaplain turned to the captain and muttered, "Where is the groom?"

All eyes flew to her.

Squaring her shoulders, she croaked, "He'll come."

The men exchanged glances. She looked down at the grass beneath her boots and let her eyes slide shut. *Please, Joshua, come.*

In seconds, the sound of feet tramping through underbrush could be heard in the woods. Heads turned. Relief cascaded through her as the children burst from the trees, beaming. Penelope carried a bouquet of wildflowers . . . tiny blooms of purple, white, and yellow. She ran to Cadence's side and thrust them into her hands.

"Sorry. We tried to hurry, but Papa Gish was insistent. Said you should have a proper bouquet."

Cadence inhaled the scent of the blossoms and cupped Penelope's soft cheek. "They're beautiful. Thank you."

She was rewarded with the child's sunny smile. "I'm so happy you're going to be my mother."

Her mother.

Cadence was woozy. She was gaining a husband and three children all in one day. James and Etta had joined them, but where was Joshua?

Her heart tripped as he emerged from the shadows of the forest. He was wearing clean trousers and a crisp white shirt that only made his tanned skin seem more golden. He had shaved, and his chestnut hair was combed, but it was his dark eyes that caused her breath to flee. They were fixed on her with an intensity that made her toes curl.

He walked toward her slowly and grasped her hand. "Are you ready?"

She could manage nothing more than a simple nod. The flowers in her left hand quivered.

His strength enveloped her as he gently led her toward the circle of austere men waiting under the grove of trees. Cadence caught Maisey's sweet smile, and a ripple of peace washed through her.

The captain eyed Joshua sternly. "Are you ready to do your duty by this young lady, Dr. Ivy?"

He lifted his chin. "It is no duty, sir. It is my honor and privilege."

She warmed at his words and watched as the faintest twinkle lit the captain's eyes. "Very well. You may begin, Chaplain."

The weary clergyman slowly opened his prayer book. "Dearly beloved, we are gathered here today in the presence of God . . ."

Cadence heard few of the words, save her own when the chaplain turned to her and asked if she promised to love, honor, and obey Joshua until death parted them.

"I do."

Yet despite the whirlwind moment, she would never erase the memory of the determination in Joshua's eyes when he gazed at her and promised to love, honor, cherish and protect her until death. A fire blazed in their depths.

"I do."

Words, actions, movements . . . all else was a blur until the chaplain's directive cut through the fog. "You may now kiss your bride."

Her pulse galloped. What would he do in front of all these people? The memory of his passionate kisses rippled through her, causing a flash of heat that was anything but proper in front of these sour-faced men. Joshua faced her fully before brushing her lips with a chaste kiss and pulling away.

She was bereft but merely dropped her gaze when the chaplain offered his congratulations and asked for signatures on the marriage certificate. After the ink was blotted and dried, Captain Archer turned to Joshua. "You may have leave for the rest of the day. No need to report back until tomorrow morning."

He shook the captain's hand. She was given little time to think as James, Etta, and Penelope surrounded her, hugging her waist. Moxley slapped him on the back as Maisey came up behind her and whispered in her ear.

"Don't worry about the children, dear. I'll watch them tonight."

"But I didn't expect—"

The matron winked. "You two go on and enjoy yourselves."

Cadence's face flamed. A hand slid around her waist as a masculine voice sounded near her ear. "Thank you, Maisey. I'm in your debt."

The older woman harrumphed. "You certainly are, young man." He laughed and kissed her cheek.

"Go on with you now." Blushing, she waved him away. Cadence braved a glance at Joshua. Her husband. That would take some adjustment.

He slid his hand from her waist, down her arm, and wove his fingers between hers. A smile tipped his mouth. "Feel like riding to Bristoe Station, then perhaps a walk?"

Butterflies fluttered in her stomach. She nodded.

Setting her atop his mount, they rode in the direction of Moxley and Maisey's farm but veered away from the road leading up to their house, instead choosing a narrower path. When the foliage grew thick and cool, he pulled the horse to a stop.

Placing his hands on Cadence's waist, he helped her down carefully.

"Where are we going?"

He merely smiled. "It's a secret."

They said nothing. The only sound was the occasional scamper of a squirrel, the distant call of birdsong, the horse's soft clop as he followed behind, and the soft crunch of leaves and twigs beneath their feet. Joshua led her with purpose, as if he had a destination in mind. How could he? What had he been doing before the ceremony?

They walked for fifteen or twenty minutes, and she relished the solitude with him, the sloping terrain leading them farther into the quiet of nature. Trees towered overhead, providing a shadowy canopy. Ferns, moss, and wild mushrooms covered the forest floor. The loamy scent of earth filled her nostrils. He glanced over his shoulder as he tugged her along.

"You seem awfully sure of your destination, Dr. Ivy."

He winked. "Perhaps."

She still clutched the bouquet in her free hand. Lifting it to her nose, she inhaled the scent. "I don't think I thanked you for the flowers. They're lovely."

He offered a sheepish smile. "I doubt it was the wedding of your dreams, but I wanted to do something for you."

Her heart warmed. "And you did."

He paused to help her over a particularly jagged rock. "Forgive me for not saying anything earlier, but you look beautiful."

A laugh burst from her throat. She freed her hand and grabbed a fistful of her skirt fabric. "In this?" She shook her head. "It's a poor excuse for a wedding gown. My hair is a mess and I've not had a chance to bathe—"

Dropping the reins, he silenced her by stepping close and studying her face before rubbing his thumb across her lips. All protests fled.

"Beauty isn't something you have to put on, Cadence. It's who you are. Believe me when I say you are the most beautiful woman I've ever known."

He stepped away suddenly, leaving her knees weak and senses reeling. It took her a long moment to realize he was continuing on. She hurried to keep pace with him. Soon the sound of rushing water filled her ears. The narrow trail turned to reveal the front of a small cabin.

Cadence breathed. "It's lovely. What is this place?"

"Moxley's hunting cabin." He grinned. "Although we've been known to use it for other things on occasion."

"Like taking slaves to freedom?"

"Perhaps."

"Are we near a river?"

He smirked like a mischievous boy. "Better. Wait."

Pausing only to tie the horse to a tree, he slipped behind her and led her down a sloping hill, stopping near the bottom to place his hands over her eyes.

She laughed. "What are you doing?"

"Getting ready to surprise my bride." His voice caused shivers of pleasure to skim down her neck.

She shuffled forward slowly, letting him carefully lead her

over the bumpy terrain. "You could just ask me to close my eyes, you know."

"I could, but I have a sneaking suspicion you would peek, Mrs. Ivy."

Mrs. Ivy.

Another long minute and he pulled her to a stop. The sound of rushing water was louder now, the air cooler. Warmth cocooned her back as Joshua murmured in her ear. "Ready?"

She nodded. "Ready."

He removed his hands from her eyes and she drew a quick breath. The spot was like something from a picture book. Stone walls jutted up from the ground. From the mouth of a cave in one of the walls, a small waterfall gushed forth, spilling into a clear stream. She looked to Joshua.

"It's not much, but I thought the spot was idyllic. Do you like it?"

"It's beautiful."

He sobered and reached for her hand, his touch gentle. "Cadence, I—" he swallowed—"I want you to know that I have no intention of taking liberties." A muscle worked in his jaw. "None of this was your idea. The last thing I want to do is hurt you."

What to say? To think? Part of her was relieved. The other part was disappointed. What was wrong with her?

"If all you want to do is bathe and catch up on your sleep, you have my promise to give you all the privacy you need."

He stood waiting for her to do something, say something. She had no way to express what she was thinking. What she needed or wanted.

Instead, she responded with "Thank you."

He squeezed her hand before releasing her.

Yet she was consumed with the thought that she had been rejected once again.

———— ✿ ————

Darkness had fallen, bringing a measure of relief from the sticky summer humidity. After Cadence had prepared them a meal of corn bread cakes and coffee, Joshua had urged her to bathe as she'd longed to do. He gritted his teeth as he listened to her gentle splashes. Even though he stayed inside the cabin to afford her privacy, his mind wandered far too much.

This was surely a way to drive himself mad. They were joined together now, before God and man, and yet he would not touch her if she didn't desire it. His heart thundered. He loved her. Loved her too deeply to let anything or anyone hurt her . . . even if that someone was him.

A piece of wood snapped in the fireplace, sending up a pillar of sparks. He inhaled the acrid odor and ran his fingers through his hair. Hadn't he hurt her already? Inadvertently shackling her to a man she didn't love, to be mother to three children and laundress to a group of grouchy Union surgeons? An ache burned in his chest. Their marriage ceremony must have been a disappointment. No family. No fancy dress or trim. Not even a ring he could offer her as of yet.

Growling, he took in their lodgings for the night. A far cry from a nice hotel with feather pillows and a soft mattress. A poor man's honeymoon.

"You'll never be anything but trash."

He slammed his eyes shut against the old barb resurrecting itself. How many times a day had he been told that very thing while living on the streets? Twenty? A hundred? Perhaps the cruel, sneering faces had been right. Look at him now. Cadence deserved so much more and he had naught to offer her.

Droplets of water hit his face, startling him from his morose thoughts. "Huh?"

He turned to see Cadence standing there in her navy dress, eyes dancing, dimples deepening as she smiled down at him. She was squeezing excess water from her long hair, twisting it like a cord. She flicked more water at him and laughed before releasing the waist-length tendrils. His breath caught. She was beautiful.

"You're glaring at the fire."

He released a long exhale and forced a smile, praying it would scatter his dark musings. "Just tired, I suppose."

"Understandable." She scooted down next to him, arranging her skirt, and tossed a handful of leaves into the fire, watching them burn. "Truthfully, I thought you'd be asleep by the time I finished."

Hardly. As if he could sleep with the thought of her being so near. Every nerve was stretched taut. *God, help me.*

"If you'd like to bathe, the stream is free."

Upon hearing the cheerfulness in her voice, he turned to study her. "You don't have to pretend, you know."

A line furrowed between her brows. "Pretend?"

"To be happy about all of this." He waved his hand toward the rough walls and crumbling chinking.

Her eyes rounded. "What do you mean?"

He ground his jaw. "Your honeymoon suite." He shook his head. "A bath in a stream. A musty cabin for a room. I can't even give you a proper meal."

He stood, suddenly angry, and stomped out the door, ready to let the cold slap of water dull the heat pouring through him.

"Just one minute, Joshua Ivy!" Cadence's hand curled around his arm and tugged him backward.

He turned to see her fuming, blue eyes snapping fire. His

own ire melted as she stood facing him looking like a riled kitten.

"This is our honeymoon, and in no way are you going to ruin it with your surliness. Look around you." She opened her arms wide. "God created this spot. His handiwork is everywhere. A waterfall and trees. Stars shining overhead and—" a blush rose to her cheeks—"solitude. What makes you think we would need anything more?"

He reached for her slowly, letting his hands slide around her waist. "You deserve so much, Cadence. And I—"

"You are more than I deserve . . . Husband."

The way she said the word ignited a fire inside. He looked into her eyes and waited, his heart hammering. His gaze dropped to her lips. A moan wrenched from his throat as his fingers moved through the wet tendrils of her hair.

He couldn't, wouldn't break his promise to her. Not if she didn't want his affection. If he kissed her, he would be unable to stop.

"I'll bathe now." His voice was hoarse as he let her hair slip from between his fingers. He walked to the edge of the stream, far away from the cabin and the light shining through the single window. It was dark here. She would respect his privacy. He carefully removed his clothes and slid into the cool water, letting the ripples wash away the thick tension cording his muscles.

Long minutes later, he heard a rustle followed by the sound of stirring water and a light splash. His senses snapped.

"Who's there?"

"It's me."

Cadence's voice, soft and timid, drifted across the water. His chest pounded.

"What are you doing?"

A thin shaft of moonlight glistened through the trees overhead, illuminating her form as she drifted toward him in the inky stream. Only her head and bare shoulders appeared over the top of the water.

"Joining you."

She couldn't do this. How did she think he could possibly maintain a modicum of self-control? Panic clawed at his throat.

She was before him now, water dripping from her hair, her lashes as she gazed up at him. Had the water felt cold only moments ago? Now it was warm. Far too warm.

She tilted her head and studied him. "Why did you think this time with you here would possibly be less than desirable for me?"

He said nothing, only stood in silence, a war raging within him.

"Being here with you, it's all I want."

His breath thinned. What was she saying?

Her lips curved, though a flicker of uncertainty flashed through her eyes. "You wanted to kiss me just moments ago. Am I wrong?"

"You're not wrong."

He knew then she was as desperate for him as he was for her. Reaching for her through the water, he found her waist and dragged her to him. With his free hand, he pushed the wet hair away from her face and lowered his head slowly, waiting and hovering, giving her plenty of time to pull away. Instead, her hands slid up his chest and her lips eagerly met his.

Then he was lost.

chapter 26

CADENCE AWAKENED IN THE DARKNESS of the cabin, wrapped in warmth. Contentment seeped through her like warm honey. Where was she? She blinked, but the night offered no light. Steady breathing filtered through her senses, along with the slow rise and fall of a muscular chest beneath her head.

Joshua.

Wonder rippled through her as she reached up to stroke his stubbled jaw. He stirred slightly and drew her closer before falling into slumber once again.

Her pulse tripped at the memory of his tender touch and passionate whispers of affection. She knew she had loved him before, but now? She buried her face against his chest and inhaled the fragrance of him. He had branded himself on her heart, irrevocably knitting them together.

He stirred and nuzzled her ear. "It's not morning yet, is it?"

"No. Far from it."

"Good." His voice was low and husky. Shivers skimmed her skin. "What has you awake, my love?"

"You."

"Snoring already, eh?"

Giggling, she shifted to her side, trying her best to see his handsome face in the darkness. "Not yet." She reached for his hand kissed his knuckles. "I was lying here thinking how blessed I am to have you as my husband." She swallowed. "And wondering if you wish you hadn't . . . that is, if we—"

He sat up. "What?"

She bit her lip. "I suppose I wonder if perhaps I was too forward, coming to you like I did. If you really don't want a marriage in that way, I—"

His arms circled her as a chuckle burst low in his throat. "I thought I made my feelings on the matter perfectly clear."

Heat crept into her cheeks.

"Do you know why Captain Archer insisted upon our marriage?"

She frowned. "Because of how it looked, with me caring for your children, my unwed status as well as yours."

"Partially, yes." His lips brushed a kiss across her forehead. "But what convinced him that something must be done immediately was the way I looked at you."

Her heart skipped. "He told you that?"

"Yes. He watched me whenever you were near and knew I was besotted." His fingers grazed her face. "Do you yet need convincing, Mrs. Ivy?"

She whispered, "I think I might."

She heard rather than saw his smile.

"Then I'm happy to oblige."

* * *

Cadence carried the bulging basket of clean linens toward the surgical tent. It had been four days since she and Joshua had wed and they had barely seen each other. He rarely left the surgical tent, performing operations continually, and had only come to see the children once, whereupon he'd fallen into an exhausted slumber. The children missed him, but she felt she was going mad with the need to talk to him, be with him, kiss his lips.

Love was a strange malady.

At least here, tucked within the seclusion of Moxley and Maisey's home, the children were safe from whatever danger lurked in Washington. How odd to find safety in the middle of war.

She climbed up the hill and paused at the flap of the surgical tent. She hesitated, smoothing the wayward tendrils of hair away from her face. She must look a disheveled mess.

She slipped inside and wrinkled her nose. The air was filled with the putrid stench of disease, mingled with the sour odor of whiskey and the sharp sting of lye. Runners were carrying away an unconscious man with his left leg reduced to a bandage-wrapped stump. She glanced to the corner where a large tub sat, filled with dismembered limbs. She turned away, sick at heart.

Another surgery was going on in the far side of the tent, but a quick scan revealed Joshua washing his hands and arms in a bowl of soapy water. His back was to her and his shoulders were slumped. Poor man.

She clutched the basket of linens and smiled when he turned and saw her. His face lit up and the shadows of fatigue disappeared. Walking swiftly toward her, he took the basket from her and set it on a nearby table. "You look more beautiful than ever, Mrs. Ivy."

"I confess I could have sent someone else up here with the clean linen, but I was missing my husband."

Private Wilson walked by and shook his head. "You two are pitiful." He winked to soften his words.

With a chuckle, Joshua splayed his hand across the small of her back and led her to a quiet corner. "How are the children?"

"Enjoying the farm. Moxley has them feeding the hogs, milking the cow. Told Etta and Penelope they can bring home a kitten if you agree. James is more partial to the dog." She smiled to soften her words. "They miss you terribly, though."

He rubbed his eyes. "Just as I miss them. And you most of all." His expression turned grave. "There's news. We are to return to Washington to assist the wounded being sent to Judiciary Square."

"How soon?"

He shrugged. "It might be days, but it could take longer. Perhaps even weeks."

She brightened. "That's good, isn't it? You'll get much more rest. We'll have plenty of able-bodied men and women to treat the soldiers." At his somber glance, she realized what troubled him. "The children."

"Yes. When we return, I'll be spending my days at the hospital. How can I keep you all safe if I'm not with you? I'll hire Zeke again, but—"

She stopped him, placing her hand against his chest. "I know! I can take the children to my father's house if need be."

Joshua blinked. "Your father." A muscle ticked in his jaw. "How do you think he will respond when he discovers I whisked his daughter away as laundress for the Union only to bring her back as my wife?"

Cadence's heart dropped. Everything had been so sudden, she'd not given a moment's thought to what this would mean to Father. "Once he recovers from his initial shock, he'll be welcoming. I think."

"Even at that, my enemies will be watching you, whether at our home or your father's."

She grasped his hands. "You can't control everything, Joshua. At some point, you'll have to trust God and leave the children in his hands."

He brooded. "I don't even know who I'm fighting."

"But God does. All the more reason to trust him. Besides, we've been gone so long, perhaps the snooping man has given up."

"Perhaps." But he didn't look convinced.

"There is nothing you can do about it today." She wove her fingers between his.

He readily acquiesced, but Cadence noticed the troubled light never left his eyes.

With the staggering number of casualties, it was weeks before Joshua's work slowed enough to enable them to pack up their meager belongings and locate a wagon and team that could carry them all back to Washington. Theirs joined dozens of others snaking their way toward the capital, carrying the wounded to the hospital.

They said good-bye to Maisey and Moxley with tears and an abundance of thanks.

Maisey pressed a small tin of tea leaves into Cadence's hands as they hugged farewell. "Don't forget our chat now. You hear?"

"I won't. I promise."

Moxley stepped forward and rested his weathered hands on the children's heads. "The Lord go before you and behind you. The Lord keep you. May his face shine upon you and give you peace."

Joshua grinned. "Why, I think you may have a soft spot for them, my friend."

Moxley swiped under his nose. "Ha! Near destroyed my barn."

Etta lurched forward, hugging him around the knees. "I wuv Mith-tuh Mock-wee."

A big tear rolled down the man's cheek. "Blamed hay fever. Always making me sick."

The journey to Washington did nothing to cheer their spirits.

Carnage colored the roadway, turning the journey into a nightmarish spectacle. Dead horses, bloated corpses, and splintered wagons choked the route, forcing the line of travelers to slow and ease around the scattered wood. Empty artillery and abandoned knapsacks littered the ground. Flies buzzed around the slack, open jaws of both dead beasts and men.

As they passed one particularly gnarled form, Cadence heard Penelope's gasp in the back of the wagon. She turned in her seat next to Joshua on the driver's bench and captured her daughter's horrified gaze. "Don't look, sweetheart."

Penelope nodded, and Cadence offered a thankful nod to James when he slipped his arm around his sister, tugged her down in the wagon bed, and pulled out a picture book.

Cadence turned and let her own eyelids slide closed. Though she was loath to confess it, the ghastly slaughter around them, combined with the lurching of the wagon, had unsettled her own stomach. Nausea crept up her throat and refused to leave.

Joshua glanced her way. "Holding up?"

"Yes, but it's far worse than I imagined."

His face was grim. "I was thinking the same thing. If I'd known, I would have requested we return some other way and spared the children these images."

"The Union would have denied you. The wounded soldiers on the wagons need you nearby. Their suffering must be intense." Her stomach twisted.

He eyed her. "Are you feeling well? Your complexion is ashen."

Bile rose swiftly. "I—forgive me. You must stop the wagon."

He halted the team and pulled the brake as she stumbled from the bench, not waiting for his help to climb down. She ran to the side of the road and retched. Strong hands slid across her back and held her as she finished. She wiped her mouth with her sleeve.

"How long have you been feeling poorly?" Joshua's concerned face swam before her.

"In truth? Since yesterday. It will pass." She forced a brittle laugh. "Perhaps your tough nurse has grown soft."

He offered a lopsided smile. "I don't think that's it. Do you feel like getting back in the wagon, or do you need more time?"

She inhaled a breath but nearly choked on the putrid air thickening the valley. "I'm fine."

He gently lifted her to her feet. The children stared from over the edge of the wagon, and she offered a smile. Penelope worried her lip, her fist clutched around the secret object she refused to relinquish. Etta popped her thumb in her mouth and watched Cadence climb atop the driver's bench.

Joshua gave her a sideways glance but didn't say anything.

"What is it?"

He frowned. "This. All of this. It's been too much for you. If you've contracted an illness in camp . . ."

"You're being too protective. I could catch such an illness anywhere."

"But all you've been forced to endure. The changes—"

"One change was particularly delightful."

He turned to her, his mouth quirking into a full smile that stole her breath and warmed her completely. "I agree."

He reached for her hand and tugged her close before urging the team back into motion.

She let her head fall against his shoulder as the wagon bounced over the rutted road. Soon they would be home and all would be well.

⸙

Joshua stood before Albert Piper's front door and pulled at his too-tight collar. They'd been back in Washington for three days, but still he felt unprepared for this meeting.

Cadence looked up at him with sympathy. "He will adore you. Stop fretting."

"Will he?"

"How could he not?" She tossed him a teasing smile. "You won me over, after all. And I was not easily captured, if you remember." Her grin dimmed. "I'm the one he'll be disappointed in. Not you." She twisted her fingers together. "I only pray he hears me out."

Joshua frowned. "Speaking of that, you didn't tell your father of my boorish behavior upon our first meeting, did you?"

"I may have mentioned your occasional propensity to be . . . unpleasant."

He cringed. "This visit should be delightful."

She patted his arm and whispered with a devilish gleam in her eye, "Perhaps you should have been nicer to me upon our first encounter, Dr. Ivy."

How he wanted to flee this moment, whisk her away, and kiss her breathless. He winked. "How else was I to guard my heart from the most mesmerizing woman I'd ever seen?"

Cadence's cheeks pinked, and he raised his hand to knock. *Lord, grant me mercy in the eyes of her father.*

Footfalls sounded just before the door swung wide. Mr.

Piper's blue eyes, so like Cadence's, rounded before his mouth tipped into a wide smile.

"Cadence!" He leaned in, kissing her cheek, and eased back, his hands on her shoulders as he took her measure. "When the papers brought word of the horrors of Second Manassas, I confess I regretted ever giving you permission to go. I know you had far too little time to write, but I worried."

"I know, Father. It was difficult, but for none more so than our wounded. They need much prayer."

"Of course, of course." His eyes narrowed. "You've lost weight."

She smiled weakly. "There was so little time to eat. We worked ourselves hard. The last counts we heard were twenty thousand dead with thousands more wounded."

"Terrible. At any rate, I'm glad you're home now." Mr. Piper's shrewd gaze flickered to Joshua. "I thank you for escorting my daughter home . . . Dr. Ivy, wasn't it?"

"It was my pleasure, sir. Actually, I'd like to visit with you for a while, if you have the time."

His silver brows rose. "I see. Please, come in."

Joshua made no protest when Mr. Piper led Cadence inside, though surely he must have noticed she brought no bags with her. Or perhaps he thought Joshua would bring them in after their conversation was finished. He led them to the parlor, where a young man with dark hair sat reading a newspaper. Upon seeing them enter, he folded it in half, cast it on the table, and stood.

"Cadence. It's good to have you home."

She embraced the man and patted his cheek with affection. "You grow more handsome every day. How are you feeling?"

"Better. Some days I don't even need my cane, though I'm not sure I'll ever totally lose the limp."

Mr. Piper gestured to Joshua. "Tate, I'd like to introduce you to Dr. Ivy. He works at Judiciary Square Hospital. He escorted Cadence home. Dr. Ivy, my son, Tate Piper."

Joshua studied the man he'd heard so much about. Slave trader. Scourge of abolitionists. Cadence had spoken little of him, but then again, thus far they'd had so little time together. The gentle, easygoing fellow before him didn't seem like the impassioned trader he'd heard reports of.

Fixing a smile in place, Joshua clasped Tate's hand and offered a hearty shake. "It's a pleasure to meet you, sir."

"Likewise."

Mr. Piper cleared his throat. "Please, take a seat. You said you had something to discuss with me."

Cadence discreetly moved to sit next to Joshua on the sofa, an action that did not go unnoticed by her father. His gaze flickered to Tate's. A bead of sweat formed at Joshua's temple.

"Yes, sir, I do." He hesitated, searching for the best way to broach the topic. "I don't know how to say this."

"Go ahead, son. It's plain to see."

Joshua startled. "Sir?"

"You have feelings for my daughter, don't you?"

"Yes, but—"

Mr. Piper chuckled. "A blind man could see that, though I admit my surprise. Months ago, it appeared you two were more likely to take to boxing than anything else."

Cadence whispered, "Father . . ."

He ignored her plea. "So you came here to ask if you could call on her? Visit her from time to time, is that it? I suppose, depending on what opportunity allows and—"

"We were wed in Manassas." Joshua blurted the truth, and a heavy silence descended.

Mr. Piper stood slowly. "You took my daughter into a battlefield under the guise of patriotic duty, then had the audacity to take her as your wife? And did so without my permission?"

Cadence stood. "It wasn't like that! Captain Archer insisted we wed."

"What?"

Joshua nearly groaned and placed himself between Cadence and her irate father. "It's not what you're thinking, sir. I had to bring my three adopted children with me. Cadence has a heart of gold and offered to watch over them while I performed surgery. She stayed with the children in a home away from camp in a small town called Bristoe Station. I slept in a tent next to the surgical tent. Nothing happened, I assure you. Yet Captain Archer thought it did not look well for an unmarried woman to care for the children of an unmarried man." He straightened and lifted his chin. "Nor could I deny my growing affection for your daughter. He insisted upon our immediate marriage."

"I see." Mr. Piper's eyes narrowed. "Since you are so honorable and want to receive my blessing in this, I assume it's safe to believe you have not touched her since the wedding?"

Cadence gasped but Joshua tucked her behind him. "The only gentlemanly response would be to say I love my wife deeply, and we have been living as husband and wife as God ordained."

Mr. Piper's neck mottled red. "Do you not understand? Cadence is not like everyone else. She needs special care. She has a condition. The phrenologist said so."

Fury mounted. "He was wrong. Cadence is the brightest, most phenomenal woman I have ever known. There is nothing amiss with her."

"Then why could she never speak properly?"

"Stop!"

Joshua whirled to see tears streaming down Cadence's face, her lips trembling and chest heaving.

Mr. Piper swallowed. "Cadence, I—"

She held up her hand. "Please, no more." With a sob, she spun and fled.

Joshua looked at her father with a hard stare. "You need to make this right, sir. Your daughter adores you, but treating her like less than she is because of one man's opinion?" He shook his head. "That phrenologist was a charlatan. Perhaps sincere, but in error all the same. There is no link between stammering and mental capacity. And believing that so-called physician has caused wounds far more deadly than his words ever could."

He turned on his heel and went to search for his heartbroken wife.

From within the confines of her old room, Cadence wiped the vomit from her mouth and moved away from the basin on the washstand. She'd not been well since returning from the battlefield, but she'd done all she could to hide it from Joshua. They had been far too busy to rest since returning to Washington. That was what she needed. Rest.

Curling on the comfort of her bed, she tucked her legs into her middle and let the tears fall. Father's words had only confirmed her suspicions of what he thought of her, but to hear them flung from his lips stung more than she'd dreamed possible. Did he really think her simple? In need of someone smarter to guide her every decision . . . like a child?

Her throat swelled, and another sob scraped. Perhaps he was right. Her only true gift had ever really been her voice, and even that last attempt had ended in failure. What good was she? She pinched her eyes closed, letting the darkness wash over her. Poor Joshua. Saddled with a simpleton.

"A lie is only harmful if you believe it."

Dear Maisey. If only she were here now. Perhaps she would know what to do, what to say to take this ache away.

The verse Joshua had penned on the card after her last singing performance rose in her mind once again.

"Behold, what manner of love the Father hath bestowed upon us, that we should be called the sons of God."

Sons of God. Daughter. She inhaled a cleansing breath. Hadn't God already taught her much about her worth in him? And yet here she was . . . wallowing because she hadn't received her earthly father's approval.

Forgive me, Lord.

The door creaked open, and she tried to wipe away the moisture staining her cheeks. The bed dipped beneath her as warm hands stroked her back and toyed with the hair at the nape of her neck.

"He's not right, you know."

She tried to squelch a sniffle but failed. "How can you be certain?"

She heard the affection coloring Joshua's low voice. "Do you know how many nurses and stewards I sent away because they didn't have the capacity or intelligence to do what I required of them? You did, sweetheart. Do you think I would entrust my patients or, even more so, my children to someone I didn't trust with every fiber of my being?"

She sat up and swiped at her eyes. "Do you mean it? You're not just telling me what I want to hear?"

His handsome face creased into a gentle smile. "No, my love. The truth is, I trust you with the children more than I trust myself. You are God's gift to me." A muscle worked in his throat as he reached up to stroke her jaw. "And I will never stop thanking him."

He captured her lips, and her scraped heart throbbed a little less as she warmed to his touch. Bringing her close, he caressed her lips and groaned. "How you undo me, Mrs. Ivy."

She nuzzled his jaw. "Can we just stay here and ignore the rest of the world?"

His soft chuckle caused her skin to tingle. "Somehow I think your father will protest."

A soft knock sounded. "Cadence?"

They eased apart as he pushed off the bed. She smoothed her skirt and attempted to school the remainder of the wayward emotions fighting to swim to the surface. Joshua moved to stand behind her and cupped his hands around her shoulders.

She cleared her throat. "Come in."

Father's face peeped around the door. Deep lines framed his mouth. "Darling, I've been talking with your husband. Or rather, he's been talking to me." He swallowed hard. "I'm so sorry."

She dropped her gaze to the floor. "It's all right."

"No, it's not." He moved to stand in front of her, and when she heard his harsh sob, she lifted her head.

His eyes were glassy. "Your mother, God rest her, fought against what Dr. Philbright said, but I—" he shook his head—"I was so heartbroken, I let his diagnosis dictate my behavior toward you." He fisted the moisture away from his nose. "Please know I only wanted to protect you. You're my little girl." A wobbly smile broke through. "In some ways, that will never change."

She lunged toward him, wrapping her arms around his middle and burying her head in his chest. She soaked in his scent of tobacco and relished the feel of his arms surrounding her.

"Forgive me."

"I forgive you." Cadence eased back and looked up. "That is, if you can forgive me for marrying without your consent."

His mouth twitched. "I think that can be done. Your new husband seems like a good sort." He winked and tossed Joshua a look of respect. "Anyone who has the stamina to keep up with this headstrong daughter of mine deserves my utmost admiration."

"Father!"

Joshua chuckled. "I'm up for the challenge, sir."

"Good to hear it." His eyes twinkled. "And I understand I have grandchildren I've yet to meet. Why don't you all come for dinner tomorrow night? We can get acquainted then." He softly patted Cadence's hair. "I especially need to get to know my daughter."

She bit her lip. "I'd like that."

Joshua tugged on his collar again. "About my children, sir. There is something you need to know. Are you, by any chance, an abolitionist?"

chapter 27

Joshua watched Albert Piper entertain the children, holding them spellbound with silly stories. Dinner had gone remarkably well and everyone was in high spirits. Whether it was because his new father-in-law was coming around to the idea of their marriage or merely for the children's sake, he didn't know, but he was thankful.

Penelope had already claimed the lap of Papa Piper, as she called him, and James stood at his side, smiling as Albert showed them a kaleidoscope. Etta toddled around the room, content to peek at various knickknacks. The only one who seemed ill at ease was Tate, who stood in the corner of the parlor, looking solemnly out the window.

Penelope gasped in delight as she held the cylinder up to her eye and spun the end. "It's so pretty! Did you notice all the colors, James?"

"Sure did. I think it'd be neat to take it outside on a sunny day. Bet it would really light up then."

"You're right, son," Albert said. "The brighter the light, the more intriguing the kaleidoscope. My toy shop is full of things like this. Say—" he reached behind the chair and pulled out a small box, his eyes twinkling—"I just happen to have a few things with me now."

The children squealed their delight as they sorted through the treasures. Albert chuckled, clearly in his element. Joshua glanced to Cadence at his side, her bright countenance communicating a hundred things. Tate, however, never moved from the window.

"You all must come visit my toy shop."

Penelope turned to Cadence, her eyes bright. "Oh, Mother, could we?"

Cadence's dimples deepened. "Of course. Perhaps this week, if all goes well."

Amid their happy chatter, Etta suddenly dropped the ball and cup she was clutching and toddled over to Tate, her gaze curious. Joshua held his breath. Etta tugged Tate's trouser leg. He startled and looked down.

She looked solemnly up into his face. "Pay?"

Tate stared for a long moment. Joshua held his breath as Etta reached her fingers out and curled them around Tate's pale hand.

"Pay wif me?"

Tate's face crumpled, his eyes batting quickly. "I'm sorry. I can't today." He extracted his fingers from her grip and fled the room. Etta stared after him, her brow pinched.

Cadence hurried to kneel before her. "It's all right, darling. Uncle Tate likely isn't feeling well. I'll play with you."

"Mama pay."

"Yes. Mama will play."

Joshua bowed his head, listening to the happy chatter of his family but lifting a prayer for the battered soul of his brother-in-law just beyond the walls of the room.

———— ·♠︎· ————

Cadence wiped the bile from her mouth with shaking fingers. It seemed all she did the past weeks was cast her up accounts and nibble on soda crackers. The poor children. She did her best to hide it from them, but surely they had noticed her fatigue. She was prone to falling asleep in her chair. And it didn't help that Joshua had been working long hours at the hospital, caring for the overflow of wounded. He returned home every night exhausted. If it weren't for Miriam's daily help preparing food and cleaning, she would be in pitiful shape.

Even now, Miriam had the children out back tending what remained of the summer garden. Autumn would be upon them soon.

Cadence's stomach twisted and she groaned, stretching herself upon the bed. Why couldn't she shake this malady? How long had it been now?

She gasped and sat up, mentally calculating the days in her head. When had she last had her monthly? With the chaos of the battlefield, returning home and all that entailed, she had failed to notice. Suddenly everything made sense.

Cupping her hand over her mouth, she felt something warm burst in her chest. She slid her hand over her stomach with sweet reverence.

Could it be?

A rap sounded on the front door. She forced her wayward thoughts into order, pushed off the bed, and smoothed her hair. Walking down the hallway, she eased the door open. Her heart lurched.

Stephen Dodd stood before her, a crutch under one arm.

His empty trouser leg was pinned up, but it was not his recent amputation that sent a ribbon of dread spiraling through her middle. It was the dark look shadowing his face.

"M-M-Mr. Dodd! It's lovely to see you again. Please come in."

He nodded curtly and entered, his crutch lending an awkward thumping sound that echoed through the room.

"Won't you sit down?"

"That won't be necessary." His nostrils flared. "I came here to see if the rumors were true."

"What rumors?"

"The horrid rumor that you and Dr. Ivy are married."

She lifted her chin. "It's true. We married at Manassas. And I would protest the use of the word *horrid*. We are quite delighted."

"I see. And what kind of indiscretion happened in Manassas that would necessitate such a hasty wedding?"

Fury lashed. Before she realized what had happened, she heard the crack of her hand slapping his face. He flinched but did not turn away.

"How dare you accuse my husband of something so vile! Nothing of ill repute happened between us, and I would advise you not to bear false witness against him again."

"You were supposed to be mine, Cadence. Mine. I wrote you. You said I could."

She fought to calm her anger. "Mr. Dodd, allowing one to write is not the same as accepting a proposal of marriage."

Stephen breathed hard. "You knew how much I cared for you. How thoughts of you kept me going during the darkest days." He laughed bitterly. "I wasn't fool enough to think you returned my sentiments, but I believed, since you didn't say otherwise, that you would at least give me a chance to win your heart when I returned. Instead I find you married to another. The very man who took my leg."

Her lips trembled. "I never intended for any of this to happen."

His voice grew hoarse. "Did you ever intend to let me court you?"

"Perhaps I considered it at first."

"But you never wrote a word against it."

"You were fighting! What kind of a person would I be to dishearten and steal hope from a man who might die on a battlefield the next day?"

His jaw tightened. "So instead you let me believe we might have a future together."

She shut her eyes. "I tried to discourage you, but I was not bold enough. Not direct enough."

"You deceived me."

Hurt and shame collided in her chest. Tears pooled and fell. "Mr. Dodd . . . Stephen. Please. Forgive me. That was never my intention. I merely wanted to give you hope."

He gave her a look rife with sadness. "Truth hurts, but it ultimately heals. Deception, though done with good intentions, always destroys. Always."

She shuddered against a sob. "Please forgive me. The last thing I wanted to do was hurt you."

He nodded. "Some of the fault is mine. I expected too much from you. But please know trying to keep people happy is far more dangerous than simply being honest."

The door slammed behind him as he left.

chapter 28

CADENCE PUSHED THROUGH THE DOORS of Judiciary Square Hospital. She unbuttoned her cuffs and rolled up her sleeves, sending up a thankful prayer for Miriam's willingness to watch the children. When she'd asked the spirited woman if she minded keeping up with the young ones for the day, Miriam only cackled.

"Go on with you. Law, I done it for a long time, didn't I? You the best thing that ever happened to them young'uns. Nothing wrong with takin' a day for yourself now and then. We'll be just fine."

Leaving the family for the day had been easy enough, but escaping Zeke's watchfulness had been another hurdle altogether. The mountainous man was always close, keeping a sharp eye outside the house, just as Joshua paid him to do. Cadence had waited until he was distracted by a near accident between two irate drivers in front of the house before slipping out the back door. She had been granted a reprieve and she would not squander it.

Ever since Stephen Dodd's visit over a week ago, she had been needled with an urge to do something. To comfort, to help, to nurse. Was it penance of a sort? Possibly. Cadence sighed and eased as best she could down the clogged hallway of the hospital, looking for one of the nurses or stewards to receive instructions.

She hadn't yet told Joshua of Stephen's visit or of her certainty of the life growing inside her. She placed her hand across her still-flat stomach. His child. They had seen so little of each other the past several weeks. Life had been a whirlwind since Manassas . . . battle on top of battle with the hospital straining at the seams. If the only way she could see her husband was to work alongside him, that was what she would do.

And she would need to do it now before her condition became noticeable.

She rounded the corner and nearly collided with a lanky man who righted her with gentle hands on her shoulders. "Pardon me, ma'am, I—"

She looked up in surprise, then smiled at the expression on Honest Swindle's thin face.

"Well, happy day! If it ain't Nurse Piper! Er, that is, Mrs. Ivy. We are all tickled pink around here at the news. Doc grinned big as a cat who swallowed a canary when he told me the news. Says he claimed himself a bride and that bride was you! Goodness, you're a sight for sore eyes."

Laughing, she squeezed his hands. "It's good to see you too. I've missed your smile."

"Say, you looking for the doc? Good luck finding him in all this chaos."

"I'll find him, but what I really came to do today is lend my assistance."

His shoulders sagged. "Glad we'll be to have it too. As you

can see, there's more to be done than we have hands and feet for doing."

"Show me where to start."

Joshua kneaded the back of his neck. Another headache bloomed. He must figure out why Private Kelsie was not responding to the quinine. And of the wounded who had arrived from Antietam, over half of them suffered from hasty amputations with unclean instruments. He could already see the telltale signs of blood poisoning setting in. What aid could he possibly give them now that the damage was done?

A soothing melody drifted down the hallway. He froze. He knew that voice. Surely she wasn't here. She was protecting the children, wasn't she?

With a renewed burst of energy, he jogged in the direction of the sweet melody and stopped at the door of the room. Cadence stooped over a wounded soldier, softly singing as she changed the bandages on his mangled arm. When the air hit his exposed flesh, the man groaned.

"I can't. The pain."

"I know. It hurts. Focus on the words." She eased back into the hymn, her voice soft.

"Through many dangers, toils and snares,
I have already come.
'Tis grace hath brought me safe thus far
And grace will lead me home."

The man relaxed as she cleaned and rewrapped his red, gaping flesh. She smoothed his hair back from his forehead. "There now. Rest. It's done."

She looked up and stopped when her gaze collided with Joshua's, but there was no masking her pleasure upon seeing him. He didn't know whether to throttle her or smother her with kisses.

Instead, he crossed his arms and affected a stern posture. Might as well have a bit of fun. "Good afternoon, Mrs. Ivy."

She quirked her mouth. "Doctor."

"Might I have a word with you in my office?"

"Of course."

He led her down the hallway and opened the door, shutting it behind her with a decisive click. "What do you think you're doing?"

She whirled to face him, jaw slack. "Pardon?"

"Where are the children?"

She blinked. "With Miriam."

He narrowed his eyes. "And Zeke?"

She stared at him innocently, but there was something in her expression that told him there was more than she was saying. "Guarding the house, I presume."

"Really? I surely hope so, since that's what I pay him to do. What else did I secure his services to do? Oh yes, guard the woman I love."

She eased to the far side of his desk. "Maybe he's not very good at his job."

Joshua nearly laughed at the meek sound of her voice and the way it lilted. So much like Penelope's when she was caught in a lie. "You think so?"

She huffed out a breath. "Fine. Would you like to know what happened? I waited until he was distracted and slipped out the door. I wanted to come here and serve, Joshua. Is that so terrible?"

He approached the desk and she remained steadfastly on the opposite side. "No, not terrible. Why didn't you just ask me?"

"Because I thought you would say no." She brightened. "Would you have said yes?"

"Probably not."

A scowl darkened her exquisite face. "Joshua Ivy!"

"Sweetheart, the children need you. Until I'm sure this fellow, whoever he is, is gone, I would feel better if you and the children were under Zeke's protection during the day. That's all."

She crossed her arms and glared. "Sometimes I think you just married me so you would have a free nanny."

"Cadence . . ."

Moisture glossed her eyes. "The real reason I came is that . . . that . . ."

"What?"

She sniffled. "I miss you."

"I miss you, too, sweetheart. It won't always be like this." He moved to go around the desk and hold her, but she slipped out of his reach. Her lip protruded like a petulant child's.

He grinned. "I thought you said you missed me."

"I thought I did, but then you boss me and I wonder why."

He laughed and came toward her like an animal stalking its prey. "Come now, Mrs. Ivy, you care for me a little more than that, or else you wouldn't have come all the way here."

Her eyes flashed. "Don't flatter yourself. I came to nurse the wounded while I still can." Her cheeks reddened.

He froze. "What do you mean 'while you still can'?"

"I—that is—"

She was slimmer, and she hadn't been eating much since Manassas. She hadn't contracted an illness there, had she? Had he been so busy he hadn't even noticed his own wife slowly consumed by a malady? Terror seized him.

He raced to her and cupped her face in his hands, searching. "Tell me. Whatever it is, we can battle it together."

She lifted her face to his, but instead of the fear he expected to see, joy sparkled in her eyes. "I'm carrying your child, Joshua. Our child."

His mind blanked, then spun. His chest filled to overflowing.

"A baby? Our baby." Saying it out loud nearly made his knees give way. Reverently he knelt and kissed Cadence's stomach, then stood, peppering her face in kisses before claiming her lips. "I can't believe it. A baby."

She sighed and murmured against him between kisses, "Are you happy?"

"Deliriously so."

"Now you know why I came. I want to do my part, to help, but before much longer I'll not be able to. Once my condition becomes apparent, society will insist I stay at home."

He nuzzled her neck and kissed her once more. "Ah, my love, I'm afraid you'll be staying away from here long before then."

She stiffened. "What do you mean?"

"Now that you're expecting, you can't expose our child to the illnesses that pass through a war hospital. It's far too dangerous."

Her dreamy expression melted into ire in a flash. It was all he could do not to laugh.

"But, Joshua!"

"Sorry, sweetheart."

She glowered. "What are you saying?"

He kissed the tip of her nose. "I'm saying that if you show up here again, I'll be forced to send you back home, even if I have to throw you over my shoulder and carry you there myself."

Stubborn, pigheaded, mulish . . .

The hack bounced, causing her stomach to protest.

Much to her dismay, her husband had hailed a hack to take

her home from the hospital without delay. Her world, her independence was shrinking each day. After fighting for it for so long, was she now doomed to surrender it?

Another sharp dip. Nausea bubbled. She could not tolerate such a conveyance. Walking would be far preferable.

"Driver? Would you mind dropping me off at the dry goods store just ahead?"

He turned, frowning. "Your husband paid for much farther, ma'am."

"Yes, I know, but I've changed my mind. It would save me the trouble of coming back later, you see."

He sighed as if wearied by the fickleness of the female mind. She ignored the silent barb, only too happy when he pulled the hack to a stop and she felt her feet connect with solid ground once again.

As the rattling hack drove away, she placed a calming hand on her churning stomach.

Instead of going to the dry goods shop, she turned left. Perhaps she would pass Father's toy store and pick up a stick of candy for the children before heading home.

The streets were crammed with shoppers and soldiers, vagrants and politicians. Truly, Washington could hold no more people.

Finding Father's shop, she breathed a sigh of relief when she pushed the door open. Instead of nameless strangers, James, Penelope, and Etta turned to her with wide smiles.

"Mother!"

They rushed to hug her around the middle.

She returned their squeezes. "However did you come to be here?"

Penelope looked up, eyes dancing. "Papa Piper, of course! He called and asked if we'd like to see the shop."

James nodded. "Miriam said she was only too glad to be free of us. Said we could drive a mad dog off the back of a meat wagon." His brows pinched. "What's that mean?"

Cadence patted his head. "It means it's time to visit Papa Piper."

"Cadence!" Father emerged from the back. "I hope you don't mind me whisking my grandchildren away for a few hours. Miriam said you were at the hospital helping your husband, and I thought—"

She leaned forward and kissed his cheek. "I'm delighted. And clearly they are overjoyed." She smiled, watching them examine a dollhouse.

Footfalls sounded. Looking up, she saw Tate enter, a ledger under his arm.

"Father putting you to work?"

"Always." His smile came easy, until his gaze snagged on the children. Crimson mottled his neck.

Cadence puzzled. Why the strange reaction?

She glanced out the display window, wondering if Zeke lurked nearby. No doubt the large fellow stood guard, carefully attending his duties.

The bell jangled over the door. A well-dressed woman swept in, her small daughter in tow. The child's ringlets were perfectly coiffed. The woman's skirts held not a speck of dust nor a single wrinkle. Her daughter moved toward the dolls, but when the mother saw James and Etta, her strident voice cut the air.

"Amelia, stop!"

The child froze, looking back at her mother with wide eyes.

The mother sniffed, pointing at Cadence's children. "We will not shop in a store with *their* kind."

James dropped his gaze. Etta ran for Tate, hiding behind his legs. He noticeably stiffened. Penelope glared.

Cadence's breath caught in her throat, a thousand words bubbling for release. "Those are my children, ma'am, and I assure you they are quite well behaved."

The woman turned to Cadence with an incredulous expression. "Yours? You cannot be serious! You have taken in—?" She used a term so offensive it made Cadence choke.

Cadence moved toward the children, squeezing both Penelope's and James's shoulders. "I'm quite serious."

Father straightened. "Ma'am, as owner of this shop, I ask you to peruse with kindness and decorum."

"Not as long as they are here. Come along, Amelia." She turned to leave before whirling back, pointing her long finger at Etta and sneering. "Trust me. Heathens like her need to know their place."

Fury iced Cadence's veins. "Etta's place is right where she is . . . being protected by her uncle from the acid tongue of a mean-spirited woman."

The stranger's eyes narrowed. "It would be better on the auction block."

Father stepped forward. "You may leave."

The mother and daughter left. Cadence kissed James's and Penelope's heads. "I'm sorry for her remarks. What she said . . . it's not true."

"I know." James frowned. "Still hurts."

She rubbed his back. "I know." Moving to scoop up Etta, she murmured, "I'm sorry, my love."

The toddler wrapped chubby arms around her neck, but it was Tate's expression that gave her pause. He stood silently, watching the little girl, as large tears ran down his cheeks.

chapter 29

CADENCE SLIPPED FROM THE TOY STORE, Father's admonition to return home and rest still ringing in her ears. She'd tried to hide her fatigue from him, but after spending the better part of an hour with the children, both he and Tate noted her sluggish steps.

"Here." He'd pushed a sack of candy into her hands. "Take this home to give the children later. You and Miriam could both use an afternoon off. Tate and I can bring them home in a few hours."

"Thank you."

She'd waved good-bye, though none of them had seemed to notice her departure, so engrossed they were in a game of checkers. Reaching into the bag, she pulled out a ginger drop and popped it into her mouth, praying it would soothe her stomach.

The streets were as congested as they'd been an hour before. Wagons rattled past. Hawkers called out, begging passersby to explore their wares. The commotion only added to Cadence's discomfort.

Holding a lavender-scented handkerchief to her nose, she had just passed an alley reeking with the odor of rotting garbage when an arm snaked out and yanked her into the shadows. Another hand clamped over her mouth, effectively silencing her scream.

She clawed at the steel-banded arms pulling her deeper into the alley. Her boots clattered against a glass bottle.

Warm breath fanned her neck. "No use fighting, princess. The Knights always emerge victorious." His whisper was a slither.

She kicked at the unyielding body dragging her backward, but it was fruitless. She was no match for the man's strength.

His hand moved from her mouth to her throat, squeezing. She longed to scream, but breath fled. Spots danced before her eyes.

A sudden crack, and her captor released her with a whoosh. She collapsed onto the gritty alley pavement in a heap. Pain burst in her hip and wrists. Groaning, she twisted to see an unkempt man lying facedown beside her. Zeke loomed overhead, a broken board in his hands.

"Zeke!" She scrambled up, wincing at the fiery darts in her hip, and threw herself into his arms.

He stepped back and glanced from side to side, while gently extracting himself from her grip. "There now, missy. Won't do for your reputation to be seen with me like that." He glared down at the unconscious attacker. "Ain't no one gonna hurt you. Not on my watch." His eyes narrowed. "How did you get free of the house without me seeing?"

She looked down. "I snuck out the back this morning and went to Judiciary Square. Joshua wasn't too happy with me, so he hired a hack to drive me home. The driver was so reckless, the wheels so rickety, that the drive made me sick, so I decided to walk the rest of the way. I—I—" She ended on a sob.

He patted her back again. "Can't protect you if you go sneakin' around."

She sniffed, wiping away the tears with her fingertips. "I know. Forgive me. It was foolish. I suppose the threats haven't been real to me until now."

Zeke lifted her chin to study her neck and grunted. "Hm. Turning purple. Ain't no hiding that from the doc." His dark eyes were sad. "Let's get you home."

Nodding, she took his arm. "Zeke? The man said something about the Knights always being victorious. What did he mean?"

The large man's lips firmed into a hard line. "It means we know who's after your husband now, and it's not good news."

Joshua picked through a broken crate, looking for any scraps of food he might find. When a fella's stomach cramped so much it felt like it was sticking to his backbone, he tended not to be picky about where his next meal came from.

It wasn't just for him. The other gaunt faces in the alley looked more desperate than he felt. They must have something to eat. Little Susan's cough was getting worse. He studied his dirt-crusted nails. They were no longer the small hands of a boy, but those of a man. A surgeon's. He held them up to the light. Crimson. Slick and glistening with blood.

Taking shallow breaths, he trembled and backed into a wall. The force of it stole the air from his lungs.

Faces crowded around him, their eyes beady, breath foul, and teeth snarling. "Trash. Rubbish. That's all you are. All you'll ever be. You can't save her. She's lost to you. They all are. Gone. Gone. Gone."

Through the crowd of faces taunting him, he could see Cadence reaching for him, far down the length of the littered alley. Her face was stricken with terror.

"Joshua, help me!"

He tried to push past the shrieking mob, but his feet wouldn't move, couldn't get free of the sticky tar keeping them in place. Before he could reach her, arms snaked around her and ripped her away. His blood ran cold.

"No!"

A sharp gasp caused him to sit upright.

His breath came in short heaves. He stared into the darkened bedroom and swallowed against his dry throat. At his side, Cadence stirred.

"What's wrong?" she mumbled sleepily.

He forced his heart rate to return to normal. "Nothing, sweetheart. Just a dream. Go back to sleep."

"Mmm."

She curled next to his side, and he studied her beautiful features before brushing a dark lock of hair from her cheek, relishing the silky feel of it between his fingers. Her breath evened and slowed as she drifted into slumber once more. His chest ached as the nightmare resurfaced. He loved her, far more then he'd ever dreamed possible. And now she was carrying their child. He shook his head. It still didn't seem real.

He pressed a kiss to her head and slipped from the bed. The dark foreboding refused to leave him be.

He stumbled to the washstand and splashed a handful of water onto his face before drying himself with a cloth. Moving to the window, he stared out, searching for the face of the nameless man who had tried to choke his wife. Who watched his house. More than one man, really. A horde of demons.

The afternoon's events had shaken him like marbles in a can. Zeke had blamed himself. Foolish notion, but the attack had rattled them all.

Joshua slammed his eyes shut. What if he'd lost her? The baby? He whirled away from the window and dropped into a chair, fisting his hair as all the horrid possibilities ran through his mind.

God, I can't do this.

Perhaps it would have been better never to have opened his heart at all. Spared himself all this anguish. Spend his time happily ensconced at Judiciary. He'd had purpose but no attachments.

This way of life was far too painful.

He'd already lost his parents and Papa John. He couldn't bear to lose another person he cared for. If one of them was ripped away, the bleeding would never stop.

chapter 30

"LOUISA, I COULDN'T EAT ANOTHER BITE."

The housekeeper frowned at Cadence and harrumphed, eliciting a slew of giggles from the children gathered around Father's table.

"You gonna turn down the only apple pie in Washington? Look at you. Gotta fatten you up, girl."

Cadence protested. "I had two helpings tonight."

"Two helpings ain't gonna make no difference. You got nothing to draw on if you get sick."

Cadence moaned. "I can't, Louisa. I fear I'll pop."

Louisa stormed into the kitchen, muttering the whole way. Laughter peppered the dining room.

Tate's eyes danced. "You've done it now, little sister."

She lifted her hands in a helpless gesture. "I can't make room I don't have." Her gaze flickered to Joshua. He had been quiet all evening. She fixed him with a meaningful look.

He seemed to understand. A small smile hovered around his

mouth and he nodded before clearing his throat. "Cadence may have even less room in the coming months." He chuckled when she pinched his arm. "She is in the family way."

Gasps of delight rose up. James grinned from ear to ear. He turned to Etta, who was busy fisting a biscuit into her mouth. "Did you hear that, Etta? Cadence is going to have a baby!"

Etta smiled through crumbs. "Baby!"

Cadence laughed. "Are you happy, children?"

James nodded. "Is it a boy or a girl?"

Joshua's mouth tipped. "We won't know until it comes."

Cadence's gaze drifted to Penelope, who was staring at her, wide-eyed. "What do you think, sweetheart?"

She shrugged. "That's good news, I guess. May I go play with Papa Piper's toys?"

Cadence's happiness deflated. "Of course."

Odd. She'd thought Penelope would have been ecstatic. Before she could ponder further, Father came around the table and embraced her while Tate moved to shake Joshua's hand and offer his congratulations.

"My little girl. A mother." His eyes misted. "If only your own mother were here to see this."

She kissed his cheek. "I know. You're an amazing grandfather already to our little ones. You'll be pure mush when the baby arrives."

He wiped his eyes. "I already love those children like they're my own. Isn't it strange how a heart knows no difference?"

Penelope's voice drifted down the hall. "Papa Piper, will you come play with me?"

"You're being summoned."

He patted her head. "I wouldn't have it any other way."

As the dining room drained of people, Cadence pushed away from the table and watched Joshua ease Etta down from her chair. The tyke toddled right up to Tate and grasped his hand, looking up into his face.

"Pay?"

He looked down and Cadence saw it then. The guilt, the shame he still carried. His chest heaved as he extracted his fingers. "I'm sorry, Etta. Not today." He walked swiftly from the room.

Joshua moved to fill the gap. "Come. I'll play with you."

Etta babbled as she led him toward the parlor, but Cadence bypassed all of it, intent on finding her brother. Where had he always gone when he was little and sick at heart?

Outdoors. To freedom.

Hastening to the back door, she slipped outside and let the cool air wash her skin. She peered through the darkness until she found him, head bowed as he clutched the narrow iron fence surrounding the garden.

Rocks crunched underneath her shoes as she approached. "Tate, what troubles you?"

In the silver moonlight, she could see his fingers tighten until his knuckles were white. "Nothing."

"*Nothing* doesn't drive you out here. You've done the same thing since we were children."

He expelled a harsh breath. "I can't do this. Every time I'm around them, it's a reminder of what I've done. What I am."

An ache knotted her chest. What could she possibly say to ease his pain? "Etta doesn't care, you know. She only seeks your companionship. She likes you."

He pushed away from the fence with a growl. "That's what makes it worse. If that babe grows up to learn what I did to people just like her, women, mothers, fathers . . ." He held his head. "For pity's sake, Cadence, it might have been her own birth mother that I captured and sold to a greedy buyer who wanted nothing more than another work mule for his field or another body to warm his bed."

She cringed. "Tate, you must stop. You'll drive yourself mad. You've asked God for forgiveness."

He looked up into the night sky as crystal tears ran in ribbons down his cheeks and disappeared into his dark beard. "Yet I cannot forgive myself."

Harsh sobs rent the air. Sinking to his knees, he clutched fistfuls of his hair. She knelt, wrapping her arms around his convulsing form, letting her own tears fall into his hair.

"Tate, listen to me. You cannot undo what has been done, but God has given you another chance. The opportunity to love as he has loved you. Give those children all you wish you could have done for those you wronged. And do the same to every human you encounter for as long as God gives you breath."

"What if this pain never leaves?"

She squeezed him. "I believe it will, but until it does, just love others and do the next thing."

They joined the children, who were happily ensconced in a game of dominoes. Etta was carefully arranging dolls upon a chair. When she saw Tate enter, her chubby face lit up into a smile. She ran to him and tugged his hand. "Pay?"

He swallowed. "Yes, Etta. I'll play."

She squealed and jabbered, showing him all the dolls and their pretty clothes. He must have shown the proper appreciation, for in moments she was carefully tucking them in his arms as he sat on the floor with her. His soft chuckle as she scolded him brought a bubble of laughter to Cadence's chest.

She turned to see if Joshua was watching but realized her husband was missing. "Where is Joshua?"

Father shrugged. "A friend of his stopped in and requested to speak with him. They are outside on the front porch."

A friend? She frowned. Who would have known they were here, save for Zeke?

Father looked at her and laughed. "Don't frown so. The man didn't seem alarmed. Come. I have something to tell you."

Forcing the dark musings away, she sat next to him on the sofa, noting the merry light dancing in his eyes. "What is it?"

"Did Tate tell you?"

"No."

Tate turned, a task made difficult with Etta climbing all over him. "I thought you should be the one to share the news, Father."

She looked between them. Father was about to burst. "What's going on?"

Father's brows rose as he beamed. "You, my dear daughter, have been asked to sing 'The Battle Hymn of the Republic' at a charity bazaar. That's not all. President Lincoln will be in attendance."

She gasped. Surely he was jesting. "This cannot be."

"It's true." Tate captured Etta's attention with another doll, distracting her for a moment. "Congressman Ramsey told me about it just today. Said the president would be attending and the congressman specifically asked if you would come and sing." Tate turned aside to his father. "The two things he speaks most often about are his son's death and Cadence's voice." Tate directed his gaze back to Cadence. "Apparently Lincoln is quite fond of 'The Battle Hymn of the Republic.'"

James's eyes rounded. "Fancy that. Singing for President Lincoln himself!"

Cadence's hand fluttered to her throat. "I couldn't. Last time I failed."

"Surely you'd not think of refusing." Father's smile dimmed.

"Cadence, it's the president of the United States! There's no higher honor. You could not think of turning the congressman down. And you'll sing beautifully, just as you always do. Don't let fear rob you of this opportunity."

The door opened and Joshua entered alone. She searched his face for any sign of distress, but he was the same as he had been at dinner. Solemn and quiet. Father waved him in.

James burst out, too excited to hold in the news, "Mother has been invited to sing for the president!"

Joshua's gaze swung to hers, brows raised. "Is this true?"

She offered a weak smile. "It appears so."

"When?"

Tate spoke up. "In three days."

So soon. She felt faint at the thought. So little time to prepare. Perhaps that was for the best. The more time beforehand, the longer she would fret.

"Perhaps I oughtn't . . ."

Father sighed. "Talk some sense into her, Joshua. She can't throw an honor like this away."

Joshua hesitated, then nodded. "I believe your father is right. You should do it."

Her eyes rounded. Never before had he pushed her when she felt unsure.

"I have not yet prayed about it. And the baby—"

"You would only be singing one song, would you not? Besides, such an opportunity might never come again. I insist."

She eyed him warily, but he looked away, carefully avoiding her gaze. Something was wrong.

"Who stopped by to see you?"

"It was only Zeke."

"It must have been important for him to come all the way here."

He shrugged. "Not really. Everything is fine."

Narrowing her eyes, she contemplated her husband. He was acting elusive.

Father enthusiastically forged ahead. "See there? Your husband is a physician, and he heartily agrees you and the baby should be in no danger. Enjoy the evening and the memories you'll make."

Tate's voice was gentler, as if aware of Cadence's hesitance. "Is it all right if I tell the congressman you'll perform?"

Joshua steadfastly ignored her, instead turning to give his attention to Penelope. Her irritation flamed.

"Yes, you may tell him I'll perform."

Three days. Three days to give the performance of her life and hopefully discover what secret her husband was hiding.

⁕

The following day, everything went wrong. Miriam left to nurse a neighbor who was ill, and Joshua was gone before Cadence awakened. She was certain now . . . he was purposefully avoiding her. But why?

The children were fractious, picking fights with each other all morning while doing their sums and reading, and little Etta clung to Cadence's skirts, begging to be held. The child's whiny pleas scraped her nerves raw. It was as if the entire family had flipped topsy-turvy.

Cadence had just given Etta her third cup of milk after no longer being able to bear her cries for more "gilk," when James and Penelope burst into the kitchen.

James scowled at his sister. "Give it back, Penelope! I know you have it."

The girl's eyes flashed with challenge. "Prove it."

Cadence fixed them with a stern glare. "What is this about?"

James crossed his arms over his chest. "I was playing with the toy soldiers Papa Piper gave me and Penelope walks by, snatches a handful of them, and just runs away."

Cadence turned to her daughter. "Penelope? Is this true?"

"Maybe."

"Penelope! Give him back his toy soldiers immediately."

She yanked them from the pocket of her pinafore, thrusting them toward James with a glower. "Fine. I didn't want them anyway."

"You've been in a bad mood all morning," James snapped.

"Have not."

"Have too."

"Children," Cadence interceded, attempting to calm their tempers while not losing her own, "think about how you're behaving. Are you showing Jesus' love to each other? And what are you teaching Etta? She looks up to both of you. She'll pattern her life after how you behave. The new baby will too."

Penelope muttered something under her breath.

Cadence speared her with a look. "What was that?"

The girl raised her voice. "I said I didn't ask for a new baby. We were doing just fine like we were. Why did you have to go and add another baby to the family?" With a cry, she ran from the room.

Cadence stood numb.

James huffed. "Likely she's just jealous is all."

Cadence squeezed his shoulder. "I pray you're right."

But when Cadence attempted to speak with her, Penelope refused. The child was sullen. Cadence was failing as a mother. Defeat washed over her.

It was late into the night before Joshua came home. Cadence lay in the darkness of their bedroom, listening as he eased the door open and began to undress. Where had he been all evening? She sprang from bed and hastily lit the lamp. The sizzling flame threw an accusing light on his surprised face.

"Cadence? What are you doing?"

She stared at the tattered green coat clutched in his hand. "I knew it. You've been out stealing slave children from their owners, haven't you?"

He sighed. "I thought it better if you didn't know. The less you know, the less trouble you'll be in if something goes wrong."

She stomped up to him and yanked the coat from his hand before tossing it onto the chair. "How dare you!" Fury unlike anything she'd ever known rolled through her, burning away all thought, all reason. "You lecture me about the danger of tending the ill at the hospital, saying it is too risky, while you play at life and death like it's a game of chuck-a-luck. I would prefer our children have their father as well as their mother."

"It's not the same."

"Of course it is!"

"Slavery is vile. I'll free as many as I can from its grip. I'm helping people."

She propped her hands on her hips. "That's what I told myself at first when I was tending the ill at the hospital, Joshua. That I was doing it for them, but I was really doing it for myself, to fill a void. To feel loved."

He pushed past her and yanked his shirt off with such force, she feared the buttons would fly. "You don't know what you're talking about."

"I was here, you know. I was the one who saw the horror on Penelope's face when you'd been shot and she was afraid you were going to die. I was the one who extracted that bullet and stitched you back up. You were nearly killed doing the very thing you were doing tonight."

He paused and stared into the wardrobe.

She placed a hand over her stomach as her throat constricted. "I want our baby to know his father."

A muscle worked in his jaw. "Are you telling me you want me to stop helping the slave children?"

Was she? "If it means you're helping them at the expense of your own children, if it means you're keeping secrets from me or putting yourself in situations that leave you cheating death each time—" she squared her shoulders—"then yes."

His eyes glinted. "Perhaps I didn't know you as well as I thought."

The words were a slap. "What?"

"I was one of those children. I was one of those hungry, helpless souls. And you want me to turn my back on them?"

"Of course not. I'm willing to fill this whole house up with them, but you're purposefully breaking the law in some cases. Deceiving men through tricks and gambling. Stealing them outright in others. You take unneeded risks." She stopped, understanding dawning. "You're afraid."

He stiffened. "What? I'm not afraid."

She blinked back the moisture pricking her eyes. "You're afraid of letting anyone get close, so you deliberately keep them at arm's length. That's what you're doing to me right now, aren't you? To the children?"

He grabbed a pillow and turned to stomp out of the room.

"Where are you going?"

"I'd rather sleep alone on the sofa tonight."

He slammed the door behind him. Etta's wail from the next room shredded the last of Cadence's composure.

Dropping her head in her hands, she wept.

chapter 31

"IT'S ALL SET THEN?"

In Joshua's home library, Zeke nodded. "Stevens says if he manages to get the child away from Billings, he'll meet you tomorrow night."

"I trust you'll guard my family for me?"

"Of course."

"Thank you." Joshua rubbed his bleary eyes. He'd sat up most of the night, his argument with Cadence replaying over and over in his head as he kicked against the too-small couch. She just didn't understand. "Where are we to meet?"

"At the Judiciary Square Hall. It's rumored Lincoln himself will be in attendance that evening for a benefit of some sort. It will be the perfect cover to carry the slave child to the next stop. With so many people there, it will make our way easy. Less interference on the streets."

The benefit. Joshua groaned and pinched the bridge of his nose. "Cadence. She is supposed to perform for the president tomorrow. How can I possibly sneak away and miss the biggest moment of her life?"

Frowning, Zeke crossed his arms. "You can't. So you make a choice."

Joshua let his eyes slide shut. "And we already promised James and Penelope they could attend the benefit with us."

Zeke sighed. "You sure you want to keep doing this, Doc?"

"I can't believe you would even ask me that. You of all people should understand what's at stake."

The large man rubbed his neck. "Hear me out. The cause is just. Always has been. But you're risking your own family for it. Are you okay with losing your wife and children to keep pursuing this path?"

"Of course not." Joshua paced, his footfalls muted against the rug. "But helping those children . . ."

"Was perhaps only for a season." Zeke shrugged. "Seasons change. The Almighty has given you children you can guide throughout their entire lives now. Don't push his hand away and continue to cling to the old. Live in the season he's given you."

Joshua clamped his jaw. "But I would be turning my back on those who need me."

Zeke fixed him with a hard stare. "Seems to me you'll be doing that either way."

His torment increased. He could do both. He had to. He must find a way to balance things better. That was all. Guilt needled, but he pushed it down.

"So you will guard Etta and Miriam while the rest of us are at Judiciary Square Hall?"

Zeke watched him for a long moment. "I'll watch them. How will you slip away from the benefit to escort the child to the next station?"

"I'll find a way. I always do. Everything will be fine, and Cadence and the children will never know."

Cadence fought to breathe, whether from the warm crush of too many people crowded into the hall, the stale air, or her own heightened nerves, she couldn't tell.

Judiciary Square Hall was packed full of men in dark suits and women in bright dresses billowed out by their voluminous hoop skirts. Laughter, chatter, and the raucous trills of the band made for an atmosphere of sheer revelry. Booths draped with patriotic bunting lined the hall, each bearing a sign for some cause needing donations or funds. Cadence had attended dozens of such benefits in the past year but never one that held such a charge of excitement. Her skin tingled.

At her side, James took in the festivities with wide-eyed wonder, saying little, though she often caught a smile playing about his mouth as he watched the antics of the band director waving his arms melodramatically in front of the musicians, his mop of gray hair flopping from side to side like the tongue of a slobbering dog. Penelope chattered continually, her excitement too great to be contained.

Joshua seemed distracted, frequently checking the timepiece in his pocket. Things between them had been strained and quiet over the past several days. She missed his easy smile and teasing. His arms and tender kisses. He was present yet further away than he'd ever been. An ache formed in her throat.

"Papa Gish, when will President Lincoln arrive?"

Joshua leaned down and tweaked Penelope's nose. "I haven't discovered that bit of information since you asked me one minute ago."

Penelope stretched on her tiptoes, trying to see over the

swarming crowd. The scent of perfume and bay rum drifted around them. "I'm too short. How am I to know when he arrives?"

Joshua chuckled. "I believe you'll know. Between his height and the whispers of the crowd, you'll know."

A man approached and bowed low before straightening and addressing Cadence. "Miss Piper?"

"Yes. That is, it's Mrs. Ivy now."

"Ah, how lovely. May I offer my sincerest congratulations."

"Thank you, sir."

"I just wanted to say how delighted I am that you'll be performing tonight. I fear Washington has been withering away to hear your beautiful voice of late. Everyone's been speaking of it."

He smiled behind his ruddy beard, but there was something in his expression that caused her a moment of unease.

"How kind of you. It's my pleasure to do so."

The stranger nodded and winked at the children before sauntering away. She watched him wind through the thickening crowd, unsure why he caused her to recoil. She shook off the sensation. He'd been nothing but gentlemanly.

The musicians began a rousing march, effectively cutting off normal conversation, and Joshua turned to her, saying something she was unable to hear.

"What?"

He lifted his voice and pointed. "There is someone I must speak to, sweetheart. I'll be back in a few moments."

She nodded. "Don't be gone too long."

He pressed her hand before weaving through the people clustering around the stage. She lost sight of him within seconds.

As the march rolled on, murmurs of astonishment rippled through the crowd.

"He's here!"

"The president!"

Cadence was tempted to jump up and down like a child herself in her haste to see him but refrained. A tall hat bobbed above the crowd. People on all sides pressed in for a glimpse.

She felt a tug on her sleeve and looked down to see Penelope's lip protruding. "James and I can't see."

Cadence scanned the area. "There. Follow me."

She ushered them to a place near the door where servers had stacked crates of supplies for the booths against the wall.

"Climb atop these crates and we'll see if you can catch sight of the president."

Giggling, they pulled themselves up, their eyes widening.

Penelope squealed. "Look, James! Look how tall he is! He's laughing at something someone is saying."

"Sure is." James was more subdued but beaming from ear to ear. "Can't believe I'm in the same room as Mr. Lincoln."

Cadence squeezed his hand. "A once-in-a-lifetime memory."

The music faded away to thunderous applause, whether because the musicians had finished or because of the president's arrival, Cadence didn't know. The harried conductor soon arrived breathless at Cadence's side.

"Mrs. Piper? Er—that is, Ivy?"

"Yes, sir."

"Are you ready?"

She inhaled as deep a breath as she could manage against her corset. "Yes. At least, I believe so."

"Come with me and I'll get you settled offstage until we receive the cue for your entrance. Key of B flat still in agreement with you?"

"Of course."

The sweating man wrung his hands as he scampered back toward the musicians, muttering to himself the entire way.

She turned to the children. "Your father should be back any moment. Stay here until you see him."

"Yes, ma'am," they answered, even as both their gazes were transfixed on the president, standing across the room. She hastened to follow the trembling conductor toward the small room beside the stage.

From her spot behind the curtain, she could scan the crowd. Where was Joshua? He should have returned by now.

She shook her head. He was likely around here somewhere. She just couldn't see him with so many in attendance. She let her eyes slide shut and tested a few notes in her throat, just as she'd done all day long. The rehearsal the day before had been smooth, but one day made a world of difference when it came to the voice. What if she floundered as she did at her last performance?

The stinging critique from the newspaper flickered through her memory, and bile crawled up her throat. The thought of failing in front of all these people . . . in front of the children, and worse yet, Lincoln himself, was more than she could bear. Word of her ineptitude would spread all over Washington with much more fire than it had from that newspaper columnist's critique. Such a thing would only prove what the phrenologist had predicted years ago. Cold tremors began in her middle and radiated to her limbs.

She couldn't do this.

I have already approved you, little one.

Her heart beat a rapid staccato even as her shallow breaths slowed. The loud din of the hall faded as the whisper reverberated through her spirit.

Whether you soar in human achievement or fail by man's standards, my love will not waver.

She looked up to the ceiling and murmured, "Thank you, Jesus."

A sharp "Pssst!" sliced across the stage, though the crowd was still milling around the president. She looked over to see the conductor staring at her.

"Are you ready?"

She nodded.

The shaking slip of a man walked to the center of the stage and lifted his hands. It took nearly a minute for the crowd to quiet. Cadence scanned the room. She still couldn't see Joshua, but Penelope and James had remained atop the crates near the door. From behind the curtain, she gave them a small wave, though she doubted they could see her.

"Attention, ladies and gentlemen. It is our profound pleasure to welcome you here tonight. Throughout the evening you'll hear many rousing speeches, music, a host of needs begging for our attention, and much more. We are supremely honored to have our great president in attendance!"

A deafening chorus of cheers and whoops rose. Cadence watched the children to gauge their reaction but frowned when the stranger who had approached her earlier sidled near them. Cadence squinted. It was definitely him. Same build, same crooked nose and ruddy beard. James shook his head. The man looked from side to side and grabbed both of the children, wrestling them to the door.

Her heart slammed. What was he doing?

She fled from her hiding spot behind the curtains and nearly ran over the babbling conductor in her haste to follow. His eyes bulged as he turned to her, yanking on her arm. "What do you think you're doing? You must sing!"

"I can't! My children—something is wrong!"

"You cannot be serious," he whispered harshly through gritted teeth as the crowd watched. "It's for the president of the United States. I'll be humiliated!"

She shook her hand and wrested her arm free. "Nothing matters but my children."

Lifting the hem of her skirt, she ran down the stairs, through the crowd, and shoved the door open. Cool night air slapped her face. She peered into the darkness, cursing the lack of gaslights near the alley. A scuffling sounded behind her.

"James! Penelope!"

Rough hands grabbed her from behind. A damp rag pressed to her mouth and a sweet scent flooded her nostrils.

The world tilted and went black.

chapter 32

JOSHUA PUSHED HIS WAY BACK into the pulsing hall. The warm air was oppressive after the cool night and his hasty sprint shuttling the slave girl ten blocks under the cover of darkness. Thankfully they'd met with no resistance and little Ruby was safely under the protection of the conductor who would take her to the next stop.

He only prayed Cadence hadn't noticed his absence.

The musicians finished the boisterous strains of "The Battle Cry of Freedom," earning the crowd's wild applause. Joshua scanned the throng for the president. With so many in attendance, spotting him was nearly impossible.

The musicians scattered for a break, and Joshua wove between chattering couples until he found the conductor, who was mopping his face with a limp handkerchief.

"Pardon me, sir. Have you seen Mrs. Cadence Ivy?"

The conductor turned to him with a scowl. "Don't dare mention her name to me. That woman humiliated me before the president of the United States! Her whereabouts are no concern of mine."

He sniffed in contempt and whirled away. Joshua stood in stunned silence. What had transpired in his absence?

He surveyed the hall. Cadence, James, Penelope . . . all three were missing from where he'd last seen them. A hard knot formed in his stomach. Something was wrong.

"Where did she go?"

He whirled to find Congressman Ramsey storming toward him. His neck was mottled crimson. The barrel-chested man jabbed a finger into Joshua's chest. "Does your wife have any idea what she's done to me?"

A sickening sensation churned Joshua's gut. "I have no idea what you're speaking—"

"No idea?" The congressman's eyes bulged. "Seconds before she was to perform for the president, she rushes off the stage and leaves the building." His brows lowered. "I had plans for this evening. Plans your wife destroyed."

Joshua could hear no more. He turned away, desperation nipping at his heels, and plunged into the crush of bodies, asking anyone who would listen if they'd seen his children or the singer who was supposed to perform. Most shook their heads until he reached a matronly woman minding a booth gathering clothing donations for the soldiers.

She smiled widely, oblivious to his distress. "Of course I remember those children. Sweet little things. Sat right over there—" she pointed to the low stack of crates against the wall near the door—"totally enthralled with the president."

"Where did they go?"

She tapped her lips with a pudgy hand. "I think a man came and talked with them. Must have been the girl's father. They sure didn't want to leave. He scooped them up and carried them out the door. They were squirming something fierce. Can't say I blame them. Shame to miss the rest of the evening."

Cold panic washed over him. "And what of the young lady who was supposed to perform tonight?"

The woman's brows furrowed. "Odd thing, that. The conductor was preparing to introduce her and the young miss just upped and left."

"Do you remember where she went?"

"Now that I think on it, the lady went out the same door."

His heart pounded. "Thank you, ma'am. You've been more help than you know."

He raced out the side door, letting it slam behind him. His breath came hard as he scanned up and down the inky alley. Where had they gone? Who had taken them? He had no clue. No leads. No starting place.

Overwhelmed, he nearly collapsed as grief and guilt crashed over him.

Oh, God, what have I done?

It was the gruff masculine voices that first roused Cadence from her thick slumber.

She attempted to push her heavy eyelids open, but they resisted. Odd. Instead, she lay against the hard, gritty floor and just listened, trying to make sense of the disjointed conversation drifting around her.

"This wasn't part of the plan."

"You told me to take Ivy's kids. *You* said there would be two. A sister and brother. That's what I did."

A grunt sounded. "It was Francis that messed up. He never should've grabbed the doctor's wife."

A whiny voice interjected. "What was I supposed to do? She

nearly stumbled atop the lot of us. Would have started screaming and brought the crowd down on our heads in a snap."

Cadence's heart hammered. Her tongue felt dry and thick. She forced her eyes to cooperate and peeked between her lashes. The light was dim, but she could make out the watery forms of at least five men, maybe more. She gulped down a breath.

A large man lumbered forward. "She's a complication, but the goal is still the same. If anything, maybe this will put a little more fire in Ivy's belly to see things our way." Footsteps stomped toward her, and she slammed her eyes shut. A dark presence loomed over her. "The Knights of the Golden Circle always emerge victorious."

She fought to keep her breathing even.

"Sure is a pretty little thing. Might have a little fun with her while we wait."

Chuckles peppered the air. Her pulse thrummed in her ears. *Jesus, help me.*

The footfalls moved away. Her sluggish thoughts began to form and race. Where were the children? Were they hurt? Why did these men want to convince Joshua of anything? Nothing made sense.

Cadence tried to move her arms, but fire shot into her shoulders. She stifled a groan and squirmed against the floor. Her hands were tied behind her back. She wiggled her fingers but felt little sensation. Numb.

"She's waking up."

Her eyes flew open when the floor vibrated beneath her. Half a dozen pairs of eyes circled her within the confines of a dirty, shadowed room. Two kerosene lanterns burned, but she could find no other source of light. She used her feet to push against the floor until her body slammed into the wall, then scrambled to a seated position. She licked her dry lips as she stared down the group of strangers eyeing her like prey.

The large man leered, his eyes glittering with deadly venom. "Hello, princess."

She said nothing. He reached out and touched her cheek. She jerked her head back and scowled.

His eyes narrowed. "We got us a filly with some spirit here, boys."

Her nostrils flared as he studied her with a greasy smile.

Before she could react, he snarled and lashed out, grabbing her face. He yanked her forward until his nose was only inches from her own. "Don't ever make the Knights of the Golden Circle angry, princess. You understand that?"

She could see the blood vessels in his eyes . . . the rage that simmered just below the thin veneer of his smile. He released her with a sudden shove. The back of her head cracked against the wall and her body weakened, head swimming.

He loomed over her with a sneer. "I'll return soon. Don't you be pining for me too much."

At his harsh chuckle, the group of men shuffled through the lone door, taking the lanterns with them and plunging her into darkness.

Penelope and James. Etta and Miriam. Joshua. A warm tear slipped down her cheek. What would become of them?

<hr />

Joshua trudged up the steps to his father-in-law's house just as daybreak lightened the sky. He'd combed the streets for hours, calling, asking those who would listen if they'd seen anyone matching the descriptions of his wife and children. His search had revealed nothing.

With every passing minute, his hope siphoned away, leaving a hollow, gaping ache inside.

He gripped the doorframe. *Lord, I don't know if I can live without them. Strengthen me. Protect them and frustrate the plans of my enemies.*

He lifted his hand to knock, every limb feeling like lead.

The door swung open, revealing Albert's careworn face. "Anything?"

Joshua shook his head, throat thick. "Nothing."

The older man's shoulders drooped. "Nothing for Tate and me either." His blue eyes glassed. "Come in and get a bite to eat and drink. You look ready to drop."

Joshua blinked away the grit coating his eyes as Albert led him into the parlor. He sank into a chair, barely noticing when Louisa came and pressed a cup of hot coffee into his hands.

Albert raked his hands through his graying hair as Tate entered the room, his uneven steps slow and weighted.

"I don't understand any of this. Who would want to kidnap two innocent children and my daughter?" Albert choked down his emotion. "It's madness."

Joshua let his eyes slide shut. Inhaling a deep breath, he lifted his gaze to the two men. "I have enemies."

Albert fell limply against the back of his chair. "What kind of enemies?"

Joshua pushed down the knot in his throat. "I can't give you their exact names because I don't know them, but I was forced to hire a bodyguard to protect Cadence and the children."

Tate's eyes widened. "Why?"

He ground his jaw. "Because someone was watching our house whenever I left for the hospital."

Albert rubbed his temple. "This still isn't adding up. Why would someone be watching them while you're gone?"

Joshua saw with startling clarity how easily he'd played with life and death for the past few years. A roll of the dice, a flip of the pasteboards . . . only this time the stakes had been those he loved.

Now they might be lost to him forever—and the fault was his alone.

He opened his mouth, trying to find the right words. "I am involved in something that is not popular with slaveholders. Something I'm passionate about but carries great risk."

Albert straightened. "Which is?"

Joshua blew out a breath. "I, along with a small group of like-minded men, work together to buy slave children from auction blocks and free them. We then carry them into free states where they can start a new life."

Albert swallowed. "I see. And has your work with these children always been aboveboard? There is no law prohibiting what you're doing. Have you always acted with integrity in this matter?"

Joshua dropped his gaze. "Not always."

Albert groaned. Joshua braved a glance at his brother-in-law. Tate's face was deathly serious, his hands moving back and forth across his chin as he thought.

"There's more. My latest excursion into Richmond proved troublesome. I fear I may have aroused the wrath of some slaveholders there, as well as stumbling into something bigger than myself. Bigger even than smuggling slave children to freedom."

Albert frowned. "What is it?"

"A secret society. A group so powerful, they have commanders, city leaders, and congressmen infiltrating every level of government."

Tate's jaw clenched. "The Knights of the Golden Circle."

Joshua's brows rose. "You know them?"

"All Southern gentlemen know them." His face blanched white. "If you have the Knights on your heels . . ."

"I know." Joshua rubbed his eyes. "I never intended to put Cadence and the children in harm's way. For years I was meticulous. But it wasn't enough"

Silence fell thick in the room, screaming an accusation.

"I think I can help."

Tate's soft voice caused Joshua's head to snap up. "What?"

His brother-in-law's dark brows lowered. "You know what I was. Who I was involved with. I know these circles. I have contacts. Leads."

Could he trust Tate? He'd been deeply ingrained in the slave trade. What if the very men who'd taken his family were working with Tate now?

Joshua shook his head. Impossible. Tate would never do such a thing to Cadence. He must trust him. There were no other options.

"Do you have any idea who might be behind this? Their names?"

Tate pushed to his feet and paced the room. "There was a group of slaveholders several years back who were known for kidnapping and executing some vigilante-style justice, but honestly, they preferred to wield their power in the courts and were based out of Kentucky." Tate fixed Joshua with a somber look. "If the Knights are behind this, there may be many men working against you in an organized movement. Were it not for your bodyguard, Etta might have been kidnapped as well. I don't know their names, but I have friends who can find out."

Joshua leaned forward at this first sign of hope. "Help me. Please."

Tate nodded, his expression grave. "I'll do everything I can, but we must move quickly."

chapter 33

SLEEP CAME IN FITFUL SNATCHES. Time ceased to exist in utter darkness. All Cadence knew was her thirst and the panic that plagued her at the thought of what the children might be enduring. She was helpless against both. She prayed between bouts of wakefulness, asking the Almighty to intervene on their behalf.

Her senses snapped when a rattling sound broke the silence. Chains. A lock? The bright beam of a lantern invaded, causing her to turn her head away. Her eyes could not adjust to such a sudden intrusion.

The lone figure holding the lantern spoke. "Time to move, princess."

A shadow came toward her. She scrambled away but only managed to press her body against the unforgiving wall. She attempted to scream but the sound was cut off as another sweet-smelling rag was clamped to her mouth with a firm hand.

Stay awake.

The shadowed silhouettes blurred as she fought. She was floating, lifted . . .

Gone.

———— ✦ ————

Joshua hunkered low in his jacket, waiting outside the seedy tavern on the outskirts of Washington. He didn't like waiting. Not when Tate was inside speaking with the very men who had connections to the demons who had taken his wife and children. Rage flooded him anew. He shifted his weight and exhaled into the evening's cool. Even now his brother-in-law might be looking into the face of the kidnappers, forcing small talk and gleaning what information he could.

It took all of Joshua's willpower not to barge through the doors and start flipping tables.

The sour odor of whiskey swirled around him. Washington had grown ever filthier and more barbaric since war's declaration, but this part of town . . . He shuddered to think of the poor souls sleeping in the alleys beyond the tavern. What hope did they have?

The tavern door swung open and he recognized Tate's lean form descending the stairs and shoving his hands into his pockets before strolling down the dark street. When he passed, Joshua fell into step beside him, saying nothing.

They walked for blocks before Tate uttered a sound. "It was who I feared."

"The Knights?"

"Yes."

"There's more."

"What?"

"I have a name."

"Who?"

A muscle twitched in Tate's jaw. "Congressman Ramsey."

Joshua pulled him to a stop with a yank on his sleeve. He hissed, "You're sure?"

Fury shadowed his brother-in-law's face. "Yes."

"I overheard a conversation between him and someone some time ago but hoped, prayed I'd misunderstood."

"You didn't." Tate's lips pressed into a hard line. "The congressman is what they call 'Master of the Rose of the Circle.' A member of the highest ranking."

Joshua's gut twisted. "None of this makes sense. Congressman Ramsey works alongside President Lincoln."

Tate shook his head. "What better way to destroy your enemy than from the inside? Working in Ramsey's office has made me privy to information that has left me suspicious to his true motives for the past several weeks. Just last week I found a stamp in his desk that bore the seal of a snake in a circle. I think after his son was killed, it twisted his mind against the Union and the entire war. I heard him whispering to another congressman only three days ago about the need to be rid of President Lincoln with all haste."

Joshua's mind raced. The congressman had always appeared to be one of Cadence's greatest supporters. He wouldn't harm her . . . would he?

Tate walked them quickly past dilapidated buildings and closed offices, weaving them back toward the cleaner part of Washington.

"What's to be done?"

"We wait."

Joshua stopped him with a growl. "What? Wait?" He cast a look about him and lowered his voice back to a whisper. "I'll not sit back and twiddle my thumbs while my wife and children are in danger."

Tate sighed. "Have a care, Joshua. You have no other options at this point. I know for a fact it is the Knights, and I heard it on good authority that they will be contacting you within the day. They want an exchange. Your life for your family's."

"I'll do anything to free them. But the thought of those men laying a hand on any of them . . ." His voice cracked.

Tate squeezed his shoulder. "I know. We pray. The Knights are a formidable foe, but God is greater. While we wait, we form a plan. You, myself, Father, and Zeke."

Joshua shook his head. "It's me they want. I'll not see anyone else sacrificed because of me."

A muscle twitched near Tate's eye. "We rescue my sister, nephew, and niece. That's priority number one. And we have an advantage. The congressman doesn't know I'm aware of his true motives. If you think I'll calmly hand you over to them without a fight, you've got another think coming. Come on. We've got work to do."

⁂

"Do you think she's dead?"

Sniffle. "Don't say that, James!"

The childish sob caused Cadence to startle. With a gasp, she pushed against the floor, slowly realizing her wrists were unbound. Bright-red marks marred her skin. Her muscles ached, but at least she could move.

She blinked and took a breath when her foggy mind cleared enough to realize James and Penelope were staring at her. With a cry, she crushed them to her chest, burying her face in their hair. "Oh, my darlings. I was so afraid."

They cried against her, pulling her close, seeking her warmth, her comfort. After long moments, she eased them back and stroked their dirt-stained faces. "Are you okay? Did they hurt you?"

Both of them shook their heads. James spoke through trembling lips. "We're fine. They kept us together."

Penelope sobbed. "How can you say that? They called you those horrible names and kicked you over and over . . ."

"Hush." He silenced her and swiped under his nose with a grubby fist. "Their words only hurt me if I choose to believe them. I don't. They're hate-filled men."

Cadence cupped James's face. "I'm so sorry."

He shrugged. "Ain't like it's the first time I've heard it."

Her heart ached with the injustice thrust upon such an innocent soul. James was the gentlest boy she'd ever met, and to be treated like rubbish . . .

She tugged him close once more and kissed the top of his head. Penelope snuggled near as they sat in the strange room. A thin shaft of light drifted down from a tiny rectangle somewhere overhead. Shelves lined with jars covered one wall. Barrels and crates filled the rest of the space. Dust coated her tongue. Cobwebs hung thick in the corners.

"We must be in a basement of some kind."

James looked around. "That's what I thought, but I can't hear a thing outside. They drugged us before they moved us, same as they did to you."

She tried to puzzle out the infuriating predicament. "They must have moved us out of the city, away from the noise and traffic."

"Why are they doing this?" Penelope's voice quaked, small and fragile against Cadence's side.

Should she tell them what she'd overheard? That the men were after Joshua? Using them as bait to lure him into danger? Her throat convulsed. No. No good could come from the children worrying themselves over such a thing.

"God is the only one who knows for certain. He's here,

even in this filthy basement. He's already working on our behalf."

"How can you be sure?"

She stroked the terrified girl's back. "You know how frantic Papa Gish must be, trying to find us? Papa Piper and Uncle Tate, Miriam and Louisa, little Etta . . . all of them must be worried, so I know they are praying night and day for us. When God's children pray, he moves."

Penelope sniffed. "Miriam always says to pray pacifically."

Cadence smiled. "She's right. I imagine if we offer up specific prayers, the Almighty will answer specifically. What would you like to pray specifically for?"

"Dear Lord, please help us get away from these bad men. Don't let them hurt James anymore, and help Papa Gish find us soon."

James cleared his throat. "And, Lord, we would be mighty obliged if you'd send us some water. Amen."

"Amen." She held them tight, trying to ignore her own parched throat. Despite her fear, a murmur of peace whispered deep in her soul.

God would see to them. To her and James and Penelope and the unborn child within her. To Joshua.

She whispered as the children fell into slumber in her arms, "Please, Lord, let it be so."

chapter 34

JOSHUA WALKED RUTS through the rug of his parlor as the next day crept by painfully with nothing but silence from the kidnappers. Tate and Albert came over, oscillating between talk of various plans and actions and sitting in silence. More often than not, Albert could be found with his head down and eyes closed, his lips moving in silent prayer.

Miriam shuffled about the kitchen, sniffling and bemoaning the fate of her babies and "that sweet Miss Cadence." No matter how he tried, Joshua could not convince her to sit and rest. She insisted preparing food kept her mind occupied. More was the pity, for her sniffles alternated with grumblings about the shortage of staples due to rising food prices. Only Etta seemed unaffected by the strain. The toddler played with her toys and chattered excitedly to Tate.

Despair shredded Joshua as the afternoon crept into evening. October's sunshine fell into twilight.

Etta yawned and held up her arms for him. "Papa hold?"

He fought back the stinging sensation in his eyes and picked her up. With a happy sigh, she tucked her head under his chin and snuggled against his chest. He continued his pacing, slower this time. Within minutes, she had fallen asleep.

His heart snagged. Was sweet Etta to be the only family he would retain when this nightmare was over?

Miriam walked up behind him. "You look done in, Doc. Let me take her up to her room."

"No. I don't want her out of my sight—not until we hear from the madmen who kidnapped my family."

Miriam shot a glance at Albert, who gave her a sniff nod.

"All right then. How about I go fetch her a blanket and you can lay her down on the sofa in here?"

"Thank you, Miriam."

As she hustled to retrieve bedding, Joshua gently leaned over and draped Etta's plump body on the couch. She heaved a deep, contented sigh in her sleep. His throat tightened. Had he ever rested that well? That free of striving? He had been pushing and working for so long, trying to prove himself—

A hand squeezed his shoulder. Joshua turned his bleary eyes to meet Tate's.

"We'll find them."

Unable to speak past the tears welling, he simply nodded and straightened.

A knock sounded on the door. They froze. Joshua's pulse tripped before he sprinted toward the entryway.

Tate stopped him with a yank on his arm. "Wait!"

"What are you doing? It could be them!"

"I know. Here."

Joshua looked down as Tate pressed the cold steel of a pistol into his hands. With a grateful nod, he inhaled and opened the door.

Zeke stood before him, his face a bloody mess. "Those men made contact, Doc."

Wincing at his friend's wounds, he ushered him inside before shutting and locking the door behind him.

"You look like you went ten rounds with a prizefighter. Come into the kitchen and let me get you cleaned up. Might even need stitches."

The big man held his side as he shuffled into the kitchen and eased into a chair with a grunt. Joshua reached for his medical bag and began pulling out bandages before moving to the sink's hand pump and filling a bowl with water. "What happened?"

"I was guarding the house, just like always, when I heard a footfall behind me. I turned around and the butt of a gun hit my temple." His eyes slid closed briefly before reopening. "Nearly blacked out. As I tried to regain my balance and fight my attacker, I was suddenly surrounded by men."

"How many?"

"Must have been at least nine or ten, best I could tell in the dark. There was a lot of them. Only a few of them were willing to fight with me, though. Maybe four." His shoulders drooped. "I should have been able to stop them."

Joshua grabbed a rag and sat across from his friend, giving him a hard stare. "You were outnumbered by a large margin. You can't possibly think this is your fault." He dunked the cloth in the water and dabbed it across the first bloody cut. Zeke hissed through his teeth and recoiled.

"Come now. If you can face down ten men, this should be nothing."

Zeke pulled an envelope from inside his shirt. "As I was lying there, trying to catch my breath, one of them tossed this at me and said to make sure it got to Joshua Ivy."

Joshua's blood ran cold. Zeke took the rag. "I can clean my own cuts for a minute. Take a look at that letter first."

Hands shaking, he grabbed the envelope and slid his finger underneath the flap, pulling the single piece of parchment free. The blocky letters were as harsh and blunt as the men who had stolen his life out from under him.

Tomorrow at midnight. Hoffman's warehouse.
Your life for theirs.
Tell anyone? The boy will be sold, and your wife and
daughter die.

Ice sleeted through his veins. With a growl, he threw the missive on the table and scratched his hands over his scalp. Zeke was silent. Joshua couldn't breathe, couldn't think. Cadence, James, Penelope . . . he was helpless to protect them. What had they already endured at these madmen's hands?

Tate entered the kitchen with needle and thread. "Miriam said you might need these. She noticed your supply was dwindling." He patted Zeke's back before his gaze drifted to the abandoned note on the table. "We have word?"

"Yes." Joshua's voice sounded hoarse to his own ears.

Tate picked up the letter and read it. "Good. Now we can form a plan."

"A plan?" Joshua rose, despair choking him. "Zeke said close to ten men jumped him tonight. If the Knights throw all their weight behind this, what hope do we have of saving my family?"

Tate fixed him with a fierce look. "If it were up to us, we would have no hope whatsoever, but our hope doesn't lie in ourselves. We're trusting God. These men are cowards, hiding behind my sister and little children. I know them. They're used to taking people to court to get what they want, or hiring guns to do their work for them. The more they are willing to dirty their own hands, the more scared they are. I think you and your friends have shaken them and they are lashing out, seeking revenge."

Joshua felt the tension in his middle relax by degrees. "You're right. Forgive me."

Zeke pulled the wet cloth from his swollen eye. "So we have a time and a location. What are we going to do about manpower? I have no intention of just handing Doc over, but right now it's only the three of us."

"Four."

Joshua turned to see his father-in-law standing in the doorway. His eyes burned with gratitude. "Albert, as much as I appreciate your courage, I have a greater task for you. I need someone I trust to care for Etta if something happens to me. The thought of her once again losing her family is . . ." His throat clamped.

Albert nodded. "Of course. You have my word."

Zeke frowned. "Three or four. Neither will matter much if they show up with ten, twenty, or more."

Tate rubbed his chin, his scowl deep. "I agree. We need help, but it's not like we have an army to summon up at will."

An idea popped into Joshua's mind, sending a spiral of excitement through his body so strong, he nearly leaped. "I think I have an idea."

<hr>

After a miserable night and an endless day, the jangle of keys and the click of a lock signaled the arrival of a visitor. Cadence and the children were met with the fading light of dusk when a spindly man entered, placed a bucket of water on the floor, tossed a loaf of bread beside it, and hastily left.

Cadence breathed a sigh. "Thank you, Lord."

James hurried to bring the water and bread close. "I was so thirsty, I could feel myself drying out."

They took turns drinking handfuls until their thirst was sated. Cadence broke the loaf of bread into three parts. Penelope started to cram it in, but Cadence stopped her with a gentle touch on her arm. "Slowly. Let your stomach adjust. It will help you feel full longer too."

The girl groaned. "I know. It's just that I'm so hungry."

"I know."

James lifted his face to the basement ceiling. "Thank you, Jesus, for this bread and water. You are good to us."

"Amen." Cadence smiled at his sweet faith. "Say, we could turn this time into our own Paul and Silas moment."

Penelope's brow dipped low. "What do you mean?"

"Remember when Paul and Silas were locked up in the jail at Philippi? What did they do instead of moaning and complaining?"

"They sang!"

"Exactly. We have nothing else to do, after all."

James cleared his throat. "'Amazing grace, how sweet the sound . . .'"

They joined in, singing one song after another. When a lull ensued, Cadence leaned her back against the wall and let the words of another hymn rise.

"Jesus, lover of my soul,
Let me to thy bosom fly,
While the nearer waters roll,
While the tempest still is high.
Hide me, O my Savior, hide,
Till the storm of life is past.
Safe into the——"

At Penelope's soft gasp, she stopped. The girl was staring at her with round eyes.

"You're her."

"What?"

"The lady."

James snorted. "Have you lost your mind?"

Penelope continued to stare. "You're the lady who spoke to me in the alley so long ago when I was upset. You sang that very song to me and told me about your mother."

Cadence lifted her fingers to her lips. The sobbing child. The gruff man who'd interrupted them. Joshua? "That was you?"

A tear streaked down Penelope's freckled cheek. "I never forgot you. Whenever I'm scared or lonely, I pull out the gift you gave me and remember."

She reached into her pinafore pocket. Opening her fingers, she revealed a hairpin. Cadence's mother's hairpin.

Penelope's tears fell in earnest, causing Cadence's to do the same. "I told God if he gave me that lady for a mother, I would never ask for another thing. He did and I didn't even know it!" With a sob, she threw herself against Cadence. "I'm sorry I was so mean about the baby. I'm just scared."

"Oh, my darling." Cadence wiped the tears from her cheeks while cradling the girl's sweet face. "Why would you be scared? Nothing will change my love for you."

"It's not that. I—I'm just so scared you'll die. It happens all the time. My mother died giving birth to my brother and left me all alone until Papa Gish found me. If you died, I couldn't bear it!"

Cadence enveloped her in a tight embrace and rocked her back and forth. Her sobs echoed against the basement's brick walls. James looked on helplessly.

"Sweetheart, listen to me. This world is a sin-cursed mess.

The Almighty never intended it to be such, but God can use even the bad things for good. When I was younger, I had a horrible speaking problem. I could barely utter a word without fumbling my way through it. I struggle with it still. Children at school made fun of me. Papa Piper and my mother took me to a special doctor who said I didn't have all my faculties. I believed him for a long time, but it wasn't true. Even though going through that was difficult, God used it to mold me into who I am today. I have much more compassion for others."

Penelope sniffed and brushed away more escaping tears. "It hurt losing my first mother, but now I have you and Papa Gish, James and Etta and Miriam. And now, even a grandpa and uncle." She gave a toothy grin. "A grandpa who owns a toy shop!"

Cadence laughed. "Exactly. And because of the hurt you felt losing your first mother, you'll be able to help others who've lost their parents too. Like James and Etta."

James winked. "Admit it, you like me, Penny."

She scowled, though a twinkle sparkled in her eyes. "Perhaps a little."

Smoothing Penelope's tangled red curls, Cadence asked, "So the man who interrupted us that night in the alley was Joshua?"

She nodded and swiped at her runny nose. "Yes. We were out because I told him of a place where some of the street children looked for shelter. He wanted to take them food, but none of them were there that night. When he said it was time to return home, I got mad and tried to run away from him." She hung her head. "That's when you found me."

Cadence rubbed her back. "All's well that ends well." She looked around their gloomy prison. But would it end well for them when it was all said and done? Her heart twisted. The thought of Joshua walking into a trap made her retch. She couldn't, wouldn't let it happen.

An idea niggled. "Say, what would you two think of trying to find a way out of here?"

James's brows rose. "How? The door is chained and locked. The only window is far too high."

"What if we tried to build a way up to that window? We might be able to pry it open and escape. I know you two could get through easily."

James frowned. "We wouldn't leave you here."

"Let's not get the cart before the horse. First we need to see if these shelves are nailed down. If they aren't, we can push them across the room and hopefully be close enough to reach the window."

Penelope bit her lip. "It's worth a try."

James agreed with a determined nod. "Let's try."

"We must make haste then. The men could come back at any time."

James stalked to the closest shelves and began yanking the dusty jars from them with gusto. "We can do it. With the Almighty's help, we can."

chapter 35

JOSHUA'S BREATH CAME IN SHORT PANTS. He forced it to even out as he stared down the dark street leading to Hoffman's warehouse. Midnight was quickly approaching.

Not a soul stirred. No sound could be heard against the gritty pavement, but he knew they were there. He, Tate, and Zeke had made sure of it. It had taken all day, but he had rounded up as many as he could. Their presence made him feel safer than the gun in his pocket did. He looked up into the star-sprinkled night sky. All of it paled in comparison to God's protective hand.

Be with us all through this night, Lord.

Miriam's muttered words from early in the morning rolled through his brain like a pounding drum. *"'The Lord shall fight for you, and ye shall hold your peace.'"*

He expelled a cleansing breath. *Fight for us, Lord. No bloodshed or violence if it can be avoided. More than anything, please keep Cadence and the children safe.*

———— ᧞᧟ ————

"James, you've almost got it!"

From atop the shelf they'd managed to push against the far wall, James wobbled on a rickety crate. He strained on his tiptoes and brushed his fingers against the window's base. "I can feel the latch."

"Does it have any give?"

Grunting, he tugged. "No. Locked."

Penelope groaned. James carefully descended from the crate and crouched on the high shelf. He swiped at the dust sticking to his sweaty forehead. "Hand me a jar, please."

"Why?"

"I'm going to bust the window open."

Cadence shook her head. "No. It's too risky. You're just as likely to break the jar and slice your hand open. And what if they are outside? If they hear the break, they'll come running."

He huffed and scratched his curly hair. "We're almost out of light. We ought to try something."

"Maybe we should pray and ask what God wants us to do." Penelope's voice was soft.

Cadence turned to her with surprise. The child's faith was growing. "I think that's an excellent idea."

James pursed his lips. "All right, but before I come down, I'm going to feel around this window some more."

Climbing on top of the crate once again, he pushed to his tiptoes and felt around the length of the window. Cadence held her breath. If he were to fall from that height . . .

A rattle jerked their attention to the door. James's sharp intake of air stole the breath from Cadence's lungs.

"Get down. Now!"

He scrambled as the locks clanked.

"Hurry!"

He dropped to the floor in a puff of dust just as the door swung open wide. Five men entered, three of them well-dressed and clean. The other two looked as savage as mountain lions.

A blond fellow with pomaded hair and an immaculate suit narrowed his eyes. "Well, you three have been quite busy, I see. Trying to escape?"

Penelope hunkered behind Cadence's skirt, but James attempted to push to the front, shielding both of them with his thin body.

Cadence lifted her chin. "Can you blame us? When our friends at the Capitol find out what you've done, you'll be lucky not to find yourselves at the end of a hangman's noose."

The man's lips quirked into a sneer. "Brody told me you had spirit. Perhaps it's time to see if we can break that nasty streak."

He nodded to one of the savage-looking men, who lurched forward and grabbed James by the arm. She rushed toward them, but another man with dark, curly hair and a mustache snaked his arm around her waist and pinned her against his chest. With a snarl, the first man picked up James and slammed him into the wall with a sickening crack.

"No! Stop!" she screamed, but the arms restraining her held fast. Penelope lurched forward, but a third man scooped her up, doing his best to wrestle her into submission despite her screams and kicks.

James groaned and slowly rose from the floor. The bully grabbed him by the throat and squeezed. Cadence tasted salt. "Please don't hurt him. Please!"

The blond man smiled coldly. "We have an accord then." He nodded to James's tormentor, who promptly dropped him back to the ground. James coughed and sucked in deep drafts of air.

Cadence choked against her sobs. "Why are you doing this?"

"All of this is your husband's fault, my dear." The blond man smoothed his hair and fixed her with a hard glare. "He brought it on your heads when he began entertaining ideas. Ideas that the black man is equal to the white man. Ideas that he and his ilk should rob honest Southern men of their property to advance his own causes, like some kind of twisted Robin Hood." The man's eyes narrowed to slits. "He angered some powerful men, and now he'll pay."

The man holding Cadence tightened his grip and inhaled against her neck. She stiffened and squirmed against his hold. He chuckled, the sound of his voice near her ear causing shivers of revulsion to traverse her spine.

"If you knew who I was, you wouldn't be so hasty to get away."

She gritted her teeth and pulled her arm, but he held fast. "Oh? And just who kidnaps innocent women and children other than criminals?" she asked.

He growled. "The only criminal involved here would be your husband. No, I'm an actor. An actor of some renown. Someday I'll be world-famous. Ever hear of John Wilkes Booth?"

"I have not."

"More's the pity. Someday everyone will know my name."

"Not for something good, I'd wager."

With a grunt, he yanked her toward the group of men as the children were pulled alongside.

"Where are we going?"

"To give your husband what he deserves."

Joshua waited in the darkness. He had no intention of showing himself until his family's captors were visible. The distant sounds of Washington's nightlife rose up around him . . . the faraway cry of a baby, the clatter of a passing wagon. Nothing strange, yet every scrape, every noise made the hair rise on the back of his neck.

Was that the sound of footfalls? He peered out from the alley. Shadows moved toward the front of the warehouse. Lanterns bobbed, casting eerie orbs of light along the street. His breath hitched. How many men were there?

"Come out, Ivy, if you've a spine."

This was it. "Not until I see my family." His voice alone would give them a fair clue to his whereabouts, but he didn't care. He'd not move a muscle until he saw for himself that Cadence and the children were not harmed.

More scuffling sounds. Penelope appeared in the lantern light, her face pale, held by a thin man with a crooked nose. Next James appeared, his hands bound behind him. His lip looked to be split and he shuffled slowly, as if moving was painful. Joshua's gut flamed. Where was Cadence?

After torturous seconds, another man tugged her forward, one arm snaked around her waist and the other holding a pistol to her temple. A cold rage unlike anything Joshua had ever known licked through him. He fought for control, nostrils flaring.

"Come out, come out wherever you are." The kidnapper's voice grated. "If you're too cowardly, trust me, we have plans for your family."

The men chuckled, and the one holding Cadence stroked her waist. She stiffened, and it was all Joshua needed. He lurched from the alley and stalked toward them with deadly intention. Penelope cried out, "Papa!"

He kept his gaze fixed on the leader of the twenty or so men who circled him. "I'm here. Let them go."

Cadence called to him, her voice a tremor. "Don't do it, Joshua! They'll kill you!"

His gaze slid to hers and held fast. "I would die a thousand times over if it meant saving you and the children."

Liquid silver escaped down her cheeks. He returned his glare to the leader. "You have what you want. I kept my end of the bargain. Release them."

"I suppose I could, but what would stop them from running to the authorities?" The blond man shook his head and tsked. "No, perhaps we should let them see your demise first as an incentive to keep quiet."

Penelope's sobs rent the air. A muscle ticked in Joshua's cheek. "I wouldn't recommend it."

"Your recommendations don't factor into the equation. You lost that privilege the minute you began stealing our slaves."

"Buying slaves on the auction block and choosing to free them is not stealing them."

A potbellied man stepped forward, his bald head gleaming in the lantern light. "Abolitionist trash! You didn't buy a slave from me in Richmond! You stole her right out of my hands!" George Proctor, the slaveholder he'd taken the girl from after his card trick failed him.

Joshua curled his fists. "And what were you planning to do with that child? I heard you bragging to your friends, you know. You said you needed another young girl to warm your bed."

Uncomfortable silence descended. Some of the men took a step away from the angry slaveholder. Joshua pressed his advantage. "That's who stirred all of you up, gentlemen. A debased man with vile intentions. Yes, I'm an abolitionist, but God help me, I have worked through lawful measures whenever possible to set slaves free. What this man planned to do was more than I could bear. No man worth his salt should excuse such an abomination."

The man holding Cadence sneered. "Yet you take in this boy as your own child? *That* is an abomination."

Murmurs followed the declaration. Joshua was losing ground.

"I promise, you do not want to do this thing."

The leader sneered. "Why not?"

Tate's voice called out from the shadows. "Because he has an entire army on his side."

The sound of close to a hundred guns clicking punctuated the air. The kidnappers' eyes went wide before they drew their own weapons, though they turned in circles, unsure where to aim in the darkness. Slowly blue-clad Union soldiers stepped out from the shadows, guns trained on the small cluster of men surrounding Joshua. Some bore eye patches and others walked with the aid of canes, but their firing arms were steady.

"What is the meaning of this?"

From Joshua's right, Steward Swindle spoke, his gaze sighting down his gun's barrel. "It's simple. We fought for the Union and paid dearly. Doc and his wife saved our lives. We don't take too kindly to you threatening to kill 'em."

One of the kidnappers cursed. "We're surrounded by demon Yanks!"

The leader seethed, pinning one soldier with a sneer. "You think you're a threat? You're missing a leg!"

The soldier smiled. "My trigger finger's just fine."

The man paled and took a step back.

Tate kept his own pistol steady. "There are at least forty more in the shadows, gentlemen. I doubt any of us are hankering to visit the undertaker tonight, so why don't we call it even?"

The leader glanced at his friends and gave a stiff nod. The men holding the children and Cadence released them. The three of them ran toward Joshua with a cry. He hugged the children, kissing their heads, before crushing Cadence in his arms.

He cradled her face and smoothed the traces of dirt from her soft skin. "Did they touch you? The baby? Are you—?"

She shook her head and kissed him between questions. "I'm fine. We're fine. Thank the Lord, we're all fine."

Tate took a threatening step toward the group of Knights. "Come near them again and we'll shoot first and ask questions later. Remember, we've seen your faces, and I, for one, never forget a face."

The leader fixed him with a glare. "You haven't heard the last of the Knights of the Golden Circle."

"For your sake, I better have."

The soldiers moved in as the Knights scattered like rats back into the darkness. When they'd left, the soldiers relaxed and offered handshakes, but Joshua's eyes were for only one woman.

He claimed Cadence's lips before releasing a breath. "Sweetheart, I'm so sorry. You were right. My priorities have been wrong. If I had been there the night of the benefit, none of this would have happened. Can you ever forgive me?"

She cupped the rough, unshaven lines of his jaw. His pulse skidded at her touch.

"I forgive you. Forgive me for making you feel like you had to choose. From now on we work together."

"Together." His voice dropped low as he nuzzled her neck. "I like the sound of that."

"Papa Gish!"

Penelope was jumping up and down in her excitement. Laughing, he scooped her up. She squeezed him tight.

"I prayed and prayed for God to keep you safe and he did! And James almost escaped through a window, but those mean men tried to hurt him. But then Mama Cadence told them off good and I'm not mad about the baby anymore because I know God is going to keep Cadence safe, and say . . . did you know she is the same lady who sang to me in the alley that night?"

Joshua struggled to keep up and looked to Cadence. She shrugged helplessly. "It's all true."

He shook his head. "Perhaps when we've had a good night's sleep I'll be able to understand all of that." He knelt and hugged James before studying him with a critical eye. "Are you okay, Son?"

James smiled, even with his split lip. "Yes, sir. Much better now that I know you're okay."

Joshua's eyes burned. "Did they hurt you?"

"They tried, but God was with me."

Joshua swallowed, squeezing James's shoulder with a gentle touch. "I'm so proud of you."

James hugged him tight. "You know, I've been thinking. Sometimes I think you're busy doing what you do because you were an orphan and all. Trying to rescue children and whatnot."

Joshua rubbed his chin. "Yes, I suppose that's true."

"But sometimes I wonder if maybe you keep so busy because you're scared of our family."

Joshua stole a glance at Cadence. She nodded toward James in assurance. He looked back at James, trying to understand. "What do you mean?"

He shrugged. "It's just that for so long you didn't have a family. You were constantly moving and running, looking for food, looking for shelter, looking for a family. When Papa John took you in, you were older. I wonder if maybe the idea of having a real family scares you."

The words pierced like an arrow. James placed a hand on Joshua's shoulder. "You chose to be a father to Penelope and Etta and me and a husband to Cadence. We talked about it and we think it's just as important for you to know that even though you chose us, we chose you too."

Joshua's throat convulsed. He nodded and tugged James into another hug. "I love you."

"I love you too, Papa Gish."

He kissed Penelope, then stood and wiped his eyes as Cadence reclaimed his arms. Her smile lit up the night. "You're stuck with us, Doc."

He chuckled and tasted her lips. "I knew you were trouble the moment you walked into the hospital."

"You did?"

"Of course. That's why I worked so hard to push you away, but it was a futile effort. My heart had already chosen you."

epilogue

June 1863
Washington, DC

"She's so tiny."

Cadence smiled as James watched her new daughter curl her small finger around his.

Miriam chuckled. "Eight and a half pounds going on nine ain't tiny."

Cadence gave her a look. "I concur."

Miriam shooed the children toward the door. "Come on now, children. Your mama and new sister need some rest."

Groans met the announcement. Penelope kissed the baby's head and murmured, "See you soon, little sis. I'll show you how to make paper dolls tomorrow."

James wrinkled his nose. "Babies can't make paper dolls."

Penelope glared at him. "It's never too soon to learn."

Etta scrambled off the bed and turned back to the baby, her hands propped on her hips. "I the baby."

Miriam rolled her eyes and ushered them out of the room as Cadence and Joshua laughed.

Cadence turned to her husband as he eased down next to her in bed. "What are you thinking, Doc?"

He never took his eyes from the bundle in her arms. The tender light in his eyes glowed as he smoothed his hand over the thatch of dark hair and reverently whispered, "She's perfect."

Cadence's chest swelled with love as she drank in the long lashes, chubby cheeks, and tiny grunting sounds. "Just like her father."

"That's not what you said while delivering her."

"Oh, hush."

His laughter wrapped around her like an embrace as he kissed her cheek. "I'm so proud of you, sweetheart. You were very brave."

"I had a good physician."

"True."

She placed the squirming bundle in his arms. The baby blinked and looked into Joshua's face, studying, memorizing. Cadence watched as his heart melted into a puddle of wax.

She leaned against him. "I'm so glad you were able to be here."

"They haven't needed me in the field hospitals nearly as much as they have at Judiciary Square. With so many wounded arriving every week, it's more important for me to be here."

She laid her head against his chest and breathed in the scent of him. "I'm glad. It's so hard when you're gone."

"And just think of all the help you'll have once Papa Piper and Uncle Tate see this living angel." Joshua grinned. "You'll never have a moment's peace."

Laughing, she eased against the pillow. "I rarely do now." Since Tate quit working for Congressman Ramsey and began taking over more of the toy shop, Father was over nearly every day, spoiling the children dreadfully. She absently ran her fingers over her daughter's dimpled hands. "Some days the congressman's betrayal still doesn't seem real."

Joshua's jaw tightened. "God sees. He'll repay. Ramsey may hold office now, but none of his deeds are hidden. The Knights may wield power at the moment, but someday their names will be blotted from history. Truth and goodness will always prevail."

He leaned over to kiss Cadence's head, then brushed a kiss against his new daughter's cheek. The baby wrinkled up her nose, and Joshua laughed, causing Cadence's dark thoughts to flee.

"Do you wish you'd had a boy?"

"Of course not. We'll have one of those next time." He winked.

She groaned as he kissed her lips.

"Well, Mrs. Ivy, there is one matter of business which begs our attention."

"Indeed."

He tilted his head and studied the little girl in his arms. "What will we name her?"

"It's not my fault you've disliked every name I suggested."

"Suggest better names then."

She sighed. "I was thinking . . ."

"Yes?"

"What about the name Liberty?"

He looked down at his daughter, their daughter, a slow smile spreading across his handsome face. "Perhaps Liberty Ann? Ann for the woman who took me in, alongside Father Hopper, and loved me as her own."

Cadence nodded. "Perfect."

"Liberty Ann Ivy. Libby for short." He grinned. "I love it."

"It only seems fitting. You fighting to free so many, and God giving each of us freedom from our pasts. It's a beautiful name."

From downstairs, the sound of Miriam's robust singing drifted through the walls.

"Pass me not, O gentle Savior,
Hear my humble cry;
While on others thou art calling,
Do not pass me by . . ."

"That's beautiful." Cadence let the words and melody soak into her spirit. "I've never heard that song before."

Joshua shrugged. "Miriam has been singing it all night. She took the children to a revival meeting last evening and said she heard it there. It's a new hymn."

"Who is it by?"

He frowned. "I'm not sure, but I think she said Fanny Crosby."

Warmth spread through Cadence's middle. *Of course.*

Joshua smiled when the baby cooed and wrapped her fingers around his own.

"Whatever will we do with ourselves when they are all grown, Mrs. Ivy?"

Leaning down, she breathed in Liberty's fresh scent and kissed her velvety-soft cheek. "The next thing, my love. We'll do the next thing."

a note from the author

WHILE *ALL THROUGH THE NIGHT* is completely fictitious, the character of Cadence Piper is loosely based on a very courageous woman named Elida Rumsey. Young, beautiful Elida was desperate to do her part in the Great Conflict but was turned away by Dorothea Dix. Elida was known throughout Washington for her beautiful singing voice and was called upon to use her gift at various benefits. She was the very first person to publicly sing "The Battle Hymn of the Republic."

When starving soldiers were released from Libby Prison in a prisoner exchange, a young Navy Department clerk named John Allen Fowle sought out Elida and asked her to sing in order to rouse the soldiers' spirits. Her popularity grew among the troops from that day forward, and she was soon labeled "The Songbird of the North." Elida organized libraries for recuperating soldiers and even took food and provisions to the battlefronts to give to the sick and dying. It was in the heat of battle that she began nursing the wounded. Upon seeing fresh blood pumping from the arm of her very first patient, she fainted. Elida resolved that would never happen again and immediately went back into the field hospital to nurse those who needed her. She eventually became the youngest member of the Massachusetts Army Nurses.

Because of their popularity, John and Elida were married in the Hall of the House of Representatives. They had four biological children, adopted two orphaned soldiers' children, and took in two emancipated slave children. I chose to honor Elida Rumsey by using her first name for one of my characters in this book—Cadence's friend, the mother of baby Rose.

While researching this story, I was horrified to learn the depths of evil perpetrated by the Knights of the Golden Circle. I had heard of the secret society before, but only in the realms of treasure hunters seeking the rumored fortune the Knights supposedly left behind. These forerunners of the KKK funded much of the Confederacy, and their influence reached even into the Union ranks. A particularly haunting memoir by Edmund Wright, one of the few who managed to leave the Knights and paid a high price, laid a rich foundation of research for this novel. My character Edmund Warwick was inspired in part by this brave man. Many historians believe that both Jesse James and Lincoln's killer, John Wilkes Booth, were also members of the Knights.

Fanny Crosby is one of my favorite songwriters of all time. When faced with the possibility of giving her a cameo in *All Through the Night*, my imagination took flight. Just before penning her part of the story, I went to sing and speak to some inmates at the Little Rock penitentiary. When it came time for worship, one of the inmates stood and led us in a beautiful rendition of "Pass Me Not, O Gentle Savior." Seeing the tears in his eyes as he lifted his face to heaven, I marveled at how Crosby's touching words still move so many today.

In the epilogue, I had Miriam humming this hymn as she went about her work after hearing it performed at a revival service in 1863. In reality, "Pass Me Not, O Gentle Savior" wasn't written until 1868. I wanted to wrap up Cadence and Joshua's story with the reminder that all of us long to be seen . . . and there is a God who sees and hears us, even in the darkest night.

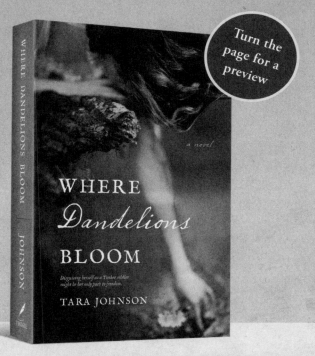

Chapter 1

April 12, 1861
Howell, Michigan

"Cassandra Kendrick! What have you done?"

Cassie cringed at the slurred, booming voice hovering just beyond the barn door. She crouched, pressing her back against the prickly wood wall, and breathed through her mouth lest the sweet motes of hay floating around her cause a sneeze. She could not let Father know her whereabouts. Not until his temper cooled or his alcohol-sodden brain plunged him once again into a sleeping stupor. For him to find her in his current condition would not bode well.

In her eighteen years, history had taught her that much in abundance.

"Come out, come out, wherever you are."

The ominous timbre slithered down her spine. She squeezed her eyes shut.

Thud, thud, thud.

Her pulse pounded dully in her ears, the rhythm far too rapid. Could he hear?

His sluggish footsteps faded, as did his familiar curses. She allowed her back to relax a fraction and dropped her head against the barn wall, wincing when strands of her hair stuck and pulled against the splinters of wood.

Breathe in; breathe out.

She waited for several long moments. He had deceived her before. She had crept from her hiding spot only to have his meaty fingers clamp around her throat.

The barn door squeaked open on rusty hinges. Her breath snagged, but it was Mother's careworn face that appeared. Sunlight streamed around her silhouette.

"He's gone."

Uttering a sigh of relief, Cassie pushed away from the wall and brushed poking shafts of straw from her skirt. "He found out, then?"

Mother nodded. "Came from town and went straight to the crock."

Cassie grimaced, imagining his reaction when his calloused fingers scraped the inside of the empty container. "He didn't accuse you, did he?"

Mother waved her hand in dismissal, though the tight lines around her eyes remained. "It doesn't matter. He laid not a hand on me. In truth, it's unlikely he'll remember come tomorrow."

Cassie stepped over tackle and crates, squinting against the bright sunlight. She straightened. "I'm not sorry. You know I'm not."

"I know." With a sad smile, Mother turned to leave, murmuring instructions over her shoulder. "Time to hang the wash."

That was all? No reprimand? Cassie said not a word. Avoiding Father was the part she had fretted over most, but fearing her actions had disappointed Mother . . .

Perhaps Mother wasn't sorry either. The thought gave her pause.

Cassie trudged through the grass-splotched yard as chickens squawked and flapped around her skirts. The worn garment tangled around her ankles.

At least she'd bought them time. Yes, she'd taken the only money to be had from the crock, but the tax man's demands were sated. If Mother had agreed with her actions, why did she not say so? Why could she never stand up to Father?

Before they had rounded the corner of the cabin, a wagon careened down the dirt road in front of the house, churning up splatters of mud and jostling with enough clatter to wake the dead. Cassie frowned. The driver was recognizable enough. Peter, her sister Eloise's husband, jumped from the bouncing wagon a hairsbreadth after he'd set the brake. His blond hair was windblown as if tossed by a dervish. His eyes were bright, sparkling with an excitement she'd rarely, if ever, witnessed from the sulky man.

Mother's face filled with sudden angst. "What's wrong? Is it Eloise?"

"Of course not." His Irish brogue lilted high as his chest puffed out with a billow. He hooked his thumbs around his suspenders. "You've not heard the news, then?"

Cassie stepped next to Mother's side. A cold stone sank in her stomach. "What news?"

His lips curved into a smile, revealing crooked yellow teeth. "Why, war, sister. War has been declared."

Chapter 2

April 15, 1861
New York City

Gabe Avery snaked his way through the swarm of people clogging Broadway, suppressing the urge to vent his frustration at the slow progress. After growing up in the city, he was rarely bothered by the crowds anymore, but this was different. Urgency bade him hurry. He must know if the rumors were true.

As he tipped his hat to an older matron coming toward him, he almost collided with a wayward boy of no more than six. The dirty moppet scurried past him without a pause, reminding him of a rat slinking between broken crates in an alley. He shook his head. The lad was likely to cause an accident.

The odor of horse dung mingled with the sharp sting of axle grease as people and carriages clattered past. Only a little farther . . .

There. The Brady Gallery was within view. A pulse of euphoria traveled his veins.

Please, God, let him say yes. . . .

He slowed as he approached the prestigious gallery and stopped to catch his breath. He'd been here dozens of times before, but never had he been so anxious. So unnerved. Tugging his vest into submission, he inhaled a thick pull of air, grasped the doorknob, and tugged.

He stepped into the gallery, his senses heightening despite the calming effects of green strategically gracing the papered room. Faces met him at every turn, each photographed form boxed within a gilt frame. Some somber, some cheery. Some lithe of form and some frumpy.

All of them were fascinating.

The faintest traces of iodine wafted toward him. Someone must be readying glass plates for exposure in the back.

His boots sank into the plush carpeting as he stepped into the main salon. A solitary couple perused the displays, murmuring softly to each other as they commented over the Imperials. The painting-size photographs were so lifelike, he felt if he reached out and touched the glass, the images would jump in response. Gabe stood off to the side and fisted his hands behind his back, willing his frayed nerves to cease their buzzing.

A man stepped through the dark-green velvet curtains concealing the workrooms from the gallery. Gabe's breath strangled as every coherent thought scattered from his head.

The man was of medium height but exuded quiet confidence with his slow, smooth gait. His dark hair was peppered with gray, though most of the hair of his goatee was still black, and he wore a cream-colored duster. The spectacles perched on his aquiline nose framed dark eyes that were sharp, missing nothing.

It was him. Mathew Brady.

Gabe wiped sweaty palms against his trousers and cleared his throat. "Mr. Brady, I presume?"

The man smiled faintly, causing slight lines to crinkle around his eyes. "One and the same."

Gabe offered his hand, and Brady shook it with a firm clasp. "Mr. Brady, sir, I have long been an admirer of your work. Your advances in daguerreotype and imprint images have inspired me."

Brady's dark brows rose, his scholarly features lightening. "You have studied the science of photography?"

Gabe paused, trying not to babble like an overwrought child. "Indeed. Your brilliant portraits fueled my interest in profound ways."

"And have you a camera?"

His tongue almost tripped over the stem of words bubbling to burst forth. "Yes, sir. I've worked and saved diligently over the past several years and recently acquired my first."

"What model?"

"An Anthony camera, sir."

Brady raised his brows higher. "Impressive. There are none better. I employ Anthony cameras exclusively in my own studio."

Gabe released a tight breath. Yes, he knew. He knew every detail about the renowned portrait gallery and the methodology of its master.

"What's your name, son?"

He'd never introduced himself? "Forgive me. My name is Gabriel Avery."

"And what brings you to my studio today, Mr. Avery?"

His mouth was cotton. "I heard a rumor you are considering undertaking a remarkable endeavor. Is it true that you are planning to photograph views from the war?"

Brady's goatee twitched in response. "News of my fanciful daydreams has spread already?"

Fearing he'd overstepped propriety, Gabe could do little more than nod. "Word travels fast, sir."

"Indeed." Plucking the wire-rimmed spectacles from his nose, Brady drew a square of dark cloth from his coat pocket and began to polish the lenses, a frown pulling his mouth into a grim line. "It's become an ambition of mine, I confess. The magnitude of such a historic event calls for an accurate record, wouldn't you say?"

"I agree entirely. Is it true that you have considered hiring photographers to complete it?"

Brady gave a nod. "I have weighed the merits of it, yes."

Gabe's heart leapt. "If I may be so bold, I'd like to apply for the job."

"I figured as much. Do you have examples of your work?"

Gabe's fingers nearly knotted. So much so, he fumbled over the clasps of his satchel. Removing the samples he'd so carefully selected, he handed them to the photographer.

Brady hooked his spectacles back over his ears and onto his nose before perusing the photographs, his face void of expression. Gabe's heart raced as he waited, each second drawn longer than the last.

Finally Brady spoke. "These are quite good. You certainly are adept at using the chemicals for the wet-plate process, although you still have some to learn about the proper use of light to acquire sharper, crisper images."

"Yes, sir." Gabe held his breath.

Brady pursed his lips. "Unfortunately, none of my plans are definite as of yet. And you can imagine the staggering expense of mounting such a venture. Equipment, traveling darkrooms, horses and their feed, chemicals, plates, tripods . . . to say nothing of the government's cooperation with such a venture."

Gabe's heart sank like an iron anchor. The disappointment tasted far more bitter than he'd imagined.

Brady rubbed his chin, his face thoughtful. "However, I see nothing wrong with striking a tenuous arrangement."

His breath hitched.

"Check back with me in one month. By that time, I hope to have permission from President Lincoln himself. If I can figure out a way to embark on such a campaign, I would like to hire you as one of my photographers."

Gabe's pulse pounded in a heady rush. His tongue cleaved to the roof of his mouth. Before he could utter a sound, Brady held up a warning hand.

"On one condition, however. You must agree to use your own Anthony camera and must purchase your own tripod and Harrison lens if you do not have one. I would provide any stereoscopic cameras needed."

Gabe tried to calculate the sum in his head. The lens would come dear. He'd had no use for a tripod as yet, choosing to perch his delicate camera on boxes or tables for the time being. There would be no such luxury in the middle of war.

He spoke slowly. "Such an investment is beyond my current means. What if I were somehow to obtain the proper funds and arrangements for photographing the war fell through?"

Brady's lips twisted into a dry smile. "That is precisely my own conundrum."

It was a risk. A big one. Where would he ever find the money for such equipment?

Brady continued, "In addition, all photographers would be required to spend several weeks working in one of my studios before travel. If I'm to fund such an extravagant and elaborate ordeal, I must be assured that my photographers are properly trained. As such, you would be representing me and the reputation I've spent years striving to attain."

Learn from Mathew Brady himself? The thought left Gabe light-headed. Such an opportunity was beyond belief. It was a priceless gift that would never come again.

As suddenly as the elation rose, it deflated. The opportunity was contingent on money . . . money he did not have. One month. Was it possible to purchase a costly Harrison lens and tripod in such a short time?

Please, Lord. I'll never ask for another blessed thing. . . .

"What say you, Mr. Avery? Do we strike a pledge?"

Gabe stared at Brady, his mind spinning like a top. How could he decline? If it was the Almighty's will, he would make a way.

Before he could hesitate any longer, Gabe clasped Brady's slim hand. Despite the excitement coursing through him, a niggling unease remained. Where could he possibly procure those kinds of funds?

Brady's brows rose. "One month?"

Gabe swallowed. "One month."

What had he done?

acknowledgments

C. S. LEWIS ONCE PENNED, "If only my toothache would stop, I could write another chapter about Pain." These past two years have been difficult ones, but a very wise author once told me my job is to write the best story I can in whatever season I'm currently living in. The journey of breathing life into imaginary worlds is made much easier with encouragers, and I'm surrounded by a mighty army of cheerleaders.

To Todd, Bethany, Callie, Nate, and Dylan: Thank you for your patience and unconditional love. You all make life fun and I wouldn't want to walk it without you.

Mom and Dad, Linda, Brian, in-laws, out-laws, nieces, nephews, and the Cousin Eddies of the family . . . I love you all. Thanks for being the most awesome, craziest family out there.

To Jennifer Pruitt: You, my dear IM sister, are seen, loved, and treasured. I don't know what I would do without you.

Spring Creek: Thank you for taking in our family with open arms. We love you. "By this everyone will know that you are my disciples, if you love one another" (John 13:35, NIV).

Savanna Kaiser and Cara Grandle: Thank you for checking in on my heart. Even more than I value our talks about writing, I treasure our chats about what God is teaching us. You girls are my soul sisters!

To Michelle Griep, Elizabeth Ludwig, and Ane Mulligan (The Golden Arrows): Thank you for shaping me into a stronger writer and for being such wonderful friends. I deeply value you.

Janet Grant: There are some amazing agents in the publishing industry, but you exceed them all. Your wisdom, grace, and kindness have been a lifeline. Thanks for guiding my career but also for showing such tenderness during the storms. You are loved.

To all the Books & Such authors: Your friendship and laughter are pure sunshine during the ups and downs of the writing adventure. Thanks for the giggles.

To the entire Tyndale team: Jan Stob, Danika King, Elizabeth Jackson, Andrea Garcia, Andrea Martin, Mariah León, Karen Watson, the cover designers, copy editors, fact-checkers, and everybody involved in the creation and production of this story: Thank you. As always, you all have been the biggest cheerleaders and have elevated this story from the diamond in the rough I began with into something much greater. I thank God each day for all of you.

A special thank-you to Bill Sparks and the men and women involved with the Arkansas Civil War reenactors. You deepened my knowledge of the Civil War, specifically in the realm of medicine. Thank you for making the book launch for *Where Dandelions Bloom* such a success and for letting me pull the cannon. Meeting you all was a joy!

Jesus . . . thank you for your unconditional love and for continually pursuing me. May my heart's desire ever be to sit at your feet. Empty me of myself and fill me with you. To you belongs all praise . . . forever my Joy, my Heart, my Everything.

about the author

A PASSIONATE LOVER OF STORIES, Tara Johnson uses fiction, nonfiction, song, and laughter to share her testimony of how God led her into freedom after spending years living shackled to the expectations of others. Tara is the author of three novels set during the Civil War: *Engraved on the Heart*, *Where Dandelions Bloom*, and *All Through the Night*. She is a member of American Christian Fiction Writers and makes her home in Arkansas with her husband and three children.

Visit her online at tarajohnsonstories.com.

discussion questions

1. How does a doctor's misdiagnosis from Cadence's childhood affect the way her father treats her—and the way she views herself—for years afterward? Think of a significant event from your own childhood. What were the repercussions of this event, and how do they still affect you today?

2. Joshua endured a difficult childhood until he was taken in by Papa John. How did his impoverished early years shape his character as an adult, for good and for bad? In what ways does he choose to channel his painful experiences for the benefit of others?

3. Dorothea Dix turns Cadence away when she asks to train as a nurse, leaving Cadence unsure about her purpose. How does Cadence react? How have you reacted to setbacks or rejections in your career or plans for your life?

4. In response to the evil of slavery, Joshua and his associates engage in the dangerous business of buying—and then freeing—enslaved children. What compels them to do this work? What injustices do you see around you in today's world? How do you typically respond to them?

5. After Cadence loses the joy she once found in singing, Joshua tells her, "The gifts God gives only continue to flourish when we pour them out through love. They dry up when we use them motivated by any other purpose." What does he mean by this? Consider your own gifts. Have you ever used them selfishly? In what ways can you use them for God's glory and out of love for others?

6. Tate is initially disturbed and upset by little Etta's efforts to befriend and play with him. Why is this so troubling to him? How is he eventually able to come to terms with his past choices?

7. When Stephen Dodd learns that Cadence is married, he tells her, "Truth hurts, but it ultimately heals. Deception, though done with good intentions, always destroys. Always." Do you agree with him? What were Cadence's intentions in her relationship with Stephen, and why did he misconstrue them? Have you ever unintentionally misled someone or been on the receiving side? What was the outcome?

8. Toward the end of the book, Joshua puts his family at risk in order to continue his antislavery work. Why does he make that decision? How would you have advised him to proceed? Why is it often difficult to balance the demands of ministry with the needs of family?

9. How does faith in God sustain Joshua, Cadence, and other characters in this story? Think of the moments their faith is put to the test. How are they able to see God at work in the midst of these trials? When do they choose to rely on their own strength rather than God's?

10. Did you learn anything new about the Civil War era from this book? Or was anything particularly surprising to you?

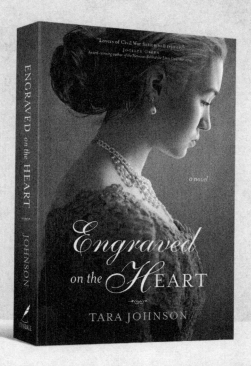

TYNDALE HOUSE PUBLISHERS
IS CRAZY4FICTION!

Fiction that entertains and inspires

Get to know us! Become a member of the Crazy4Fiction
community. Whether you read our blog, like us on
Facebook, follow us on Twitter, or receive our e-newsletter,
you're sure to get the latest news on the best in Christian
fiction. You might even win something along the way!

JOIN IN THE FUN TODAY.

 crazy4fiction.com

 Crazy4Fiction

 @Crazy4Fiction

CP0021